Anonymous

El Reshid

A Novel

Anonymous

El Reshid
A Novel

ISBN/EAN: 9783337001360

Printed in Europe, USA, Canada, Australia, Japan

Cover: Foto ©Andreas Hilbeck / pixelio.de

More available books at **www.hansebooks.com**

EL RESHID

A NOVEL

ANONYMOUS

Los Angeles, Cal.
B. R. BAUMGARDT & CO.
1899

THE FACE

My love ! her eyelids close,
So soft asleep is she—
A milk-white dreaming rose,
Her soul is waiting me.

Somewhere in shoreless space
Our eyes will meet and part—
Sweet rapture on her face,
And bliss within my heart.

CONTENTS.

PREFACE

This novel is founded upon the principle that life is the opposite of death. If so, man only lives when he reaches his full self. His Nirvanic poise implies nothing other than that rapid motion which a top manifests when its spinning is too quick for the eye.

The people neither live to order, nor marry and die in conventional fashion, nor are they trotted out on the stage at the call of the manager or the signal of the orchestra. There is something behind a man, when he begins objective existence, other than heredity and pedigree.

Causes far-reaching bring him occasionally in his rush and battle with his kind to a dead stop, and whirl him about face, as though he were gripped by a god.

Over all is Will, which is free and sovereign, and which has been the prime cause eternally of apparently irresistable effects.

The story tells something of the incipient stages of the Master ; and by the Master is meant *any one* who aspires to the regal distinction of the possession of power—any one who will pay the price of wisdom, and submit to the experience which evolves understanding.

El Reshid is a hard nut to crack for these who believe in nothing except that which the five senses demonstrate ; and a still harder to the devotees of the pseudo Mahatma, who materializes letters, precious stones and roses on one side of the globe, while his sacred body lies in a dead trance on the other.

But to get a glimpse of the book you must open it ; to pronounce judgment you must read it through.

CHAPTER I.

WHO AM I?

It was in Stamboul; rain had fallen, and washed the minarets and domes of the mosques, but the streets seemed filthier than ever. Alas! there is dirt that water exaggerates, and Stamboul, the vilest, yet fairest of cities, presented its dual aspect on this rainy morning, when Aleppo tried to disentangle his troublesome locks of hair, after a sound night's sleep. Had it been Edmund Sallus Smith junior, we should have said a night's debauch; but it was only Aleppo, and he had slept well from sunset till dawn. His hair bothered him; it was thick, long and beautiful, and knew little of the barber; for he never visited the tonsorial adept, unless driven by snarls and despair. The room where the young man was so dexterously busy, was bare, and quite out of order; in fact, a young woman of his age would have rejected it in toto. Gloomy, damp, upheaved, with but one thing of beauty in it, and that was the boy himself. He was neither small nor large, and his suppleness was evident in every movement of his arm as he critically arranged the parting of his black hair a little to one side of the right brow. The eyes that looked back at him from the mirror, were tender yet bold; there are some people whose eyes so draw you that you forget to make discoveries elsewhere; but Aleppo was *universally* distinguished. His smile revealed perfect teeth; and his nose told a tale of pedigree, which he had thus far failed to trace.

Suddenly he dropped his comb and paused to listen.

"I believe that's Smith; it will be the same old thing over again," and he threw open the door with a commanding air, to let in Edmund Sallus, Jr.

"Drunk are you?" said Aleppo fiercely; but Sal (this was his pet name) was too far gone to speak. A look of ineffable scorn spread over Aleppo's face; he threw his companion with no gentle hand on the bed, and began to tug away at his boots. The task was a hard one, but eventually he had him undressed, and under cover; then he sighed heavily and tossed back his hair which had fallen over his brow; a habit of his.

"This room is polluted; it is sacrilege to write to her here; but where else can I go; it is raining, Sallus calls them 'great guns,' outside."

He stopped a moment, and looked puzzled.

"I have it; I'll open the window and sit with my back to the bed; 'tis the best I can do."

To think was to act. He arranged the furniture of the room with considerable noise, wheeling up

a lame desk to the window, which he had thrown
open to the storm; then casting another look on
Smith junior, who snored away unconscious of
the fine distinction in ethics drawn by his room
mate, he threw himself into a chair with his back
to the bed, and sighed again.

"I haven't had my breakfast yet, have I? But
what of it; it will keep. I would rather write to
her than eat."

He opened the desk; it was in a terrible state.
Evidently this young man had brought himself up;
but he found somewhere in the medley a pen,
paper and an envelope; then, uncorking his bottle
of ink, he tossed back his hair again and looked
out pathetically into the rain. It dashed in every
now and then over his face and eyes, giving him
the appearance of a weeping Romeo, hopeless of
his love. Suddenly, as if struck by a lightning
inspiration, he began to write; and his pen made
the queerest, most unreadable scrawls imaginable.
The letters, or hieroglyphics, or whatever they
were, would be utterly untranslatable to one unaccustomed to the tongue in which he wrote; so we
will transcribe them in English.

STAMBOUL, Thursday.

My Dear Miss Somebody:
I will write you to-day in spite of everything—
lack of breakfast, a rain storm, and a drunken
chum. Nothing can come between you and me,
sweetheart, not even a bed fellow who snores. I

hear him, and yet I do not; instead I listen to the
trees sighing in Arcadia, and your singing. Ah!
love, how you sing! Where are you this minute?
Who is so happy as to hear you? I am jealous of
somebody, somewhere. But I must keep my
promise to tell you more about myself of whom I
know nothing. This is literally true; I am without parents or country. Whether I am oriental or
occidental, of the south or north, I cannot tell. I
have studied myself in the glass, I have asked
others, but nobody knows. My eyes and hair are
so black that I seem to have hailed from the east,
but my skin being white the west can in no
way deny me. Who am I, sweetheart? Even my
age is unknown? How can anybody tell? I was
left, a child, on the steps of a hospital; I might
have been five, I might have been seven. All my
early years in an asylum; later, adopted by Aunt
Serena (so she was called), who died and left me
in Italy, in an artist's studio; where, having
studied a few years, I came into her property, and
have been traveling ever since. Who knows my
exact age? I don't.

Aunt Serena never had a lover, never in all her
life; so I heard. She was wofully plain; she found
me in the asylum, and thought me beautiful. That
was years ago, remember, before I had grown
coarse and into a man. She adopted me, and made
me her heir. As I told you, yesterday, she was
not over rich, but I have enough. She taught me

to be frugal, and put me to work in a studio, as a
sort of apprentice pupil. I loved Aunt Serena, but
not as I love you, dear one. I can quite understand why she never had a lover; but I will tell
you of that another day. How it rains! Who
am I, sweetheart? If I could but find you, I am
sure I should read my history in your eyes. Yesterday I met some American girls; one of them, I
thought, for a moment, was you. How pretty she
was! but when she spoke I was disillusioned. No
dearest; she is Estelle; but where are you?
That fellow on the bed is talking in his sleep; it is
raining harder than ever, and the drops are dripping from my eyelashes like tears; besides, I am
hungry. To-morrow I will write again. Can you
not answer me in some way? Shove a letter under
the door, will you? Toss it into the window; or
mail it and send by post. It's so dreadfully one-
sided you see. If it were not for your singing,
which I am forever hearing, I should despair.

Look for another to-morrow.

Your true, true love,

ALEPPO.

This pleasant task over, he kissed the missive
many times; then enclosing it in an envelope, he
addressed it thus :

" Miss Juliet Somebody,
Somewhere."

He found a box in his desk where he dropped the letter, among hundreds of others, all addressed in the same way, with the exception of a change in the first name; which seemed to vary periodically, like the seasons of the year. On some it was "Miss Helen," on others "Jeannette;" again, "Viola" and "Kate," but the surname was always "Somebody," sacredly cherished, and never altered.

Having locked his desk, and deposited the key in his inner vest pocket, he began the most beautiful whistling that a boy of twenty or thereabout is capable of; imitating every bird in Italy, to say nothing of the stray singers in Stamboul. He tortured his debauched chum, by whistling into his ears; he rolled him over and over on the bed, and whistled at the back of his head; in fact so inundated him with a rain of notes, that Sallus sat up, and rubbed his eyes.

"Come on, get out of this! Here, wait till I give you a douse."

Aleppo brought the pitcher of water, and poured a quart or more on Sallus' disheveled head, regardless of consequences. This seemed to wake him and to clear his liquor-soaked brain to the fighting point. He sprang out of bed in a fit of rage, and the two had a hand to hand tussel, worthy of a better cause, but Aleppo pinned him at last, after the room had been turned into bedlam, and brought him to terms. A half hour later they went arm in

arm to breakfast, where Aleppo drank water and
filled Sallus with coffee, strong and hot.

The sun came out and re-gilded the mosques of
Stamboul. On the shores of the Bosporus the
beautiful villa cities, new-washed, appeared from
the distance like the seraglios of a Mohammedan
heaven, while through the forests of masts and
rigging on the Golden Horn, were caught glimpses
of towers and turreted minarets ; with great and
little domes, intermingled in incongruous proximity, that tantalized the charmed eye. East, on
the promontory of Asia, lay Scutari, whose pink
houses, half buried in gardens and trees, would
indicate, were it not for the cypress groves, that
the homes of the dead were even more cheerful than
those of the living. On the heights, one finds Asia
and Europe at his feet; the sinuous Bosporus
rolling between ; and far off in Bithynia the hoary
head of Olympus, white with eternal snows. Back
again from grandeur to the glittering water, where
the caique glides in and out among the larger craft,
with all the grace of a Venetian gondola, and up
afterward to the sky, where the eyes are lifted
naturally to seek relief in simple azure from a sur-
plus of beauty, that turns pleasure into pain. But
this is the veiled Byzantium, draped with the mist
which distance brings. Asiatic Rome on her seven
hills, is the breeder of everything, from the pests,
vermin, and horror of dirt, to the paradise of the
Hareem. Here the Ottoman and the occidental

races shake hands ; extremes meet, and hell and heaven have naught between but a metaphorical Bosporus, where they blend at last in the craft-laden Golden Horn.

Out from the narrow streets Aleppo dragged his half dazed companion, and settled him at last with his back against a grave stone in the cemetery of Scutari. The millions of dead under the great cypress trees made no sound, unless, in their upward trend toward life, their souls had entered the moaning trees, that sighed and whispered mysteriously, as the wind stole in and out. Everywhere were sculptured tomb-stones with their arabesque carvings. Aleppo saw none of them, however, but stared in a puzzled, affectionate way at Sallus. The latter had thrown off his hat, half closed his eyes, and looked, as he leaned against the marble, like one dead. Aleppo planted himself firmly on his two feet in front of him, ran his hands down into his pockets, tossed back his hair, with a jerk of his head, and began:

" Now it seems to me that you are a sight better off than I am ; you know who you are, and I don't ; that's one thing in your favor ; then you are the most deucedly handsome cur, that I ever set eyes on."

Sallus winced a little at this, and straightened himself a bit.

" You are a downright beauty ; that's why I stay by you so close; I'd chase beauty across Siberia, or Hell for a glimpse, you know; and here you are right in my hands—a veritable Apollo; by jingo! I believe you are prettier drunk than sober."

Here Sal sat upright and opened his blue eyes.

"Look here Lep, for heaven's sake leave go that slang—" he was thoroughly roused—"it's all right in me, but it's horrid in you; you got it in pretty straight this morning, but as a rule you can't do it, it's worse than an old woman singing."

Here he sank back in a sort of stupor again, and closed his eyes. Aleppo was right, Sal was beautiful, with yellow hair, blue eyes, and a girl's cheeks. He might as well have been a young woman; save that for all round dissipation, and reckless immorality, few girls, even of the dance houses of Constantinople could compete with him. Aleppo had fallen in love with Sallus a year before, and begged him of his distracted father, promising to make him into an angel in a given time, provided they were allowed to travel together. After investigation, Mr. Smith, Sr., having ascertained that Aleppo was strictly abstemious and correct, turned over to him his poor baggage of a son, with a forlorn hope, that the young man's influence would eventually be beneficial. The boys had wandered about together for six months, or more, and on this particular day they found themselves under the cypresses at Scutari, the preacher delivering his afternoon sermon, and the audience dozing off into drunken dreams.

"You see," said Aleppo, "I can't make head nor feet out of you." Here Sal roused himself again; "Let up on that slang, I tell you, you are going wrong already."

"Well then, head and something—it isn't any fun, I want you to understand, not a bit."

"I know better," growled Sal.

"Well, in the first place, you get that confounded headache on you, that makes you see snakes."

"Nonsense! you make me tired. Should think I would see snakes; for you everlastingly take this opportunity, when you know I am not myself, to drag me into the grave-yard and sermonize. You did it in Paris, you did it in Vienna, and here we are again."

Having said this with as much venom as was in him, he spat at the tomb-stone behind him, and dragging himself clear of the sacred dust, collapsed into the grass near by.

"There's nothing like a cemetery to point a moral—" and Aleppo showed his beautiful teeth in one of the rarest smiles, that the human face is capable of—"for my part, I like it. Here am I in Asia with the dead; I feel wonderfully at home; don't you Sal?"

"Y–e–s," drawled Sal, who had reached the pathetic stage. He rolled and lighted a cigarette with trembling fingers, then lying flat on his back, blew clouds of smoke at the patches of sky, which he saw between the interlaced trees. His eyes were as blue as heaven ; and two tears gathered in them which he immediately became ashamed of, and attributed to the smoke.

"Now look here Sal "—Aleppo had seen the tears, though he made no sign ; for he loved this bad boy to the point of sacrifice—"I'll tell you what I'll do "—the words came out with difficulty, for he felt that he was choking—"you go a week without touching the stuff, or lighting yourself up, and I'll promise you on the Koran and the Bible, that I'll go on one of the most hell-inspiring sprees with you, at the end of that time, that the devil ever dreamed of. You will find yourself nowhere ; I'll drink more and sin more in one day than you can in a month ; upon my word and honor I will ; that is, if you say so. "Look here Sal,"—and he gave him a punch on the shoulder that made him wince —"will you do it"? Sal sat up—he was as sober as a desert owl, and as solemn—"I'll be d——d if I do!"

"What of that? two of us in hell are better than one. Let's be sober together for a week, pious and everything, then go to the other place."

"Now you just shut up on this." Sal got on his feet and shook himself, somewhat after the manner of a dog that scents danger.

"I'm one of the devil's own, any how ; but as for you talking slang, and wallowing, you shan't; that's just all there is of it, do you see?"

He pulled off his coat ; and any delusion one might have harbored about his feminine incapacity and like stuff, must have vanished at sight of his muscle and brawn. American, pretty and dudish in face, herculean in form, he was about as fine an animal as one often gets a chance to gaze at.

"Now it don't make one straw's difference whether you are in earnest or not, (the man had woke up in him) you shan't carry it out, that's all ; but I'll tell you what I will do,"—here he took in a long breath, as if to wash his soul clean—"I'll let you see that I can go a week in spite of the painted faces of Constantinople ; but on one con- dition—*you* listen now, the tables are turned, you see. You've just got to quit that slang, business; it grates on my nerves, worse than Oriental music. Promise me, that you will give me back the slang dictionary and the concert songs, and I'll swear on this tombstone, that I'll go sober for a week."

Aleppo squeezed the tears that were welling up, back into his eyes, delicately arranged his hair, in fact made great show of hesitancy, but at last con- descended to speak.

"Well I suppose I'll have to, for a week."

" Not much, *for a week*, but forever."

" Forever " ?

" Yes, forever ; do you suppose, if *I* had a Miss Somebody to whom I wrote love letters every day, as you do, do you suppose, that instead of absolutely knowing that I was the son of an

American stock-raiser, that, on the contrary, I had
the chance of surmising that I might be a wandering prince in disguise, do you suppose that if I
were you, I would foul my tongue with swear words
and slang !''

To be preached to by Sal, gave Aleppo a thrill
that was almost intoxicating; besides his allusion
to Miss Somebody held him to the cypress tree
against which he was leaning, as though he had
been welded there.   Sal was king, and he a
mortified, Constantinople cur.   But this passed off;
he pulled himself together, and looking the blonde
beauty straight in the eyes, said smiling, " It's
agreed ; now for dinner.''

'' Wait a bit ; you don't expect that I'm going
around with this stuff in my pocket do you ? ''

He pulled a brandy flask from the depths and
laid it with some dignity on the adjacent grave ;
then a dozen or more cigarettes, and a package of
tobacco.

'' There, if that corpse gets dry and nervous, it
has its chance.   Remember Lep, it's only for a
week. sabe ? ''

'' Yes, I s—— understand.''

'' There, you saved yourself this time but your
promise is eternal. See ? ''

'' Yes, I s—— comprehend.''

'' Come on then.''

Sal led the way and Aleppo followed in a strange
frame of mind ; the kingly American had got in his

work ; and the man without country or name, went after him, as the great St. Bernard follows its master.

CHAPTER II.

A STRANGE MEETING.

A woman, whose age it would be impossible to determine, but about whose beauty there was no shadow of doubt, came out of the Vienna Opera House, and made her way rapidly toward the carriage in waiting at the entrance. She stopped suddenly, as if transfixed, and stared wildly into a pair of eyes, that answered her's with a similar look; then the heads of the two were bowed with conventional courtesy, and the apparent strangers passed each other as though they had never met before. The man (for the eyes that brought the widow—Madame Cressey—to a sudden halt, were masculine and stern) turned rapidly on his heel and proceeded in an opposite direction from that in which he had been going, plunging into a side street, and thence into the dark. She, however, cold as ice, climbed somehow into her carriage, and fell back among the cushions in a dead faint. When the coachman stopped at the entrance to her hotel, she made no attempt to alight, in fact knew nothing, and had to be lifted out and taken to her room. It was late at night, under the ministrations of her physician, before she understood who she was and where. On the contrary, Henrique Romanes seemed to be fired with the strongest cordial that the grape could produce; for, having found his room, and locked his door, he walked the floor till morning in a fury of excitement, utterly inconsistent with his correct conventional dress and hotel surroundings. His face spoke power, even in its frenzy, and the very wildness of the storm now blowing over him, implied an oncoming calm, which must later be formidable. At daylight he threw himself upon the bed, and fell into a sound sleep, which lasted until late in the afternoon; when he awoke he was obliged to make some effort to collect himself. As the memories of the preceding evening thrust themselves upon him, a spasm of pain knit his brow into a fierce scowl; but it passed, and a fixed look took its place, which set his features, as though in marble. It was not, however, the repose of indecision; it spoke determination and power. Dressing hastily, without aid of a valet, he seated himself before the window, where the afternoon light flooded his stern countenance, and took, from a concealed pocket over his heart, a worn and faded letter. His face grew a shade whiter, and his eyes more intense, if that could be, as he touched it; otherwise he showed no emotion. It ran thus:

"Farewell! If misery can be condensed, it is included in this word; if sorrow can be told, it is

spoken now. Farewell! O, tell me, can it be, that
we who have loved for love's own sake, that we
who have defied the world, and even God, that
we must part. I could not have dreamed it; I
could not have believed it; but the bitter fact
stands. Fate forced us together, and wrenches us
asunder. Fate! We are masters of nothing; the
wind blew the pollen to the flower, and tore it to
pieces.

" I care for naught in the universe but *you.* Alas!
the one out of the innumerable, that I love, is sent
adrift. I neither drown myself in illusions, nor
drug my heart with hopeless dreams; boldly I face
the fact. I love you, I love you! May the sin in
which I glory be mine forever. I shed no tears on
my rebellious heart, nor do I wring my hands and
supplicate an unseen God. On the black night of
myself, one star gleams fiercely, eternally—the star
of Love. *Forever, fare you well!* "

To this scrap of paper, from which age had
failed to tear the passion, there was signed no
name. It was written in a bold, almost masculine
hand, interspersed with dashes; and had been read
and folded so often that it was cracked and worn.
The date took it back many years to a former
generation, though Henrique Romanes looked
scarcely thirty-five. His chin was powerful and
firm; his eyes keen, mysterious, dark; his face
clean shaven, his hair black, and his frame slight,
but well knit. Altogether, he would seem to have

scarcely reached his prime, were it not for a certain
air that betrayed a depth of experience, undis-
coverable in youth. Age is betrayed by a certain
flabbiness of the tissue and skin. Romanes had
hard flesh, tense muscles, and the erect carriage of
a man of thirty, while the depths of shade that
lay under his eyes, spoke of feeling, rather than
years. There was one thing quite out of the ordinary about this man, and which stamped him as of
different coin from the jingling mass. He made
you *feel* his personality. To pass him in a crowd
was to turn your head ; to touch his hand was to
receive an electric shock; to glance in his eye was
to wilt as does the morning glory in the sun; to
enter a room where he *had* been, was to realize his
presence still. To some he brought pain, to others
pleasure, but to all a consciousness of himself. In
plain speech, he looked like a fallen eagle, that
had dragged its wings in the dust.

He was a long time reading the letter ; save his
eyes, he showed no sign of especial interest; but
they, as he pierced the very paper with their
glance, took on a new fire, and flashed with the
glow of self-illuminating stars. He folded it at
last, and laid it again over his heart, then, after
striding the room once or twice, rang for coffee,
which he took, black and hot, with a crust of
bread. Consulting his watch, he ordered a carriage, and shortly after left the house. He directed

the driver in a positive way, addressing him in the
German tongue.

Several hours later, at about nine in the evening,
he alighted at a certain well known hotel in Vienna,
and demanded audience with Madame Cressey.
He was informed that the lady was ill and could
see no one. Romanes, not the least perturbed,
turned his back a moment, and drawing a pack of
playing cards from his pocket, from which he
extracted the ace of hearts, inclosed it in a small
envelope, and ordered it delivered to her at once.
In a short time the messenger returned, with a
similar missive, on which was written the word,
"Aleppo."   "Conduct me immediately," said
Romanes. The boy rushed off in the direction of
the Madame's apartments, as if his life hung on their
quick arrival, and Romanes followed with a dignified speed, that savored as much of indifference as of
haste. The door of Helene Cressey's salon swung
back noiselessly at his approach, and was closed
again after his entrance, as though muffled in felt.
The two stood face to face beneath the shaded
light of the chandelier, and looked once more with a
half startled, half defiant expression into each
other's eyes.

" You have broken your vow, Romanes."

" Pardon, Helene, it was not I, but that which
you term fate. We had promised never to meet
again, but our childish vows were scorned, our
word of honor broken, *for us* last night."

"Are we in truth such puppets?" said she, with a sneer.

In reply, he held her letter before her blazing eyes.

"Fate forced us together and wrenches us asunder—fate!

"We are masters of nothing."

As she read, she grew whiter, if possible, and colder.

"Read," he said sternly, "every word."

She became more rigid, as her eyes turned the words into symbols of fire. At last, she hissed between her teeth, while steadying herself by the table, "Cruel!"

"No, nor kind," said Romanes. "It is twenty-five years since this letter was written. You are as young in feeling as when you penned it, and so am I. You have known me to some purpose, Helene Cressey; she who weds an Olympian is endowed with eternal youth."

"Words are but will-o'-the-wisps, when the heart speaks," she answered, then burst into a storm of sobs, and sank into a chair, completely mastered by the frenzy of her sorrow.

With the alteration of mood, his changed also. He sank at her feet, and, taking her hand, held it caressingly to his lips. In time she grew calm, for he dried her tears. Then mixing a drug, which he discovered upon the table, he brought her the glass and ordered her to drink. A very child in

his hands, she obeyed, when, drawing a long sigh,
as though with it she had thrown off the incubus
of a score of years, she leaned back upon the cushions and looked trustfully into his eyes. He drew
a chair to her side, and spoke, as would a man of
the world. "Helene, we will drop tragedy now
and talk with calmness. The subject which
demands our utmost attention is vital. First, let
me say, that neither of us would have broken our
vow, which we signed jointly, years ago, had not
Fate pushed us, like two wandering meteors,
together, and mingled us once more into one; and
by Fate, you know that I mean the *Powers* that
are. Well then, you see," and he tossed his hair
back in a peculiar way, "there can be but one subject between us now, and that is Aleppo."

At the mention of this name Helene shivered,
but remained dumb; looking into the fathomless
depths of Romanes' eyes.

"Yes, Aleppo, who is he, and where?" And
Helene answered, in a half-whisper, as though her
word were an echo, "Where?"

"That we must ascertain," said Romanes
emphatically.

"I thought," said she, "that we had agreed to
remember him as one dead."

"True, but on condition that we considered each
other in the same way; our coming together makes
the finding of our son imperative."

"I believe you," said Helene.

"And more," said Romanes, who rose and paced the room rapidly, "he must be what his father was not; he must succeed where I have failed. Our lives must be given, from now on, not to each other, but to him, at any cost. Do you understand, Helene, at any cost." He looked her straight in the face, she met his gaze boldly, and replied in the affirmative, in the same far-off voice in which she had been speaking for some time.

"Tell *me exactly*," said he, drawing his chair still closer to her side, "all that occurred after we parted, in regard to Aleppo." She remained silent for some time, then began talking as if she were in a dream.

"The nurse, Edena, kept him from the hour of his birth, till she vanished with him, as I bade her do, seventeen years ago. No mortal but Edena and yourself connects Aleppo in any way with me, except," she drew a long breath, "except Jacob the Jew."

"What!" Romanes sprang from the chair. "Jacob the Jew?" He fairly hissed the words.

"I had no other means," said Helene defiantly, "I knew he would be secret, and the work had to be done."

"Go on," said Romanes.

"I had never seen the boy until the day before Edena's departure, when she brought him to me in the Swiss Mountains. Here, Jacob, by appointment, arrived also; when the sign of the Order was burnt into his back, just over the left shoulder blade.''

'' Was it clear-cut ? ''

'' Perfectly; so said Jacob, though I had no heart to look.''

'' Helene, you have made a fatal blunder ; first, in trusting this task to Jacob; second, in not scrutinizing the sign *yourself*. Aleppo undoubtedly has a mystic symbol tattooed upon his back; but what the symbol is, is of vital importance, however let it pass. We have no means of proving the identity of our son save by this scar. If we succeed, it will be, I fear, through the diabolical assistance of Jacob the Jew. Is he still alive ? ''

''He is,'' said Helene, scornfully; '' He will never die ; I saw him but a month since on the Rialto.'' Romanes began his tireless walk again.

'' Did you give Edena instructions as to what to do with the boy ? ''

'' None, whatever, she begged him of me, and promised that she would educate and start him in life. The large sum which you had handed to me for that purpose was given over to her, and from what I know of her in the past, I am sure she fulfilled her trust.''

'' And you never saw Aleppo but once ? ''

'' But once ; at the time the brand was made.''

'' His eyes, his hair, what color ? '' Romanes walked faster and faster.

'' Black,'' said Helene, in a still more dreamy

tone. "He had a trick like yours, of tossing his hair from his brow by a shake of his head."

"Even then ! "

"Yes," said Helene. She had gone back into the past, until her present surroundings had utterly vanished; her eyes were closed, and her face, white as snow, caught the attention of Romanes, and brought him to a sudden halt. The years had left no mark on her. Her hair, of a reddish gold, was abundant, and of the fluffy kind, that makes still softer a soft face. Her complexion, extremely fair, was relieved, as a rule, by a flush in the cheeks, giving her the coloring of a pink pearl; though to-night all glow had left it and a deathly pallor had taken its place. Her eyes had the gleam of amber, and her features, while scarcely of the Greek type, were refined and youthful. Altogether she was fair, fair ; and Romanes gazed at her in wonder. Then, turning shortly, he walked resolutely away, and knit his brows.

"You see," he went on, and she heard, "it will be difficult ; perhaps impossible. He may be dead." She moved no muscle. "However, we two must give our lives, every hour, to the undertaking ; shall we begin now? "

He reached his hand to Helene.

"Do you love this boy?" She drew a long sigh and came suddenly to herself, as though out of a dream; then sat erect, and opened her eyes which beamed on him like fiery stars.

"I do not; why should I?" He has stood
between you and me, since first his little heart began
to beat beneath my own; he drove you to the south
and me to the north; he divided us by continents,
by seas, he stole in upon an ideal love, and painted
it black. He wrenched the sign of the order from
you, and tossed it into the Bosporus; he degraded
your powers till you lay prone in the dust, a fallen
giant. He drove me an exile to the Swiss Mountains.
and fouled my tongue with lies. And now, when
we were getting upon our feet, he comes again to
intrude between us, and hold us apart." She
towered over Romanes; the negative had become
positive, the poles had shifted—he bowed his head.
"Yes," she went on in the same impassioned tone,
"in spite of my unnatural hate, in spite of the
sacrifice which he entails, in spite of age and
death, I will seek and find Aleppo Romanes, and
restore him to his own." Henrique lifted his eyes,
his face beamed with admiration and awe.

"Helene Cressey, you are great. No one can
understand why I say this, except ourselves. In
taking such a step, all that which we have struggled
to obtain is given up; certain powers, which we
have acquired, are sacrificed; life is laid down.
Fate you claim is powerful; our wills, I have reason
to know, are more so; yet in spite of this we yield,
and shackle ourselves"—He stopped abruptly—
"what must we do?"

"Part."

" And then ? "

" Search ; you in your way, I in mine. Whoever succeeds, notifies the other and we meet. Till
then adieu." He hesitated a moment ; but in her
face was an unalterable détermination. He swayed
slightly, as a sapling does, that has lost its support;
she stood erect like a granite shaft ; then backing
slowly toward the entrance, keeping his eyes
intently fixed on hers, he left the room. The door
closed silently after him, and the instant it was shut,
Helene *turned out the light.* The darkness could be
felt, as it sometimes is, when a pall is drawn over
the stars of heaven, and the moon.

CHAPTER III.

ON THE RIALTO.

Aleppo and Sallus were on the Rialto, stopping
now and then to dicker with a shop keeper, and
pushing ahead later, to catch up with " the
philosopher." This unique individual, captured
by Aleppo the second day after Sallus' reform, had
remained with the young men ever since. He was
long-visaged, slim and brown, with a shrewd eye
which might have graced any other Yankee ; but
his chief charm lay in the fact that he could talk,
and touch up his word paintings with as much
pessimistic bile, as could any old cynic of ancient
times. He had more venomous wisdom than

Diogenes himself, and rivaled all the iconoclasts
that ever were born, in his power to upset precon-
ceived ideas, and overthrow castles in the air.
With all, he was clean and square, and reached the
skeleton of truth straightway, having no respect
for her veils nor her varnish. His name was Regan
with a Patrick attached, for Aleppo and Sallus used
his surname as a fixed thing, adding on the other
when it came to their minds. The three got over
the Rialto at last, and later on, established comfortably in a gondola, prepared to enjoy themselves.
Their method of doing this was peculiar; in fact
for the last ten days, since their flight from Stamboul, the boys had done scarce else than listen,
while Regan, with a piece of tobacco tucked safely
under his tongue, did nothing but talk. To be
sure, the young men interrupted with questions
continuously, but aside from that they were all ears.
When young fellows get hold of such a disciple
of realism as was Regan, who proceeds to unmask
everything, they are aged forthwith. Whether
this is good or bad for them is not in the question;
they are as fascinated as is the green medical
student in possession of his first "stiff."

"You see," said Regan, spitting tobacco juice
as far as he could send it into the blue water, "You
see, Venice did the best she could to commit
suicide; I suppose you know that Aleppo?"

The young man had been gazing on the bright
scene with the eye of an artist.

"She is a dream," he answered.

"Yes, she is pretty fancy," and he sent his second fire of tobacco juice at the water on the other side, "but she is nothing to what she was, nothing."

"What was she?" demanded Sallus.

"A good deal; you see it's the way with cities; they reach their prime and their decay. There is no use in pretending that you can perpetuate a city or a government, for you can't. Eternity is a long time; its forever. See?"

"Yes," said Sallus.

"Now, this pretty place about which poets tear their hair and painters rave, this place is dead."

"Don't look much like it," said Sallus, "they ship enough glass beads from it each year to delude all the darkies in Africa, besides it's a Mecca; you know very well, it's a Mecca."

"When a former seat of government and a medieval center has degenerated into a Mecca, mark my word, boy, *it is dead*.

"Venezia la bella," sighed Aleppo.

"But what of the Venice of the Crusades?" answered Regan; "born of mud and crystalized in marble; foremost among the states of Europe, unassailable in locality, stuffed with gold, embanked with granite, and tied, island to island, with four hundred bridges; the center of art, unrivaled in the world." He smiled, and showed a complete and even set of slightly discolored teeth. His noiseless laugh implied an immense deal about to be revealed, which would completely disillusion any fanatic, who looked upon Venice as other than a corpse, over which the scum of humanity crept, in its ceaseless trot around the world.

"As I said," went on Regan, "she was in at her own death ; although her case, as regards longevity was hopeless even had she had no hand in it, you see?" He was fond of saying, "you see." "Foremost in geographical research, she helped to circumnavigate Africa, and find the New World; the discovery of which took away the great commercial value of the Mediterranean, and Venice died, you see."

"Yes," said Sallus but she is coming to life."

"A sort of an electrified corpse;" observed Regan, rolling his tobacco into his cheek, " to be sure it looks a little more lively than in 1840, when it was down to a hundred thousand, and the grass grew in the squares. It has a new bridge, its skies are way up, just as they used to be, its climate is tip-top, and its palaces for which those old larch forests gave their lives, that the city might have legs to stand on, still set the Ruskins singing requiems and psalms. In spite of her hundred and seventeen islands, her hundred and fifty canals and three hundred and fifty bridges, Rivo Alto is dead. To be sure, she has her Moorish-Italian architecture, her Rialto over the Grand Canal, her masterpieces of Titian, Tintoretto and

Paul Veronese ; to be sure she has her tourists'
hotels, and her modern gondola, nevertheless she is a
shrine ; and to find this out we must go backward
in years and behold her alive." He paused again
to cut off more tobacco, and the young men,
enthralled, sat speechless.

" Well then, there was a time, when she stole
marble and porphyries, like a first-class thief, from
Rome, from Byzantium, from the ruined cities of
Heraclea, Altinum and Aquilea, indirectly also from
Numidia, Egypt and Arabia—all kinds of treasures,
as you have ample chance to see yet on the palaces—
red porphyry from Egypt, green from Mount Lay-
getus, ancient granites, alabaster, Phrygian pavon-
azzetto, and the amber-blue proscenium. The columns of the ancients were sawed up and turned
into mosaics ; besides these, look at the gold and
silver, and the famous ultramarine. But let me
tell you, it's all shoddy, every bit, and nobody pre-
tends it isn't; it's a thin coating of veneer, nothing
more; look inside Saint Mark's. See ?

" But," interrupted Sallus as though roused out
of a dream, " Venice is the second commercial city
to-day, in Italy."

" Don't care if she is, nor the first ; she isn't the
city of the Middle Ages, I can tell you, by a long
shot. Places have a rhythm as sure as the sea has ;
perhaps she will rise again, but 'twon't be Venice.
Look at those ugly iron bridges, and that steam
engine. The genius of the Nineteenth Century

rides rough-shod over tesselated pavements, and erects suspension bridges where Rialtos ought to be. There's no use talking, the dunes of the Doge and the Council have gone under ; and a cross between a mechanic and a water swan has brought forth something with a new motive, and a modern name "—here he smiled again. " Yes, I tell you she's dead; she has quit stealing, she has stopped conquering and overhauling, she is too good to be alive; her game is up."

" But the beauty of her ! " said Aleppo.

" She is pretty enough, no doubt ; so is a corpse, if you paint and powder it, and get up a modern two-step fantastic in the near vicinity. Why even this gondola is a new-fangled institution ; the thing they used to have is as black as an old man's hearse, however "—here he smiled once more.

Aleppo shook himself and tossed back his hair ; he had been slowly drawn out of his water dream of years by the bait on Regan's hook. The ideal Venice floated off into the blue on tearful clouds, and the modern canal city with its beautiful decay, its rain storms and hot winds, took possession of his soul. Sallus was not so deeply stirred ; he stood for the spirit of the age. There was nothing back of him but an American plough and a flint lock ; he had his fancies, and beauty was his aim ; but he was wofully young both in country and in object ; a modern, out and out. He might have risen, clean-washed from the sea, or descended from

heaven, as far as anything behind him was concerned.

Later, after the three had returned to the hotel
for supper, Sallus went out for an hour and Aleppo
sat down in loving proximity to Regan and made
this proposition. " You have smashed my ideal of
Venice to bits, you can go on smashing things to
the end of this trip—which will be a long one, I
fancy—on one condition ; and that is, that you'll
keep Sallus straight. I've managed it for a week,
but I tell you, if you hadn't turned up, 'twould
have been all over with him by this time. You're
a marvel. I turn him over to you, understand ? "

" I do," answered Regan, stretching his legs,
" guess I'll get after him now. I know about
where he is. I'll give him a revelation to-night, a
regular inside view. He'll take it straight without
any liquor in him, and I'm sure he'll be disgusted.
You see he was always boozy when he got into the
worst of things and didn't know what he was
about. Its quite another thing for a man to make
the tour of the Inferno with his perceptive and
reflective faculties in normal condition, from that
of dragging himself along, stupified with drink."

" You are right " answered Aleppo, " Sallus is
anything but bad, when he is himself; it is the
drink that has spoiled him. You have set him to
thinking—you certainly have ; he's brainy but
young. Wake up his ideas, and keep them active

till he conquers this craving that's driving him wild, and you'll see what a fellow he is."

"That's all right," answered Regan, "but a shock is a heap better ; there's a way of turning love into hate you know in double quick time. Of course if he were old, and hadn't the wine of pure youth in him, 'twould be a harder thing to do ; he has rich blood, that Sallus ! he makes himself over about once a week, and goes "the pace" again, good as new, that is the privilege of youth, but he's a beauty lover ; and beauty and nastiness don't go together you know. He has to get drunk before he can soil his wings ; when he is sober, he is too dainty, see ?

At this stage of Aleppo's development he was easily convinced that most of Regan's conclusions were right ; so thinking a moment, he asked, "What kind of a shock are you going to give him ?"

"That's not for you to know," said Regan emphatically, drawing himself up to his full height and plunging his hands into his pockets, "I have done this sort of thing before with young fellows ; with some I succeed, with some I don't. I reckon I've got Sallus ; I don't mind telling you the principle of the thing, but beyond that it's my secret. I am going to work by the law of antithesis, see ? Catch him sober when his squeamishness and daintiness are on top, and duck him into about the filthiest pool on the planet ; of course he'll get a shock—can't help it; and you know what shocks mean, eh ?."

" Well, after a fashion," said Aleppo yawning—he only half grasped it.

'' I'm off now ; we'll make a night of it. Don't *you* go to meandering ; our crowd needs some one to maintain the reputation."

Regan laughed, got out his tobacco, and went off, leaving Aleppo in his own company.

He enjoyed it too, he always had ; in this sense he was a strange young man ; he loved to be alone —utterly, without a soul within miles of him. As a child he would hunt solitary places as naturally as most children seek a crowd. He had a curious power of ignoring outer environment, and creating an inner one after his own fancy—literally reversing himself and looking inwardly rather than without.

That this condition was to him extremely fascinating, can be better understood, when we explain a certain phenomenon which often accompanied these inner explorations. Over and over again, in some pretty dream world of his, had appeared a *face*, young, beautiful and feminine, with eyes that met his, lovingly, adoringly.

Since his first sight of her, he had lived in a sort of interior transport, irrevocably in love with the vision which was so especially his own ; ever longing for its reappearance, and firmly convinced that its counterpart lived either in flesh or among the angels.

This mysterious tendency of Aleppo's to live the interior life was inherent; he had received no instructions to that effect, nor had he, in the few short years of his existence, met with any one who could in the least degree sympathize with or understand him in this respect. He wrote to "Miss Somebody" regularly, as we have before stated, and although he had privately informed Sallus about her in one of his confidential moods, aside from that, he kept his experiences to himself. Nor was the vision of the girlish face his only source of rapture. He beheld places, which he was convinced must be on earth ; and heard music that charmed him, like the song of the nightingale. He remembered also, some of his early past ; a little of his nurse, Edena, and a vague and beautiful woman, whom he saw once when a mere child ; also a revolting personage that he felt sure had in some way tortured him, though how, he could not recall. To-night he made several attempts after Regan's departure to enter his interior domain, but without avail ; no vision presented itself which gave him the slightest satisfaction ; so, seizing his hat, he started forth to make a night of it also, after his own fashion.

The moon was full ; and Venice lay like a silvery dream on the water ; her voice, heard now and then in the song of a gondolier as he paddled noiselessly up and down the calm lagoon, or paused before the steps of a marble palace, whose age and decay had been painted out by ghostly fingers.

Aleppo was drunk with glamor, debauched with beauty, as he shifted his point of view, now here, now there, appropriating the still splendor, as the earth absorbs the sun. To him the illusion was the real, and the real the illusion. Venetian scars were sanctified and made lovely, by the magic touches of the moon. The ideal city had descended from the blue above, to float upon the blue below, more content, more at rest, than in celestial spaces.

At last Aleppo found himself on the bridge of the Grand Canal, and unable to account for a strange nervousness which had suddenly seized him, and to which he was entirely unaccustomed. He was at one moment exhilarated, and the next depressed; fear set him trembling, to be followed by an ecstatic spasm of the heart. In this perturbed state of mind, he sought the Rialto, as if driven there by the whip-cords of fate. Wandering aimlessly over the long bridge and peering in mechanically at the shops, he had gone part way, when two people coming in his direction arrested his attention, and brought him to a sudden halt.

The elder was unmistakably an Assyrian Jew, while the younger resembled the sweet-faced vision of his dreams. The former coming out of the past, unchanged, save by added ugliness, was the counterpart of the demon, which had lodged in the brain of the child, Aleppo, seventeen years before,

while the latter *seemed* to be " Miss Somebody " to
whom he had written since his hand could hold a
pen.

They passed so quickly that before Aleppo had
recovered from the shock, they had vanished, and
left no sign. The young man took off his hat,
tossed back his hair and rubbed his eyes. Had
he been deceived—was it after all but a return of
his vision? No, they had been so near that he
could have touched their garments, and *together*.
What had they two in common? The face of the
girl, he remembered, was pale, the eyes tear-stained.
He recalled, however, that he had been deceived
before, many times, and sadly disappointed. This
young lady's hair was different—lighter and more
wavy—than that of the vision of his dreams; he
must be mistaken, it was a resemblance only. But
of the Jew he had no doubt. He had noticed as
they passed, that he had fixed his eyes on him as
though his attention had been arrested, and a suspicion aroused. Had the remembrance been
mutual? Had this strange man, with his parchment visage, and claw-like fingers, discovered some
resemblance in Aleppo's face, that made his identity plain? The Jew, was uncanny, antique, revolting, and might, for aught he knew, possess extraordinary powers.

Aleppo was utterly at sea; he could neither
understand himself, nor his dread. He put the episode of his sweetheart aside, and exaggerated his

meeting with the Jew, apparently out of all proportion with the event.   He hurried back to his hotel,
and locking himself in his room, strove by all the
power within him to get at a clue to himself.
This Jew he must find at any cost, for he was
undoubtedly the key, by which Aleppo might
unlock the door to his undiscovered past.

CHAPTER IV.

THE JEW.

The next day after his experience on the Rialto,
Aleppo became skeptical, wary, and altogether
unsettled in mind as to the identity of either of the
parties, met the night before.   He said to himself,
"The Jew of my childhood is undoubtedly dead;
or, if not, his diabolical face was exaggerated in
my terror.   A baby forgets—I must be a fool.   Of
one thing I am certain, if I stumble on him again,
I will 'draw my skirts;' 'tis pollution to touch
him.   Rather than cultivate his acquaintance, I
will leave Venice; better lose my past forever than
seek it through such a source."

This was Aleppo's cogitation.   He had remained
in his room through the morning, debating with
himself ; after the departure of Regan and Sallus
in search of more experience along doubtful lines.

In the meantime a Jew had entered the hotel,
and was diligently inquiring for a young man

named Aleppo. He was asked if the name was
Aleppo Bracciolini. Having satisfied himself that
it might be, he sent his card to Aleppo's room,
who received it with a shock of astonishment.
The name inscribed on the curious looking tablet
was Jacob Issachar. Almost before Aleppo had
time to consider whether to admit him or not, the
door was pushed softly open and a strange figure
entered. He wore the dress of the ancients, and
presented, in his face and form, a picture that must
necessarily throw one back in memory or imagination thousands of years. His undergarment was
loosely girdled at the waist and over this was
thrown a cloak, which fell gracefully from one
shoulder, leaving the other exposed. On his head
was a cap-like hood, which was drawn squarely
across the brow, and fell in a cape at the back of
his neck. His black hair, stiff and straight, fell a
little out of his head-gear on either side of his face,
and that, with his tawny skin and piercing eyes,
contrasted fiercely with the creamy white of his
garments, which fell in folds of great beauty over
an erect and powerful frame. His height was phe-
nomenal—he towered above Aleppo, who was of
average size, like a giant patriarch over a degen-
erate modern—and as he elongated, seemingly taller
and taller, his broad mouth spread into a beaming
smile, displaying the perfect teeth of an untamed
beast. He spoke in Aleppo's favorite tongue,
which was English; his language being beyond

criticism, though the words fell slowly and with great precision from his lips.

"Pardon,"—Aleppo instinctively drew away and placed a chair between them—"I seek one Aleppo Romanes."

"You have certainly struck the wrong man." Aleppo tried in vain to assume a haughty and indifferent air, but the same terror that he had felt as a child was creeping over him, wholly unaccountable, and utterly beyond his understanding.

"Ah! Not Aleppo Romanes?"

"No!" thundered the young man, in a ridiculously loud voice.

"May I ask your name?" The Jew was faultlessly polite. Aleppo, feeling his own actions to be absurd, pulled himself together, and answered in a more moderate tone, "Aleppo Bracciolini."

"A—h!!" Issachar posed like a statue, turned his eyes far back into his head and remained rigid a full minute, then, coming to, as if from a dream, blazed in dark splendor once more on the young man, and shot flashes and sparks into his very soul.

"Yes, Aleppo Bracciolini, 'tis the same, from Italy?"

"Well?"

"Brought up in an asylum ; later, adopted by a celibate; afterward, in an artist's studio ; to-day, on a long journey. Am I right?" He smiled again in the same beaming way.

For the first time in his life Aleppo deliberately
concluded to lie. His dread of this man had increased with every minute of his stay; his uncanny
knowledge of himself was revolting ; so, turning
his full face on Issachar, and looking him straight
in the eyes, he proceeded to tell a full-fledged false-
hood, as glibly, aye, even more glibly than he usually told the truth.

'' You are all wrong (becoming affable suddenly,
and smiling back, while courteously offering the
Jew a chair, which that gentleman declined.) '' You
are all wrong. I am traveling with my father,
(here he hesitated) Patrick Bracciolini, and my
brother Sallus; we shall make the tour of the
world. What, pray tell me, is this to you? ''

Before Jacob Issachar had time to reply, the door
flew open, and Regan and Sallus entered. They
stopped, as if brought up with a round turn,
when their eyes caught those of the patriarch,
who, though apparently .but middle-aged, seemed
to have all the pride and mystery of an ancient.
Aleppo, caught in the act of lying, was greatly
confused by this turn of affairs, and, driven to
bay, took desperate measures at once.

'' Jacob Issachar, this is my father, Mr. Patrick
Bracciolini, and my brother Sallus.''

Regan allowed his lower jaw to drop for a
moment, showing a whole row of saffron-tinted
teeth, and the tobacco besides ; then smacked his
lips together, and with a curious look of under-

standing in his eyes, held out his hand to Jacob. This the Jew rejected, but, elevating his voice a little, said, without the slightest loss of dignity, "Your son does not resemble you."

"No; it's the way with families—odd sheep. See?"

Sallus, convulsed with laughter, stuffed his handkerchief into his mouth and steered toward the window, but the Jew stood utterly motionless, and Regan, catching the appealing expression in Aleppo's face, went on:

"He's an odd one; so is Sallus for that matter; out of six 'tisn't strange that two should look like —well, their grandmother."

"When do you go from here?"

The Jew uttered the words with a pause between each.

Regan had no idea, but glibly answered;

"We shall get up into Scandinavia next midnight sun, and all that; may keep on to the pole; but who is it that you seek?"

"Aleppo Romanes."

"Ah, I understand. Aleppo Romanes! Yes; met him in Stamboul; let's see, on the Asiatic side, skulking around among the grave-stones. Fine lad, he, given to poetry and romance; had a talk with him at Scutari; was just about to do up Siberia, hunting for weird subjects for a great picture; may be in Constantinople yet;—that all?"

The Jew, during this harangue, had turned his

eyes backward again, far into his head, and seemed not to have heard a word; then, coming to himself, shot sparks from them straight into the lying soul of Regan, and bowing slightly, marched, with long and dignified strides from the room.

"Great Scott!" What a figure!

Regan drew a long breath, and wiped the perspiration from his brow.

"We are in for it now," said Sallus. "What on earth are you up to, any way; who under heaven is that son of Adam that just passed out?"

For answer, Aleppo locked the door; then went to the window near by, and took a long survey.

"It seems to me I've grown ten years older—lying comes hard. Yes, we are in for it, and I see no way out of it either, except to run."

Regan seated himself in a big arm chair, like a privileged sire, took care that his spittoon was handy, and then drawled, in a paternal voice,

"Come here, my son, and explain to your anxious father the nature of this event.

For the first time since the entrance of the men, Aleppo laughed, then recited, in a few decisive words, the account of his adventure, beginning on the Rialto the night before. The two listeners fell into the spirit of the thing with avidity, and though they could not in the least understand the reason of Aleppo's nervousness, each, in his way, discovered in the event the means to an end. Sallus' love of adventure found full play, while Regan saw

a chance to carry out a standing joke which would
be a never ending source of amusement for the
three.   Aleppo, on the contrary, was tragic to the
core, and with difficulty threw off the numbness
and dread which had set him trembling an hour
previously.

" Now, look here, boys, you've introduced me as
your father, and as it's the first time I've tried the
role of paterfamilias, I propose to keep it up to
the end of this trip.   It'll be an awful sight of
trouble, to be sure, for I'm used to the name of
Regan ; but I'll get round that somehow, and make
you fellows toe the mark, if I know myself.   If
the Jew has designs I can settle him perhaps.
He's after you, Aleppo, of course ; but you don't
want him nor none of his sort.   In my opinion he's
a kind of Mahatma."

" A what? " said Aleppo.

" A Mahatma, I believe that's what they call
them.   Did you see how he rolled his eyes up
when he posed? "

" But what on earth do you mean by Mahatma ? " said Sallus—the two boys drew closely
to the newly-made father.

" Well, they do say, those that are supposed
to know, that there's seven or eight of them on
earth to-day, and I guess he's one."

" Seven or eight what ? "

" Oh, they're men of course ; that is they look

like men, but I'll tell you what it is boys, they are not; they're Dyhan Chohans."

"Good gracious!" and Sallus kicked over the chair on which his feet were resting, "why do you need to be so allfired mysterious, why can't you let a fellow know what you are driving at without all this jaw breaking language?"

"Well you see," deliberately rolling his quid, "these beings won't tolerate English; Sanscrit is hardly good enough for them, to say nothing of Pali."

"But what are they?" put in Aleppo, who was taking it all seriously.

"Men, as I told you; but did you observe the ancient look of Issachar? Well now it's just possible"—here he lowered his voice to an uncanny stage whisper—"that that man was born before Moses."

"Bosh"! said Sallus, rising and restoring the chair to an upright position, "What are you giving us anyhow?"

"Well you see it's this way," went on Regan, if there are Mahatmas they must be about the same as Dyhan Chohans. And if they can build worlds, and walk on water, and appear and disappear, why seven or eight of them are enough on this planet, it strikes me, and I shouldn't be more than surprised if this fellow that's got after Lep is one of them."

The faces of the young men were a study during

this harangue. Sallus' showed supreme disgust, and Aleppo drank in the words as though they were gospel truth—then Sallus caught Aleppo's eye—

"You are not going to make me hate you by believing this stuff are you Lep," he said with a sneer.

"Hate and love cut no figure in the question," answered Aleppo tartly. "I believe Issachar has strange powers."

"You'd better believe he has ;" went on Regan, "you took the Jew to be about forty, but I shouldn't wonder in the least if he were the bona-fide son of Jacob and Leah. You see, Jacob was always hankering after Rachel. Leah had blear eyes, or something of that kind, so this son was a sort of an odd stick ; and those that the gods desert are generally compensated by some unnatural power. This Jew is a master piece ; he's one of the seven wonders. Anyhow I think it's an excellent plan to go on the supposition that he is a Mahatma, otherwise he'd be seducing us with miracles, subduing us with delusions, making passes over us and staring us out of countenance till we didn't know which was which. Then he'd hypnotize us, and that would be the end—once hypnotized, we'd be done for, sure. Why boys, he'd make us go anywhere, just calling us; we'd follow to the verge of the universe. It's the most deucedly hellish power there is ; and what's worse, if he wanted to kill us,

he'd just make a wax image of you or me and stab
it to the heart—that's killing by proxy, but it
works with a Mahatma every time—his powers are
simply infernal."

"I'd like to get at him," said Sallus, bending
his elbow, and displaying a tremendous knot of
muscle near the shoulder—"I could lay that Jew
flat with one blow."

"Don't know about it," continued Regan, "you
see he's a head higher than you, and square at the
shoulder like an American Indian. What's under
that infernal night-dress of his, 'twould be hard to
tell. In my opinion, he's pretty tough, both in
giving and taking; wouldn't be an easy one to
tackle by a long shot. But as I was saying, if he
is a Mahatma it's all right, if he isn't, it's the same
—we'll be ready for him anyhow."

"Yes," said Aleppo nervously, we'll be ready by
running. I am going to clear out."

"I never knew you to be such a coward," said
Sallus with astonishment.

"I will admit it. I am scared. Nor do I understand myself in the least, nor this sensation of fear.
Of one thing I am certain however, this man is the
link to my past. Up to the time I met him, I was
most anxious to learn about myself; but now I am
not. Besides, though I know very well that Regan
has been joking, I believe, without comprehending
why, in the Jew's diabolical arts. A man with
great powers is not necessarily good—if Satan is

alive, Issachar is he. Matters sift down to this—
I'm going to run, you can come on with me if you
like, or,''—here he stopped.

"Stay here, I suppose you meant to say—'whither
thou goest, I will go,' and Sallus also. As my
two dutiful sons I propose to show you the world;
and if the black Mahatma gets after us there'll be a
race worth watching.''

Sallus gave a sigh of supreme satisfaction; if
anything had been needed to complete the reform
which Aleppo and Regan had initiated, it was this
touch of adventure, this spice of danger, that,
though it did not appeal to him in the least in the
latter sense, was nevertheless so thrilling to Aleppo,
that he enjoyed its effects on another almost as
much as though feeling them himself.

After a long pause, Regan began again—'' You
see, it's about time we made some regular plan
instead of gallivanting around hap-hazard. Finan-
cially I expect we are fixed ? ''

'' As for me,'' answered Sallus, '' my father will
pay anything to keep me out of his sight; he won't
care if I go on till doomsday, so that I don't dis-
grace the Smith family; he's very sensitive about
the Smiths—they're so *few*, you understand ? ''

"My case is different," put in Aleppo. I havn't any
father—nobody but myself; however, I can make the
tour of the world; it was my aunt's desire, and I
have arranged for it.''

"Now see here boys,'' said Regan, "you know I'm

rich—I don't mind telling you, and what's more, I know how to spend. The time was once when I was as poor as a religious mouse, fully didn't know where my next bite was coming from. I was a failure up to thirty, out and out. It's a pity too, for if I had had anything, I should have married—but I hadn't, so that settled it. She went off with a richer man. She wouldn't let me go out to day's labor, so I ran for pound master, coroner and district-attorney, but they all fell flat. It seemed as though the more effort I made, the poorer I grew; at last, she threw me over altogether, and I vowed I'd get rich to spite her. As I couldn't make something out of something, I just went and got it out of nothing— I invented an egg-beater.''

"What!!"

"An egg-beater that beat any beater that ever was beaten before; and I followed it up with two or three other unmentionables, that went like wild-fire. I got hold of a fool bigger than myself—he spent all his money on them, and to-day is dead.''

"Whew!!"

"Yes, but his widow isn't; her new husband enjoys the profits—he has a good time I can tell you; so you see I'm fixed.''

"Why didn't you marry later?'' asked Sallus curiously.

"Because '*twas later*, that's what's the matter— too late. My only sweetheart turned sweetness to gall, but she's the one that's bothered, not I. She

repents a hundred times a day. When she found
out how rich I was growing, she wanted to get a
divorce and return to her first love—that was me.
See? But of course she couldn't. Her husband is
a respected member of the Chamber of Commerce,
and doesn't desert her, nor give cause. Is home
every night at sundown, drinks nothing but tea,
chews nothing but gum, and smokes eucalyptus.
So there 'tis; she's doomed, and—well I'd rather be
here. Now boys where shall we go next? Understand please, that if either of you run short, I'll
back you. Easy come, easy go; the stuff flows in
on me, and I don't know what to do with it. Ah!
I have it, I'll hire you as travelling companions on
condition that you take pot luck with me. I'll pay
you a salary, see? I'm getting on toward forty-five,
need youthful society to keep me from ageing, and
all that."

The boys laughed and agreed, that if times grew
hard with them, Regan should hire them at so
much a month. The financial part arranged, Regan
started in again.

"Now about this paternal business; I believe it's
a good scheme; it will throw the Jew off the track.
and give us no end of fun. I'll assume Aleppo's
name, though I wish to goodness 'twas Sallus'.
Smith suits me better. We'll do the world up in
fine shape—millionaire father, two fractious sons—
eh?"

"Seems to me, Lep and I are too near the same age to be passed off as brothers," said Sallus.

" That's all right—twins of course."

" Bosh! who ever heard of twins that didn't match better than we do? "

" Well then, one of you will have to lie. How nearly of an age are you ? "

" A few months apart, I imagine."

" Which is the oldest ? "

" I guess I am," said Aleppo.

" It's easy then, just change the months to years, see ? "

"But I don't look that old," protested Aleppo.

" Sure, you could pass for forty easy. Now that's fixed, where are we going ? "

" I'd rather like to get out of the beaten track," said Aleppo, "everybody does Europe. America, Australia, Malay Archipelago, Siberia, anywhere except France, Holland, Switzerland, Italy. Europe's done to death ; besides I have seen a good share of it."

" America and Siberia are some distance apart," answered Regan, "however that cuts no figure ; time and space are counted out. Now if we could penetrate into Lhasa, I should be perfectly content."

" Into where ? "

" Lhasa—Lhasa."

" Why it's the hardest place to get at imaginable, and still harder to get out of. To be within the atmosphere of the Grand Lama, is a thought that stirs my blood."

" Never heard of the place,' said Sallus.

" Ever so many people have though, but mighty few of our kind ever get to see it; however, that's in the far off—what next? "

"Pack," said Aleppo. "I'm going to get out of this "—the fear of the Jew was still on him. " I don't care where we turn up, so it's not Venice."

" 'Pon my word, we've got a girl to look after."

Sallus was disgusted with this new phase in his friend's character.

" Said and done," interrupted Regan. And the three, at this call to action, bustled about, and stuffed their wallets and bags, man-fashion.

The city of the Doges knew them no more; and the Jew Issachar, retired within himself, to work out the problem of Aleppo and the mystic mark.

CHAPTER V.

RHEA.

Mrs. Hancock and Rhea had been at Brindisi for several days ; they were traveling leisurely, and would embark later on the P. and O. steamer en route for Cairo. They had turned a couple of hotel bed-rooms into pretty places, by perching a few artistic photographs in perilous positions, fill-ing a vase with green leaves, picked while on a walk, and strewing the tables with magazines and papers. Besides, they had brought out their dainty tóilet bottles and an oriental tea-pot which a man would have smashed forthwith.

It's strange, but American women (particularly American) can be set down anywhere—by the sea, in a hut, on the desert, in a tent or a hotel bedroom, and with a magic wave of the hand—lo! *home*.

Mrs. Hancock was Rhea's aunt, and all-round adviser. She was, she said, doing her duty by Rhea, who lived in a chronic state of resentment. She had been known to complain to her beloved pastor, the Reverend Joseph Hitchcock, that her niece had no feeling of gratitude nor comprehension of the meaning of the same. Rhea had an annuity of her own, and was in no way a dependent; but being without father or mother her aunt had dutifully brought her up, and was now voluntarily chaperoning her around the world. Mrs. Hancock, according to her own account, lived a life of continual sacrifice, and had whispered in the Reverend Hitchcock's ear, that her reward would come later, if not on earth. The fact was, she was getting her recompense each day; and thoroughly enjoyed herself (deny it as she would) the posing, advising, displaying of virtues, rolling of religious eyes, the martyred expression which circumstances gave her a chance to assume, all these brought her supreme satisfaction, and abundance of matter to send in the form of weekly letters to her "beloved pastor." ·

Orthodox by persuasion, to say nothing of profession, she used the unbending rod of blue Presbyterianism to pierce a hole through the azure of heaven, into which she expected eventually to crawl. But Rhea was a heathen. She had lived now some twenty-six years, and would suffer no "ism" or "ist" to be attached to her; literally daring the devil, and traveling the broad path of wickedness—so her aunt called it—with as much self-respect and contentment as most young ladies when on the narrow road to heaven. Mrs. Hancock had never been able to frighten her, even when a child, though she had threatened her with all the sorrows of this life and of the other, if she continued to ignore the admonitions of the Reverend Hitchcock, and refused to enter the door of the church. But for that gentleman, Rhea had an absolute dislike; which was ill-concealed; in fact between herself and her aunt there was but little love, save that which creeps in through ties of blood. The two tolerated each other, extracting a mosquito-like pleasure from their relative positions, stinging right and left with their tongues, and preventing in their intercourse all monotony and stagnation.

Rhea was beautiful—if beauty is in any way akin to fascination. Whether she could stand the test of sculptor or painter is a question, but one thing is

certain, she always succeeded in impressing one
with her mysterious eyes, and slender white hands,
that seemed to be made either for models or for a
harp. The face of Rhea carried in it strength and
witchery—such an expression as must have been in
that of Cleopatra or Phryne. Her brow and speech
indicated fine intellect and conquering will, while
in the dimples, where the angels had kissed her,
nestled little cupids, restless to take wing. She
was a New England product, but far back of her
were Spain and Scotland—the flower of a hard-
headed, passionate ancestry. Thriving under the
wintry blasts of Cape Cod, she grew straight as an
arrow, cold as an iceberg, and hot as a tropical sun,
with logical mind and stormy heart she represented,
in her own sweet self the two poles of being that
drew to her side both men and women—lovers of
either sex and of all ages.

As I have said, they were temporarily at Brindisi,
but Mrs. Hancock had an abundance of work to do
nevertheless. She had a rival in Massachusetts,
whom she remembered well, even in Italy; this unreasonable personage was a Mrs. Ellsworth, who was
liable to get the pastor's ear while Mrs. Hancock
was traveling, and this worried that lady unceasingly. The rivalry did not stop here however;
these two women had vied with each other from
the days of their youth in fancy work and embroideries ; and just at present were working on table
linen and centerpieces, Determined that her trip

around the world should but emphasize an honest competition, Mrs. Hancock spent every spare moment, when not writing to the pastor, in embroidering the initial "H" in napkin corners, or adorning elaborate table centerpieces with somewhat weak imitations of innocent flowers.

Rhea had once told her that the Americans could never grasp the secret of color. and, in high disdain, she had left the room—but this aside.

Mrs. Hancock came bursting into Rhea's parlor the day before their departure, with her hands full of work; and it must be confessed that she was a picturesque figure, as, comfortably adjusting her eyeglasses, she covered herself with embroidery silks. She had a certain type of New England mouth that shuts itself with a snap. She was ceaselessly looking forward to a reward, and working on no matter what, as though she expected to be paid for it. Undoubtedly this was New England thrift, honestly come by, and well maintained; the only difference between her's and that of any other Yankee lay in the fact that she had transferred her right and title from property on this side to a piece on the other, having taken a deed to a literal mansion beyond the pearly gates, which she expected sooner or later to rule over in genuine Yankee style. This was evidenced in her face—it had a by-and-by expression, peculiarly its own.

She was scarcely more than seated, when, with

the first plunge of the needle into the linen, she
addressed Rhea:

"Feminine graces, my dear, are always sought
after by the men."

Rhea raised her eyes from the book she was reading, and looked straight at her aunt; there was
defiance in her expression but none in her tone, as
she said calmly, "Well?" The young woman
was always polite; frigid oftentimes in her manner,
yet strictly the lady, from head to toe. She hated
ugliness, coarseness and vulgarity; so, while full of
inward revolt at the tirade she felt in the air, she
answered Mrs. Hancock in a calm tone.

"Of course, Rhea, you know that you must
marry, sooner or later—you have put it off now
longer than most girls would dare—and the way to
really capture a desirable man is through your truly
feminine qualities. Men have enough of the male
element in themselves; they seek in woman the
very opposite."

"Do you think me decidedly masculine?"

The girl's eyes were sparkling with fun; the conversation had taken an amusing turn.

"Not to look at, but you are a regular man to
talk with; men admire you till they know you, then
you frighten them."

"But that is what I live for; what better amusement could I have than that of frightening men?"

"That is all very well while you are young, but
'twont do forever; you will find yourself among the

list of those ' left out ' in a year or two; your
chances are growing less all the time. When we
have completed this trip, your education will be
entirely finished, and if your prospects are as vague
at the end of the journey as they are now, I don't
know what will become of you."

"I shall probably go into a convent," said Rhea,
more and more amused, "but say, Aunt Carrie,
what do you mean by ' my chances '? "

"Your chances to get married, of course."

"But I never had an offer from anybody in my
life, so I don't see how they can grow less."

"You might have had a hundred; its your own
fault; you have men dangling after you continually
—all sorts, young and old, but as soon as they
show a sign of coming to terms, you spring the
subject of spontaneous generation on them, or the
cellular theory, or some cult or other, that shuts
their mouths tighter than clams. I've seen you do
it over and over again."

"But suppose I want to shut their mouths, havn't
I the right so far as I am concerned?"

"No you haven't, Rhea Nellino, your first duty
is to marry."

She was somewhat wrathy and stabbed her finger
with the cambric needle till the blood flew. Rhea
bit her lip to keep from laughing, and dropped her
eyelids to hide their mischief. To get Mrs.
Hancock into a rage while she remained utterly
unconcerned, was one of Rhea's chief delights.

"You talk exactly as Mr. Sylvas does—exactly; he informed me, that men sought clinging imbecile women—gentle, unlearned women—madonna-faced women—" lean-to " women—he also whispered in my ear that I had but to suppress my inclination to study and logic to find a man like himself, or perhaps, even himself, my devoted slave."

"And his advice was good," said Mrs. Hancock, snapping her eyes, and pricking her fingers again.

"But you see, Aunt Carrie,"—in her sweetest fashion—"while those after the style of Mr. Sylvas might enjoy me in that phase, I *shouldn't enjoy myself*. The wonder of it is, that men never consider *me ;* as it happens, what they would like me to be and what I enjoy being are quite different. I live, I imagine, *to live*. The main question with me is how much of life can I get; but unfortunately Mr. Sylvas' idea of me is just contrary. He would reduce me in height a few inches, in order that he might be the taller of the two. It is mostly that way with men, Aunt Carrie; they can't bear to look up, but love to look down."

"Talk is cheap, and that's conceit"—this time Mrs. Hancock snapped her needle in two—"but I tell you, after you've passed thirty you will change your tactics."

"Why?" said Rhea innocently, assuming an aggravating expression—

"Because you'll want to be loved mighty bad, just as any other woman does."

" But I want that now "—she looked more child-like, more ignorant if that could be, than before—

" Then why don't you take your chance while you can get it: Sylvas is dying for you; all that he asks is that you spare his pride a little, and become • dutiful and humble as a woman ought to be. Ralph Logan would marry you too, but for the same cause."

Rhea sighed as if her last hope had vanished, though one with sharp ears might have translated the sigh into a laugh.

" Then I'm doomed to be a spinster, and against my most ardent wishes too. I want love more than any woman on earth, but I desire it for the whole of me, not for a part. If I must sacrifice two-thirds of myself in order to get the other one-third adored, I don't know what I am going to do. You see auntie, 'twill be suicide—nothing less. I should have to kill my logic, my imagination, my dreams —all that part of me which I enjoy the most, whether it gives anybody else pleasure or not."

" Wouldn't you rather have a third of yourself loved than none at all ? "

" Not a bit of it!" said Rhea energetically, toss-ing her book on the table—" in fact I have that now; my tom cat, Noah, at Sandwich loves that much of me, so do my six white hens, and my pug Bascom. No Aunt Carrie Hancock dearest "—and she went over to her aunt and caught her face in her hands and kissed her—" just in proportion as I belong to these men, they love me, don't you understand. I suppose I appeal to each one of them somewhat, so they dangle about, but I appeal to myself more ; that's just all there is of it. If I ever marry, and alas ! I fear I never shall ''—here she stroked her aunt's hair consolingly—'' I must marry completely: to be a little bit married isn't after my style. I want to be married altogether or not at all— do you comprehend ?''

''No I don't.''

Mrs. Hancock was mollified, however; she always gave way under Rhea's caresses—'' You're the strangest mortal I ever saw, without exception, but we must dress for dinner,'' and she gathered up her flosses and linen and rustled out.

When she had gone, Rhea threw herself into the chair and gave way to a fit of hysterical laughter— O, auntie! You'll be the death of me yet! Mr. Sylvan! Mr. Logan!'' It was too much; she abandoned her dignity and allowed her amusement full sway. This was a trait of her's, to drain the last drop from the cup, though it contained nothing but water.

Completely rejuvenated, she proceeded to dress, and looked much like a girl of sixteen when she met her aunt at dinner an hour later.

As it happened, Regan, Aleppo and Sallus arrived in Brindisi that very day on their way to Cairo also, and were placed at the same hotel table with Mrs. Hancock and her neice Rhea. The three men, one

after the other, caught the eyes of the young lady,
and each felt in his own way a peculiar little shock,
at the same time a warmth about the heart and a
desire with it to be good, and do good, to all the
world. This was the first emotion that Rhea called
up in the soul of a man, when she chose to look him
in the eyes. It was always the same, with old or
young, but later, her aunt had remarked, she spoiled
it all.

Regan sat opposite Rhea, and the two young men
were on either side of him. For a few moments
they devoted themselves energetically to the dinner,
but later, Mrs. Hancock who was rather nervous,
dropped her fork, which Aleppo instantly restored
to her; this called forth thanks and apologies, and
before they knew it, they were all talking as
though old friends. Regan informed Mrs. Hancock
that he and his sons were about to take the steamer
for Cairo, and learning that the lady and her neice
were going there also, the three men beamed at
each other unconscious of what they were so happy
about ; while Mrs. Hancock took account of
stock as she usually did whenever Rhea and a
husband were concerned.

Bracciolini, the *elder*, and Rhea took a fancy to
each other at once, and having ascertained that they
were both Yankees, and from the same state, their
right to a travelling partnership was conceded by
all. The boys, already jealous of Regan, vowed
by the powers, that on no account should Miss

Nellino be disillusioned about their relationship;
they called Regan, father, continuously, and he seeing through the ruse proceeded to tease them forthwith by making the matter of his paternity so
emphatic that Rhea suspected mischief. It took
but a few moments of companionship with this
beautiful and tantalizing young woman to set the
men on edge with each other, while plunging them
"head over ears" into certain states of feeling
which they had never experienced before.

Rhea revealed·to them new worlds and excited
potentialities into action which had previously lain
dormant. Aleppo longed to tell her of "Miss
Somebody," and adopt her as a sort of muse-mother
to whom he might. fly and pour out his soul.
Sallus on the contrary had already·vowed that he
would marry her or die; while Regan warmed by a
spirit of comradeship, felt that at least he had found
his match, and prophesied for himself more downright fun for the coming trip than he had deemed
was possible an hour before. But she had thought
little about any of them except perhaps Regan,
whose Yankee face and sharp tongue had tickled
her fancy from the first.

The steamer was to sail the next day, and they
met in the evening on the hotel porch to talk over
plans and prospects. Mrs. Hancock took the
young men under her maternal wing, and Regan
found a seat near Rhea. The moonlight struck her
full in the face, and Regan's sharp eyes discovered

numerous and unreadable expressions there, as he went on, glibly lying to her. He was trying to concoct some sort of a story, by which he should justify his relation to Sallus and Aleppo to whom he was loyal to the core, but it was hard work.

"In the first place," said Rhea "I don't know anyone in the Bay State named Bracciolini; to be sure I am not acquainted with everybody there, but it seems rather queer, seeing that you are on such good terms with a number of my friends, that they have never mentioned you to me."

"'Tis, rather," said Regan—"I expect it just happened so; you see the name's a hard one to pronounce." He bit off a piece from a twig on the porch and put it into his mouth; he had given up tobacco—since supper.

"Nevertheless" went on Rhea with a contented little sigh "it's nice to meet you, especially as you know so many of my friends. There's one thing that puzzles me though—"

"What's that?" and Regan drew a little nearer.

"You seem too young to be the father of these men."

Regan was both disturbed and flattered—"What the deuce," said he to himself, "have I got into this fix for?"—out loud—"I suppose I do look somewhat young; just a boy with them, as a father should be, see? Married in my teens." Then a bright idea struck him—"wife died," he saw per-

dition yawning at his feet, but he was in for it—
"have been a widower a long time."

The girl's face was a study. Regan could have
killed himself for posing before her as such an ass,
but what could he do? He liked Rhea exceedingly,
and was far from anxious that she should consider
him in the paternal light; but there were the boys,
he liked them too, and read revolt in their eyes, if
he deviated in the slightest degree from the prè-
arranged plan; he saw that neither Sallus nor
Aleppo would tolerate him as their rival unless he
played the paternal role. Ah! it had its advantage
—it would give him a degree of freedom with the
girl and a hundred opportunities to enjoy her
society, that would be otherwise hard to get.

"So your first name is Rhea," said Regan, "are
you the mother of Zeùs?"

She laughed exultingly—"I may have been, in
some far away life, when the Olympians were casting longing eyes on Greece: it's a wonderfully
maternal name, isn't it?"

"Quite out of the ordinary" Regan answered,
chewing his twig vigorously—"Greek myth is
about as pretty as any I know of—eh?"

"There let me shake hands with you Mr.
Bracciolini, I love Greece, every inch of it," her
face positively glowed—"old Mitylene, Athens, the
Acropolis, Olympus, how the names thrill and
charm me. If it be true that man dies to be born
again, I have sometime lived in Greece. I dream

of Hellas at night; a Corinthian column makes my
heart flutter; the names of Phidias, Aspasia, Damon,
Pericles sound in my ears in echoes to this very
day."

She rose and paced up and down the room, the
moon transforming her to a reincarnated Phryne,
reveling in the memory of Praxitiles.

Regan was somewhat appalled, and sent his twig
over the railing instanter. The impassioned being
before him, in white serge had changed from a
Cape Cod Yankee to an enraptured child of Hellas,
pouring out her soul's complaint—not to him, but
to the moon.

He had nothing to say; for once his tongue was
glued to the roof of his mouth; he wanted to run,
and he wanted to stay. At last Rhea herself broke
the spell.

"You must think me crazy, Mr. Bracciolini,"
dropping into a chair and drawing back into the
shadow—" I have these spells once in a while—
can you explain them? "

Regan felt better—" Yes, I think so; you see
'tisn't exactly hallucination; it's the poetry in you
that's all. Those folks in Attica were first class,
as far as culture and art go, and you've got a fellow
feeling—it takes the moon to bring it out though."

"Of course you will think me a fool, but I am
pretty sure I have lived there," answered Rhea.

"'Tisn't for me to say you haven't, answered
Regan—" as long as it is admitted that there are

adepts, there's no telling but reincarnation may be true."

" But what in the world have adepts to do with the question?"

"Only this, just the minute I admit of one thing outside of the well known, I admit all, see? As long as I am swallowing adepts, reincarnation goes down with it."

" But *do* you swallow adepts—Mr. ———— I forget your name—Bracciolini?"

" I'll tell you later, I'm in the act of making a test now."

Rhea drew slightly away from him; she was getting afraid of this riddle.

" Don't be frightened Miss Nellino, it's all right." And adroitly changing the subject they began to discuss the coming trip to Cairo.

In the meantime Sallus and Aleppo had been whistling to the moon; Mrs. Hancock, unable to do anything with them had sought her own room. Suddenly Sallus burst out, " Say Lep, let's play a joke on Dad?" "All right "—as a rule Aleppo scorned practical jokes; but he had fallen from grace.

"Ten to one," went on Sal—"he's palming himself off as a widower; 'twont do."

" Not much " answered Aleppo, forgetting his vow to abandon slang--" not much—come on !"

They both shied over to the animated couple, and Sallus blurted out, " Dad have you written to mother to-night?" but Regan was one too many for them.

"No my son, I shall do so later." You see, Miss Nellino I've had the habit ever since she—hem—departed" he bit his tongue here—"of writing her a letter, just to keep up the memory you know—old times—see?"

The young men began to whistle again, directly at the moon, and Rhea who found Regan beyond her, rose and smiling bewitchingly at Sallus and Aleppo, bade the three good night.

CHAPTER VI.

EL RESHID.

It was raining in Paris; the storm had been tempestuous since sundown, and as the evening grew apace, sleet and hail fell on the shining roofs and sidewalks with increasing fury. Indeed it was difficult for the pedestrian to make headway at all, while the street gamins crawled into their holes and crannies like cats and dogs, but with less discomfort. It was severely cold, and as disagreeable a night to be out in as one could select. Nevertheless, a man came from Gare de l'Est, took a carriage, and proceeded along the Boulevard Sebastopol in the direction of the observatory; about mid-way he ordered the driver to stop, and alighting, continued on foot, somewhat after the manner of a hound, following an unseen trail. At last he brought up suddenly before a house which looked exactly like its two neighbors on either side.

Within this particular residence Henrique Romanes had been for the past two hours anxiously waiting for some one, and betrayed his nervousness in a hundred ways, but chiefly by walking up and down the full length of his dimly-lighted library, pausing periodically before the doors and listening a long minute, to be rewarded by the slamming of a shutter, or the rattle of the sleet.

The house, furnished in the conventional French style, had, nevertheless, a secluded and refined air, that proclaimed the individuality of Romanes. First and foremost, it was instinct with him—the things about seemed half conscious servants, ready on all occasions to do the Master's bidding.

He grew more impatient as time advanced, and consulted his watch continually, even unbolting and opening the outer door, to peer into the storm. At last a sort of despair took possession of him, and throwing himself into a chair, and closing his eyes, his face assumed a drawn look, which aged it at once. He had been in this downcast mood for a full half-hour, when, glancing up, as if brought to himself by a shock, he beheld the calm but brilliant face and erect figure of El Reshid. How this gentleman had entered he could not surmise—the servant must have been silent and swift. Romanes stared at him for an instant, then, rising, bowed

nearly to the floor; in fact he failed to raise his
head, but kept it bent, till El Reshid stooped and
compelled him to look up. Romanes' eyes were
streaming with tears, which he tried in vain to
hide, and which his guest affected not to see.
From the first to the last of their interview, which
continued for half an hour, Romanes avoided the
glance of El Reshid, and betrayed humility and
shame, utterly foreign to his ordinary self.

El Reshid was scarcely of average height, but
his carriage was so erect, and his air so imposing,
that he appeared even larger than Romanes, who
was somewhat above him. Though dressed in the
civilian's garb of black, of true Parisian cut, but
a glance was needed for one to discover that he was
of oriental extraction; his eyes and hair being
extremely dark and his skin of the tint of cream.
Twice during his interview with Romanes he consulted his watch, the case of which was studded
with emeralds, imbedded in the gold in such
a manner as to reflect a peculiar symbol, utterly
untranslatable to the mass of men. On his
finger he wore a ring, the seal being a highly
polished gem, cut in Egyptian hieroglyphics not
easily understood. Otherwise he was free of orna-
ment, and unobtrusive as to attire.

He stood during the whole interview, and though
utterly still as to body, he had such an appearance
of action and power that he seemed to quiver from
head to foot.

" Romanes, you sent for me—I have come."

Romanes bowed his head even to his breast.

" And may I presume by this," his voice trembling, "that I am to be reinstated?"

"What matters it?" answered El Reshid, with slight scorn in his tone.   "A society is but a shell; you had passed into the kernel—the worm appeared."

" True,"—he evaded his guest's eyes—" can the injury be repaired?"

The stern look on El Reshid's countenance vanished before Romanes' pleading aspect; his face brightening with a peculiar smile, which had the effect of sunlight flashing through clouds.

" Romanes," he said, " time may heal a serious wound, but it leaves a scar. You joined the Order, you aimed to acquire cetain powers—the law of exchange holds good in the psychic world; even there one pays for what he gets—it is not a question of sentiment, but of fair dealing. You agreed to give a certain price for a certain return; you understood very well what that necessitated; to acquire one thing, you gave up another; you were not persuaded, you volunteered. For many years you were true to the transaction; your dividends on the investment were large; you acquired powers and secrets which, abused, might make of you a fiend. Already, at this stage, you were master of circumstances and men; but alas! not of yourself.

Though unable to *hurt the Order* in a vital part,

you injured your own life, and threw us into confusion. The result of the fall from a pure love, with no taint in it, which was sanctioned by us, was the child Aleppo, upon whom you entailed, when he came out of Eden, a life of sacrifice. You have thrust earthly existence on him under conditions that will be well nigh fatal to his peace of mind. Endowed with the powers (from close affinity with yourself and Helene) of the Rajah, at the same time cursed with your physical fall, he stands to the world in a far different aspect from one born in ordinary sanctioned or unsanctioned wedlock; from parents living according to the rhythmic law of normal man. You have stolen an angel from the skies and thrust him into the mud. Having crossed the Rubicon of the flesh, you turned back, and, cannibal that you were, ate from a table where your own kind are devoured. But regrets are vain—'tis done. The nemesis of Fate, which is nothing other than a wolf-fanged, devil-eyed causation, is throwing her effects at your guilty head. You are bruised and bleeding. Results, full-grown, give heavy blows. For seventeen years you have striven to forget, and to thrust from your life a lotus flower, that told its grievances to the moon—for seventeen years you have obeyed strictly the laws of the Order, and have striven by penance to undo your mistake ; to an extent, you have won. Time passes you and leaves no finger marks, you speak the languages of all races, sickness scorns you, you

know the secret of the bird and the bee, you hear
the heart-beat of the flower, you behold the far-off
without eyes and revel in the song of the stars
without ears, but *love* is denied you ; Aleppo has
stolen it all—his heart is bursting. The icy realm
of intellect is yours, but your passion, alas! is but a
stone.

"Forgiveness! Ah ! can pardons piled to heaven,
and sealed and stamped, thrust out Aleppo from
your thought? Forgiveness is a word and nothing
more. Atonement! Nay, for justice with its two-
edged sword is on your track. What mortal, or immortal, can pay Aleppo's price but *you ?*

" 'Tis spoken, Henrique Romanes, thou shalt stop
where thou art, and in thy place shall step thy son;
advance, thou cannot—'tis he that marches on.
Through this, thy mortal life, till death doth free
thee, himself thou servest; on thy crushed body
shall he rise to pinnacle of power. In finding him,
thou shall discover age, the grave, Kismet !! This
life thou payest, but in the next, thyself shalt find
again."

He quivered from head to foot with that still
motion which the bird reveals when poised upon
the wing.

Romanes looked El Reshid in the eyes. Romanes ! !—the fig tree blasted by the Master's
curse.

" 'Tis *thou* hast spoken? "

"Not I, for, by the Eternal, *this is law*,"

He backed toward the door, never taking his eyes from his host, who bowed his head, as he had done at his entrance, nearly to the floor. An instant's pause on the threshold, and El Reshid had gone, leaving Romanes hopeless, fearless—facing the effect of a fatal past, with clear and steady eyes.

Rising, he staggered to his desk, for his firm step had left him, and, finding pen and paper, began immediately to write ; his letter ran thus:

" *Helene :*

" I am at last calm; El Reshid has been with me for one-half hour. I am neither happy nor sad; hope and fear I know not. I shall fly no longer from the effect of a cause that it will take my whole Unit of being to face, for ' it is spoken.'

" El Reshid will stand behind Aleppo—he has said as much—he will reveal him to me when the time is ripe. Though you and I can never unlearn that which is ours—though in no sense can we go back in mind and comprehension, our bodies will pay the price of this new object upon which our energy must needs be spent. This is Law—the unit of strength which has been ours, and which, by certain principles that we have learned, we have utilized to keep ourselves in perfect poise and health, must now be directed toward another end. Force is constant ; there is power within to generate the same in limited degree; directing it all, as

in justice we must henceforth do, in a never varying endeavor to further the welfare of our natural
son, our bodies must needs wither with age and
stiffen in death.

"Helene, my eternal love, we, *we* must die! "

"I am utterly calm; we have but a few more
years, and you—feel you the same? Can you
watch that pink pearl face, in its fading, day by
day—a veritable blush rose, wilting in the cruel
light of an avenging cause; can you bear that your
eyes retire far back into your head, to look out on
the world through the blear of age ; can you tolerate the sight of your sun-lit hair turning to gray,
crisp and withered like sere grass? Will you suffer
the twinges of pain and the gnawing of the worm?

"Ah, Helene, I *fear* you. For me, you would
go to the rack; but for the thief, Aleppo, who stole
me from you, I have great dread. Already you
are in the clutches of Issachar, whose magic is
beyond me—the war is on. The Unit of Energy
shifts rapidly from pole to pole—the light of heaven
is eclipsed at high noon, and the dark brings forth
a midnight sun.

"Helene, consider well your far-off future—the
unborn child of this fateful hour.

Yours,

ROMANES. "

Romanes always wrote and spoke with a romantic dignity, seemingly far-fetched to the occidental,
but normal to the oriental soul.

Having sealed and addressed his letter, he staggered like one drunk, through the long hall, out on to the front vestibule, where the storm struck him in the face. However, he found a box in which he placed his missive, where, strange to say, he discovered another addressed to himself, or rather an old envelope, covered with the scrawls of a lead pencil. He knew it instantly, and though written in Hindoo dialect he read to the end without difficulty.

"Romanes—Brother, I pause to address you a note before leaving. It is the last that I shall direct to you, personally, in *this* life. But you will receive many letters from me for Aleppo, and these it will be your duty to forward to him. Direct always, 'Aleppo Bracciolini, Cairo.' Wherever he may be, they will reach him. Do not in any way betray your identity nor mine; simply mail the papers sent by me to his address, and leave the result to—himself.

Yours,

El Reshid."

Romanes bit his lips, which had turned pale, and found his way into his library, where he closed and locked the door; then, throwing himself face downward on the floor, gave way to hysterical sobbing, unnatural in a man, and hitherto unexperienced by himself since reaching the condition of prime. His calmness, which had been a sort of

inertia after intense excitement, had utterly abandoned him; he had lost his nerve, and his convul-
sive sobs were pitiful to hear. Though a man with
the cold wisdom of a sage, yet was he entirely
undone by a spasm of jealous pain. Enslaved not
by physical passion, not by its results, his towering
genius and cool logic had no power over the
petty fires of a half-dead heart. His grand passion
smouldering, tingled and burned him with the darts
of a small flame. He was jealous of Aleppo; his
flesh and blood stood not only between himself and Helene, but usurped his place with the
beloved teacher to whom he had bowed to the
floor. Those precious letters, which should have
been his own, were to be transferred to his more
fortunate son; and he, an Ishmaelite, was to bear
them across the desert of his life with their un-
sealed covers laying a dead weight on his heart.

For an hour he hated Aleppo with the hate of
Helene, but no longer; the spirit of sacrifice, like
a dove from a clear sky, stole into his life, bearing
the green leaf in its beak. He kissed the crum-
pled envelope, on which was inscribed El Reshid's
name, passionately, and taking from his breast the
letter written years before by Helene, placed the
two together, and buried in his own bosom the
grand passion of his life. Then, standing before the
long mirror, where a strong light fell, he carefully
scanned his troubled face. He was older—a pallor
of the skin and lifelessness of the eye, told of

change. He remembered El Reshid's countenance, as he had seen it that evening—that of a man of thirty; almost boyish in its purity of color and fire of glance; he recalled his erect carriage and quick action; his abrupt and positive speech; his radiant smile; and then, sighing, he turned sadly from the glass where, in after life, he never looked again.

CHAPTER VII.

OFF THE IONIAN ISLES.

Our party of five, headed by Regan, had steamed out of the Adriatic and were off the Ionian Isles. Sallus, healthy on shore, had gone to bed sick, so also had Mrs. Hancock. Aleppo, possessed by strange dreams of late, was crooning to the moon alone ; while Regan and Rhea, ridiculously well, had arranged two steamer chairs in most comfortable quarters, and, between watching the play of the moonlight on the waters of the Mediterranean, and discoursing on subjects divine and infernal, were having the best kind of time. Mrs. Hancock was utterly disgusted with the turn affairs had taken ; Regan was well enough—rich, to be sure, but a married man. Nothing that Rhea couid have done would have so set her aunt on edge as this flirtation, so she called it, with the father of two boys. He had stated that his wife was dead, but she didn't believe a word of it.

"It's the way with the men; when they go traveling, they leave their wives, not only at home, but out of their memories. Writing to a wife in heaven, nonsense! Didn't you see how the boys tripped him?"

"I don't care a straw," said Rhea, tossing her head, "whether he is married or single; he is the first man that I have ever met that I could talk sense to."

"Sense!! Such stuff—Theosophy, reincarnation, Piato, induction."

As much scorn as could be condensed into words, she packed into these; but it did no good. Rhea and Regan were inseparable; and the boys, after listening to one or two of the conversations carried on between them, were quite content to be left out, preferring her ravishing smiles which she was very indiscriminate in bestowing, to her puzzling medley of phantasy and logic, that Regan took in with pitcher-plant ears.

As I have said, they were on the steamer deck; it was moonlight and balmy, with an ideal sea and sky.

"So," said Rhea, after humming a snatch of opera, "you don't exactly grasp reincarnation?"

"Not exactly,"—he wished that he did—"you see, somehow, I take more kindly to evolution, though, after all," brightening, "I don't discover much difference; if you have come up from the oyster to Miss Nellino, you've been in some sort of flesh all along, haven't you?''

"I don't know, Mr. Bracciolini, I very much fear that the evolutionist makes no claim to an extended individuality. I suspect the fellow that animated a certain far-back oyster isn't the one that . animates Mr. Bracciolini to-day, according to the believers in the survival of the fittest." ·

" Maybe 'tisn't; but now I have put in an appearance, I've come to stay."

"There is the trouble," said Rhea, brusquely, "why do you object to extending me backward as well as ahead? It seems to me that I would be of much better proportions to have a past that in some degree balances what is to come."

"To that I haven't the least objection, Miss Nellino; the longer you are, the better—there can't be too much of you any way you fix it. Shake hands on that, will you?"

They had grown quite accustomed to shaking hands. Whenever they came to terms, Regan shouted, "shake!" and Rhea's pretty fingers were grabbed with a daring that shamed the boys.

They shook, and Rhea continued;

" Of course, it *may* be all a dream; I am possibly a clod, that appears but once in human shape, or any other, but I do like consistency. I am one of two things, or logic is a fake—either an eternal being, or not ; *now* if my life is endless, there never was a time when I didn't exist, and never will be one when I shall not be. If, on the contrary, I am simply mortal—the puppet of a capricious deity—I shall turn to dust when I die, and go back to the nothing, as regards individuality, from which I came."

"It seems to me there's no getting around that," said Regan.

"Which?"

"Either one."

"I have to establish myself somewhere or nowhere. The inconsistency of nine out of ten of · the religions, to say nothing of the cults, makes me shudder. I am either an out and out materialist, who believes in this life and no other, or the rankest spiritualist that ever was born—that is, I have an indestructible past that always was and ever shall be. Which is it, Mr. Bracciolini ? "

"I expect it's the latter, as far as you are concerned."

He really had not made up his mind, nor could he without his tobacco. He had taken to chewing gum since his acquaintance with Rhea, but it was a failure. He had been a slave to his one habit so many years that even Rhea and evolution were insufficient to free him. A sudden craving came, that broke the conversation at its very climax. He complained of dizziness of the head, and Rhea, laughingly, said that he was sea-sick, dismissing him forthwith.

The next morning he was still to evil habits inclined, and his chair being vacant, Aleppo slipped into it. He was to have it all his own way. The lynx-eyed Mrs. Hancock was very ill; Sallus beyond the throes of love, and Regan in solitary bliss, like an isolated cow chewing her cud.

Rhea glanced Aleppo over and decided that he was a very different figure from Regan—much handsomer, much younger, and not a bit like his father. He had puzzled her from the first—there was a page back of him that she could not read.

Mysteries are fascinating, and he "put a spell" upon Rhea at once. Now, in reality he admired Miss Nellino amazingly, but as yet he had but little tact; and any man, young or old, who is without tact, is, in slang phrase, "in a peck of trouble."

"You quite puzzle me, Miss Nellino," naively—"sometimes I take you for sixteen and sometimes for forty."

"O my!—forty."

"Well, you see, when Sal and I first saw you in Brindisi, we thought you were in your teens; later we changed our minds, and I told Sal that I thought you could not be less than forty."

"On what did you found this wise conclusion—did the sunlight bring out some wrinkles when you beheld me next day in its cruel glare?"

"No, 'twasn't that; I can't see any wrinkles in

your face now, and I am sure the sun is bright
enough—but you talk on subjects that most women
of forty take up.''

''Do you know a great ·deal about women?''
asked Rhea, exceedingly interested—

Aleppo sighed. ''Not as much as I would like;
you see I had Aunt Serena, and I have met a few
girls in traveling.''

He looked at Rhea adoringly. She had a fresh,
pure countenance which the sun improved; her
jaunty sailor hat was rather back on her head, and
her rebellious brown hair, having its own way.
She had the philosopher's square brow, the poet's
eye, and the mouth of a Venus, with its pretty
smile and dimples—altogether she was a '' rare
bird.''

''I think,'' said Aleppo, ''of all the girls on
earth that I have ever seen, I like the American
girls the best.''

''But you have not placed *me*,'' said Rhea laughing—'' am I a girl or not?''

''·That is what puzzles me,'' said Aleppo
seriously.

''Well I will tell you, so that you may set your
mind forever at rest—I an just twenty-six.''

''Ah! He was not quite sure yet where to put
her, and he looked straight out at sea.

'' What do you think?'' persisted Rhea.

'' You are better than either,'' he answered—you
look sixteen and talk forty.''

"But most women of forty are as unendurably stupid as mother-hens."

"Not all," said Aleppo with an air as though he knew, though he did not. "Now I've the chance," he went on, "I want to confide something to you."

Rhea's heart beat faster. Regan had never raised her pulse in the least—was she falling in love? She hoped not.

"It is about Sallus—I want you to like him."

Rhea was piqued. In reality Aleppo was on the verge of making a great sacrifice. He was half in love with the beautiful American himself. He longed to put his arms about her and kiss her on both cheeks, in spite of "Miss Somebody" or anybody—she was so sweet that morning, yet in spite of it all, he was going to bestow her upon Sallus.

Women are queer composites, every one of them —even the most sensible is vain; hurt her vanity and you set every nerve quivering. Rhea was no exception ; she was wonderfully charmed with Aleppo, and wanted him for a dear, dear friend— nothing more of course, she said to herself. His half-oriental face, his innocence, the veiled genius of his eyes, the mystery of the boy, had stormed her heart. He had implied that he liked—yes, more—adored her on this very morning, and just at the point where she felt that their friendship was about to be sealed, he had turned her over to Sallus.

For a moment she hated him—he caught her mood, and was silent.

"Go on"—her tone a little hard. He was "in for it," and he went deeper and deeper.

"It is this way," he said haltingly, "though I expect Sallus would hate me for telling, yet it is for his own good. Regan and I are pulling him up a little; he had got down pretty low—and it was not his fault either."

"Who's Regan?" said Rhea tartly.

Aleppo was caught, and he lied stupidly; however, there was no help for it.

"Regan? that's my father—we always call him Regan at home. He says it makes him feel more like a boy—hem!"

"Go on," said Rhea, her lip curling.

"Well, as I was saying, it is not Sallus' fault. He was brought up on wine and champagne—always on his—our—father's table—understand? Regan is to blame"—Aleppo was blushing to his ears.

"Now, I don't believe a word of that," said Rhea, bridling; there is no better man than Mr. Bracciolini on earth."

"Of course not," said Aleppo, gaining gall as he went deeper. "Father is all right, and did not realize till the last year or so, what it would come to with Sallus—that is why we are here; and he is doing better too. I am sure Miss Nellino," he sighed, "I am sure you can help him. It is the

craving that bothers him now.   Once he gets over
that, he is all right—dantiest creature you ever saw,
and so handsome.''

He looked pleadingly into Rhea's eyes.   She bit
her lip and winked hard to keep from crying—not
for Sallus, but for herself.   It was very bitter to
have the first fascination of her life snapped in this
way, and by an innocent sinner too.   She could not
say, "Aleppo be my friend first and foremost, and we
will work together for Sallus ''—not at all.   She
was so little thought of by him, she argued to herself, that he was using her like a missionary, or
Salvation Army woman—as a means to an end.
He was making of her a cat's paw to pull Sallus
out of the fire—so she felt, and the emotion was
hard to bear.

''If you could but be a mother to him,'' went on
Sallus, blundering more and more in his vain
endeavor to right himself.

''Now look here, Mr. Aleppo, I was scarcely
four years of age at the most, when Sallus was born.
I am not old enough to be his mother, nor do I
desire in the least to assume the maternal role,
especially to an *adopted* son ; on no conditions
would I take a boy to bring up.''

Aleppo was confounded, he failed to understand
why Rhea was so emphatic.

''I am sorry, Miss Nellino, I am afraid I have
made a mistake.''

Rhea's mood changed instantly ; Aleppo was

unhappy.   She took the boy's hand and pressed it
softly—" There dear friend, I'll do what I can for
Sallus.   He is perfectly safe at present—in bed;
between the three of us, I am sure he will not go
wrong; and if he should, later—we will turn him
over to Mrs. Hancock."

"O no, not to Mrs. Hancock," said Aleppo recoiling—"please   promise   me"—reaching   and
taking her hand again, it made him so happy to
hold it.   " Please promise me that you will never
speak of this conversation to Sallus or Regan; it is
because I love Sallus so much, and believe so
entirely in you, that I have mentioned this."

Her pique was gone.   She felt a sudden desire to
force Sallus inside the narrow gate of the straight
way, even though she remained outside herself.
Aleppo still held her hand, and looked so supremely
content, that she felt that in spite of Sallus and the
whole world, she had in him a dear friend whose
love would be of heaven.

There was something about Aleppo that lifted
one upward in thought—a fine magnetism which
inspired and fascinated.   The purity of the boy's
intent, together with the dream world in which he
lived—his innocence and virile power produced the
effect of glamour, and whoever—especially of the
feminine sex—came near him, was charmed.   He
longed for love and one felt it, yet at the same time,
he was so selective and exacting, that but few were
allowed near.

Rhea had sighed from childhood for a friend—one whose heart-beat she could feel. Friendship to her was the ideal—the supreme; it had no taint of earth on it. In vain she had sought consciously or unconsciously among women and men, and though she found comrades here and there, no friend had been her's—but Aleppo! If he would but sit beside her, they would utter no sound—the speech of silence would be their's, happy—happy—happy. The vast expanse of sea, the vaster sky, the long infinite line, where earth weds heaven, and the music—the subtle half-heard music, which two hear better than one. Just here, (they were both dreaming, hand in hand) Regan appeared.

"Aleppo, Sallus wants you ; says he's going to get up."

The tables had turned. Aleppo had no longing for Sallus; he suddenly remembered, however, that he had disposed of Miss Nellino, and with this recollection came a spasm of despair. He looked wistfully at Rhea who translated it all, and smiled.

CHAPTER VIII.

CAIRO.

In due time, "the five," as they called themselves, reached Alexandria, and later steamed into Cairo, where they expected to remain for some time.

Though Aleppo had never been in the Orient,
except at Scutari, this first glimpse of Africa, and
his nearness to Syria, had a strange effect upon him
—he grew more and more introspective, and less
inclined to talk, except to Rhea, who was so in
demand on all sides, that he obtained but little
chance with her. She had taken Sallus " in tow,"
as Regan expressed it.

"The peculiar charm of Egypt," she went on—
the beauty-loving boy drinking in every word—
" lies in its long lines;"—they were rushing toward
Cairo—" even the camels move in a string, and the
date palms are slender and tall. Egypt is entirely
consistent with itself. The Nile, the green fields,
the mud huts, the date gardens, the azure, wonder-
ing morning-glories, which stare with open eyes all
day; the Arabs in blue gowns; the dome and mina-
ret; the eternal sky, beside which the camel
marches with the dignity of a ship at sea; the
Libyan sands, glittering like jewels in the sun; the
majestic pyramids, tawny with age; the Sphinx,
with fixed and untranslatable eyes, gazing straight
ahead."

"That's all very well," said Mrs. Hancock, listening with disgust on her face at Rhea's rhapsody,
"but it's the greatest country for flies on earth ;
they stick all over the Arab babies, which I don't
believe have ever been washed since they were
born."

"You see," put in Regan, "if old Pharoah had

given these Israelites half a show, he wouldn't have got 'cussed' as he was."

"Nothing grows here," went on Mrs. Hancock, "unless you give it water; you are not sure of any rain, and the glare is something terrible. I never realized what a pretty place New England is, till I came down into Egypt."

"You are not up to the majesty of straight lines, I suspect," said Regan. "Now, Rhea—"

"Yes, it's always and forever Rhea; Rhea this and Rhea that. If she chose to rhapsodize on an ant hill it would be beautiful in men's eyes. She raves more over ugly things than she does over any person on earth. I've half a mind to set her down on the desert and leave her there; she'd change her tune, I imagine."

Mrs. Hancock was all out of sorts. Her seasickness had made her cross, and the three unwelcome traveling companions aggravated her troubles. The "boys" disliked her and she knew it; while Regan, she hated on principle. The more Rhea appreciated her new friends, the more her aunt distrusted them, taking every opportunity to imply that they were not what they pretended to be, and so forth, and so on; which Rhea, in spite of her admiration, half suspected was true. She felt that she was entering the land of mystery with three riddles to guess, more puzzling than the unsolved Sphinx itself. And of the three, Aleppo had her thoughts the most. They arrived at Cairo each in a

perturbed state of mind. Mrs. Hancock cross
and suspicious, Rhea puzzled, and half in love
with—she knew not what. Sallus, swinging
between qualms of a persistent sea-sickness and
spasms of delight; Regan, minus tobacco, and
cursing gum; Aleppo, in a dream, disturbed now
and then by a strange influence, which, in all his
life, he had never felt before, that seemed to be
drawing him from these new-found friends, far, far,
to a life of isolation and sacrifice.

Over him still hung the dread of the Jew. He
had fled to the " Black Land " in the hope that he
might escape this cursed vision, but in memory
Issachar still hovered—a veritable buzzard, ready
to pounce upon him and pick his bones. Even
Khem, guarded by deserts and hemmed in by a
rampart of low mountains, might be accessible to
this son of Leah. Aleppo was at the gate of Africa.
The dull, yellow Nile, sometimes shading into
brown, went unconcernedly by. The bare rocks,
tawny in hue, made a rhapsody of color, as sweet,
in its way, as is music beneath the deep azure of
the sky. Unobtrusive as to outline, marvelous in
tint—Egypt—uniform, various, unique, mysterious,
set his heart palpitating with a kind of rapture
that the Occident had never roused. But when, at
times, the still fog of the Nile veiled the vivid
green of the far-stretching fields, the dread of the
mystery of himself, the seeming antiquity of Issachar, the future which Isis had concealed, so

enwrapt and subdued him, that his eyes took on a look of melancholy that Rhea, alone, observed.

The age of Egypt forced Aleppo to feel his own. The awful weight of years, that lay prone upon the pyramids, yet insufficient to subdue them, pressed on himself also, as though he had *been* and *been* since earth began, yet stable still, a changeless entity of change, a paradox, a sphinx. And the mystery of Libya! !—the jeweled sands challenging the sun—stretching to their meeting place with heaven, appealed to him in vague prophesy, as symbolic of himself.

" 'Tis the great waste of water or of land that the sky comes down to meet. Ah, Libya, thou art *myself*—barren, yet wedded to the blue. Thou bearest neither blossom nor fruit; too well, *too well* thou lovest thy adored—the sun."

In Egypt the poet in Aleppo was born. He had studied art and failed, but looking into the eyes of Khem, the singer, for the first time, sang; and the muse, Rhea, listened and sat apart.

'Twas night. Aleppo had longed for Rhea, but, true to his sacrifice, had left her in Cairo with Mrs. Hancock and Sallus, and substituting Regan, as best he could, in her place, had sought the sight of Memphis, where he unbosomed himself to his friend.

"You see, Regan," he said, with a half sigh, "I'm in a strange frame of mind. I never felt far different from other boys, that I know of, till after

I met Issachar. Something happened to me on that morning in Venice; I told my first lie and have been a changed being ever since."

"Are you unhappy," said Regan, sympathetically.

"Yes, and no. Is it possible to be happy and miserable at the same time? If it is, I am that. I live in a sort of rapture, but it is shaded with despair. I feel like a Rembrandt—one half of me in broad glare, the other in the dark. I wonder if heaven isn't a place that hangs over hell. Just imagine peeping out of the pearly gates once in a while, and looking down into a fathomless abyss, blacker than midnight. That is my case, Regan. What's the matter with me, can you tell?"

"Maybe you are in love."

"I should like to be in love with Rhea," said Aleppo, simply.

Regan winced perceptibly.

"But that is not it," went on Aleppo; "this feeling of ecstacy which comes on periodically, is caused by Egypt, I am sure, unless—I don't know," here he hesitated, "unless some one *unseen* is influencing, and—yes, I must say it—loving me. I feel as people say they do when Christ loves them. I don't understand it, in my case; for I never took any stock in that sort of thing. But that is not all—I have a horrible dread of Issachar. I never was afraid of any mortal before. Just

think, Regan, he made me lie. I'm living a lie
now; we all are.''

''Don't you worry about that,'' said Regan, set-
tling down in a comfortable frame of mind once
more, '' we are not deceiving Rhea and Mrs. Hancock one bit; they know we are traveling incognito
—they've guessed it I am sure; and we've a right
to get over the world that way too ; even kings
do it.''

''Sure,'' said Aleppo, somewhat relieved, '' but
that's not the main thing. What I don't like is the
power that Issachar wields—no other mortal could
have made me lie.''

'' That's just where it comes in,'' said Regan,
winking perceptibly '' he's not mortal, if I know
myself. Didn't I tell you in Venice, that he was
older than Moses ? You see, it's this way ''—quite
emphatic, and imitating Rhea's method of debate
—either there are magicians, or there are not ; if
there are, Issachar's one. See?''

''What makes you think so,'' said Aleppo, walking restlessly back and forth.

''The look of the man. No mortal ever looked
like that. He doesn't die, I tell you.''

''Now, say.'' said Aleppo, though inclined to be
credulous, ''do you really *believe* that; no joking,
now; *do* you?''

'' I'll be switched if I know what I do believe—
that's a fact. I never was side-tracked before. It's
Rhea that's done it; always knew where I was at

till I met that girl, but since then I've got north
and south dreadfully mixed. She believes more
trash than any mortal woman I ever met, except
Miss Dunnigan. I knew a school-marm once that
could match her. But Miss Dunnigan only made
me more confirmed in my own way, while Rhea
knocks me all sixes and sevens. She has a way of
laying down premises and towering up to conclusions that's kind of dumbfounding. Of course, when
I think of it afterward, I see that, as likely as not,
her castle was erected upon air. But I tell you
that girl can reason; give her any sort of a base
to build on, and she'll make a syllogism out of it or
my name's not Regan. That's where she's so con-
founding ; she's not a fool, and Miss Dunnigan
was."

"She's a New England product," said Aleppo,
reverently. He had thought of Boston with a
species of awe.

"Yes," went on Regan, "the best type of the
New Englander is like a roasted chestnut—he's
hot and hard. 'Tough nut,' burning inside, hard
shell. You see the climate is peculiar, especially
down at Cape Cod—hot as blazes in summer, regular Arctic in winter. That's Rhea."

"So, then, you half believe he's a magician,"
replied Aleppo, his feelings somewhat mixed.

"No, I don't, to be downright in earnest ; but
bad men are common as dirt; add shrewdness and
intellect to one of them, and you get a fellow that'll

match Satan himself. That man, Issachar, is dangerous. See?"

"But what do you suppose he wants with me?" asked Aleppo, anxiously.

"That's the mischief of it. I'm sure I don't know. If you had not remembered his face, should say that he was after somebody else; but the fact that you recognized him, and that he came after one named Aleppo, would seem to indicate pretty strongly that he is seeking you."

"He has my name dreadfully mixed, it seems to me. Romanes! Who on earth is Romanes? Can it be " here Aleppo paused, shocked by a sudden thought. "can it be that *that* is my real name?"

"Might be; stranger names have been tagged on to a fellow lots of times."

"How did I come by the name of Bracciolini, then?" said Aleppo, somewhat dazed.

"Don't know, unless it was bestowed later, in place of the other. I expect when you were deposited in the asylum, you were booked by that second title—fine name; I'm getting used to it myself."

There was nothing more to be said. They found their way back to Cairo. Aleppo, uneasy, yet with a strange thrill at his heart, and Regan greatly puzzled about his newly adopted son. Patrick Regan was loyal to the uttermost; his heart had been a desert for many years, but since these stray boys had crept into it, he had found an object for which to live. Deep down in his soul he had resolved to

make a man out of Sallus and a son of Aleppo—
they both seemed to need him, and to be needed in
the *real sense*, was all of happiness that Regan
desired. Aleppo was drifting about the world
alone,—homeless and without kith or kin ; while
Sallus, a victim to an evil habit, was even in a worse
condition. They had taken to him from the
moment the three had met, and the pathos of their
earnest but wordless appeal, had wrung his heart.
So Regan was determined to stick to these two
young men through thick and thin ; not only for
their sakes, but for his own.

It was late at night. Aleppo, tired, had returned
from the site of Memphis, and desirous of being
alone, sought his room at Shepherds' and locked his
door. He had met Rhea on the corridor, she had
smiled and touched his hand—he sat down to dream
of this. He was always calling up in memory a
look of hers or a word, in fact she seemed to haunt
him, though for the sake of Sallus he strove hard
to put her out of his thoughts.

On the table lay a pile of letters. After resting
a little, he picked them up with some curiosity, as
he was quite unused to an extended correspondence.
Two or three he found were from stray acquain-
tances who had happened to have him in mind at
the same time. Another was from Caesar Catus, a
man who had studied at the same studio with him
in Italy—a half oriental who had taught him to ·
write in the Hindoo dialect and a number of other

things to be discussed later. Aleppo had taken a
great liking to Catus, and they had kept up an
active correspondence since his leaving Italy. . The
epistle was a long one; so he laid it aside to read at
his leisure, and took up the last letter on the tray.
It puzzled him before he laid his hand on it. It
was mailed at Paris, and had arrived on time ; he
turned it over and over before opening; the writing
though strange gave him a peculiar sensation—it
seemed exactly like his own. At last he broke the
seal and found enclosed a smaller envelope,
addressed in an entirely different hand and Hindoo
dialect—the very same that he had learned from the
artist Catus.

Translated, it read: "For Aleppo Bracciolini."
He lifted it reverently—why he could not tell—
and slowly drew forth the closely written pages,
and held them to the light. His head was dizzy ;
he seemed to be on the verge of something wonderful—was it a narrow path at a great height ?
For a moment it was impossible to read; then, his
brain clearing, he traced out the writing as well as
his astonished condition would permit. It was as
follows:

"THE MASTER.

" You have wondered a little if there are magicians. Read carefully what follows and decide for
yourself:

" The world is full of fads and fancies. The
Twentieth Century is drawing near and will usher

in an epidemic of credulity fully a match for the
wave of skepticism which has lately passed.   Man
runs to extremes—to-day, he seeks the miracle;
to-morrow, normal fact.   One hour, hard stuck on
the rock of science, the next, adrift on the sea of
superstition.

   " The idea has gone abroad, and is bolstered by
self-styled philosophers, and others, who use the
credulity of men to an end, that there are, most
likely, in far-off China and the inaccessible haunts
of Thibet, great souls (Mahatmas) whose powers
are beyond compare—*so great* that the term
' a God ' has hardly enough dignity to apply to
their august selves. They are supposed to walk
on water, rise in the air, pass through fire, transmit
to a long distance messages by occult means,
materialize letters at a given point, appear and disappear before one's eyes, live countless years, or
die, to rise in body from the tomb. To be masters
of all tongues, knowing, by intuition, the sciences
and arts; backing and controlling large bodies, rep-
resenting various cults; behind societies and innumerable organizations; silent, secret dictators, compared with which the Council of Ten played but a
child's foolish game.

   " Farther, mediums here and there, who are, or
are not, as the case may be, vehicles for the passages
of spirits from the unseen world to this, have been
suddenly seized with the notion that secret masters,
still alive, are making of them dignified agents to

do their silent work. The fascination of this strange encounter with a living being, unseen but felt, has so grown and flourished that there is scarcely a town of any size in Christendom that fails to shelter one or more of the favored ` many who make this claim.

"Now, let us sift the matter, once and for all. Was there ever smoke without a fire? Mahatma! What means the word? Simply a great soul. Out in the open, they are often discovered; and have been since man began. Each race has produced them, from the Egyptian Trismegistus to the German Mozart; from the Greek Plato, to the American Edison; from the English Shakespeare, to the French Napoleon; from the ancient Cæsar to the more modern Angelo—rare but accessible, and proof positive of mastership, if proof need be.

"If, in full light, there come and go men of *genius*, is it out of order that there are others who walk in the shadow?

"But let us examine this 'great soul,' who uncovers his head to the sun; what manner of man is he? Always a being of *power*—a unit of energy, that makes itself felt along the ages. We call him immortal because he will not die. He persists in remaining *in memory*, if nowhere else. He is as little superior to law, as is the veriest worm that crawls, yet he differs from others in that he seizes upon and utilizes principles where *they* do not. Instead of being caught by lightning, he, himself,

catches it.   He masters human nature, ere it master him.   He forces the marble into semblance of
life before it marks his grave.   He dominates num-
bers by will, and controls an army with a silent
glance.   He brings down heaven to the strings of
his violin, and calls up hell by a sweep of his bow.
He has *power—power*.   He forces law to bear *upon*
law.   This is the Master; to that degree in which
he has energy and understanding to do, so much is
he supernatural and great.   He may be evil, he
may be good.   Though Cosmos is now upon the
throne, while   Chaos,   exiled,   wanders   restless
across the trackless waste.

   " Take note, the Master does no miracle.   What
he is, you, too, may be.   Seen or unseen, in the
sunshine or in the dark, he moves upon the line of
the least resistance, and reaches his goal by the
shortest route.   Consciously or unconsciously, he
has power to *concentrate* and is the most deadly
specialist on earth.   Knowingly, or unknowingly,
he has the art to generalize with a certainty that
amounts to a fiat of Fate.   The Master sees the
soldiers as individuals, and the army as *one*.   He
has a sweeping glance, and while grasping the
whole he grapples with the parts.   His eye is
quick, his grip is certain.

   '' Consciously, or unconsciously, he wastes no
energy; or if, unfortunately he does, he shortens
his span of natural life.

   " He stamps his letters and sends them through

the mail, and no more makes something out of nothing than can the triune God. He travels by coach or by steam and wears the garb of the people with whom he dwells. He is as probably in New York as in Thibet, as likely in Japan as upon the Himalayas.

"If in great necessity he resorts to extreme measures—to clairvoyance, thought-suggestion, or hypnotism, the result is no more a miracle than is a sonata of Mozart or a play of Molière. If a specialist along the line of the occult, (which means the generally unknown) he is as much a slave of law, as was Beethoven or Comte. The fairy web, spun by the spiders of philosophy to-day, has never caught a *true* Mahatma in its mesh. A Spencer would tear it to bits, a Mill would reduce it to atoms.

Yet, in face of this, we boldly state, that men exist upon earth even now, who have discovered the elixir of life—the philosopher's stone and the secret of youth. They read the pages of the book —*Time*—backward, as well as ahead, and condense the past and the future into *to-day*. Having found the extreme limits of being, they have discovered the poise of Nirvana, and know that the Law of Polarity means the fiery equator of life itself.

Yours,

————————."

Here it ended. Where the name should have been was a dash. Aleppo felt as though suddenly transferred from Cairo to a garden of Damascus, where a subtle teacher spake the words on the paper before him into his very ears. What could it mean? Was he dreaming? The letter surely was there—the strange symbols, as clear to his mind as the English alphabet. Could it be from Catus? He dismissed the thought at once. To be sure, Catus had spoken at times in the same way, but never with such authority. He, Aleppo, had come to Cairo to receive this *particular* letter; of that he was certain; what else had brought him here? He read it over and over again, then, hiding it both on his person and in his heart, went day after day through the streets of Cairo, as though he had it not.

CHAPTER IX.

AT THE SITE OF MEMPHIS.

Aleppo was fond of the graveyard and mausoleum —this was an Oriental trait. If he desired to think or dream, he went among the dead. A few days after receiving the letter which by its extreme of mystery was rivaling the riddle of the sphinx, he sought the site of Memphis, taking a Nile boat rather than the railway, and disembarking at Bedrasheyn. The palm grove bewitched him with its play of light and shade among the columnar trees—things of beauty, all alike, with tufted heads,—the place was akin to the joy and sorrow of his heart. Behind the grove spread the fields, green, tilled, and wide; and from the chief mound of the ruins he beheld the extended landscape once occupied by the city of pyramids. West, his eye swept the limestone range—a yellow wall, shutting out the view, of itself undignified, boasting neither snow-crowned peaks nor mighty domes, a simple, monotonous, golden chain, wedded to the pyramids which overtopped it, seemingly as hoary as itself. Man had vied with God, and had built a wonder which defied time, and looked down upon the everlasting hills.

Before Aleppo's eyes lay the site of Memphis founded by Egypt's first king, but naught now save a heap of rubbish, and a few monumental ruins. Its temple pillars were firm and fast in the mosques of the thief Cairo—an upstart that had reared its head on the ruins of a shrine.

But while he felt the charm of the spot, he spent but little time in musing over its sublime antiquity; on the contrary, he dreamed of Damascus, though why, he could not tell. The letter which had become a part of himself was mailed at Paris, yet he saw in vision a rose garden, wherein stood a peculiar little building, with dome-like roof, and columns instead of walls, through which swept the sweet-scented, aromatic air of an out-door paradise. He tried to *feel* Memphis, to mentally bend beneath its weight of years, instead, he realized Syria, and the perfumed breath of the rose.

He was alone; he could dimly see in the distance a blue shirted Arab, who seemed but a part of the landscape, and nothing more. He had never beheld a lovelier sky than bent over him on this remembered day, nor felt such aspiration and strength as he was conscious of then.

He had aged in Egypt; the boy who lectured Sallus in Scutari had departed, and a man stood on the site of Memphis, and scanned the peaks of the pyramids. He thought of Rhea—had she made him older? He believed so. To talk and think with her, he must needs expand. To be sure, he saw her only for a few moments now and then, occasionally he was allowed a short walk or a stolen chat; but Rhea—he had gone thus far in his dreaming when on his soul fell the music—the song—he had heard for a lifetime, which had ceased in the land of Khem. It was a simple little melody, and these were the words:

SONG.

I told you that I loved you
Nor did you listen then;
My voice was faint and distant
But now I sing again.

I loved you in the *old* time;
I love you in the *new;*
Forever and forever
My heart belongs to you.

It was all within that he heard it; the stillness without was that of the dead. The first verse was sung softly and seemed to come from far away; the second, nearer; the words "forever and forever," so close that he took up the strain himself and chimed in with the beautiful treble, as though it were a part of his own clear voice. "Forever and forever my heart belongs to you."

The last word had scarcely fallen from his lips, when he turned with a start—beside him, outlined against the Egyptian sky like a resurrected patriarch stood Issachar, the Jew.

He was clothed in the same immaculate robe that he had worn in Venice—without spot or blemish. On his face was the identical bright but cruel smile betraying the teeth of a perfect animal, that Aleppo had beheld before. He bowed his head, and approached the young man who shrank from him, looking wildly in all directions for a spot in which to hide.

"Pardon—but I have followed you here."

"That is quite evident," said Aleppo trying to be brusque.

"It is important—and you evade. I seek Aleppo Romanes."

"But have I not told you distinctly and emphatically that I am Aleppo Bracciolini?"

"Ah! yes," said Issachar hissing his words a little, though extremely polite—"you have told me; I do not believe."

" Why ? " said Aleppo pretending wrath, though his heart beat fast.

" Because Patrick Regan is not your sire."

These words came deliberately and with great. dignity, while he looked with piercing glance straight into Aleppo's eyes—the young man dropped his lids.

" Have you"—there was still more of a hiss in his tone—"have you a mystic symbol tattooed upon your back ? "

Issachar had stepped nearer, and Aleppo realized his towering height and terrible force as though he were a mountain in a thunder cloud. Cowering, the young man endeavored to shrink away, but the Jew advanced toward him, using no weapons but his eyes. Aleppo had lost all power to think, he *felt* only a presence, that like the sea monster was extending on every side its long tentacles and drawing him to itself. He saw the peaks of the pyramids, the walls of yellow hills, the receding Arab all vaguely melting and blending into one personality, which was that of Issachar, the Jew.

" Have you?"—he heard it again close to his ears; the site of Memphis seemed to rise toward him and then retreat; the pyramids at last were over-thrown and the sky fell upon his head; then, as far as Aleppo knew—nothing !

It was night, he opened his eyes, and discovered the moon directly over his head, staring down at him with a sort of cold pity. Where was he ? He

rose to a sitting posture and looked around. The
dead were busy whispering among themselves—
sepulchral voices on every side. The mound on
which he sat teemed with phantasmal life—half-
naked Egyptians muttered in strange tongues as
they glided past, veiled women peered at him with
wanton eyes, and mummies suddenly instinct with
life, arrived from nowhere and went back to whence
they came. At first Aleppo imagined himself dead,
but catching sight of the moonlight on a quaint
ring that he wore, he concluded that he must be
going mad; then slowly there crept upon him the
memory of a fatal magnetism which was that of
Issachar the Jew.

"Ah !"—he sprang to his feet and shook himself; he walked rapidly back and forth and inhaled
deep draughts of air— at every step his mind grew
clearer. He noted that his coat was lying on the
ground and his under garments disarranged—the
symbol ! Had Issachar made sure—could he have
stripped him and found the mark upon his back ?

With a shock he remembered *the letter*; he delved
into his pockets one after another; he tore open the
bosom of his shirt and felt around his heart ; he
scanned the ground right and left everywhere—
IT WAS GONE.

On Aleppo there fell a great cloud—the song of
Acadia and the sweet rose of Damascus had
vanished from his heart. He wandered aimlessly
over the site of Memphis until the sun came up

to greet the Sphinx and drive delusion from his mind.

To return from a terrible experience to the ordinary, the hum-drum, is indeed a transition. For a few days after Aleppo's experience with the Jew, he kept his room, being both physically and mentally ill. He had contracted a severe cold on the night of his exposure at Memphis, and worse, had learned, as he bitterly complained to himself, that he was a coward. He was ashamed of the whole affair, and of the dread of Issachar which still possessed him. He had told none of "the five" of his adventure, not even Regan. He bitterly regretted the disappearance of the precious letter, though it had been engraved upon his heart; but more bitterly the loss of his nerve, in acting the craven before the Jew. He tried to fight the battle out with himself and exorcise his terror, but his superstition got the better of him in spite of his efforts: more to his shame, because he had always considered himself especially strong and courageous. The unhappy part of it lay in the fact that it was not physical terror that he felt, though Issachar was much his superior in muscle and size, but a dread of his magnetism which he looked upon as invincible. He had no idea of what the Jew might desire of him, but he was positive that whatever it was, he would have it, in spite of all his own efforts to the contrary. His past, to which he felt that Issachar was the key, was becoming a terrible present,

like a thunder cloud foretelling a storm. Who
were his father and mother? What sin had been
theirs that this diabolical Jew had become so
in league with them, that he knew of the very
tattoo upon his back? This mark had always been
a great mystery to Aleppo, who had shown it to no
one in his life excepting Cæsar Catus. That gentleman had informed him that it was a symbol which
·probably a mystic could interpret. He remembered,
in recalling his childhood, that at the time he had
seen Issachar, he had awakened from a sleep, and
that his back had caused him to cry with pain.
Had he been drugged, and had Issachar, himself,
deformed him? He also recalled a beautiful lady,
vaguely, as if in a dream; he remembered the color
of her hair—like sunbeams. He began to pace the
floor. Could it be—was she his mother? How he
hated her! As the conviction grew, taking the
shape of a certainty, he shuddered, and wiped the
damp from his brow. His mother! He had
thought of her heretofore as an angel in heaven ;
now, there was no escaping it, this golden-haired
vision was his mother—this woman of light and
beauty. Then the most damnable idea that had
ever blackened his soul, for an instant turned him
into a fiend. Was Issachar his father? Great
Heaven ! he could have killed himself then and
there; but it passed, and the reaction came with its
indifferent calm. He began to think—was he a
bastard or a child of wedlock—had he been born

of beauty and the beast, or—it was no use; thought helped not a whit.   It was guess work from first to last, but he shrank and shrank from the revelation, which he felt was being forced upon him in spite of his tight hold on the door of his past.

Of course "the five" were to make the Nile trip, and that very soon.   Aleppo could scarcely wait to be off; the desire to run was still on him— to flee to any spot where Issachar was not.

On the morning of their departure he received his letters and among them was another with the Paris postmark.   It set his heart beating much as does a lover's whose sweetheart has favored him.   He sought his room to be alone, and tearing off the outer covers, found the inner epistle as before.   He absorbed it with his eyes, his brain, his heart.   It was entitled,

"FEAR.

"To be afraid of a thing is to give it *power*.   He who fears nothing is never in reality hurt; his body may succumb, but his soul is too white to be bleached. Fear of God, man, beast, or the devil, is to install each or all as avenging deities, before which a poor mortal must needs cringe.   It is not the magnetism of man that can hurt you, but *your own fear* of the same.   This talk of a subtle fluid emerging from a black, white, or any other kind of magician, is meaningless, and without weight.   This nonsense about auras—red, pink, and blue—is the laughing stock of true science. Magnetisms and auras in the sense in which they are interpreted, are but chimeras of diseased brains.

'' Each human being, to say nothing of the brute creation, has will and power to do; some more, some less. If you fear a stronger will than yourself, a subtler and more logical brain, you are as much by *this very terror*, the slave to its owner, as though he had a veritable magnetic fluid which could envelop you forever.

'' One in pursuit of another, who *fears* him, is a poisonous spider after a half-paralyzed fly.

'' *Be not afraid.* Knowledge is power. Know, that every mortal that walks the earth is an *immortal*—this paradox is worthy of the Sphinx. The immortal, by its very nature, is indestructible. He who realizes this in truth, knows naught of fear.

'' The mass of men *believe* that they must die. They prate of eternal life, they gossip of heaven, but by their extremity of fear, give the lie unto themselves. If once thou art convinced, that thou canst not die, fear, and hope—its everlasting mate —will flee, and certainty will stand, firm-footed, where they once were.

'' Fear and hope are for the world of men who strive to annihilate the eternal with time; who would run their span of four score years and ten, and bury the everlasting in the yawning grave. Fear and hope are for him who barters his soul for a span of sentient life. But one who beholds the

eternity in the now, and the all in himself, fears
nothing and hopes for naught.

"Wouldst thou serve a relentless will, that would
bend thee as does the blast the sapling, or wouldst
thou marshal thy whole potential force till giant
face giant, and king face king? The Master in
thee struggles with the man—the immortal with
the mortal. *Fear not.* Thou art destined *to be.*

Signed, ——————."

With the reading came courage born of conviction. The sudden consciousness forced upon him
by its own self-evidence, that the immortal was
indestructible and in reality safe, while the danger
lay in his own condition, rather than in anything
that Issachar could do, braced him like a draught of
wine. It gradually dawned upon him, that he had
fainted from sheer terror at the site of Memphis;
Issachar taking advantage of this weakness and
using it for all it was worth. But here came the
puzzle. How had this unknown writer, evidently
in Paris, in spite of Damascus roses, how had he
forestalled any further advantage that the Jew might
take, by opening his eyes to the philosophy of the
situation?

The letter must have been written long ere the
event of his meeting with Issachar. The author
must indeed be Seer and Sage combined, to bring
about such a concatenation of circumstances—coin-
cidence was out of the question. He had mused

over the first letter, but he puzzled more over the second.

What unseen entity at Paris was following him with a telescopic eye, guarding and directing him as might the spirit of one dead? He knew that for some reason, powerful influences were being brought to bear to prove the identity of Aleppo Romanes. To a certainty, the pursuit and investigation of the Jew, and the anonymous letters from Paris, were directed toward the same end. Opposing influences were undoubtedly at work, but Aleppo, though groping in the dark, understood which way to lean. The two letters appealed to him as a finality; they spoke with the authority of Holy Writ, because of the truth on which they were based. He was braced beyond expression by the second communication. A sort of rugged scorn of Issachar had to an extent allayed his fear; a ray had pierced the darkness which had well nigh turned his head; the letter gleamed as though engraved in gold, and flashed on the night of his soul like a fixed star.

CHAPTER X.

HELENE

Helene Cressey was a young widow when she first met Henrique Romanes and bore him a natural son. He being a sworn recluse, far advanced in the art and practice of Hermetic

Mysticism, and vowed to strict celibacy, had, through his passion for her, broken his pledge and betrayed his order.

During all the years since their separation, Helene had lived in the rapture of her love for Romanes, never suffering him to die out of her mind and heart, though until she met him on that eventful night in Vienna, she had never seen his face. In fact the two had lived in a sort of mental contact, conscious in a vague way of each other's sufferings and joys, and striving to climb again the height from which they had fallen. They tacitly agreed to ignore Aleppo, having arranged for his physical comfort, they concluded that for his sake as well as their own, it were better that he remain in ignorance of his illegitimate birth. It was not the illegality that troubled them, but the indignation which their natural son must necessarily feel at Romanes' disloyalty to a Sacred Order, and Helene's acquiescence in the same. To condone their offense they had agreed .to part, and thus removed from all personal temptation to strive to get back into the pure Eden where love is of the soul alone.

Romanes, in his early infatuation for Helene, had confided to her all the secrets of his cult ; for, having resolved to exchange honor for herself, he had become, for the time, utterly reckless. Later, when they began to drink the dregs of the cup, Helene (the first to recover and repent) had almost

driven Romanes from her; he being wiser than herself was exceedingly dubious as to his power of
regaining lost ground ; she however was hopeful
and persistent.

"I have paid a great price for our unborn child,"
he said to her as they parted ; "not only have I
defied law, which some would look upon as entirely
inexcusable, where love ties the knot, but I have
broken a vow and betrayed a trust. I doubt much
if there is any way to regain what I have lost."

"And I," said Helene, "have given nothing,
and have acquired much. What is my fair name,
when weighed against your love ?—what are living
lies compared with the joys of memory ? Romanes,
go !—and our unborn child shall be as if he were
not."

Thus she spoke to him, though she cursed Aleppo
in her heart. This was all years and years before.
Since her meeting with Romanes at Vienna,
Helene Cressey had begun to fade; the shock of the
contact with one who had been to her as dead, the
renewal of the old anxiety which she had hoped
was buried with the past, the sudden and inevitable
assumption of responsibilities that mantled her
cheek with shame, and caused her proud head to
bend, all these sprinkled her golden hair with
silver, and brought lines upon her brow. True to
her promises she used the means within her reach
to recover Aleppo, though in disposing of her
strength thus, she wrote the death warrant upon

herself. She believed in another life—*on earth;*
the cult of Romanes had taught her this;—she
would wash the pages of it now, that she might
begin with a white sheet.

She saw herself afar,—she lifted the veil of Isis
and beheld Helene again. Her feet trod a virgin
soil. Vestal once more, she raised her eyes to the
mighty Sierras, and challenged the blue above
them with a steady glance. Born among primeval
trees, of alien stock, new-made out of heaven,
white as the sea gull, strong with awakened energy,
she gazed fearlessly across the waste of the Pacific
to the unseen Orient, and dared all the Buddhas to
wipe her out. But the realization of this fair
vision,—this pristine strength and Edenic beauty,
hung upon a price; she must make of herself a very
stepping stone whereon Aleppo might ascend. She
must lose her life, that she might find it, where the
sun sets to rise over the East. Her love must fall
asleep; her beauty wane; herself buried, would rise
again with the freshness of the morning dew,
where the west wind blows off the ocean, and
eternal roses bloom.

She would come into this pure consciousness with
difficulties—the birth pangs would be hard. She
saw in vision, dark days, when storms not only
shook the giant sequoia, but herself also. She
repented in advance of grave mistakes made in the
romantic audacity of new-found youth. But over
and above all, she beheld the glittering stars of

a California sky, and the purified peaks of the Sierra Madre, cleaving the thin air with the boldness of great height. She breathed the breath of the pines and felt the salt brine of the Pacific on her blooming cheek.

"All a dream," you say: and we answer; "Possibly, all a dream; so, too, may be the Methodist heaven, with its paved streets and pearly gates; so, too, the Mohammedan's hareem in Paradise, or the Buddhist's Maha Meru."

Fact or fancy, Helene believed, and found in the face of truth, *as she saw it*, but one thing to do. She was intense for good or evil, as the case might be. The selfish once becoming unselfish, *gives all*. She neither calculated nor considered, but began immediately to act. Alas! She was not altogether wise; Romanes was a sage, Helene—a woman.

She saw no way to find Aleppo, save through Jacob Issachar, to whom she had resorted once before in her extremity, much to Romanes' grief; so, prompt as her attention was strong, she once more retreated to her chalet in Switzerland and buried her life beneath the awful, glittering crags of the Alps. Her first thought was Edena; she had lost all trace of her after her departure with Aleppo, but she knew the whereabouts of her home in Saxony, and communicated with her relations immediately. She ascertained that Edena was dead, but that a younger sister, Silvia, now an old

woman, was still alive, and could account for the
history of Edena to her last hour. She immediately sent for the old lady, begging a visit from
her at her chalet.

It was a bleak night; snow was piling up on all
sides, and the cold in the mountains was so intense
that Helene's man servant had piled the enormous
fireplace with huge logs, which blazed and smoul-
dered, causing weird, shadowy shapes to appear
and disappear in the corners of the great living
room of this mountain retreat. The apartment
was wainscoted in dark wood; the ceiling being
relieved by heavy beams, which were enriched in
color by the uncertain smoke that the wind often
blew at them, when it came in its mad rush down
the chimney on stormy nights. The fire furnished
both heat and light; not even a candle glowed on the
dresser, nor illuminated the ancient shelving which
rose from over the mantel to the very ceiling.

Silvia, who had arrived at the chalet that day,
sat over the blazing logs, crooning an old German
song, and knitting vigorously with fingers that age
had left untouched. She had a benign but severe
countenance, and white hair, combed smoothly
under a black cap.

Helene drew her chair close to her side, and
began to ply her with questions, listening intently
to catch every word that fell from her lips; for the
storm outside was doing its best to prevent conver-

sation by rattling the shutters and shaking the doors.

"So Edena was with you when she died?" said Helene, in German.

"Yes," said Silvia, knitting a whole round before raising her eyes—she was naturally secretive and mysterious—"but she had another name."

"Had she been married?" asked Helene, anxiously.

"No, but she ought to have been; she adopted a son."

"Ah! What was her name?"

"Serena; 'twas as much like the other as she could get."

"Did you ever see this boy?"—Helene's voice trembled slightly.

"Yes; when I visited her in Italy, and when she died, at the old home."

"What manner of child was he?"

"Good, I guess, as young folks go; went to school right along. Edena was very fond of him; and if I do say it, who didn't approve of her having him, she was like a mother, no doubt. Aleppo loved her in his way, same as all boys."

"How old was he when Edena died?"

"Don't know exactly, he was pretty well grown; at work in a studio. Not very much of an artist I guess, though Edena thought to the contrary; she believed he was everything. That boy could do no wrong in her eyes; whatever he said and did was right. She spoiled him, 'and I told her so."

" Did he suffer or want for anything ? "

" Suffer!—'twould have been better for him if he had. Edena gave him money, though where she got it, I don't know. I'm sorry any cloud should rest on my sister, but she seemed to have plenty for herself and the boy; and I have had my suspicions. Edena, in spite of her plain features, was romantic. I am afraid she had a lover, and that Aleppo was her own flesh and blood. How else did she come by so much gold?" Helene moved with a start.

" She would not confess anything, even when she died; but the boy had been provided for—a good round sum. He started off traveling a few months after Edena went out."

"Can you tell me where?" Helene had grasped Silvia by the arm and spoke with a kind of spasm. Silvia looked at her with surprise; all sorts of vague surmises ran through her head.

" I'm sorry, but I cannot; he was with us when Edena died, afterward went back to Italy, and never wrote us a line."

" If he were Edena's son, how did it happen that he was in an asylum ? "

"Just as a blind, I think—to temporarily mislead people as to his relationship. I expect it was to throw our family off guard. Edena was very shrewd, and we, for poor folks, are very proud."

Helene shuddered, and the wind howled through the pines outside.

"Nothing of the sort ever happened in our family before; in fact," tossing her head, "Don't know as it ever did happen. I expect I have misjudged Edena; the money is what puzzles me though; it made a coldness between us from the first."

Helene was walking the room rapidly. Pride! Where was her's? She must begin her atonement now—this very night. Turning abruptly toward Silvia, her eyes flaming, her face red—not from fire, but from shame—her hands nervously clutching each other, she said :

"Silvia, you do your sister a great wrong. I am the mother of Aleppo, and the money that has troubled you was mine."

Silvia had passed the age of enthusiasm; tragedy to her seemed far-fetched. She knit a whole round on the sock, then raising her eyes to Helene, said severely :

"You should have lifted that shadow off from my sister before."

"In truth, Silvia,"—Helene was trembling like an aspen—"I never dreamed that you had put such a construction on Edena's care of my son."

"How else could I look at it? A poor woman suddenly becoming rich and adopting a lad; it carries evidence on its face. I am glad, for the honor of my house, that she was innocent; but 'tis the more shame for you.''

Silva was a privileged character, she spake her full mind, and Helene took the ethereal slap with a meekness heretofore unexperienced by herself.

The roar of the blast outside had subsided into a kind of wail, the logs in the great fireplace were smouldering, and the cold had crept in through the crannies and cracks. Silvia was inclined to be dumb, and the click-clack of her needles spoke of a certain condensed scorn for the woman by her side, which words could never express. Helene felt it, and broke the silence:—

"I know now, that you'll not care to prolong your stay, you will leave me to-morrow; be thankful, however, that I have cleared up Edena's character and restored your family to its pristine state." But Silvia was not as hard as she looked.

"Tut tut!"—she dropped the sock in her lap—"so you'll turn an old woman out in the storm; well I shan't go; understand, I'll stay my week out as I came to do, perhaps longer, for that matter." She made great show of anger, but Helene felt the crude kindness to the depths of her soul, and went over to old Silvia, who was looking very severe.

"You are Edena over again." She threw her arms around her neck, buried her face on the old woman's shoulder, and sobbed as though her heart would break.

"There, my beauty,"—this was the only time

that Silvia had spoken tenderly—" you've not aged
enough yet to spoil your eyes; when you get like
me 'twon't matter." But Silvia let her stay, and
stroked her hair a little. It was the sweetest
touch that Helene had known for many a year.

The room grew colder and the fire went down,
till the corners were black with shadows; still the
golden head rested on Silvia's shoulder, and Helene's
low sobbing mingled with the gale outside. She
was neither repenting of her sins, nor regretting
retribution; Silvia *had found her clean*, and was
holding her in her arms. It takes a strange thing,
sometimes to break up the ice-floe of the heart.

Edena's sister staid her time out; and after she
had gone, Helene waited restlessly for a visit from
Issachar. Having ascertained nothing from Silvia
that could give her any clew as to the whereabouts
of Aleppo, she had resorted, almost against her
judgment, to the Jew. Not aware of his precise
address, she directed a letter to Venice, in hopes
that by some good fortune it would reach him,
requesting a visit as promptly as possible, and
appealing to the mercenary side of his nature with
a large bribe. The days went by, but brought no
news. Almost in despair, and frozen by the savage
peaks of the Alps, she made up her mind to go to
Venice, and make personal search, when a letter
arrived, addressed in French, and mailed in Egypt.
It was from Issachar, and read as follows :

Madame :   .

Your epistle received in Venice. Have since
been following one Aleppo Bracciolini—young man
with his father and brother. I am suspicious that
he may be Aleppo Romanes. Will go after him to
the end of the world, provided that ¸you bestow
upon me a sum worthy of the task. Issachar is a
prince, remember. No other on earth can prove
the identity of the son of Romanes; for was it not I
that burnt the sign of an order into his back ? The
devil knows his own mark.

Shall await your command at Cairo.

JACOB ISSACHAR.

What the pecuniary demand of a self-styled
prince might be, Helene had no idea; nor could
she, nor any but Issachar decipher the devil's mark.
The Jew had stated truly, that he, alone, of all on
earth, could prove the identity of Aleppo Romanes.
To be sure, the boy adopted by Edena might be
verified by Silvia, but he had been in an asylum
three or four years, and might, for all they knew,
be a different child from the one booked as Aleppo
Bracciolini. The mark alone was the test; and
from the hint in Issachar's letter, Helene had grave
doubts as to its being a sign of the order to which
Romanes belonged. A subtler brain than Helene's
might have seen that proof positive was not even
to be found in the oath of the Jew. Capable of
deception once, why not again? The signer of the

devil's mark, could easily perjure himself, but, subtleties to the contrary, Helene believed that Issachar was the one and certain clue. Her fortune
was large and her sacrifice had already begun. If
Issachar must have money, she would pour out her
own to the last penny; with the rash audacity of a
woman who had known no half-way experience in
all her life, she dashed off the following reply to
the Jew's letter :

Jacob Issachar:
Sir : Make your terms, by telegraph. If within
my power, will acquiesce.
Address.
HELENE CRESSEY,
Vienna.

Upon sending this, she returned to Vienna to
await events, while the fire of her life burned
rapidly toward its end.

CHAPTER XI.

ON THE NILE.

" The five " had increased to seven; two rather
ancient sisters, friends of Mrs. Hancock, had met
her by appointment at Cairo, with the understanding that they were to make the Nile trip together.
They were harmless ladies, and called the Misses
Richard. The older by perhaps a year or two was

Sarah, while the younger answered to the giddy name of Bess.   With Mrs. Hancock they balanced the party, adding enough of conventional dignity to overcome the Bohemian tendencies of the other four.   They were to make the Nile trip in a dahabeah, about which Regan had employed himself for several days.   He had hunted for a dragoman till he found just the " right thing," so he said; though why this individual should be styled a "thing," he never explained.   They had eschewed Cook and steam and taken to wind and sails ; for time, being of no account, and the Nile everything, they had all voted to go up to the first cataract with the pace of a snail.

Their dragoman made a picturesque figure with his turban and slouchy trousers, and his English equalled any pidgeon vernacular that a Chinese was capable of.   He took the pride of a titled lord in his small but nicely furnished dahabeah, and showed the passengers over it as though it were a floating palace.   It was like all dahabeahs, with its flat bottom and forward mast.   There was the outdoor parlor with its Oriental furnishings, the indoor saloon, its mite of a kitchen, and tiny state rooms.

Their dragoman was a musselman named Haggi, though his religion counted for very little.   He was literally all things to all men— a kaleidoscopic chameleon as regards color of thought and tone of speech.

It being Autumn, they were to sail against the current and float down with it on their return to Cairo. The day of their start was a fine one, the Mohammed hurried along like a bird, flying by palaces, temples and gardens; while the pyramids in their majesty pursued her like veritable avengers. . She passed vanishing groves of palm, huts of mud, and yellow hills; thus floating on and on, till night set in, when, staked like a weary ostrich, she slept by the side of a little village that dreamed, as it had for centuries, the Hareem-tinctured dreams of a servant of Allah.

In a few hours after leaving Cairo they were all at home, their belongings settled and adjusted, and themselves in a frame of mind amicable in the extreme. Aleppo felt that for some time at least he need have no dealings with Issachar, while Rhea was in literal rhapsody, realizing a cherished vision, where the Nile had wound and coiled like an insinuating serpent of yellow and green in and out of her life for years. Sallus rejuvenated, was becoming conscious of powerful ambitions, while Mrs. Hancock gloated over the long hours in prospect where table linen and embroidery silks should reign supreme. The addenda, called Sarah and Bess, were as benignly conventional as it was proper to be, and Regan—Regan!—king! In spite of the musselman Haggi, in spite of dead calms and the tracking of Arab sailors, in spite of Mrs. Hancock's scornful snubs and the cook's preeminence, *king!* There was no denying it, this was the place for Regan.

" 'Pon my word, I wonder I've never tried this before ''—it was the brightest kind of a morning, the second day on board.

" It seems to me you like to have but few people about,—you're a natural boss,'' said Mrs. Hancock snappishly.

" No, that's not exactly it; bossing isn't after my style. The fun of this thing lies in its opportunities. I've always wanted to be lazy, but never had a chance before. To move and be lazy at the same time is happiness done brown. It's as much like a massage as anything I know of—you are exercising, and yet you are not. To lie on your back and be kneaded is very much like going up the Nile— See?''

" How horrid!'' Mrs. Hancock looked scandalized and the conventional Misses Richards turned their backs.

" Well it's just this way—you're going along and seeing the identical mud hut, duplicated from Cairo to Karnak; at the same time you are sitting still. Besides you feel young and frisky down here in old Khem ; comparison makes kids of us, don't you see, Mrs. Hancock?''

"They say,'' said Rhea, " that one never realizes his ideals; it's a mistake, for I'm realizing mine.''

" That's just it ;'' answered Regan, " your ideal is up to the Nile; Mrs. Hancock's isn't. Folks are different—two peas to the contrary. My ideal is realized in active laziness or lazy activity—one way of putting it is as good as another. I like to be doing and yet not doing, see? Going and keeping still is the sum total of happiness—the Nile suits me."

"You ought to have been happy at Stamboul, where, metaphorically, you embraced two continents at once"—

"That is a kind of paradox, sure—East and West tumbling into each other's arms; but 'tis nothing to this calm motion which the Buddhist describes as Nirvana."

"Wait till the wind lulls and those Arabs get to "tracking;" you'll sing a different song most likely," said Sallus whistling.

"I expect so; I hate to be pulled anywhere by one of my kind. No help for it though, if the wind lulls, unless I get out and join in."

"Yes; you'd make a pretty figure along side of those Arabs"—Mrs. Hancock snapped her eyes at him as she said it, but it was all wasted on Regan; he was proof against Mrs. Hancock's eyes in any shape; their flashes either celestial or terrestrial were as harmless as sheet lightning, as far as he was concerned. Regan loved two boys and one girl and Mrs. Hancock was utterly shut out. She knew this and a woman scorned, or rather ignored, is bitterer than aloes. She tolerated the young fellows because of their youth, but Regan, from the fact of his utter indifference and extreme good nature, was beyond endurance. She enjoyed herself however, exceedingly; to have a grievance was to her a source of great delight, so she nursed her petty hatred and poured out her feelings on the innocent heads of the Misses Richards much to their enjoyment also. In fact the Nile voyagers, while outwardly one, were inwardly *two* — the forces being diametrically opposed.

Rhea had assumed the role of mother confessor to Sallus, and had maintained it with so much dignity that the young man had completely changed his mind in regard to her. That he had determined to marry her, he remembered with a species of awe. How he could ever have been so audacious he failed at present to understand. He would die for her gladly, but marry her—never ! She had talked to him as though his senior by twenty years. She had raised herself so high on her pedestal of dignity, that he thought of her as a denizen of another world—here by mistake—but sure to return to whence she came, when the time was ripe. Whatever of passionate love he had conceived for her on their first meeting in Brindisi, she had succeeded in putting out, and in place of it, had arisen in Sallus' mind a sort of worship such as a devotee bestows upon his idol. Rhea was Sallus' church and Sunday School; more—a veritable flesh and blood goddess to whom he said his prayers. Aleppo had discovered this peculiar condition of affairs between

Rhea and Sallus long since, and felt particularly content in consequence.

Sallus was saved; his redeemer was Rhea. Aleppo had no more anxiety about his beloved chum, and Rhea was the sweet friend of himself for though their tongues were silent—their eyes spoke.

The "tracking" came according to Sallus; the patient Arabs pulled like mules along the bank of the Nile, and so slowly that there was plenty of chance to investigate and take notes.

They had reached the region of the Dom palm. Here they had opportunity to exercise, and instead of motionless motion, according to Regan, they went for a walk through a small Arab town. It had the squalor of Cairo, without its splendor; it was a typical place—Bazaar, flies, shops, rugs, saddles, flies, dogs, camels, donkies, flies, men, women, children, flies—this is an Arab town.

They were moored at night as usual, and the party, tired after their walk, were lolling about on the deck parlor, each dreaming or plotting, as the case might be. There was a soft, seductive moon, which flooded the Mohammed with a fantastic glow. The Nile, on whose bosom lay a phantom of her lunar self, was glittering and flashing in a sort of rapture, to which Rhea responded with full heart. She had thrown herself among the cushions, and looked, in the splendor of the night, like a dream-child of the Orient. She was dressed in a white, clinging robe, with loose, half-open sleeves, that

displayed the sculptured beauty of her arms, whose
ivory tinting was intensified by the light on high.
Her face, as she reclined among the cushions, with
those beautiful arms clasped above her head, had in
it the expression of rapture that an unrealized passion sometimes brings. She revealed in her look
and pose, the ecstacy of a waking dream, untrans-
lated, save in song. Aleppo was near her, and
with half-veiled eyes, watched the celestial beauty
which the moon had made. There was a hush on
the Nile, and in his heart. He seemed to be waiting for something—what, he could not tell. The
others had stolen away, and he and Rhea were
alone. He thought of the queen—Cleopatra. He
forgot the blackness of her character, and remembered but the charm. Something in Rhea recalled
her, as one star brings out another. He thought of
icy peaks and lotus flowers, of pine trees and palms,
of the mystery and witchery of color, of the magic
and majesty of sound. He beheld the flashing eyes
of Egypt's queen—the starry eyes, veiled to hide
their passion, or opened wide in the deadly splendor of their power. He saw her challenge Cæsar,
and conquer Antony, and felt, stealing over
him, the charm of life, *life*, LIFE !—the voluptuous
spell of the poet—the Sapphic cry of an exultant
love. He was conscious of the teeming luxury of
earth. He melted moonlight pearls and drank
them in cups of magic wine. He felt the Greek
heart beat in Egypt's breast, and while he dreamed,

the serpent Nile coiled and uncoiled, and flashed
and quivered—its million glittering scales alive
with color, speaking in their Iris glow and glitter—
life! life! life!! Entranced, half lost in rapture,
there stole upon his ear, a voice—the same that he
had heard since time on earth began.   It was
Rhea's; her soul went out in song, and her voice
--pure contralto—floating on and on in Aleppo's
heart forever and forever :—

> "I loved you in the old time,
> I love you in the new—
> Forever and forever
> My heart belongs to you."

He was shocked to his feet.   Was he dreaming?
Where had she heard it?   It was his !—the song
of his soul—and Rhea was pouring it out to the.
moon with the rapture of a singing-bird.   He dared
not speak.   The powerful, thrilling rhapsody died
—died away, till only an echo floated softly through
the Dom palms on the shore, mingling and losing
its sweet cadence in the ripples and the glitter of
the Nile.

She ceased; her beautiful white arms fell listlessly
in her lap, and her head dropped on her breast.

" Rhea!   Rhea!"

She lifted her face and looked Aleppo in the eyes.

" Where did you learn that song ? "

" I have known it forever."

" *And so have I.*"

She looked at him like a startled fawn, then turned away.

"Rhea! Rhea!"—he came very close and took her hand. "How happens it that you and I have sung the same?"

Even in the moonlight he saw the color steal up from her rosy neck to her brow and hair. "Can you not speak to me? Rhea!"

"Since I can remember, I have sung this song."

"And I," said Aleppo, "I have it written down."

In startled speech, hardly knowing what she said, she went on: "I have always *known* that somewhere on earth this dear love dwelt. I have sung to this *unknown* forever. Some one there is who loves me—some one." Here she paused and turned away.

"It is I, Rhea! it is I! Can you not understand? I have written to you a thousand times; I have sung to you a thousand more; I have seen you, since I could dream at all. To-night, in the moon's soft glow, you came again—the virgin face —within my soul. Sweetheart, it is I; our song is one; we respond to the same love note; the stars have told us, and the moon; the Nile is alive with light. Oh, Rhea!"

She shuddered, and drew her hand away. "The light is for you, dear heart, the *shadow* for me."

She sat erect, the soft languor gone, her eyes fol-

lowing the sinuous river, as though within its serpent coils she read a tale of doom.

"It is true, we sing the same song; but, ah! there
is something—a shadow; it comes between us like
a veil; on one side it is bright—the white light of
the sun, on the other, *dark!* I see you, Aleppo,
on a shining height; myself out in the night,
alone!

"Oh, Rhea, too much of happiness has made you
sad; it seems to me my heart will burst with joy.
I have the letters—all; this very night I will place
them in your hands; and the song—it is written
down. They will tell you what I cannot say—
the story of my life—my *love.*

She arose and reached both hands to him; a little
taller than he, her robe falling in classic folds about
her form, her perfect profile touched by the waning
light of the moon, she looked a pure Greek, and
sent Aleppo back to Attica with the swiftness of
thought.

"Aleppo, I am older, and I know by some
strange insight, that you and I must part; yet,
wherever you may be, I too shall dwell, in soul,
with you."

"Dear love, for once you are wrong; this voyage
upon the Nile will last—*forever.*"

She smiled, it was both sweet and sad; there was
a hush upon the river; the moon had paused a
moment in its downward course.

"May you be right, but speak to no one of this

blessed night; it is as sacred as our song—'I love you.'" For one short, but eternal moment, he held her in his arms, and pressed that loved form to his own—the first kiss, *and the last*. Never on earth, again, through the years that came and went, did their lips meet.

CHAPTER XII

KARNAK.

The mighty pillars of Karnak preach the sermon of the ages, not only defying time, but telling of the bold grandeur in the mind of man at the dawn of history. Thebes with its sitting colossi, its magnificent propylon, its avenue of sphinxes, and its temple of Ammon points unceasingly backward to the flower of Egyptian splendor, Ramases the II. Whether or not this Pharaoh of Pharaohs lashed on the Israelites to the building of the temples whose ruins are the world's wonder, whether the stiffened mummy of the tyrant of the Pentateuch lies in the museum of Bohlak, or somewhere else, it is nevertheless true, that Ramases the Great made the Thebes of to day a spot of unrivaled ruins, to whose giant remains our modern monuments are as pygmies and dwarfs. If the splendor of ancient Egypt is to be guessed by its decay, the moderns have no great cause to boast. The colossi still sit solemnly on the banks of the mystic Nile, while headless sphinxes hide the secret of Ammon whose mighty temple challenges the centuries. Defiant in its deathless decay, it cherishes its columnar perspective ; and steadfast as is Isis, remains the translator of old Egypt, and the revealer of ancient Thebes.

When Aleppo first beheld Karnak, his intellect rose to its greatness, though the shadow of its propylon fell like a cloud upon his heart. He had been supremely happy, as man is *once* in a life. On the right of the Nile was a range of mysterious mountains—in his soul was the song of Rhea. There was nothing to show him that the great ruin was at hand, nor to warn him of his coming life. Suddenly, as if from nowhere, appeared the propylon of a temple, and with it the *shadow*, beside which the sunlight of his after days must always glow.

At Luxor, he found two letters—one from Caesar Catus, the other from the beloved correspondent whose name was a mystery. He kept the more precious till the last, and read the words of Catus with great interest : `

"*Dear Aleppo:*

"This letter will be waiting you at Luxor. What do you say to a trip with me later to Damascus? I will meet you at Cairo on your return, and we will run off together to Syria. Don't disappoint me; there is no reason why you should not go—you have no ties. Let us see the charmed spot together."

There was much more to the letter, but the suggestion in regard to Damascus was of chief interest. Aleppo smiled to himself—"Caesar thinks I have no ties; if he only knew! No man was ever bound as I am. Even Catus cannot drag me from Rhea—whose eyes of late are sad."

He opened the second letter—it was entitled:

"PERSONALITY.

" Persons belong to themselves; the truth behind them, to everybody. The person of the teacher may be dear, but the maxims taught are priceless. Guatama is dead; the Tripitaka lives. Jesus has departed, his truth remains.

"Personality is transient, principles are eternal.

"Climb on the ladder of your teacher to a height where you can tower above his head. Make of him a way to an end—a door through which to pass to the Ultima Thule of your soul's splendor. The person may be loved as is a fading flower, the eternal principle for which he stands, adored. He who puts his trust in persons is floating on the glittering sea of *change*, but one who dwells on *Law*, *is fixed*."

This letter, like the propylon, was unutterably dreary. The *Great Gate* through which he was doomed to pass, was the entrance to a boundless unknown country, upon whose broad expanse, though extending to the sky, was no familiar face. He found it difficult to explain the cause of this apprehension;

the fear of Issachar had departed—he felt himself
a man, in his secret heart he kew the soul of Rhea,
and yet the glitter of the heaven-kissed desert,
upon which the shadow of the propylon fell like a
band of mourner's crape, predominated all, and
subdued his joy, till his song thrilled with a sad
rapture like that of the dying swan. He went
among the ruins of Karnak day after day, sometimes accompanied by Rhea, more often alone.

The party had no idea of the secret compact
between these two; in fact, Aleppo and Rhea were
less often together than before ; yet, somehow it
was realized that there was a change in both of
them, that it was hard to understand.

Rhea's eyes were sad, Mrs. Hancock declared,
" 'twas enough to make anybody cry, to be in a
heap of rubbish,''as she styled Karnak.

" Aleppo," Regan remarked, "must have caught
a Luxor fever—don't kuow whether it's of the
body or the mind; but it's apt to come on amid
ruins. It might be the microbes of old age, or it
might be the ghosts of the ancients. Aleppo, you
see, is a sort of a mystic, and as susceptible as a
medium. I think some old spook of an Egyptian
is trying to use him. The East will make an adept
out of Lep, if I kuow myself. Never saw a fellow
like graveyards as he does; if he wants to dream,
he hunts out a headstone; if he wants to fight
with himself, he crawls into a tomb. Cypress
trees are after his own heart, and the wail of the

banshee the sweetest sound on earth. I never
could understand"—here he looked at Mrs.
Hancock mysteriously, "why Aleppo and Sallus
are so fond of each other; of course being brothers
cuts no figure. Sal has no more respect for the
dead than he has for the living; don't believe as
much. That fellow Sal likes *live* beauty, if ever
anyone did. He's getting mopy down here at
Luxor."

Mrs. Hancock tried to prick Regan with metaphorical needles from morning till night, but he had
the hide of a rhinoceros.

"You can't make me believe"—there was malice
aforethought written all over her—"that those
two fellows had the same mother, if you are their
father—which I don't swallow either."

"'Tis a big gulp—so diverse in each particular.
They show it more in photographs than when
together; types different—see?"

"Yes, I see with my eyes shut." She was angry.
Regan slipped away from her as easily as an eel;
she could neither get a grip on him nor make him
speak truth. He was the most optimistic pessi-
mist that ever walked the earth. He kept up the
spirits of the party at Karnak in spite of his owl-
like hoot and frog-like croak. Not in the least
awed by the sitting colossi or the headless sphinxes,
he slandered the ancient children of Khem with an
apparently malignant tongue, though in reality
there was no poison in his fangs. He had no

respect for relics, and called a scarab a beetle without biting his lips. The cartouche of Ramases the
II made upon him no impression whatever, and he
spoke of the tragedy of the children of Israel as a
myth. Regan tore glamour into shreds and stuck
his rugged New England head through the window
of the past without regard to the smashing of the
pane. He was so much of an iconoclast that he
toppled over Karnak's last pillar and would have
cleaned up no end of rubbish had he not desired to
be busy elsewhere.

Sallus considered Regan the greatest philosopher
on earth, and agreed with him from first to last.

"You see," said Regan leaning against a pillar
of the temple of Ammon, with his feet on a block
of stone as high as his head, "I've always had a
fancy, that to whitewash Rome would make it a
heap healthier; the dust of ages is full of small-pox
and typhoid fever."

"I suppose," said Mrs. Hancock indignantly,
" that you'd advertise your egg-beater on the walls
of Karnak; 'twould be as good a place as any,
according to your idea."

"Well now, that depends; trouble is, 'twould be
taken for a hieroglyphic, and relegated to the first
Pharaoh. No, 'twouldn't do; besides the thing has
been advertising itself for ten years."

"Don't you feel," said Rhea, in love with the
quaint humor of Regan, "the majesty of these
ruins—the age?"

"Now Miss Rhea, that's a question; the majesty does impress me, must confess. I've been trying to puzzle out in my head ever since I came, how many tons of rock there are in this thing anyhow. As to the age, it doesn't count for much; the rock *anywhere* would be as old as the world, however you fix it— one part of the earth is as aged as another for that matter."

"Of course, as far as the material is concerned," answered Rhea, laughing, "but the putting together of the thing—the building ?"

"Time's all a matter of comparison. I don't believe Karnak holds a candle to the Kitchen-middens in the Swiss lakes. Historic man is quite a young biped compared with the other fellow who got in before history. In my opinion, the world is a heap older than we think it is—and man with it."

One day—it was as bright as any other—Aleppo stood at the door of the little hotel at Luxor, and looked with half-frightened eyes upon Rhea—"I am going over to Karnak alone; do not worry if I am late to-night."

Rhea bent forward as though to kiss him, then restraining herself, touched her fingers to her lips, and threw him an airy salute which he never forgot. Often in years after, in strange countries and stranger conditions, he remembered those soft, half-mischievous eyes and the pretty finger tips that had thrown him a tantalizing good bye.

She stood in the full glow of morning, with a

smile on her lips and in her eyes—the sweetest
promise that man could crave—and yet his heart
was a stone in his breast.

The Luxor sky was in its usual condition, of
cloudless serenity. The great temple was isolate,
like himself, and a relic of a life long gone. He
felt that he belonged to another age and race, and
had somehow fallen upon a century with which he
was out of tune. Why had life been thrust upon
him in the dark, with no ray anywhere to light up
the mystery of himself. He longed for a family
record to show to Rhea—the extended pedigree of
an honorable house. Even a Bible with the
account kept, something—anything, to present to
the woman he loved, as a clean page behind him.
He had dared speak no word to her of the future,
for the years ahead are the legitimate children of
the past—*he had no past.*

And here he was, on the verge of life—his Paradise, as he had said to Regan—hanging over hell.
He wandered, restlessly, among the ruins, brooding.
There was but one thing for him—he *must know.*
Never would he take Rhea to his heart and life on
this uncertainty. She had seen the shadow on the
Nile; it was cold, like a night mist. He had given
her the letters; she knew what he knew, but that
was not enough. This beautiful woman had a
proud, Puritan ancestry behind her; every line of
their history was written; the pages had faded in the
sun. For an instant—only for an instant—Aleppo

pitied himself. He had led a clean life—he was
as chaste as a pure-souled girl, and had followed
his higher instincts as naturally as he had breathed.
All the passion and power in him had gone out to
beauty and truth; burning ever with that inextinguishable love for the great, the supernal, he had
wings as white as the sea-gull's, and as strong. He
came to the propylon, and leaned wearily against
its inner walls, looking upward at the arch overhead with tears in his eyes. Beyond was " the
way." Through this mighty gate, he would travel
somewhere, over the wreck and ruin of a life. Had
he deserved it all? Was justice but a name?
Softly, in the depths of his own soul he heard a
voice: " He that would climb on a ladder to the
stars, must have the courage to look down." He
dashed the tears from his eyes, and stood erect; the
propylon bore his weight no more. With head
thrown back, he went through "*the gate*" and
stood face to face with Issachar the Jew. He
stopped abruptly, and the ancient bowed his head.

" So you have followed me again." Aleppo
had passed the crisis of his life and *feared no man*.

The Jew, with quick glance, noted the change;
instead of a half-terrified boy, he was facing a
young David, whose sling-stone was as deadly as a
cannon-ball. But Issachar was shrewd. The
whitest child of heaven ofttimes is more than
matched by the wily servant of the god—"on
change."

" Yes, I have come to try again the common speech of human kind. If that should fail, I know well what to do."

" You are right; hitherto I have acted the craven and the cur. Speak on, but let there be no *lies*."

" Lies! 'Tis thou that liest.

" I lie no more."

" Who art thou ? " said Issachar.

" Aleppo Bracciolini."

" Dost thou know thy father and mother ? "

" I do not; but what is that to you ? "

" Much ! Much ! " Here the Jew moved from head to foot like a snake. " I have proved thine identity, as thou well knowest. Shall I reveal to thee thy past ? "

For a moment Aleppo seemed to turn to stone, then, getting power of speech, said calmly, " Yes."

The Jew tried the effect of his eyes, but without avail; the young man looked beyond them into space.

" Thou wast born out of wedlock. Thy mother was a young English widow, and thy father a member of a sacred order, sworn to celibacy. The symbol on thy back, is my *own*, put there by the command of thy mother, and known only to myself."

Again Aleppo's heart stopped beating ; but finding words once more, he faced Issachar with a challenge in his eyes. " Are *you* my father ? "

The idea was new to the Jew; for a moment he

lost his poise, and calculated the value of the suggestion, then threw it aside as of no account.

" *Are you* my father?"

Aleppo spoke in the low voice of one in deadly
earnest.

" No."

The Jew smiled; the revolting white teeth were
all displayed, as suggestive as those of a hyena.

The reaction came. Aleppo wiped the beads of
sweat from his brow, tossed back his hair, and
breathed. The Jew went on.

" I know thy father well, and thy mother; they
desire thee. I am their messenger; wherefore
otherwise should I follow thee here, or take thee by
force at Memphis? It is not I who pursue thee,
but thy parents."

The blow had fallen; the young man saw Rhea
vanishing, the airy kiss gone with her. Sallus
and Regan, dim memories of the past, and himself alone, with Issachar the Jew. No! What
subtle power had wafted to his spiritual sense the
garden of Damascus; what dream was he still
dreaming that he caught the scent of roses and the
breath of Syrian vales?

He stood an inch taller, and looked down upon
the Jew.

" What proof have you? "

" Come with me," said Issachar; for the first
time bowing low to Aleppo Romanes. " My

proof is all in writing, clear and clean, in yonder hut; come, follow me.

Aleppo walked proudly behind the Jew, an illegitimate son of a disloyal father! Never in all his life had he held his head so high.

CHAPTER XIII.

CÆSAR CATUS.

In a room at the hotel at Luxor, six anxious people were holding council, drawn together for the first time, and all of one mind. It was the morning after Aleppo's departure for Karnak, and he had not returned. Mrs. Hancock bustled around nervously, suggesting this, that and the other to the Misses Richard, who looked as dreary as pallbearers. Regan was worried to that degree that he had lost his humor, while Sallus, wildly impatient to take some step in the search, was rapidly pacing the room ; Rhea, alone, said nothing, though her eyes were beyond fathoming.

The excitement had begun at breakfast; no one had known of his absence save Rhea, who had watched all the evening for his home coming, and had walked her room the remainder of the night. The party had been in the habit of dividing and going off on exploring trips each day, meeting the following morning to relate their adventures and

start out again.   At first, with the exception of
Rhea, whose divine intuition rarely failed her, they
took the matter of Aleppo's absence lightly,
remarking to each other that he would come in
later; but as the morning grew apace a cloud settled
over the whole party, culminating in a downright shower of surmises and suppositions, which
multiplied on themselves every instant.   What
could have happened?   Was he murdered?   Even
Mrs. Hancock found in her woman's heart an affection for the *absent* Aleppo, whose *presence* she disliked.   In her feminine inconsistency she manifested true anxiety, and revealed her better side,
much to the surprise of all.

When something really serious falls upon one,
the depths of the soul are moved, and the kinship
of humanity is discovered.

Regan called the party together at once to hold
council, and, after a few moment's conversation, it
was decided that the two men should start immediately for Karnak, making a thorough search of the
ruins; but Rhea would, on no account, be left
behind.   So the three departed hastily, leaving
Mrs. Hancock less comfortable than she had been
for many a day.

A week was spent in untiring search ; they went
everywhere, notified the authorities, and moved
heaven and earth; but Aleppo "was not."   The
dread that hung over them at first was lifted ; they
expected to discover his dead body at any time,

and each undecipherable object that startled them, they shrank away from, for fear of a revelation. Regan's humor was all gone and his pessimism with it; he neither smiled nor complained, but Sallus was a distracted Damon without his Pythias; he would have followed Aleppo to the end of the world, and here in Africa his friend had vanished. Each night, after the day's failure the six met and made new plans, trying át the same time to decipher the riddle. That Aleppo had voluntarily left them they never once considered. He was utterly loyal. Foul play, they spoke of in whispers; though the motive for such a thing they failed to discover; that is, the most of them. At the end of the week, however, Regan called Sallus into his room and locked the door.

"Sal, I've sifted it down to this—the Jew is behind the whole business."

"The Jew!"

"Yes—the arch fiend!"

"But we left him in Venice."

· "He didn't stay there though, mark my word. Aleppo's terror had some backing; he was in constant fear in Cairo, for he told me so."

"Did he meet Issachar up there?"

"Not that I know of; if he did he kept still about it ; he was ashamed of his terror, perhaps. I'm right though; it's the one probability out of the innumerable possibilities. That Jew was determined to have Aleppo Romanes, and what was to hinder him from slipping down here and carrying him off from Karnak."

" Why didn't he strike at Cairo? Lep was always wandering about alone."

" Possibly he wasn't ready, he may have heard some news that changed his mind. There's a mystery back of Aleppo, as you know, yourself, and it's deepening."

" Does this idea relieve you any ? " asked Sallus, anxiously.

" Yes, and no ; I believe his life is valuable and will not be tampered with ; in a sense, that thought is comforting ; nevertheless he'll see no end of trouble if my conjecture is correct."

" What do you propose to do ? "

"Get after that cursed son of Satan, if I know myself."

"Shake on that, Regan; I was a hog till Lep got hold of me; I have something to live for now. If I don't lay that Jew may I be the cursed son of the devil himself."

Sallus rose to his six feet. There was something inspiring in his knotted muscles and set teeth. He had never fully comprehended the spiritual side of Aleppo, and for that reason loved him with devotion. He had felt himself a huge bear in comparison with his friend's fine figure and beautiful eyes, little knowing how Aleppo had hung over him when he slept, filled with admiration, tinctured with envy, of his superb Greek proportions and hand-some American face.

They loved, because they were entirely different and needed each other beyond telling. Sallus expanded to the occasion with the elasticity of a true son of Columbia. He was the typical Ameri-can, and required something large to draw him out; evolving rapidly through opposition, and surpris-ing everybody who had previously pronounced judgment upon him. The more bitterly he was interfered with by environment, the more ready was he. He needed hard knocks, and the loss of Aleppo was a downright blow. Regan, in his heart, had adopted Aleppo and this was his first real grief. So the two men combine, and the Jew must indeed be a magician to escape the Nemesis upon his track.

Rhea had passed all possibility of a surprise; she had dreamed, night after night, that Aleppo had vanished, and when, one beautiful, sunlit morn-ing, he went away, she watched his retreating form and sad face (for he continually turned around to look back at her) with a consciousness that her dream had come true. When the sun had set and he failed to return, she knew that the shadow of the Nile was upon her, to be lifted, if ever, under another sky.

During that dreary week at Luxor she read, over and over again the letters he had placed in her hands. It was the strangest courtship that woman

had ever known. These passionate words of love
had been poured out long before he had met her,
and were the innocent, spontaneous expressions of
a full and devoted heart. He had translated all of
the missives, written in a tongue unknown to
Rhea, and had enclosed them with the originals, so
that she had no difficulty in making them out.
The song was in a number of them, sometimes
recorded in foreign tongue, and again in English.
About this bit of music she wondered and wondered, and indeed it would have puzzled a greater
psychologist than Rhea. A hard-headed, matter
of fact individual would have emphatically asserted
that the explanation was easy. The word coinci-
dence covers a great deal; they both had some
time read the lines in early youth, had taken a
fancy to the same, and had retained them in memory, forgetting that they had ever seen them. That
the same identical words could have sprung up in
the minds of two individuals of different nationali-
ties and thousands of miles apart—not only the
same words, but the same air—was too much for
even a credulous person to believe. Whatever the
fact may have been, however, Rhea looked upon
this song as the seal of her soul's kinship to Aleppo,
and she hummed it over and over, all through that
melancholy time at Luxor, as though it were a
funeral dirge. She kept her own sweet secret; it
belonged to no one on earth save Aleppo, and he,
alas, had flown. But her eyes betrayed her with

their unutterable longing; and Regan read the sad
story, though he made no sign.

The six returned to Cairo as rapidly as
possible, discarding the dahabeah and resorting to
steam; for as Regan declared to Sallus—

"We shall never find Aleppo down here; Issachar
has hustled him off, as sure as you're born. We'll
try Cairo—everywhere; the Jew is a striking figure;
somebody may have seen him up north."

They were scarcely more than settled at
Shepherd's when a card was sent up for Aleppo
Bracciolini, on which was engraved the name,
Caesar Catus. Sallus had heard Aleppo speak of
him a hundred times and rushed into the parlor at
once."

"A thousand pardons," said Sallus, "you have
not heard—Aleppo has disappeared; no trace as yet,
vanished at Karnak. I am glad you have come,"
all this in one breath.

Caesar manifested no surprise whatever, but said
rather quietly, "Yes, I understand."

"How on earth did you know?"

His visitor smiled and stroked his beard. He was
a man of medium height, in the prime of life. His
head was large and finely shaped, and though, as
Aleppo had stated, he was of oriental extraction,
his appearance failed to bear it out. He hailed from
Italy and was of the type of ancient Rome. He
had a handsome, powerful nose with the true
aggressive curve; deep-set, quick-moving eyes,.

under heavy imperial brows; and a smooth cheek, without prominence of bone, which was slightly flushed where his tawny, well kept beard had failed to intrude. His complexion was surpassingly fair and his brow, where the hair was thin about the temples, white as sun-tinted snow. Punctilious in dress, and slightly pompous as to form, he was as striking and clear-cut a figure as one often sees, and might have been a reincarnated Caesar of ancient Rome, being distinctly an aristocrat without the malignity of the tyrant. In spite of his aristocratic lineage he had the shyness of genius, which set peculiarly on his erect personality and gave in him the touch of eccentricity, always manifested in men of this type.

To be sensitive and at the same time masterful is to present a contradiction to the world.

Behind Caesar Catus was one of two things.— He was either the relic of a pedigree that had been born to rule, or in some far away life, he himself, had ruled. He stood for a domineering ancestry, or for another Caesar whose shoes he still wore. Whichever was true, Catus was backed by something that he evidenced in himself; for he revealed from the crown of his head to the sole of his feet, the aristocrat, cursed or blessed by a versatile genius which enabled him to turn in any direction and to conquer innumerable obstacles. Nevertheless this very versatility was in a sense a detriment; because .lost in the charm of variety, he had, in times past,

either as his great, great grand sire or another self,
failed to discover that unity which makes the
master out of the man. He quivered with masculine nerves, the power of which he took off and
transmuted into something that flashed from his
eyes like the gleam of gold. He was impetuous
for or against a thing, and as quick to get a grip on
himself as the steersman is of the helm.

Whether we are drawing a pen-portrait of Caesar
Catus or some other Caesar we are not prepared to
decide. We imagine, however, we write of some
other Caesar, for the man who stood before Sallus
was not exactly the one here pictured. If the
patronizer of the extremes can strike a poise, Caesar
Catus had done it, and must have got, by some
mysterious means, a new conception of himself within
the last few years. He had a certain air of authority
which was not that of blood or of aristocracy,
but rather derived from an influx of wisdom lately
acquired, and which gave him such a puzzling
aspect that one not expert in human nature would
have found him hard to translate. He made himself unpopular with the Regan party, because of
his indifference about Aleppo. Catus could be run
after and liked, or avoided and disliked, as he chose.
He had the power of not "putting himself out"
when the mood struck him, that procured for him
an array of enemies, bitter indeed. On the contrary, with apparently no effort he could win right
and left, if he so desired, making for himself hosts

of friends; both popular and unpopular, sometimes affable in the extreme, again insuperably bored, he had friends and foes enough to send him to Paradise and the Inferno at the same time ; consequently he went to neither, and remained content.

As we have said, he was unpopular with the Regan party; all except Rhea, who read more deeply than most women. He had manifested little or no surprise at Aleppo's absence, and expressed it as his opinion that he was in safe hands, and would put in an appearance later. This all seemed childish and unreasonable in the face of facts; but Rhea felt that Catus knew more than he was disposed to tell, and took a deal of concealed comfort from the thought.

The whole " family " had gathered in the parlor to talk with Catus and had learned, that he expected to be in or near Cairo for some time; later on, however, he was to take a trip to Damascus and the Holy Land. After he had gone, the six looked at each other without speaking; then Regan spoke out—

"I like the face of that man better than any I have seen for many a day, but his actions give the lie to his looks. How he can show so little loyalty to an old and true friend—'pon my word, I don't understand."

"I think he knows more than he tells," said Rhea.

" Pshaw ! " Mrs. Hancock bristled, " You're

always ferretting mysteries out of nothing; we've got the bona fide thing now in the vanishing of Aleppo without turning that Catus into a Sphinx too.''

'' It seems to me,'' said Sallus, "that he might have shown a grain of interest; we don't need him, that's certain; he'd be worse than nothing on the track of Aleppo with his blamed indifference.''

Sallus doubled his fists unconsciously.

'' I believe Rhea's right,'' said Regan.

'' Catus never spirited Aleppo off, that's certain, but he suspects lots; and if he don't get after him in his own way, I can't solve conundrums nor guess riddles.''

The search went on in Cairo much as it had in Luxor. Sal was indefatigable ; Regan stopped occasionally, but Sal never ate nor slept, as Mrs. Hancock remarked, but just kept going till he lost color and flesh. He was no more tempted to badness than he was to fly, the veiled beauties of Cairo were out of his sphere and the weed and glass, things of the past. His heart was lead in his breast. He visited revolting places, interviewed disreputable people, and penetrated the most dangerous localities without regard to his health and life.

The roué had brought forth a hero, whose loyalty to friendship none could surpass. The same "hail fellow well met " feeling which he had shown in

the bacchanal debauch of his former days, had
grown to the immensity of "your's until death."

Regan was amazed at Sallus and called him a
book that had never been read.

One night he came to the hotel in a hurry and
called for Rhea; the young lady had retired, but
hastily dressing, emerged from her apartment and
met Sallus in the long hall. He was intensely
excited and the words came from his lips with a
rush.

"Miss Nellino, I've seen the Jew!"

She had been informed by Regan of their suspicions and understood perfectly what Sallus meant;
the color left her face but she said nothing.

"I was prowling 'round Cairo, seeking some
clue, when Issachar came out of a little shop and
passed into another, where he disappeared."

"What did you do?" said Rhea, her eyes fiery
with excitement.

"Rushed over and plunged in; but he was nowhere; the shop-keeper looked as innocent as a
girl, said he hadn't seen him; but he lied—where's
Regan?"

"Gone with the detective."

"I wish to goodness the detective was in Tophet;
if ever I wanted Regan, it's now."

He remained for no comment from Rhea, but
rushed out, leaving her in an indescribable state of
anxiety and hope. Was Aleppo in Cairo? So near!
She walked back to her room like one drunk,

steadying herself by the stair railing as she went, but nothing came of it.

The Jew, if in truth it were Issachar, could not be found ; and Regan with his detective (he had given up the rôle of father and had made himself known to the whole party) and Sallus, alone, went their weary round of search for a clue to the whereabouts of one who, for aught they knew, was dead.

CHAPTER XIV.

ARCANA CŒLESTIA.

Henrique Romanes lived like a recluse in his house in Paris.

He received no guests, and with the exception of an occasional letter, had cut himself off from the outside world. He was waiting for Aleppo, expecting that in some way El Reshid would discover him and bring them together. As for himself he never lifted a finger in the search, feeling that a master detective was on the track, and that whatever efforts he might make, would be but child's play. Nor had he any idea of what would be the outcome of this meeting with his son. In fact, from the time of his half hour's consultation with El Reshid, he had locked the door of his Paris house and remained inside, forcing himself by pure will to a state of calm, which had become a condition of cold. He had

presumed, from his having written to Helene of the
visit of El Reshid, that she would abstain from all
further efforts in regard to Aleppo, trusting entirely
to one in whom they both believed ; and, having
heard nothing from her to the contrary, rested upon
that conclusion.

The days passed one after another, all alike; the
only break in the monotony being the occasional
reception of a letter from El Reshid to Aleppo;
otherwise his life was as quiet as is the stagnant
pool, but without its lillies and lotus-blooms. This
stillness was ominous, and seemed freighted with
woe. He tried, with his powerful energy and
intense will, to lift the load from his heart, and to
tear off his shroud, for he felt himself already
wrapped in the garments of the tomb. He strove
to pierce the darkness with the eyes of his soul, but
the opaque veils of shadow defied and frightened
him.   He seemed already dead and though he
moved and talked with a semblance of life, his
heart beat time to a funeral march ; each throb
bringing him nearer to the coffin and the clod.

It was a tempestuous winter in Paris. Ice, snow
and sleet followed or vied with each other, half
freezing the poor and killing the aged.

Romanes was cold—no heat could warm him ;
and when the raging gale without, struck the house
like an enemy, he drew farther and farther within
himself, and sat over the smouldering fire of his

own soul, striving to get warmth from the burning wreck which had lost its power of flame.

It was a night even wilder and bleaker than that out of which El Reshid had come. In his usual place in his library, with an unread book in his hand, he had listened to the voice of the storm for hours; and, the sash being lowered, the weird and majestic music struck full upon his ear. For the first time for long months he felt an exhilaration and renewed life; a something akin to the thrill which he had known when for the first time he saw Helene Cressy—an emotion like that with which El Reshid had inspired him over and over again.

A servant rapped softly at the library door, and receiving a summons to enter, glided in like a grave phantom and bowed low; he was a Hindoo and as lithe as a snake. In soft, melodious voice, and looking as unconcerned as a dummy, he announced that a lady was in a hack outside, who desired to see him. Had he stated that an angel had arrived, Romanes could not have been more surprised.

" Did she hand you her card ? "

The servant shook his head in the negative, and bowed again. Waiting no longer, Romanes hurried through the passage and down to the street curb where the carriage was in waiting.

" Romanes ! "—He would have known that voice on the farthest star. I wish to see you, take me in."

Helene was the last person on earth whom he expected to meet at his Paris house; she had never visited him in her life, but her word was law. An hour later she was seated in his library, or rather propped up with pillows on a couch where the fire light struck warmly on her face. She was very ill, and talked rapidly to Romanes, as though to condense all that she had to say into a short space of time.

" I went to my physician in Vienna before coming here, and he informed me that there was no ray of hope; my life hangs upon a thread. I feared that I should die without seeing you; there is so much to tell." She twisted her fingers nervously, and the hectic flush mounted to her temples. Romanes, for her sake, suppressed his emotion, though his heart was breaking.

" You see," said Helene, " this did not come to me as it will to you, by slow degrees—the shock of our meeting, my renewal of the responsibility of Aleppo, was a sentence of death. I shall never lose my youth—my beautiful hair and bright eyes, Romanes." She smiled with pathetic coquetry that seemed odd in one in the shadow of the tomb. " Death will be kind to me and take me quickly, with the roses still on my cheek. I love beauty, I hate decay." This tortured Romanes, but he made no sign. " The time is so short," she went on, "only a day or two at most."

She reached to the little stand near, and lifting a glass of cordial to her lips, drained it to the dregs; then, taking a letter from her bosom, handed it to

Romanes. He perused it at one glance, and what
of color remained in his face left it instantly.   It
was dated at Cairo, and ran thus :

" *Madame :*
  " Upon receipt of a deed to your Vienna estate, I
will introduce to you, in good health, Aleppo
Romanes. Should you fail to comply with my
request you need make no attempt to discover
either myself or your son.   We shall vanish
forever.

Yours,
JACOB ISSACHAR."

  " What did you do?"
  " I telegraphed to him that the estate should be
his."
  She was extremely pathetic; her eyes had the
light of death in them, and were unnaturally
bright.   She kept clasping and unclasping her
hands, and watching the stern face of Romanes,
with the intensity of one conscious of having made
a mistake; yet, withal, so noble in her complete
self-abandonment, that a heart of ice must needs
have melted.
  Romanes felt that Helene's compact would perhaps be fatal to the finding of Aleppo; yet in this
supreme moment, with death knocking at the door,
all care for his son vanished.
  Helene !—Helene !   There was naught else in
the universe now; the stern precepts of El Reshid

were forgotton; the order was a dream. Only
those anxious, beaming eyes, with earth's last flash
in them, and the nervous hands, clasping and
unclasping; only those hectic cheeks, blushing at
their meeting with the bride-groom, death. Only
Helene. What were the few years of stress and
fever; what the one mistake; even the sad soul,
wandering, lonely on earth without parents or
country—what of him? Weighed in the balance
with the love eternal they were light, like vapor,
and invisible as air. She was grand in her dying;
she had given all, and the cursed Jew would force
upon her the dregs of the cup.

In this supreme moment, Romanes saw his life of
a day like a passing shadow, already vanishing into
memory's dream. He felt himself cold, wretched,
selfish, debauched. What was his great wisdom, in
the face of this passion, which could warm up
to death with the fire of self-sacrifice? Her lip
quivered; she discovered no approval in his face,
nor love in his touch. She strove to read the book
of his soul, but finding it closed, the tears welled
up in her dying eyes. The saddest sight on earth is
the tear of one half dead.

He would have given all the world if he could
have told her that he cared nothing for the order,
the teacher, or Aleppo; that she, herself was everything—*everything;* but his lips refused him speech.

It was bitter to be so judged, yet he had forced it
upon her—the misapprehension, the despair. Even

in dying she was proud; and he, more abject than a slave in her sacred presence, carried himself with the demeanor of a prince. Such is the anomaly called man.

Helene picked up the letter; tears fell on the page. She folded it carefully, and returned it to her bosom; then, lying down calmly, turned her face to the wall. Her beautiful brown-tinted hair had loosened and fallen over the pillow, a plaything for the firelight, which flashed in and out with fitful shimmer. For a moment Romanes clung to his chair for support, then, forgetting everything save Helene, he threw himself down by her side, and buried his face in the tangle and mesh of her beautiful hair. An occasional spasm shook him from head to foot, but no word could he find in which to tell her the depths of his woe.

The fire went out on the hearth, and the icy wind blew in at the open sash. At last, rousing, he softly touched the cheek of the woman beside him; the hand. *She was dead.*

CHAPTER XV.

A PROBLEM.

There are men as easy to read as a child's primer, and others harder to decipher than the·Book of Revelation. Only a magician comprehends a magician. The Sibylline scroll is revealed to none save those who have the key.

Caesar Catus was a problem to Sallus and Regan;
they had met him a number of times after his first
call at Shepherd's and they grew less acquainted
with him, but more fascinated every day. One
night, on a street in Cairo, they came plump against
him, and he insisted that they visit him at once.
They went to a house, whose bird-cage balconies
hung over the street, and were introduced into
apartments, the like of which they had never seen
on earth. It was a room, impromptu, he said and
got up for a temporary habitation, but one would
have thought that he had fixed himself for eternity,
so elaborate was his environment and so numerous
were his belongings. It was a sculptor's den, an
artist's studio, and a musician's retreat. He
worked in clay, he dabbled in paints, and scraped
the strings of his violin with a ready bow. There
were books, portfolios, curios, bronzes and rugs.
He occupied a number of apartments all blending
in and intruding upon each other in an indescribable fashion. His audacity in the rainbow tints
made him their master; his color blindness, as he
called it, resulting in combinations that bewildered
and charmed. He was daring with red, and the
absence of the mezzo shades was noticeable at a
glance; but he reveled so much in the shadows and
browns, that all things were toned and softened in
a way that no son of the Occident can manage.
Jewelled lamps hung here and there, giving a subdued, smoky light, that added a clouded brilliancy

to the place. He had " slung things together " he
said; but some people's slinging so far excels other
folks' studied art, that comparisons are out of order.

No sooner had they arrived at this unique suite
of apartments, than Catus retired to his dressing
room to appear five minutes later, as a thorough
Oriental, having on a mysterious robe with droop-
ing sleeves, which was a cross between that of a
Japanese and a Hindoo. On his head was a red
fez which set off becomingly the tawny coloring
of his beard and hair, while it emphasized the
Roman cast of his face. That he was devoted to
tobacco no one could deny who looked about, there
were pipes of every description, oriental and
occidental; cigars, small and large, pale and black,
beside cigarettes and plug cut. Regan trembled; he
had become a total abstainer, and this array was
almost more than he could bear. Catus had filled
the apartments with fumes of incense—aloes,
sandalwood, myrrh, and the curling smoke ascended
ceilingward like ethereal snakes.

" Now then "—Caesar was a fine host—" we'll
have our coffee." He clapped his hands sugges-
tively, and a slim Arab came upon the scene as
though materialized then and there. He must have
been concealed behind the arras, but from appearances he was an effect without a cause. In his
hands was a tray upon which were three tiny
jewelled cups, containing the far-famed coffee of

Egypt, black and strong.   It exhilarates one like
wine, and set the men's tongues all going together.

"I declare," said Regan, " this is the first time
I have been comfortable since I came to Cairo;
somehow I'm not worrying as I was," and a flash
of the old humor lighted up his rugged face. "It's
strange how one fellow will get a hold on another ;
that Aleppo anchored me; since he vanished, I've
been scudding like a ship under bare poles.   I
wouldn't have thought anybody could have held
me like that. Sal's case is different. But I'm
beyond myself, that's a fact."

"Everybody is, for that matter," answered Catus,
at the same time lighting a prime Havana and
establishing himself in a chair, whose fat padding
threatened to bury him altogether. He looked
supremely content. " Everybody is," he went on;
" we express about as much of ourselves in a lifetime as is good for us; but I tell you, we're bigger
than we seem."

" I've heard it said," replied Regan, sighing with
inward regret for his vanished quid, "that we
would extend from here to Jupiter, if we were
expanded to our final possibilities ; of course we'd
be rather vaporous, but we'd get there all the
same."

"I'd rather be more condensed." said Sallus—
the boy was weary and half asleep; he had scarcely
rested since his return to Cairo, and this was his
first chance at luxury. Catus scanned him admir-

ingly ; he was the final touch to the room, the masterpiece of Greek art. Phidias could have well turned him out, or Praxiteles. Sallus said nothing more, but succumbed at once and lay the whole evening, a beautiful, dreaming statue, from which Catus scarcely took his eyes.

"Do you suppose he'd let me do it ?" Catus said at last, looking at Regan.

"Do what ? "

"Make a copy of him; he's the finest male specimen I've struck in this incarnation."

"Don't know; guess he's too restless ; he isn't what he used to be, he's pining for Aleppo, same as I am—beats all what a hold that fellow had."

Catus said nothing, but rose and lifted a damp cloth from a life-size clay head, which stood upon his moulding board.

"Great Scott! that's Rhea," said Regan with amazement.

"I'm glad you recognize it; 'twas meant for her."

"Don't tell me she's been sitting down in this den." Regan stared at the head with a glare in his eyes.

"Not exactly"—Catus took out his cigar and looked lovingly upon its red end; then stuck it back in his mouth and puffed vigorously.

"But it's a perfect likeness," said Regan with suspicion.

"What of it; don't you remember I saw her at Shepherd's ? "

"You don't mean that you can fix a face like that in your mind!"

" 'Twas easy enough to fix Miss Nellino's it's a veritable Phryne, and takes me back to Greece."

" I'll buy that of you," said Regan shrewdly.

" It's not for sale." He covered it up with as much reverence as he was capable of showing—which was very little, and sitting down once more, lighted a fresh cigar.

Regan failed to settle himself so quickly; he was puzzled about the clay head of Rhea.

" It's hard to find a face like Miss Nellino's; it has the Mono Liza charm and the Greek caste. There are plenty of Hellenic heads, with no expression whatever, and hundreds of magical faces with no purity of form; but Miss Rhea, as you call her, has the witchery and the outline. I never have seen just this thing in life before—that is, *this* life. " By the way," abruptly changing the subject, "do you like music?"

" Yes, if it's fiddle playing; there's nothing like the cat-gut and bow to my mind."

"You are right, if ever you were; but do you suppose 'twill wake him?"

Regan cast his eyes over Sallus; " Don't believe a thunder-clap would bring him out of it; he's half dead. I guess it's the best thing that could have happened—your dragging us in here; he's getting a rest at last."

Catus began softly to tune his violin—taking but

an instant about it; he drew the bow across the
strings with such exquisite delicacy that one was led
to expect a love rapture or the plaint of a nightingale.   To the surprise of Regan he burst into a
queer, mysterious song, with something of a rollic
in it.   He played a few, fantastic strains, and then,
scarcely touching the strings of his bow, dashed off
into a tarantella; afterward singing one stanza in
baritone, the next in tenor; to fall upon his violin
again, and draw forth more weirdness and melody.
It was a peculiar performance, a sort of medley of
Tyrolese extravaganza and Japanese wail.   A cross
between oriental and occidental music, which produced a tipsy banshee, that both amused and
frightened the listener, with its sorrowful merri-
ment.   And this was the song :

Two dancing girls from Cairo !
Ha ! ha !—ha ! ha !
An expert and a tyro !
Ha ! ha !—ha ! ha !

One tripped from eve till morning,
Ha ! ha !—ha ! ha !
Her lover's kisses scorning,
Ha ! ha !—ha ! ha !

The other perished grimly,
Ha ! ha !—ha ! ha !
Her dream is cherished dimly,
Ha ! ha !—ha ! ha !

Two dancing girls from Cairo !
Ha ! ha !—ha ! ha !
An expert and a tyro !
Ha ! ha !—ha ! ha !

"Well, I don't know," said Regan, scrutinizing
Sallus, to see if he still slept, " whether I like that
or not; you see it's beyond me.   I never tried to
shine up to dancing girls but once, and then got
snubbed.   I guess we aren't elective affinities."

Catus was not a smiling man, but his eyes
laughed a little.   Regan had stopped abruptly in
his talk and was staring at a picture which hung
right in front of him.

" Did you do that, Catus ? "

" Yes, why ? "

" Never mind; though I'll say this much; I
wouldn't sleep in the same room with that thing
for a twenty dollar gold piece."

" Ah ! What's the matter? "   He lighted a
third cigar.

" Everything, or nothing; I don't know which."

" It's called ' The Devil and the. Angel ;' an
original design.   Do you consider it good work ? "

" Too all-fired good.   If I had the thing, I'd cut
it apart; I'd keep the angel and send the devil to
sheol."

" They are better together ; they show you your
two selves, or, rather, your extremes of possibility."

" Bosh !   Excuse me, Mr. Catus, but I could
never be one nor the other ; that angel is as much
beyond me, as is the prettiest woman in Christendom, and the devil—I couldn't touch him with a
ten-foot pole."

" That's because you think you are smaller than

you are. The fact is, in Jupiter you'd be the
devil, on earth the angel; you've got a long stretch,
Mr. Regan.''

" May be,"—without the least air of being convinced, " I wouldn't have that thing in my bedroom, though ; but what's this ? "

He took up some parchment, covered with what
seemed to him hieroglyphics, and scanned it searchingly.

" I'll be blamed if that isn't exactly the style of
writing that Aleppo used to indulge in.''

" True," said Catus, unconcernedly, "I taught
him the dialect and the symbols. That scroll con-
tains an outline of the cult of the Olympians."

" Do you mean the twelve apostates on the
Greek mountain ? "

" Hardly, there are hundreds of these."

" What do they do—what's their profession? "

" They do a great many things, out of sight; and
they profess the law of antithesis.''

" Strikes me that's a good thing; how do they
work it? "

" About as polarity is worked in physics. Action
and reaction's their hobby; the meeting of
extremes, and all that.''

" Exactly ; it's clear as mud."

" I told you that they kept out of sight.''

" Well, the wicked love darkness rather than
light ; I suppose they're bad."

" That depends," said Catus; " 'twould have

been rather uncomfortable for them about the time
of the middle ages, if they had shown a hand."

"So old as that! must be antiquated," said
Regan.

"The so-called mummy is not dead, though; you
can't kill an immortal."

"Are you one of them?" said Regan, more
blunt than polite.

Catus, as though deaf, clapped his hands once
more, and the invisible became visible in the shape
of the Arab, this time· bearing cream, cakes and
fruit.

"Have a bite," said Catus, "shall we wake up the
Greek ?" But Sallus, through some sub-conscious-
ness of the good things awaiting them, was already
rubbing his eyes, and looking lamb-like in his
humility.

Nothing more was said of the Olympians, and,
after the supper, the visitors left.

"'Pon my word," said Regan, when he reached
the street with Sallus, "I believe Catus is a sort of
magician, second only to the Jew. Can do no end
of things, and one's as good as another. He has
painted the most diabolical picture on the planet;
the background is a blending of light and shade,
and right about the center of the uncanny thing is
a figure made up of two—an angel and a devil;
they blend together, like the sky and a thunder-
cloud ; the angel is beyond compare, and the devil
worse than Faust's conception, they are the

queerest couple that were ever conceived; the Siamese twins can't hold a candle to them; its a pity you didn't see it."

" I don't know what's the matter with me," said Sal; "I was so dead gone I just turned in. I could't help it to save my life."

" Plain enough," answered Regan, " 'twas the incense; some.folks can't stand incense, but he did something else."

" What was it?" said Sallus, interested.

"He sang a song, about two Cairo dancing girls."

" What! He?"

" Yes, he !"

"He must be hard up," said Sallus, whistling.

" Don't know about that; sure's you're born, you never can tell what a man like Catus will do next; he springs surprises on you just as he did the Arab; he has no more reverence than a long-billed eagle, yet, he has made a clay bust of Rhea."

" Good heavens !" It was Sallus's turn to wake up. " Of Rhea?"

" Yes, of Rhea; it's good too, caught her likeness, that day he called at the hotel, carried it around in his head, or his heart, till he imprisoned it in clay; now he has got her."

" He must be uncommon smart," said Sallus in a maze.

"Smart's no word for it; it's uncanny, I tell you."

"If he would only put some of his brains into hunting for Lep, I'd like him better."

Upon Sallus saying this, they were both swallowed by the great hotel, and lost to view.

After they had left him, Catus lighted another cigar; his capacity in the direction of the weed was enormous; then, clapping his hands again, the Arab appeared, carrying a beautiful South Sea shell upon which lay a letter. The moment that Catus was possessed of it, his aspect changed; he had been, through the evening an indifferent, nonchalent sort of person, but with the touch of the letter he became nervous and reverential, and, tearing off the envelope, he read it out loud. It was entitled:

"FACT AND FICTION.

"You are too apt to settle down upon yourself as *you are*. The potentialities of your being to a great extent, you let alone. Of course you are busy and extremely energetic along the lines on which you have started, but there is danger of getting into the ruts even there.

"We have driven you to reason with a whip of knotted cords. We have insisted on it; in fact, our philosophy has no basis other than logic; yet, the fact that logic is at the bottom, proves that sentiment, imagination, and emotion are at the top.

"It is a poor animal that is all bones and no fat; a skeleton, whose ribs shine through his drawn

skin, is not after our fancy. Logic, if intense
enough, can move a man to tears; it is the mountain whose grandeur is overwhelming; it is the tor-
rent that sweeps all before it; it is the whirlwind
with fury in its breath., The splendor of a logical
syllogism turns ice to fire. A terrible result of logic
will carry conviction that culminates in passion.
Let an orator pour a volley of logic on the heads
of an audience, and he rouses them to frenzy.
Extremes meet; passion flames, and action follows.

" Our logic means nothing if it has failed, by this
time, to rouse you to emotion. We believe that it
has; the fact that fiction is running riot with you
is a good sign; fiction is the mate and opposite of
fact. You would freeze on fact, if fiction had not
blown at the flame. The severe nakedness of truth
sometimes calls for cosmetics and dyes; bald truth,
nude truth, exposed truth, palls after a time; so we
dress her up. She is truth still, for however you
may turn her, fiction is fact, and truth is error.
This is a paradox. Notice, truth is many sided;
she is false when she shows a rim of herself, to this
extent—that she implies that she is exposing all.
She is true, in that whatever manifestation is laid
bare, it is an exact manifestation of herself, in a way.
She is false in her specialization, true in her generalization; that is, she misleads by her exhibition of
the part as to the consistency of the whole. She is
true, in that every part stands for the spoke of its
relative wheel. Thus truth and fiction are two

poles of one. To the Master there is no fiction; to the Master all is fiction; that is, he goes by steps —specialization, or by bounds—generalization; he leaps from extremes to extremes, or walks slowly, saying one thing at a time. Thus, he who has not reveled in the opposite of truth, which is fiction, is but half-fledged.

ADDENDUM.

The fiction of truth lies in this, that when you see but one spoke, the chances are, that you will relate it to the *wrong* wheel. The spoke is a true one, but you find the fallacy in attempting to place it. An expert can tell what kind of a wheel a certain spoke fits. To get into the real charm of fiction, one must utterly ignore the wheel, and con- sider an unlimited number of spokes.

The fiction of theology and orthodoxy, and so- called philosophy, lies in putting yellow, green and blue spokes together; some longer and some shorter; and he who enjoys superstitiously his church or his cult, is the one who never wakes up to the fact that there is a wheel at all.

The true sage makes no such mistake, and con- sequently revels understandingly in parable, story- telling, fancy and fable. Christ was the poet of Syria; he wrote the epic of the Jew.

In studying character, the most of us commit this grave error, we take a yellow spoke of a man and put him beside a blue one, where he wiggles and waggles, being too short for the rim. We grumble and growl, because he fails to fit, and finally decide that he is no true spoke at all. Let me tell you, that he is just as much of one as yourself, but you have stuck him into the wrong wheel, and betray your own insufficiency in considering him afterward.   .

The Master knows how to fit the spokes, or to ignore the rim altogether. He never spoils the fancy of his fable, by thinking it untrue, on the contrary he turns fiction into fact by believing in it for the time being, in toto. Nor does he dream that each event in his history is fallacious, until he intentionally throws off the glamour, as a bird shakes the dew from its wings, when new washed, he starts after fact again, with a vim which a clean man always has.

The paper was signed with a peculiar symbol. Catus read it over a number of times, then putting it on file with other similar letters, went to his writing desk and dashed off the following :

Have postponed my visit to Syria; hope to go later; will let you know all facts. Have a strange feeling that something has happened in Paris ; will make certain.

Yours,

A like symbol to that on the letter just received was stamped at the end. Then the Arab entered with the South Sea shell, to depart in an instant

with the second epistle, whereupon Catus threw himself on the divan where Sallus had been lying, and
went, as though with a clear conscience, into the
region of dreams.

CHAPTER XVI.

A CANTANKEROUS OLD LADY.

Regan and Sallus held a consultation the next
day after their visit to Mr. Catus.

"Understand," said Regan, "I don't condemn
him; simply can't grasp him. His indifference
about Aleppo would imply that he knows something; if he does it is his duty to come out and say
so; that's my opinion."

"And mine too," said Sallus; "of course, if it
is sifted, it amounts to this: He either knows or
he does not; if he does not he is the most milk and
water friend conceivable; if he does, he is in league
with the Jew. Which ever way you look at it, he's
not to my liking."

"Maybe you're right," said Regan, "though
somehow I don't feel like committing myself. One
thing is certain, however, we must keep in with
him till we settle our minds. If he is Issachar's
ally, we ought to know it; if we are convinced
that he isn't, we can cut him at once."

"I hate playing the hypocrite," said Sallus.

"True, but this isn't exactly hypocrisy; we

don't put our arms around him and kiss him, do we? Nor get on our knees? We just exchange visits, hover about, etc. We are neither enemies nor friends; most people in the social world are indifferent to each other. We are just like the rest; it isn't hypocrisy, it's mutual understanding.''

But Sallus was not going to be a good detective, that was evident. For downright hard work and complete self sacrifice no one could beat him; but when it came to sitting on the fence, with one leg in the enemies' quarters and the other in his own, well, he was not the man for it; so he went on his '' own hook,'' and Regan fraternized with Catus.

Mrs. Hancock took Rhea to task one morning, though it was understood, at the beginning of their trip, that her aunt should follow her to the earth's end; for that matter, the young lady was her own mistress, and paid all Mrs. Hancock's expenses, yet the old lady was becoming exasperated, and broke out in open rebellion one fine day in Cairo.

'' We've staid here long enough; I'll not remain another week for anybody.''

'' Do just as you like, Aunt Carrie; I have no power nor desire to compel you; nevertheless, even though you go, I shall stay till Mr. Regan an Sallus give up the search for Aleppo. I have made several lady friends here, both English and American, and really have no need of you, unless you desire to be with me.''

'' What I want to know, is, what Aleppo Bracciolini is to you, that you throw yourself at his head,'' said Mrs. Hancock.

Rhea bit her lip and turned white, but her power of transition from anger to humor was marvelous.

'' If I remember rightly, Aunt Carrie, in Brindisi you gave me a lecture, the text of which was just the contrary. You advised me to use all the arts and wiles of a first-water society girl to catch anybody in the shape of a man. You even requested me to go so far as to give up the best part of myself, presenting humbly to whatever suitor might appear, a perishable thing only. You more than advised, you insisted, informing me that I was already on the verge of middle life and would soon be out of the market. You implied that it was all a question of supply and demand; and here you are going back on what you have said.

But Rhea was really too sad at heart to indulge in much humor; though hope, of late, had set her soul singing again, and enabled her to do battle with her aunt in the old fashion.

'' You might as well be dead as to get in love with a mystery like him; there is no telling who he is, nor what his parents are.''

'' We'll leave Aleppo out of the question, Auntie, if you please; though I'll say this much, once and for all, to set your mind at rest, if I loved him, or any other man, it wouldn't make the slightest difference with me, what his parents turned out to be, or whether he were legitimate or illegitimate, a prince or a pauper; if I *loved* him, I say. But enough of this, one thing I want you to understand from now on; I positively insist that upon the subject of love and matrimony you never speak to me again. On this condition only can we remain together. Do you comprehend?"

Mrs. Hancock did. When Rhea was emphatic. her aunt knew what it meant; besides Mrs. Hancock was a financial dependent; so she closed her lips as you shut a desk, and said nothing; her hot temper, however was boiling.

" Now about Cairo, Auntie, you can do as you please, stay or go. I can get along either way."

Mrs. Hancock was dangerously mum, and Rhea, discovering that there was no answer forthcoming, arose and left the room. She had scarcely gone, when the Misses Richards slipped in; they had heard every word. As eavesdroppers they could nowhere be excelled. Their zest in life lay in the world's contentions. They, themselves, never quarreled, not even with each other. They were like a large proportion of the saints, that sin by *proxy*. They enjoyed evil in its reflex, and licked the platter after the gravy was gone. No sooner had they arrived and properly seated themselves than Mrs. Hancock burst out.

" She's going to stay, and I can't help myself."

" How long," said Bess, in apparent surprise.

" Forever, I hope; then, perhaps, she'll get enough of it."

"How sad!" said the Misses Richards, in one voice.

"It's more than sad; it's scandalous; the whole town will be talking if she don't look out. What's that Aleppo to her, that she has to be dangling around as though she were married to him." ·

"Perhaps she's keeping a secret," said Miss Richards, "could't you discover? Maybe Bess could find it out."

"Rhea can't stand a spy; neither can I," turning on them; but the ancient ladies were altogether impervious to her mysterious hints, and answered again in an angelic voice,

"Too bad!"

Mrs. Hancock was no fool, and was Yankee enough to know on which side her bread was buttered; so she swallowed her wrath and declared to the Misses Richards that they need not alter their plans in the least on her account; that she expected to become a martyr; it had always been her fate, and always would be.

"I don't hope to get my reward here, but on the other side; if it wasn't for the Rev. Hitchock I should pray the Lord to take me now, but I do want to sit · under the ministrations of my dear pastor once again. I was born to suffering, as the' sparks fly upward; only a few are so privileged."

"Too bad!" again responded the female doves.

"Rhea's a black sheep," her venom getting the better once more. "From the time she was born

she would have none of the Rev. Hitchcock, nor
sit under the droppings of the sanctuary. In my
opinion she's afraid of hell. She would run when
the minister came, though scarcely more than a
baby, and hide her head in the bed-clothes. If we
dragged her out she would shut her eyes and
wouldn't look at him."

', How sad!"

" It grew worse as she grew older, and though I
must say she wasn't a liar, nor a thief, nor a mur-
derer, she persisted in thinking for herself, in the
face of revelation, and I felt sometimes that the
burden was more than I could bear."

Mrs. Hancock wept angry and uncharitable tears,
and the Misses Richards, wiped them away.

" And now,"—the irate woman was about to
make an awful revelation—"she is secretly loving
an idol-worshipper.

" How dreadful !" The ancient sisters positively
shuddered.

"I am positive I am right: She's ashamed of it,
or she'd tell; she wants to stay here because she's
stuck on Isis˜and Osiris. I know it, as sure as I am
born; it's not Mohammedism she cares about, it's
the original. She has a half a dozen little sinful
idols more or less, on her dressing table, and in my
opinion she prays to the whole lot."

" Oh! Oh!"

" Yes it is, Oh! Oh! What would my poor,
dear sister say, if she could look out of heaven at

all this wickedness. She's that fixed that I've no hope of turning her.'' Here the Misses Richards drew near and adjusted their eye-glasses. '' She's a rank heathen; that's why I call her a black sheep. 'Tisn't Aleppo, so much, though he's at the bottom of some of it; it's innate; and all she needed was this country and these lying Arabs to bring it out. I believe she's thinking of entering an order.''

''What?'' The two sisters drew very near.

'' She used to get hold of books, at Sandwich, that made my eyes ache, about mysteries, and a lot more ungodly stuff. I burned up two or three of them, and she never knew where they went to.''

''She must be a crank,'' said Bess, speaking for the first time to some effect.

'' Pshaw! you put it too mildly; she's a lost soul, and it's my mission to save her.''

Mrs. Hancock shed a few more tears, and the Misses Richards again dried her eyes.

'' Her mother was only a half sister of mine, and not a bit like me. If I had had my way, Rhea would never have been born.''

'' Is there no hope?'' asked the curious Bess.

'' Not the slightest, unless I get the power to work miracles. I don't despair, though; for what would I be ordained to look after her for, if 'twasn't for her good; never mind about me, my sufferings are nothing, compared with the awful fate ahead of her.''

Here the door opened and the beautiful sinner entered; she took in the whole situation, smiled beamingly, and passed out, closing the door as softly as though it were the entrance to a minister's study, or the class-room of a New England Church.

CHAPTER XVII.

SALLUS.

As we have said, Sallus discarded detectives, and hunted for Aleppo alone. Since his vision of Issachar, he had spent much time around the shop where the Jew had vanished, in a vain hope that he might see him again. Neither he nor Regan had veered from the idea that Issachar was at the bottom of Aleppo's disappearance; and the fact that Sallus had seen him in Cairo, when he was supposed to be in Venice, confirmed them in their former conclusion.

"I'm working along the line of the smallest evil," said Regan, in a cheerful pessimistic drawl; "men talk about choosing the least of *two* evils; it seems to me that there are always about forty to pick from. I never was reduced to two evils yet; I see the sense however, of grabbing the littlest one in the pile. They're heaped up pretty high around us now, that's a fact, and the least evil just at present is that Jew; without him we'd be nowhere. If ever a man vanished, Aleppo did;

and if it wasn't for that cursed black clue of an
Issachar, I should think he'd been translated or
confiscated by an ancient. As it is, I feel that he's
alive; mark my words, that son of Leah is after
money, and whoever owns Aleppo will have to buy
him, see?

" I've a notion," answered Sallus, " to take up
my quarters down near that shop; where the devil
was once, he's likely to go again."

" That's not a bad idea," answered Regan, "you
don't sleep as it is, and you might as well live in
the street as anywhere else."

It was done. Sallus managed to wedge himself
into a small hired apartment, not over clean, in the
thickest of Cairo where he had a window-eye that
stared down at the shop night and day.

One morning, very early, he had come in from a
night's work, as he called his still hunt for Aleppo
and was looking up the half deserted street. It was
scarcely four o'clock, and a dim smoke lay over
everything. Suddenly there appeared a figure
looming, white, out of the gray haze, which Sallus
stared at with the glare of a crouching cat. It
was Issachar—the hooded head, the immaculate
robe, the claw-like hands and the smile. Beside
him was a young girl, somewhat disheveled in
appearance, as though she had come hurriedly from
her sleeping apartments, half dressed. She was
expostulating with the Jew, who answered her with
naught save smiles—smiles. Even in the dim gray

of the morning Sallus could see those gleaming teeth
and scintillating eyes. The girl pleaded with the
Jew as though her life were at stake, but he shook
his head and smiled again; then waving his hand
imperiously, turned and vanished through the door
of the shop.

Sallus waited no longer, but throwing on a long
cloak which effectively concealed his figure, and
drawing a slouch hat over his eyes, he hurried into
the street, where the disheveled young lady stood,
looking at him in a bewildered way as he approached
her. She was evidently not an oriental woman,
for her hair was fluffy brown, though her eyes were
large, dark and full of sentiment which had culmin-
ated in tears. In spite of her hastily donned attire
she was very pretty and singularly pathetic.

" Pardon," said Sallus, stepping close to her and
speaking in a low tone, " but may I have a word
with you--it is on business—very important."

She scanned him for an instant, gazed all around
her in a half frightened way, and then stepping
close to him said,   .

" Yes."

" That man whom I saw with you just now—will
you tell me where I can find him ? "

She looked startled, but whispered.

" Come ;" leading Sallus into a side street, "walk
with me a pace and I will tell you what I know."
Then turning her great dark eyes on him, swimming

with tears, she exclaimed, " For the sake of Allah
will you help me ? "

" You ! yes."—every drop of his chivalrous,
American blood boiling, " what is it ? "   ·

She wiped the tears from her eyes, with her
beautiful bare hands, and poured out the story of
her woe into his shocked ears so rapidly and with
so many pauses and breaks, that he could scarcely
catch its meaning; she spoke in French.

"I've lived with him always—that man you saw,
since I was born ; but he's not my father—nor
relation.   I am stolen; my mother was stolen
before me. Oh!''—here she broke down completely.
"I have told lots of people, but no one believes."

" What do they think," said Sallus, his voice
choking with anger at Issachar.

" That he is my uncle; that's what he tells everybody—his sister's child by a French father, and
they believe."

" But you—he tells you differently ? "

" The old nurse did, who took care of me; and
when I accused him, he did not deny. I begged
him this morning—I'm always pleading with him
to take me back to Europe—I want to escape. I
was in Venice with him last year, but he suddenly
brought me here again."   ·

" It was getting lighter and Sallus looked up and
down the street anxiously.

"Can you come to my room—will you be
missed ? "

"Who should miss me," she said, her lips curling. Even Issachar doesn't care now." Then she looked the young man over with a quick glance. "Yes I will come."

He hurried along a little ahead; she following, even into the bedroom of this stranger. In the eyes of the world this would seem scandalous; but there are evils and *evils*, and this, at the time, appeared to be the least.

"Now," said Sallus, handing her a chair, "you have begun by trusting me; don't worry, I shall never betray your confidence. I should not have brought you here, but time is precious; we could not talk safely in the street—no harm can come of it."

The girl looked a little startled and dropped her head.

"Tell me," went on Sallus, assuming a very business like air and drawing a chair near her, "all you know of Issachar; and I will then state to you the reason why I desire this information.

"I don't know much;" she said, still keeping her eyelids down. "He kidnapped my mother a few months before I was born. She was a wealthy French lady. He strove to negotiate with her family for a large sum of money. My father was dead, and he took my mother by some means from my father's grave, when she was decorating it with flowers. He brought her here and kept her on the desert, where I was born, and she died. This

upset his plans; her life had money value, or
something else, I don't know what, but mine
doesn't seem to have any.   He has been trying for
seventeen years, for that is my age, to negotiate
for me, but my relatives have lost interest, and I
am of no account.   Still he will not let me go; I
shall always be a prisoner, Oh!''—as she broke
into sobs.

Sallus was intensely moved, but he controlled
himself; it was no place to comfort her here.

'' What have you been doing all these seventeen
years?'' he asked excitedly.

'' I had a governess until last year; then Issachar
sent her away.   I think he is tired of me.   He had
hoped my relatives would come to terms, so he
educated me a little and all that, but he finds they
won't; it was my mother they wanted, not me.
Besides, I believe he has some new scheme on
hand.''

Sallus sprang to his feet—'' Tell me quick, what
is it?''   The girl looked startled.

'' I'm not sure that it's anything; but he brought
me suddenly to Cairo and one day I saw a young
man ''—the beads of sweat started on Sallus'
brow—

'' Yes!—yes!—when? where?''

'' In a room of our house.''

'' Where is your house?''

'' Over the shop.''

'' How did he look—quick!''

The girl seemed not to understand this anxiety,
and stared in amazement at Sallus.

"Oh, speak!" said Sallus—he was pacing
rapidly.

"He was dark, very; with beautiful eyes. He
seemed to be sick; he staid but a short time, at the
house, and was taken away."

"Taken away! Who took him?"

"Some Arabs—Issachar's slaves."

"Slaves!"

"Yes, the same as slaves."

"Can you tell me, have you the least idea where
they have taken him?"

He had come very near to the girl and pierced
her eyes with his own.

"No," she said shrinking, "my mother was
taken to the desert, and died there; yes, and I was
born there."

She wondered why he had forgotten her case so
quickly and was thinking only of the dark young
man.

"Forgive me; but I have been searching for my
brother for weeks"—he still called Aleppo his
brother. "I'm crazy about him. I have suspected
the Jew; now I am certain. Where is Issachar
this minute, can you tell me?"

"Gone away; far, far, while we have been talking; he goes and comes, no one knows where."

Sallus' conscience smote him; ought he not to

have followed Issachar; he feared that he had made a great mistake—" When will he come back? "

" I con't know. I hope never," said the girl bitterly, rising at the same time.

Sallus was wild; what could he do? He had let Issachar slip, and had this poor child on his hands whose sorrows appealed to his tender heart. But Aleppo was first and above all—even this pretty girl must stand aside. He walked back and forth a few times, then stood between her and the door.

" I have made a mistake; I should have followed the Jew. My brother is all the world to me. Now listen, my poor girl,"—he could scarcely think of her as other than a child—" I swear to you that your cause shall be mine also. I'm going to find that Jew or die. He has kidnapped my brother as he did your mother. We must work together—you and I. I shall live in this room, you must watch, and spy, and connive, and cheat, and lie and do everything wicked to learn the facts. Get on the track of Issachar as you prize your liberty, and leave the rest to me."

" But he is so slimy," said the girl, shivering ; he is like a snake."

" Has he abused you, poor child; " his eyes snapping.

" No, not that, he has been very good ; till last year I was kept like a princess. Now he neglects me, he has sent away the governess, only old Spino, the nurse, remains; and she hates him venomously.

I'm afraid if he gives up all hopes of obtaining a ransom for me that he will sell me to a hareem—Oh!''—

"Never," said Sallus, biting off an oath before it was out. "And this Spino,—is she faithful?"

"True as steel; an Arab—a servant of Allah."

"Ah! and you,—your name?"

"Cicily."

"Cicily! What a strange name."

"Yes, Cicily."

"How did the Arab woman know your history?"

"From her husband, who helped to kidnap my mother."

"And your governess—did she understand?"

"She was indifferent, utterly; she was well paid to keep still, and she was very wise."

The sun was now up, and flashed into Sallus' bare room, all over the girl who stood in its full glow. Then it was that Sallus saw how dazzling she was. Her dress but partly fastened displayed her beautiful, young neck, daringly. The color had come to her cheeks; and the disheveled hair, "every which way," enhanced with its soft, yellow tint, the startling splendor of her eyes. She was in a state of intense excitement, her bosom rose and fell and she now and then clasped her hands as if in prayer, raising her great eyes, full of ecstasy one moment to Sallus, the next, dropping the lids, as though half-frightened at being with him there, alone.

"You must go now," said Sallus decidedly, turning his eyes away; "but can I not visit you; Spino will be good, and understand; tell her all the moment you return; make an ally of her at once. This evening I will come."

For the first time Cicily smiled. It was a dangerous thing to do, but the girl's apparent innocence was more of a protection than all the guardian angels of heaven above. Sallus opened the door for her as though she were a queen, and Cicily glided out with a swift, serpentine movement, more oriental than otherwise, and wonderfully suggestive to him of Constantinople and former days.

Had he been deceived, or was she what she claimed to be; she had stated that no one believed her. How intoxicating she was ! How beautiful ! Yes, there could be no mistake, unless Issachar himself were using her as a decoy to trap him also. He had failed to read her ; she was too blindingly beautiful, too seductively sad. Through her he would either find Aleppo or walk into a trap. As he grew cool-headed and more sober, he realized how either might be true.

Issachar well knew that both he and Regan were making search. He had probably discovered Sallus' proximity to his own headquarters; what was to hinder him from using this young girl with her pathetic story as a means to capture him also. On the contrary, there were some things about Cicily that spoke to his very soul. But Catus !

who could tell whether Catus connived with
Issachar,—his head ached; he had been up all
night; his adventure of the morning was abnor-
mally exciting. He was thrilled with a pair of
beautiful eyes; altogether, he was in a bad way.
The sun was pouring into the room, and the flies
were a million. Coffee! Ah ! Egyptian coffee !—Ah !
Shepherd's !—Regan ! He got out of that quarter
of Cairo as quickly as he could go, and went for his
breakfast at a haunt of his own; then hunted up
Regan, whom he found in bed at Shepherd's.

"'Pon my word this is out of order," said the
philosopher, sitting up and yawning; "never knew
you to make such a break as this; what's the
matter?"

Sallus took Regan by the two hands, dragged
him out of bed and jumped in.

"It's my turn now," said he, "let me doze off
for an hour, and then I'll tell you—am dead tired."

He turned over with the last word, and nothing
more was heard of him till noon. When that hour
arrived, he opened his eyes, and met those of
Regan who sat by the window with his feet on the
mantel.

"Have I slept an hour?"

"Several."

Sallus sat up and rubbed his eyes.

"The problem gets stickier every minute ; this
morning I saw Issachar."

" You did ! " said Regan, opening the door to let in some breakfast.

" And the prettiest girl on earth "—Regan whistled softly. Sallus, between munching his rolls and sipping his coffee, told Regan everything, even to his fascination and fear of Cicily.

Regan sat in a brown study for a good ten minutes, then began—

" It amounts to just this; we've got down to one evil—that's Issachar, he's the biggest and the littlest. If it's a trap, you may be caught; but I am afraid you'll have to try it, or let Lep slip altogether. Of course you know, I'll be on the watch with a strong guard; may be 'taint a trap; perhaps the girl is all right, but I'm scared."

" Can't help it," said Sallus, getting out of bed in a hurry. I am not the coward to let Aleppo go that way, trap or no trap ; besides that's the prettiest girl I've ever seen.

" She's a trap anyhow ; you're bound to be caught however you fix it. Count on me Sal, first, last and all the time, from now to the day of judgment."

CHAPTER XVIII.

MYSTERY.

Regan found Mrs. Hancock alone in the hotel parlor on the day of Sallus' escapade with Cicily, and that fair daughter of New England poured all

her venom upon his head at once; she scolded,
threatened and blamed Rhea, without scruple, for
keeping her in Cairo.

" Why don't you go," said Regan, " I'm sure
you're of age, and can do as you like. Rhea has
plenty of friends and will be perfectly safe without
you."

" I'm sworn to stay by that girl till she dies or
gets married, and l'm going to, in spite of you or
anybody."

" Married ! " said Regan, thrusting his hands
into his pockets; I wonder any decent girl dares to
try it, in these days of pulpit oratory and priestly
advice."

" What on earth do you mean ? " shrieked Mrs.
Hancock.

" Why, it was just before I left the States, that
I strolled into an influential church in New York,
and the parson was talking on matrimony, giving
advice to his young flock, and all that, and what do
you suppose he said ? "

" I'm sure I can't tell," snappishly.

" He told them the same thing I've read a hundred times, or more, and always swore at; " Dearly
beloved," he drawled, " marriage, to a man is but
an incident, to a woman, 'tis her whole life !" And
he thought he had said a fine thing. I should have
sworn at him, if it hadn't been for the usher ! Such
beastly stuff to teach young women. So man goes
into this church-ordained business of marriage

as a sort of side issue, or by-play, exactly like a
Mormon, if I know myself; and woman, beautiful
woman, talented, educated woman, is ordered by
these wolves in sheep's clothing to give her whole
life, and that in free America, where justice is supposed to be done.   What's the man going to do
after the *incident* is over, I'd like to know; seek
another and another, incident piled on incident,
event on event; and she was requested by that
same gent in the pulpit to solace herself with
memory—the recollection of the incident, I suppose
—*the incident!!*   I got the hymn book ready to
throw at his head, when I caught the eye of the
usher, and stopped short.''

" I wish that usher had caught you by the nape
of the neck and thrust you out of God's house, into
the street; you were blaspheming divine truth, and
putting out was too good for you.''

"Maybe, but I got after that parson all the
same.''

"You did!''

" Yes, I did!   I went to his study and informed
him that I wanted a consultation about a lost soul;
he rubbed his hands with invisible soap, and anxiously inquired if it were I that were lost.   I tried
to catch his eyes, but they shifted like moonbeams,
and I gently instructed him that it was *he* that
couldn't be found.''

"What did he do,'' said Mrs. Hancock, in an
awed whisper.

"He just put a chair between us and pointed to the door with the majesty of a justice of the peace; he was choking so that he couldn't speak; but I smiled and coughed, and gaped, and looked at my watch, and tied one shoe, and dusted off my sleeve, and wiped my eye-glass, but he kept his index finger straight out, till he looked for all the world like a yogi practitioner. 'Not so fast,' said I, 'you're lost, because you taught those lambs in your flock a cursed lie'—he still pointed, and I yawned again, and tied the other shoe—'you advised those young women to take up with men who treat marriage as an incident. I'd bet on you as against old Brigham, every time. It's another form of hareem you're advocating, or my name's not Regan.' Then I bowed very low, and backed out, while that parson was still pointing."

"You are the most disrespectful man on God's footstool; you haven't the least reverence for the church nor the minister; you'll have to answer for this some day."

" As for reverence, I guess I can bestow it, where it belongs. My father was a respected parson and text expounder, and if I do say it, who shouldn't— there was never a better man. He and I didn't agree on all points; we quarreled over the Bible, that's what parted us—the Bible; but for all that, I'd like to find one who could beat him. When he got to singing those psalms and hymns the whole congregation roared, their voices blending into one

monotonous thunder peal, that was just about the
grandest thing that ever struck a fellow's ear. Yes
ma'am, Mrs. Hancock, that father of mine was
worthy of reverence, if ever a man on earth was,
and whether he was right or wrong, he had a soul
as white as swan's down."

" You don't take after him! " spitefully.

"Couldn't preach a sermon to save my life," said
Regan, "nor speak in meeting either—suppose you
do, though ?"

At this point Sallus entered and called Regan
out.   Mrs. Hancock was left alone with her cogitations, which were more or less of a tumultuous
kind.

" I'm going, now, said Sallus, "to keep my
appointment with Cicily; if it's a trap I may not
come back."

" 'Twont be sprung yet, trap or no trap. You're
safe enough for a time; will send a detective after
you though, so don't fret.   Get on the good side of
Spino, that's the first thing—Spino."

After Sallus had gone, Regan sought Catus; these
two were great chums. To-night, however, Regan
proposed to spy on him a little, and get him, if
possible to commit himself in regard to Aleppo.

" Mr. Catus," said Regan, stretching his long
legs on a stool and sipping his coffee, "have you
ever met a particular Jew, called Jacob Issachar ? "

His host reflected a moment, and said, dreamily,
"The name is familiar; how does he look ? "

"About as infernal as the prince of darkness; that is, if you don't happen to admire his style. He's a giant in size, wears a woman's dressing gown, parts his hair in the middle and allows it to stream down the sides of his face; teeth of an animal, swarthy complexion, and four or five thousand years old."

"Yes, I know him," said Catus indifferently; "he looks comparatively young, though, but adopts the style of a patriarch; literal descendant, I presume—a Syrian Jew—eh?"

"That's he, now what of him?"

"Oh, nothing much; makes his living by the black art, same as lots of orientals."

"What's the black art?"

"He got hold of a few secrets, in fact they had come down from time immemorial; there's money in them, any amount; that Jew knows a heap." And Catus lighted up and settled himself in his fat chair.

"Is it out and out magic or a fake?" urged Regan intensely interested.

"That depends upon what you mean by magic. Anyone can know magic who acquires certain laws and makes use of them; a little hypnotism, a good bit of human nature, a subtle logic, immense concentration, knowledge of chemistry, a quick eye, a quicker hand, and lo! the magician."

"Black or white?" said Regan.

"Either; power is power—used for good or evil, according to the man."

"Now you talk sense. I never could believe in these fakirs who get something out of nothing; they're sharpers. See?"

"Of course," said Catus, "they have their hands down so fine they can pick a man's pocket right before his eyes, and he never knows it. They have a way, too, of looking at you, and absorbing your soul; there's no mistake, they're great men. The fellow who would be an expert must begin before he is born. The way they can concentrate is beyond telling; patience! patience is no word for it, they're simply sublime; they run an idea to the ground, they suck their subject till it's like a squeezed lemon; they never let up when on the trail, no matter what interferes; they follow scent like a hound. Obstacle! They climb over it as they would a mountain; if it were as high as Everest it would make no difference; they would get on top and come down the other side, or die."

"Die! Do they die?"

"Yes, after a fashion, but not like other folks; they go into a hole, as a frog does, and exist without eating or drinking till they're made over; it is a sort of prolonged fast, accompanied by stagnation and inertia."

"And is Issachar that kind of a man?"

"Shouldn't wonder."

"Would he kidnap anybody, do you suppose?"

"He might, if there were money back of it; there's one thing they can't do."

"What's that?"

"Transmute base metal into gold; on the contrary, base ideas are turned to filthy lucre with a wave of the hand."

Now, in my opinion," said Regan, mysteriously, and drawing closer to Catus, "Issachar has his clutches on Aleppo, and money is back of the whole business."

"Ah," said Catus, puffing at his cigar.

"What is your idea," said Regan, edging still nearer."

"How do you know there is any money behind Aleppo?"

"I don't, except that Issachar's after him, and what on earth but money could animate the legs of that Jew?" 'Tisn't revenge, nor enmity, for the boy had never seen the fellow but once, since he was a child. No, 'tis money, sure."

"What are you going to do about it?" said Catus, indifferently.

"Move heaven and earth, till I find him. Fight money with money, what else? If everything else fails, I'll stake my egg-beater, that little thing weighs heavy in the market—income from it alone would set a Jew crazy: then there are several other unmentionables. Oh, we've got him in the long run, but first I'm going to try for him in another

way: that fellow's committed a crime, did you
know it?"

"You haven't a scintilla of proof; you're surmising that it's Issachar because he happened to call
on Aleppo in Venice; the young man was afraid
of him, etc. Very likely you're doing a great
injustice."

"May I ask you an out and out question?"

"I don't object."

"Then tell me, please, why you are so utterly
indifferent about the disappearance of Aleppo
Bracciolini; you, who were such a good friend to
him in Italy, and such an excellent correspondent
afterwards, you puzzle me."

"I am a sort of conundrum, everybody thinks so;
well, about Aleppo, what's the use, the inevitable
is the inevitable. If he's dead, I can't bring him
to life; and if he's hid in Cairo, I might as well
save my energy as to waste it hunting here,
'twould be of no use. If he's spirited out of the
country, how on earth can I tell whither. No, Mr.
Regan, 'tis the law of cause and effect; I accept ·
the inevitable.

"To hell with your fatalism!" said Regan,
more emphatic than polite. Will is on top of fate
and effect and everything, if you did but know it.
Why, man, 'tis a cause itself; it always was and
always will be; it's first and foremost. How
would your protoplasm ever sprawl around in an
Ameba if will or desire wasn't back of the whole

business.   You can change an effect as quick as a
wink, if you can get will enough—that's the way
the world is run.   Will is sovereign, or there never
was a king on the throne; from everlasting to everlasting you've been willing something, and have
got it, too, in the long run.   The mills of the gods
grind slow, but they grind, I tell you; and that
god in you, is *your* will.''

''But what of fatality,'' said Catus, not moved
an iota by Regan's effort, at the same time yawning, as though bored, and lighting a fresh cigar,
''what of fatality?''

''Oriental fatalism knocks me silly.   'As you
sow, so shall you reap,' but you're always sowing,
and 'tis the will that's the sower, or my name isn't
Patrick.   In my opinion, this excuse of fatalism is
only a blind to cover something.   When a man
is up to mischief he talks fatalism from morning till
night; he's revelling in evil, and excuses himself
for wallowing, because of his Nemesis called Fate.
No, you're on the wrong track, Mr. Catus. If Fate
is after Aleppo Bracciolini, I'll get after Fate, and
we'll see see whose legs are the longest.   If you
must make Fate to blame, my back is broad, I can
stand it, far I am that very gentleman—Fate, himself.''

'' *You*, Fate ! ''

'' Yes, I, or you, or anybody that gets his finger
in the pie—the Jew, if you'd rather.''

"You're a slippery one," said Catus; "I half believe you're a philosopher."

"Which is another name for Yankee," putting his feet as high as his head and looking longingly at his host's cigar.

It was no use; he gained nothing from "the riddle," for that gentleman failed to commit himself, and wending his way back to the hotel, he inwardly decided that he had found a match for his own sharp practice in Cæsar Catus, of ancient Rome.

Catus clapped his hands, as soon as Regan had departed, and the Arab materialized with another letter on the South Sea shell. It was stamped with the symbol. He opened it forthwith. These were the contents:

"Caution! Remember that there are tombs all along the Nile, in the mountain range; also, that about two hundred and fifty miles from Cairo, on the desert, is an oasis; also, Serapeum, the tombs of the sacred bulls; also, that the sands of Libya retain no tracks; also, that something of grave importance has occurred in Paris; also, that upon one man alone must you bring yourself to bear.

"A bove majori discit arare minor."

Symbol.

Catus sat in deep study for an hour, lighting one cigar after another, and throwing them away. When sure that he had deciphered correctly, he clapped his hands, and remarked to the waiting Arab, " Have my traps all packed to-night; I leave Cairo immediately."

Bowing, the servant vanished, and Catus, going to the pile, placed the latest with the other letters, and sank down among the cushions of his couch and fell asleep.

CHAPTER XIX

SPINO.

Spino was the strangest old hag that ever wore shoe leather; if she had any shape at all, it was so variable that she was never twice alike. Sometimes she was tall and sometimes short, now bent almost double, again straight as a barber's pole. One shoulder was higher than the other, one day the right and the next day the left. Her legs and arms differed according to the time of the week, and her eyes were the worst match on record. That which grew on her head, which people called hair, was much like the stub of an old clothes brush, uncertain as to color and changeable as to length. Her skin of the hue of pale molasses, was written all over with a net-work of hieroglyphics which the world called wrinkles, but which the wise read like the pages of an ancient book. She had not a tooth in her head save one which forced her mouth open in spite of herself, betraying a deep and awful cavern behind her thin lips, from which came a variety of sounds from the profundo of a guttural to the high treble of a screech. Her nose was a beak, with nostrils that betrayed blood of race, but whether her pedigree were black or white no one could tell. She was so utterly ugly that she was not ugly at all; grotesque she might be, artistic surely, but hideous, never. Besides she was interesting like a sixteenth century manuscript or a scroll of black magic, and shrewd and keen and sharp and wise, with no touch of senility anywhere, but quicker, brighter, more apt than the young folks of her time. This was Spino, the constant companion and perpetual foil of Cicily.

When Sallus arrived, according to appointment, at the house of Issachar he found himself in a strange place; it might have been a continuation of the shop below were it not for the fact that nothing was sold above stairs. The rooms were in irredeemable disorder, but wonderfully enticing in their chaotic splendor. If Issachar had been pitching things right and left at the heads of the occupants they would have assumed about the position that they occupied at the time of Sallus' call. Such beautiful things ! or sins, as the toothless Spino called them. There were stuffs, oriental and occidental, of the rarest bronzes, embroideries and rugs, curtains and hangings, treated with as little reverence as so much old junk and so many rags. The rooms were lighted by stuffy candles stuck into the most elaborate hammered brass sticks, or behind greasy bits of glass of every color, that flashed dimly at the shadows, where the curtains hung here and there without object or purpose, save simply to hang—shameless exhibitions of their own embroidered splendor.

There was but one homely touch to the place—a brass tea-kettle hung over an alcohol lamp and sang madly while it sputtered into the eyes of an intrusive bronze dragon that had the curiosity to investigate.

Spino greeted Sallus with a cork-screw bow which made her ancient skeleton crack from head to toe; then bustled around the tea-kettle like a witch with a caldron. She went on the principle of tea, or die. She looked quite scandalized when Cicily entered, and bowing to Sallus took her old head in her arms and laid her face against it in the most loving fashion, saying, "Granny, this is Sallus."

Cicily could have done no more coquettish a thing, were she artful or artless, and about which of the two natures that young lady had, Sallus was more puzzled than ever.

To lay her face against that of Granny was to enhance her beauty a thousand fold—her youth, her charm. The force of contrast threw her into a halo of magical splendor, from which Sallus could never disentangle her in the years to come. She was dressed like a tawdry Oriental princess

who had had no new clothes for a year. Her garments must have cost a pretty sum, but were shabby
from over and ill usage; still they gave a touch of
pathos to her irresistible beauty which Spino was
destined to foil. She was a conscious or unconscious
coquette—an artful child of sin, or an artless angel.
From her surroundings and manner she might have
been either; but whichever she were there was no
mistake about one thing; she was fascinating—
fascinating, with that witching glamor of the flesh
and the Orient, that made Sallus an easy prey. He
stood in awe of Rhea, but Cicily was a warm-
blooded creature of earth ; a woman of dimpled
arms and half-clad bosom, with red cheeks and
seductive eyes.

"Now this tea," said Spino—she began her
sentence in French, but Sallus interrupted.

"Can you speak no other tongue than that ? I
can make it out, but it's mighty hard."

"Talk English," said Cicily with a coaxing
smile; so Spino finished up in English—" this tea
is good."

"You see," said Cicily in a whisper, "she speaks
every known tongue under heaven; she is as wise
as Issachar."

" Is she his mother? " said Sallus awed.

"No, she hates him. It is a constant battle
between them."

" Why does the Jew keep her ? "

" He likes the opposition, I guess."

Spino came wriggling toward them in a rotary motion, and presented the tea which was strong and bitter; on the saucer was a lump of sugar wet with brandy.

" We drink tea constantly," said Spino, " from morning till night."

" And always with brandy? "

" Always with brandy."

"I can't go that," said Sallus throwing the sugar at a bedraggled dog that was curled up on a Smyrna rug. He was a toper, no doubt, for he nestled up to Sallus forthwith and begged piteously with his eyes for more. " I've given it up; a drop is one too many for me, for it leads on to a second and then a third, till I get where I can't stop."

Cicily looked amazed. " In that you are like Issachar, who never touches a drop. He's as abstemious as an Arab, but it doesn't hurt me; and she picked up the sugar and placed it between her red lips; those lovely lips that sugar was powerless to sweeten, those luscious lips made for kisses— kisses. So thought Sallus and how could he help it. He was young; the brandy he had thrown to the dog, but her lips !!—ah ! !

" Madam," he said, turning to Granny, " is Issachar as base as he seems? " This question was put to open the subject.

" He is black," said Spino, shaking her head.

" Do you know one called Caesar Catus?"

" Yes," croaked Granny like a mournful raven.

" Is he a tool of the Jew; did the Jew send him to Italy to study with one Aleppo Bracciolini, years ago ?"

" You ask too much ; I know not that. Caesar spake twice with me, but with Issachar I know not."

" And may I inquire what he said to you."

" It was about the young man whom he called Romanes, who staid in these rooms a few hours."

" What did he say," said Sallus excitedly.

" He inquired if he were better; he came twice in the same day to ask."

" And that was all."

" That was all."

" The rascal ! " said Sallus, biting his lips to keep from giving vent to a volley of oaths. "Would you take him for a friend of Issachar, or an enemy."

" That I know not."

" Curse him; if he were a friend, he would have captured Aleppo by force ; he's in league with Issachar, and Regan and I are in his clutches like mice in the claws of a cat. I expect he has been spying on Aleppo for years; undoubtedly he went to the studio to be near him—curse him ! "

" It would not have been easy to have taken the young man from the Jew by force, even if he were here longer. Issachar has ways and means of hiding one instantly."—She wriggled like a polly-wog ; her English was beautiful in its dignity; her manner supremely grotesque.

"What was the matter with Aleppo; can you tell?"

"He seemed to be very sick. I think it was one of Issachar's drugs; he was hardly conscious when brought here, and though he roused a little was taken away in about the same state.

"Is the drug dangerous," said Sallus nervously.

"No, I imagine not, except that it prostrates one for a time."

"Where do you suppose Issachar has taken him?"

"Of that I haven't the slightest idea," said Spino, pouring out more tea and swallowing it with a great noise.

Here Cicily came closer to Sallus and looked appealingly in his eyes; "Your whole thought is for the young man; what of me?"

He blushed; he was proving a great cavalier indeed.

"Really, Miss Cicily, I shall do as I said; I must find Aleppo and steal you; there is no other way.'

"When you have found him, it will be too late to steal me; Issachar will put me out of sight. Spino and I must get off somehow, but—we have no money."

"That's easy enough to remedy; but wait"—an awful thought had shocked him—"you will have to be patient till Aleppo is found; there is no alternative. Should we spirit you and Spino away, the Jew will take revenge on Aleppo."

"Then his life is more important than mine,"—
she said this in a piqued tone.

"His life is everything!" said Sallus, rising and
walking the room, "but don't you worry, Miss
Cicily; I have a powerful backing and plenty of
money. I can buy you from Issachar. You say
you're of little value to him since your relatives
have thrown off on you; he will be glad to get a
customer. Stay here quietly with Spino and act as
though you had never heard of me. Keep on the
watch though, and send your old nurse out with
letters to my room when there is news; it is the
only plan. Trust me, sweet girl, will you?"

A rosy blush spread over her neck and face ; but
pouting she said, "It seems strange to be bought."

"'Tis, rather, but never mind Miss Cicily; I'll
tell Regan all about it, and he'll back you too."

"Who is Regan?"

"My best friend since Aleppo vanished—a philosopher and a Yankee. You can trust him too."

The girl seemed mystified, but said nothing.
Sallus discovered a tear dropping from her long
lashes, and his heart smote him. Yet, it might be
all a part of the trap, a fictitious sorrow conjured
with a purpose. He was becoming suspicious of
Catus, of Spino, of Cicily. Were they all a band
worked by the Jew? Yet, she was pretty, this
Cicily, and so pathetic. He must leave instantly ;
he was afraid of himself. If he failed now, or lost
his bearings, or varied from his fixed purpose, what

would Aleppo say, to whom he had vowed to be loyal unto death ; so he put on a stern look and faced Spino.

" Do you not think it rather strange that Isaachar should have brought Aleppo here? How did he know but that you might betray him ? "

" Do you think we are fools ? " she answered ; " Issachar considers our gabble as harmless as rain drops. No one believes us, understand ? "

" Ah ! " Sallus backed toward the door. " I shall be in the room across the street ; send me word if you have news—any news." He reached his hand to the old lady, then to the young, and bowing, drew back the curtain and began to descend the stairs. A cold sweat broke out over him ; he knew not why. The passage way to the region below was narrow and dark. He glanced nervously right and left and then behind him.

Ah ! a claw-like hand was drawing back the portière through which he had just passed, and Issachar, noiseless as a cat, stepped from the dark passage near the stair-way into the lighted room he had just left.

The young man shivered from head to foot ; then bracing himself, for he was no coward, began to think. Should he face the Jew then and there, or was it a part of wisdom to slip out, leaving Issachar misled. Sallus condensed an hour's cogitations into a minute. "The Jew," he thought, "imagines he has played the spy without being caught. He

heard all that I had said ; nevertheless I am fore-
armed because forewarned." And during this
minute of condensed thinking Sallus' eye was
fixed intently on the arras at the head of the stairs.
"Should I open Issachar's eyes to my knowledge
of his presence here, it would be the worse for
Aleppo ; yes, I must go." He swallowed his
wrath, which was rising with his hot blood, and
deliberately finished his descent ; passing out into
the street, the most mystified man in Cairo. He
had gone but a few steps when he met Regan
sauntering before the shops. He had finished his
visit to Catus ; had been to his hotel and returned
to watch for Sallus. The two started homeward
arm in arm.

"Well," said Regan.

"Whew ! ! "

"What's up ?"

"The devil's to pay."

Sallus recounted everything to Regan, who whistled between sentences one melancholy minor note
that filled into Sallus' impassioned speech like
a musical accompaniment to a stage tragedienne.

When he had finished, Regan remarked dryly,
"A trap after all."

"As far as Issachar goes, yes ; but the girl I
can't fathom."

"Nor I ; but say, how much of this business
does Rhea know ?"

"She understands a little about Issachar," said

Sallus, "and thinks we have a clew; she's braced by hope.. In my opinion, though I've never spoken of it before, there's something between Aleppo and Rhea." '

"Shake on that," said Regan, squeezing his companion's arm, "she never says anything, but no girl on earth would wait 'round for a young man unless there was something like that. She has the tour of the planet before her, and her aunt is raging. She has a cause for staying, or I'm off my base."

Sallus was silent.

They were nearing the hotel when the men both turned suddenly, conscious that some one was following them. Getting over the ground very rapidly was a peculiar figure wrapped from head to foot in a black shawl. Sallus recognized the gait and bearing of Spino, and said directly,

"What is it?"

She came very near, displaying her grotesque face to the astonished Regan.

"The Jew is back," she hissed; the words piercing the men's ears like needles; then without waiting for comment she vanished down a side street, leaving Regan and Sallus rooted to the ground.

"Good God!" said Regan, "what was that?"

"A woman."

"Heaven save us!"

"It is Spino."

"I've seen women and women," said Regan, "but she takes the cake. Has she ever been married?"

"Probably."

"He had lots of nerve," said Regan.

CHAPTER XX.

THE LIBYAN SANDS.

A skin tent was pitched about a hundred miles west from Cairo, on the trackless waste. The Khemseen had been blowing all day, but, as the sun set, a hush fell on the desert, and the tent was thrown open to the fresh air.

A young man, on a pallet of straw, looked out on the broad expanse, stretching, stretching endlessly, even to the blue depths, where the stars floated. He watched the celestial splendor with patient eyes, whence longing had departed, and where only a resigned self-reliance remained. They were dark, beautiful eyes, somewhat sunken beneath a forehead, whose pallor betrayed both weakness and pain. His face was white as the driven snow; even the hot wind of the desert had failed to paint it; its thinness being more apparent from the heavy masses of black hair, which had been brushed back carelessly from his brow. He was too weak to get upon his feet, but, raising himself upon .his elbow, he leaned out of the tent and watched a slim Arab, as he moved back and forth in the shadow, preparing sticks for a fire.

From another goat-skin habitation, near by, there emerged a remarkable individual, a Bedouin, a monarch, a desert king. He gave directions to the Arab in a commanding voice, and then approached, with dignified strides, to the young man's tent.

" Aleppo Romanes, I have come to instruct thee yet again."

" As you please," said Aleppo, wearily.

" The map of heaven I read like a book,"—his voice rose and fell in a sing-song monotony—"from the stars I gain strange revelations, warnings, omens. See'st thou that fiery sun that banishes all others from the sky, and cuts the blue with its million keen blades of light, as though it were armed against the entire heaven; it sends its rays even into thine eyes, and reflects thyself to thyself. It is Sirius—the star of thy nativity, the self-illuminating, the mystic, the all-absorbing; it is typical of thee. In the forming of self thou shalt melt to a white glow, and burn with the fire that never goes out. Thy handmaid is Vesta; she serves thee well.

" What mean you by this talk," said Aleppo, mournfully. " It seems to be a vague monologue, that carries no weight."

" I mean," said the Bedouin, "that thy fate is

written on thy hand, and in thine eye; thou art destined by the centuries behind thee, to the majesty of isolation; thou art *constrained to be great*, for the march of events has lifted thee above low passion, into power."

"Indeed, I am very weak, said Aleppo, brushing a tear from his eye, yet looking on the star-lit face of the Bedouin with fascinated gaze.

"Thy body is prostrate; thy soul is in the crucible; but the day cometh when thou shalt wax strong."

"You have befriended me," said Aleppo, "without you I should have died. Can you not tell me the purpose of Issachar, and the meaning of this delay?"

"The purpose of Issachar is naught to me nor thee. The Jew is great, but signs are greater. Thy fate is written in the stars; not even Issachar can stay Aldebaran in its course, nor stop the march of Hercules."

"Astrology is blank to me," said Aleppo, sighing; "nor do I believe, either, in the scroll of heaven, or this thin palm of mine hand; in you, however, I have faith. You are more subtle than your creed, and would know me, were no mark upon my body, nor star in the sky. And you speak truly; the past has forced me to the desert, where, alone, I shall see heaven; no golden mean remains for me; the extremes, alone, are mine—either to blanch, a skeleton, upon this trackless waste, or rest mine eyes in ecstacy upon the star of stars. Aye, Sirius, to thee I look; a burning splendor, majestic and alone."

" He, only, who can endure isolation, is worthy of the crowd."

"You speak well," said Aleppo; "man must know the desert, if he would be worthy of life. There was one in Judea who spent forty days in the wilderness; I feel myself banished for a lifetime. You are wise, my faithful friend, but will you not rid yourself of the rubbish of superstition, which sticks to you like rags to the beggar."

"Already thou hast begun to teach, said the Bedouin, a peculiar expression lighting his face.

" It strikes me," replied Aleppo, " that pure wisdom needs no veil. Truth should be clear-cut, like a cameo. Why blur it with astrology, alchemy, delusion? Is not science good enough, and fact?"

The Bedouin cast on Aleppo a strange look, and said calmly,

" Canst thou read a riddle?"

"I might," said Aleppo, "if I puzzled long enough; but why the riddle? Are not the eternal principles inscrutable without making mysteries out of self-asserting truth, which refuses to be hid?" Nay, my friend, get rid of your rubbish, and polish your gem; it will be bright enough if you will but let the sun bring out its glitter."

" Canst thou read a riddle?" repeated the Bed-

ouin, who still maintained the same peculiar
expression of face.

Aleppo looked at him with surprise.

" What mean you ? "

" Consider well; to-morrow evening I shall speak
to thee again." He walked into the haze of night,
leaving Aleppo tired, but astonished.

He was getting better, and would lie for hours
recalling as much as he found possible of the events
which had followed each other in his life since he
had met Issachar at Karnak.

He remembered well, following the Jew to the
Arab hut, where he had been shown the papers
that proved his identity, beyond a doubt. He
recalled the sensation of faintness that had overcome him, and the glass of water which Issachar
had placed to his lips; then nothing for days.
Later, he had opened his eyes to watch the moon on
the Nile and feel a phantom—Rhea, kissing his lips.
He recalled how his consciousness had come and
gone. Once he had looked about a strange room,
and had seen Issachar preparing a draught; also a
witch-like woman and a beautiful girl.

He had been on the desert for weeks, though at
first he had realized but little of it, conscious only
that they had changed their location again and
again, and that once he had waked up to gaze at
the walls of a tomb, where Issachar and the Bedouin
were sitting side by side, on the ground, deeply
engaged in earnest talk. For a long time, now, how-

ever, be had been of strong and lucid mind, though
his body still failed to do his bidding.   For the past
week they had remained in one place; Issachar
being absent, and the Bedouin on guard.

Aleppo, in his mental wanderings backward, had
come to the conclusion that since he had been at
Karnak, something had been given him continuously, to keep him in this helpless state. He could
neither surmise the reason of this, nor prove the
·fact; nevertheless, he felt certain that his judgment
about the matter was correct.

Strangely, he neither regretted his past, nor the
fate that was overtaking him, but felt dimly, yet
surely, that he was destined, by the very nature of
events, to realize something better than he had
ever yet known.   Nor did he feel that Rhea was
lost, save to the eye and the touch.   He was so
conscious of this and the vague ecstacy of spiritual contact, that his deprivation in the physical
seemed as nothing.   He was as one who sensed
Paradise and realized the golden age.   Never more
would the old delights overwhelm him, nor gross
pleasures subdue.   He had had a drop of the elixir
on his tongue and the taste remained with him. All
else was now judged by comparison; the divine
charm throwing the lesser into the shadow.   He
felt his celestial destiny; not for the reason of his
environment, nor through the persuasion of others,
but because of his consciousness of self.   When he
passed under the Propylon, he was flooded with

light—his former years were to him as nothing; his
future a dream; only to-day was of value, with its
majesty of desert stretches and its arch of blue;
only the stars, and his illuminated soul, which felt
causation and futurity as one and the same; and the
present hour as a throb of rapture. He had come
from the narrow by-path of specialization, to the
broad expanse of a full view, where his eyes swept the
meandering roads of his past with a clear glance,
and focussed all that was behind him on an isolated
spot on the sands of Libya, where his body lay
prostrate in a tent of skins. He had lost his life to
find it. His friends, phantoms, whose voices were
dying echoes; his passionate love, a far-off throb of
bounding blood; his ambitions all in the past, long-
gone ; and he, with mind attuned to celestial music,
with eye fixed on Sirius--his natal star—saw,
clearly, the meaning of himself. Something in
him had awakened, which clarified his intellect and
purified his emotions. A comprehensiveness of the
purpose of his life, a quick and subtle logic, an
ecstacy of sensation, that in other days he had but
dimly known. There was nothing in this new
splendor of himself which savored of sickly sentiment, or the froth of feeling; on the contrary, he
had begun to be conscious of the masterly poise,
which is struck through the realization of the subtle
limit of the power of head and heart.

He thought of other men, young men, who, like
himself, loved. He saw them wedded and settled

in life, and, as the years went by, falling into the wearying drudgery of the commonplace. He felt the fate of the mortal and shuddered. Doomed to sully his ideal, man crushes the wings of the butterfly and cripples the soaring bird. But he, outside of conventionality by the fatality of his birth, beheld the short road to immortality, clear-cut and direct.

Some discover the breadth and power of being by slow degrees; lighting a million little tapers, one after another, they pick their way out of the darkness into the glare of noon. Others take but a step, and lo! the dungeon is behind them, and the sun overhead.

Aleppo had no plans, nor much philosophy. Some things, however, were clearly revealed. He must elude the clutch of Issachar; turn his back on his parents and his past, hold a last, sweet interview with Rhea, then seek the rose gardens of Damascus to sit at the feet of one whose name was a mystery and whose face was veiled. To accomplish this, he must recover his strength, and seize upon an opportunity when Issachar was absent to make his escape. The prospect was certainly gloomy. He had no idea on what part of the desert he was hid; but surmised that they were either near Cairo, or an oasis, for several times fresh Arabs had arrived and deposited water skins, while the old ones had departed. The Bedouin would make no communication about their situation and prospects, and he was left, in this respect to his own cogitations and plans.

The next evening after his talk with the nomad, that strange individual appeared in his tent again, finding Aleppo much stronger, and sitting cross-legged on his bed of straw, like a Turk.

"The sickle of the moon has appeared in the heaven," said the Bedouin; "and when it hath grown to a full orb, thou wilt be well."

"Most gladly will I get about once more," answered Aleppo, with his old beaming smile. "But will you not tell me the plans of Issachar? I have continued to beseech you, but in vain."

"Issachar's plans are naught to me or thee, as before thou hast been informed."

"You seem to be my friend in spite of appearances; I trust you, although you are acting in harmony with the Jew, and depriving me of the right of liberty, if not of health; still, I feel your friendship and wisdom, and doubt not but that you, yourself are deceived as to Issachar's real motive, and are doing his bidding with a clear conscience."

The strange, half-veiled smile that had been on the Bedouin's face before, appeared again; he looked searchingly at Aleppo, placed his hand to his breast, then dropped it, speaking sharply at the same time, as if impelled by a power beyond himself.

"And what wouldst thou do with thy liberty if it were thine?"

With these words he gazed, with a keen, intense expression, into Aleppo's eyes. The young man felt the challenge, and tossing back his hair in the old fashion, said, promptly, as though no other answer were possible,

" I would seek the feet of the Master, and lean on him, that I, too, may become great."

" Thou hast friends, ambitions, love," said the Bedouin, " what wouldst thou do with these?"

" I would make myself worthy of them; till then, my friends and I must part. He only is fit to have, who can do without. He only is able to rule who has first served. He only is worthy of love who can abide alone."

" Aleppo Romanes, thou hast stood the test; take this." He drew from the folds of his robe a sealed letter, and placing it in the young man's hand turned and left the tent.

The light was dim, but the keen eyes of Aleppo caught the familiar symbols and tearing it open, he ravished the self-illuminated scroll with his very soul.

THE LETTER :

" The *mortal* passes from the womb to the grave, reversing all things. He acquires learning without wisdom, and love without service. He reproduces without regeneration, and dies ere he has lived.

" The *immortal* wrenches victory from the grip of defeat, and life from the clutch of death; he makes the desert to blossom as a garden, and hell to glow with the light of heaven. He turns despair to ecstacy, and frenzy into rapture. He extracts honey from bitter herbs and the dregs of the cup are sweet upon his tongue. Losing love in the flesh, he gains it in the spirit, and escapes the vulture and the worm.

"Arise! Thou art chosen! To-day thou dost look up; in time thou shalt look down."

Aleppo struggled to his feet and stood in the door of his tent. The heaven was blazing with star-light and a thousand eyes beamed on him from the arch overhead. He breathed deeply the soft, warm air of Libya and felt his blood rush through his veins.

To whence had vanished the half timid boy? The eyes of Aleppo had suddenly acquired the quick glance of the Master, who mocks at fate, and *defies* destiny.

A half-fledged bird had stood on the edge of the nest; challenged by hunger and mocked by death; but spreading his wing—lo! space universal, height, motion, freedom, *life*.

CHAPTER XXI.

WHEREFORE ?

Cæsar Catus was a man of affairs. He left Cairo promptly on the morning after his interview with Regan, and appeared again at a railway station in

Genoa, where, cigar in mouth, he walked up and down the platform awaiting the arrival of an incoming train. It was near dusk and the depot was already lighted. Catus consulted his watch a number of times, but without any appearance of restlessness, and stopped to reward two or three vagrants for doing nothing, carrying himself altogether like a man of the world, even to having a word or two with a dissolute woman who flaunted her shame in the eyes of the railroad officials with unblushing audacity. What he said to her was not heard on the outside, but it was noticed that she departed from the station straightway with a smile on her lips. A street boy caught the glitter of gold coin in her hand, as she went out, and yelled loudly, "Struck it rich, didn't you." Later, that same imp of the pavement sauntered up to Catus and began a pitiful tale; he struck it rich also, for that gentleman collared him on the spot and gave him such a scathing look that he did not get over it for many a day. Catus accomplished a good deal in the few minutes of waiting; he made a number of notes; read and answered a letter; sent a telegram and drank a cup of coffee; all without any fuss and with great dispatch. He was dressed in a strictly correct English costume, and looked quite a different figure from the one that lounged in the oriental den in Cairo. The epicure was metamorphosed into the man of action, who carried his load of responsibility with great ease, as though used to the wear and tear.

The engine of the incoming train came snorting to the station like a roaring bull in harness, and wheezed and puffed as it slowed up as though it were the victim of an incurable asthma. Catus placed himself instantly at the door of a *particular* car and watched the passengers as they alighted. The last individual that came forth arrested his attention at once, and following him to where the light struck full in his face he intercepted his further progress and placed his hand to his head and heart. The eyes of the two met for an instant and the salute of Catus was returned.

The traveller stooped somewhat, and looked care-worn and anxious; his thick black hair was sprinkled with white and a stubble of gray beard covered the lower part of his face. His counte-nance, which was that of a very handsome man, seemed prematurely aged; the only sign of youth still retained being a lock of dark hair, untouched by the ash of time, that fell on a lofty brow, in Napoleonic fashion, and which his soft hat, set back on his head, brought into full view. His eyes, restless as though impatient of life itself, had in them a composite expression of bereavement and anxiety, as though they were ever weeping for some-thing vanished, and searching for something to come. The two men began a conversation in oriental dialect.

" I recognized you at once," said Catus.

" How," asked the other wearily.

" By that lock of hair on your forehead; it is famous."

The stranger tossed it back with a shake of his head—" In another life it will be blasted,"—smiling grimly—" it has been both my pride and my worry; but speak—what news? "

" All is well," said Catus, touching his head and heart again.

" And Issachar? "

" A match for the Bedouin."

" Ah! "

" The combatants are unequal," went on Catus; " we shall have to reinforce."

" And I in the meantime? "

" Be patient," said Catus; patience is a virtue that you have need of; acquire it now."

The stranger took a letter from his pocket and handed it to Catus who, without glancing at the superscription, placed it inside his note-book.

" It shall be delivered."

" Now Mr. Catus," he said, " though I have never met you before, I place myself entirely in your hands; do with me as you will."

At this Catus glanced begind him, and an individual loomed up from the shadow, who announced that a carriage was waiting. Catus took the arm of the stranger, and the two emerged from the station, to vanish into the black recesses of the vehicle at the door. `

Two or three hours later Cæsar Catus, prowling around some of the low haunts of Genoa, found himself in front of a disreputable house that boldly announced itself to those who understood its vile vocation in the scheme of the universe. Scanning the number, aided by a squint between the. eyes, he made himself manifest in a peculiar way and the door flew open as though swung on fairy hinges. His companion of the railway station, dressed with reckless daring as to arms and neck, greeted him effusively, and ushered him into a tawdry, flashy apartment that spoke of the hand to mouth style in vogue among people of her class.

Catus seemed perfectly at home as though used to such places and women. '' I announced to you at the station that I should call later, and I gave you some money, do you remember ? ''

'' Yes,'' she said laughing, do you suppose money slips out of my mind as quickly as it does from my pocket? I'm sure you're a pretty gentleman, Mr. Jackson.''

'' Wait a minute,'' said the improvised Mr. Jackson, looking fixedly at the woman who was not half bad; '' I must tell you a little of myself; I want you to understand me.''

'' Oh, do you ? that's a new departure,'' said she archly.

'' I'm accustomed to visiting places like this when

I pass through a city, and on my return going over the same ground again."

"Well"—something like a blush stole up and edged the rouge on her face.

" I correspond with a hundred women like you."

She was slightly piqued ; it was an unusual sensation for a woman of her kind, and she wondered what was the matter with her; she was amazed too, at such an eccentric visitor; she had never met a man like this before, and simply had nothing to say, but sat looking at him.

"Yes," went on Catus; "now and then I see a face that I think is worth cultivating. You had gone pretty far though to prowl around a railway station; you are too young and good looking for that."

In spite of herself a couple of tears fell from her eyes and left their tracks in the rouge on her cheeks; she had not wept for a year! what did it mean?

"I should like very much to correspond with you," said Catus.

" Me ! "

" Why yes, you—I write very good letters."

She lifted her startled eyes and looked him over; was he crazy, or was she?

" I am going to leave you some money, and I shall be back to see how you use it, later. In the meantime write to me."

A new idea struck her and she asked timidly, "Are you a priest? "

"No," he replied, "nor a philanthropist, nor a religious specialist. I am interested though, in about a hundred women, whom I feel sorry for. It seems to me they are literally driven to be bad by us men. Our physicians instruct us that we need you; our city government winks at this unevenly distributed Yoshiwara where you and your kind abide. Virtuous women have a sword continuously suspended over their heads, which means nothing other than a threat from their pastors and husbands, that unless they walk the path laid out for them, they will force their abused helpmates into your very arms. Society demands you, and poor scape-goat that you are, more sinned against than sinning, it curses you, and dumps you without coffin into a pauper's grave, when your three year's work is done.

The woman stood up; the tears were streaming down her face, "I haven't cried for a year—my God!"—she burst into a frenzy of sobbing, and tore her hair and clenched her hands like one gone mad.

"There,".said Catus, "I am glad to see this; you have a big heart—more's the pity; the bigger the heart the oftener the people trample on it; that is the way with us men; we dry your last tears, we squeeze the last blood from your veins, then we kick you out. The more beauty you have, the more pleasure it gives us to blast it. We never dream of coaxing the bud of your charm into a

flower; we tear open the petals before it has bloom-
ed and throw it away with a curse."

"But you," she said, looking at him in a bewildered way, through her dishevelled hair that
had fallen over her face.

"I, well, I am sorry," before he could prevent it
she threw herself at his feet, and on her knees as
though she were praying, with clasped hands, and
sobs she poured out her woe.

"Go away from here " she said, " go ! It is useless; even God cannot help us. The priest came
and I drove him off; we are bad entirely. The
men are no worse, you mistake; we—*I am bad.*"

"Yes, I know it," said Catus, "You are very
bad, about as evil as you can be; and that means
that you can be very good."

"What—I ? O, I should *hate* to be good."

"I don't blame you," he answered; "I should
too, if good meant to me what it does to you."

"I have a horror of heaven," she went on, "and
angels, and virtuous women, and churches, nor do
I want a respectable funeral, nor a tomb;" and
while she said it the tears flew in gushes and washed
away the powder and rouge.

"Nor do I," said Catus, "we are out and out
Bohemians both of us; but you see, my dear woman,
your idea of what good is and mine, are different;
to be good is to be happy; are you happy?"

"Happy, I don't know exactly what you mean."

"No, I presume you do not. To be happy is to

get the very best there is out of life; in my opinion
you are getting the worst."

She seemed dazed, but looked at him with that
wistful expression, which comes from a half-clouded
intellect. *He was a fact* however, this man who
sat before her, and he had expressed in her behalf
and those of her class a certain kind of sympathy
which she had missed in the priest and a few Bible-
women who called to level scripture texts at her.
She cared nothing for goodness, nor gentility, nor
religion, but she did admire him in that respectful
way that made her ashamed of her room and herself.

"Now," said Catus, "I'm not going to stay any
longer; promise me that you will go to bed and try
to sleep all night. I don't leave money with some
women, not a penny, but with you it is safe. I have
made no mistake about you I am sure. In a month
I shall pass through Genoa again and shall call to
see you; but you must not be here, understand. Get
a respectable room and modest clothes; keep off the
street and rest and grow strong, for you are sick,
did you know it? Write me a long letter once a
week; here are the envelopes." He handed her
four of them stamped and addressed. "I shall
answer them all. Tell me where you are living,
and everything. Now Nita, don't be afraid; here
is more money than you can possibly earn—good-
bye."

He held out his hand to her; she took both and
kissed them passionately, while the tears fell in

showers, and he let the precious drops dry on them as though they brought comfort and strength.

When he had gone she threw the gold pieces up and down and listened to them jingle, then stowing them away very carefully, she fastened her door and windows, and drew the shades so as to give the room on the outside an appearance of darkness; after that she sat down before the dressing table and examined herself in the mirror with the eye of a connoiseur.

"Three years," she said out loud, "and I have gone through about half of it; only eighteen months and then I'm done. It takes more rouge and powder every day to make me up. I'm getting thinner too, and she examined the visible bones of her chest. And he says it's all the men's fault, but I know it isn't. Nobody tempted me, that I remember; I just deliberately came here. I don't like being good or virtuous, now that's the plain truth; yet—three years is an awful short time. He said that I'm not happy "—here the tears fell again —" that's one word of truth he spoke anyhow; but I wasn't happy before, never was happy—I don't believe he is either. I could be happy though "— she took out the pins and let the luxuriant hair fall over her thin shoulders—"if he'd come once in a while and talk like that. I can't work for my living, and I don't want to, but—I'd work for him. I wouldn't mind blacking his shoes even, but for anybody else I wouldn't lift a finger—not I. He wants

me to go away from here; I wouldn't do it for any
other person, not a soul on earth. I like it here,
and moving is a nuisance, but I expect I'll have to,
yes, and he told me to go to bed and sleep. It
seems queer to be minding anybody; I never did
that before, even when I was a child—I wonder if
this is being good."

She washed her face and threw her rouge and
powder boxes all into a heap in the corner, and
turning up the light to get a full view, she began
making up faces at her regenerated image in the
glass; "the uglier the better," she said, and she
squinted and scowled, and contorted her once fair
visage into innumerable grotesque and ugly shapes.

"Now Nita you are good," she said; "you'll not
paint nor powder, nor sell yourself for a month;
you'll grow fat maybe, and pretty again, if you
sleep nights and keep off the streets—if it wasn't
for him it would be stupider than dying, but I guess
I can manage it. I'll not tell another woman in the
house a thing about this affair either, and she tossed
her head as though already she had attained a
height they knew nothing of and never could.

The next day she managed to vanish from her
old haunts as though she had been annihilated; not
a vestige of her remained; we take that back; there
was one—the girl upstairs found a gold piece under
her door which somehow she attributed to Nita
though why, she never knew.

CHAPTER XXII.

THE MISSION OF ISSACHAR.

. Sallus continued to reside in the house opposite the dwelling place of Issachar, but that individual had again disappeared; nor did he see anything for several days of Spino or Cicily.

Regan spent a good deal of time with him, and they planned, and threatened, and waited, but nothing came of it, They dreaded to bring direct legal action against Issachar, for fear that he would take revenge on Aleppo; so they worked under cover, in vain hope that they might, in some way, outwit him, and save their young friend from personal harm.

One day Sallus and Regan were conversing together, when the door was softly opened and Spino ambled in.

" Pull down the curtain," she said, " so nobody can see me from the outside; I'd be uneasy if I were discovered." She was uglier than ever, and more interesting.

" What is it—have you any news? " said Sallus, after introducing her to Regan.

" Nothing special; only I wanted to talk.   Issachar has been gone a week, and I said to Cicily, ' now is his chance.' ''

" No you don't," muttered Sallus to himself; "we want to get our bearings first."

" By the way," said Regan, " may I ask you some questions about Issachar ? "

" You may," she answered, solemnly.

" In the first place, what is his profession, any-how ? "

" Stealing."

" But you know as well as I do that he's no ordinary thief; how do you think he manages it ? "

" As far as I can make out, it is this way," she answered; " somebody vanishes from somewhere, Issachar, perhaps, is a thousand miles off, but he knows all about it; has his emissaries at work in every part of the earth; later he cultivates the bereaved relatives, and poses as a magician, who discovers lost treasures and victims that disappear, agreeing, through his supernatural powers, and for a price, to restore the lost."

" And so he is responsible for the very disappearance itself," said Regan.

" Always, though in nine cases out of ten he never sees the victim. Issachar is at the head of a band; my husband,"—Regan winked at Sallus—" was one of them; they have a mysterious symbol, which is called the devil's mark; and make themselves known to each other in any part of the

earth.   Issachar stole Cicily's mother, and he has
the young man you seek.''

" How is it that he is never apprehended ? "

" He!   'Twould be impossible; I defy you to find
a victim of Issachar, or to implicate him in any
way.   Should he deliver up the young man to his
parents, he would so stipulate, and they would be
so implicated, that their mouths would be sealed ;
besides, Issachar knows the whole Sahara, to say
nothing of Libya, his allies are faithful unto death
—every one; the life of a man who betrays Issachar
is not worth a farthing."

" How about you ? " said Sallus.

" I might talk to all Cairo and he'd not turn his
hand over.   He looks upon my gabble as rain
water; in fact, he rather likes it; the more that
Cicily and I talk, the better."

The two men stared at each other greatly puzzled.   What did she mean?   Whether she were
working for, or against the Jew, they could not
make out.

" It seems to me one person's talking is as bad as
another's."

"No, it is not; I used to express my opinion
before the whole band, but they shed it as a roof
does water.   What we Arab women say has no
weight; we're all grumbling and lying, from morning till night."

" But Cicily ? "

" Oh, she repeats me; everybody knows that.

She was born on the desert and understands nothing but what I've told her. The whole world believes that she is Issachar's niece; you're the first folks I've found that listen to my story."

''How do you know that you are correct in your surmises?''

"How do I know! Haven't I heard them scheming for hours, when the band met—Issachar calls it a corporation—wasn't my husband a member? Mark me,"—her voice rising to a shrill shriek—" I know, and what is more, I warn you, that all your puerile efforts to outwit Issachar and save the young man are useless. It takes a magician to compete with a magician; only another as subtle as Issachar, and as shrewd, whose eyes and hand are trained to quickness, who has devoted allies and unusual powers can hope to match Issachar—the son of darkness and the devil's own."

Her voice rose to a screech, but her words were those of an orator.' The effect was amazing; she looked, in the dim light of the room, like a witch of antiquity, whose rattling bones and mummied visage were animated by a ghostly Cæsar, or a phantom Demosthenes.

'' In my opinion," said Regan, getting up and shaking himself, as though to throw of the uncanny atmosphere that had settled on them all, '' in my opinion, Issachar is a blackmailer of the first water. You rate him too high, Madame; can show you a half dozen of his trade in New York. He's pretty smart, no doubt, but you put him a peg or two above his mark. See?"

Spino shook her head. "You haven't got the better of him so far, have you?"

"We've only begun; get a Yankee after a Jew and they generally keep neck to neck; don't know which one will skin ahead, but it will be a close race, I can tell you. Now, my good woman, how did it happen that Issachar was at the top of the stairs, behind the arras, the day that Sallus called?"

"That's a question I can't answer," said Spino; he appears and disappears, like any other wizard."

"Moral," answered Regan, "shake every curtain, and set a trap at the stairs when you call on Cicily, Sallus, my boy. See!"

"Can you make anything out of this," said Spino; "I found it in Issachar's inner pocket the last time he was here; I put another in its place."

She handed Regan a blank envelope, inside of which was another addressed in oriental dialect.

"Not much," said Sallus; "it is probably from one of the Jew's correspondents."

"I know better than that, although I can't translate it; but I know a man who can."

"How does it concern us," said Regan, doubtfully.

"Trust to my instinct that it does," she answered. "There's a dried-up old specimen of a linguist at the end of the street. I'll bring him here, if you say so; makes a business of deciphering all sorts of hieroglyphics, to say nothing of languages; have to pay him though."

The two men hesitated. To steal a man's letters was not to their liking, but the emergency was great.

" I have it," said Regan, "we're not obliged to read the inside, if we find the outside doesn't concern us. Get him, Spino, and I'll shell out."

She was off before he had finished, and shuffling down the stairs, in an incredibly short time she returned with a specimen of humanity almost as queer as herself. The four made an odd set; the long-legged Yankee with his hollow cheeks and quick eyes; Sallus, too handsome for a pen picture, with his Apollo head and athletic figure; the hag of hags—Spino, and a wizened interrogation point of a man, whom she called Quiz. He seemed to be asking questions whether he spoke or not, and curiosity was magnified in every part of him, as it is in a cat. He touched things curiously, he looked at them inquisitively, his nose had a why and wherefore scent, and his ears listened for answers to the never ending questions which he seemed to be propounding from morning till night. He looked, "What is it?" when he entered the room, though his tongue was still.

" This," answered Spino, handing him the letter. He opened and questioned it, mumbling a few sounds with a rising inflection, then, turning to

Spino, spoke in French, which she immediately translated to Regan.

"He says that the letter is addressed to Aleppo Bracciolini."

"What!" exclaimed Sallus and Regan.

"Listen," said Spino; "I will repeat after him in English."

LETTER.

"To get the full force of the opposite, drive a man to an extreme. Corner a peaceful stag if you would see fight. There is a limit to the power of sorrow; its other pole is joy.

"The Master emerges from a pedigree that has forced him to the wall. Desperate, he transcends one law by another, and resorts to the principle of extremity, which is the opportunity of God in himself.

"Imprison a man in the dark and he realizes light; starve him and he appreciates food; he discovers health through pain, and beauty through ugliness.

"On earth, at a given time, but few live who have reacted from the wilderness to the gardens of Hesperides—from the cross to the crown.

"The logic of events has taken you from much to naught; finding *nothing* at one pole of yourself, you rebound to the other and discover *all*. You were bereft of country, parents, and that which men call love; the gates of conventionality clanged behind you; the world of respectability was ready to turn its back, you faced a blank, which was as clean and white as a new scroll. Reaction was true to itself—from nothing you recovered everything—the void brought forth a universe. A famished Keats braces his ladder to heaven, in his attic window, whence he struggles upward to the stars. The desperate artist paints in his strong touches with blood, and destines his canvas to immortality. A wretched Pygmalion breathes upon his Galatea and parts with the fire of himself that the statue may live. If you would compel all things, give up all things. When a Master is forged in the furnace of being, the Magi come from the East, and a new star appears in the sky; there is a commotion among the wise, and bitterness in the camp of the foe; the news is carried to far countries and secret dispatches are sent from mind to mind. There is electric contact between the great, and the uprising of a thinker, and a seer braces them anew. Thou didst lay a spell upon thyself in ages past; to-day it takes effect."

Spino had translated slowly, and Sallus had written it down.

"That is beyond me," said Regan, with a more serious countenance than he had ever worn before.

"I grasp it," said Spino. Sallus and Regan looked at her and said nothing, but the inquisitive Quiz was all ears.

"We, in the Orient, believe that desperate circumstances, that which you call opposition, drive men to fortune. The poor, when all else fails, scratch at the breast of their mother, like hens, and pick out gold. Genius is the legitimate child of hardship. To wake up the whole man we know that the gods set devils on him like a pack of wolves."

"That's true, I forgot; the Lord permitted Satan to interview Job, and get the better of him for a time, it seems to me," said Regan.

"Only for a time," went on Spino, as though teaching a Sunday School class. She was a marvel; how she had managed to acquire such fluency of language and keenness of thought under conditions like her's, was beyond the understanding of Regan and Sallus.

"You see you don't know me, gentlemen; I was ugly as sin at the time I was born, and have never improved since; that's why I know something; learning was all the show I had. If I had been beautiful 'twould have turned out differently; as it is, I'm up in languages and experimental science."

"But the letter," said Regan, "what does it mean?"

"Just this, Issachar has intercepted it; 'tis addressed to Aleppo, and is from Damascus. I expect it was enclosed in another envelope and remailed; it was Issachar's business to intercept it. He cuts telegraph wires, pillages the mails, rifles pockets, and walks the streets of Cairo, or any other city, like a king."

"Who is the author of this letter, I wonder." Sallus picked it up reverently.

" It's beyond me again," answered Regan; then both men stared at Spino; she had a curious, sly expression in her eyes, which aroused suspicion in their minds at once.

"That letter," she said, " was sent to the young man by a servant of Allah."

" A Mohammedan ! "

" By a servant of Allah."

" Mohammedan ? "

" Yes."

" Is that your religion ? "

" It is."

" How comes it that you go unveiled, and ignore all Mohammedan customs ? "

" I serve a Jew; besides I am a woman of independent thought." Again a sly look came into her eyes.

" You really don't believe that the young man has been clutched, not only by a Jew, but by a buzzard of a Mohammedan also, do you ? " put in Sallus.

" Shouldn't wonder."

" 'Pon my word, you're wrong; 'twasn't a Moslem that wrote that letter. Say, Sal, Aleppo Bracciolini must be a mighty important personage. that mysterious people, good and bad, should be so hot after him. I wonder if he is a prince out and out?''

Quiz and Spino exchanged significant glances.

''Look here, madame, you're keeping some things back, why can't. you make a clean sweep while you are about it ?''

Spino's eyes snapped, and looked like little red coals, away back in her head.

'' If I am an Arab, no one can drive me, not even a man,''—she made a great show of indignation—''give me back the letter.''

'' Not at all,'' said Regan, placing it in his breast pocket and buttoning his coat.

'' What do you propose to do with it ?''

'' That I can't tell at present; it may come handy though. Now Quiz, what's the damage? The ' standing question ' named a ridiculously small price, and the two eccentricities departed, leaving Regan and Sallus as puzzled as ever.

'' I am afraid,'' said Sallus, '' that she is a tool of Issachar.''

'' Why this letter, then ? ''

'' It is just a blind; something she's copied somewhere; how in the world could Aleppo come by such a correspondent ?''

''Ask me something easy, When you get in with Jews, Moslems, and Mohammedans you don't know where you're at.''

'' Issachar would stop that woman's tongue if he hadn't an object in letting her talk. However, if

the letter is genuine, and I can't get over the idea
that it is, in spite of all indications to the contrary, what shall we do with it? ''

"Show it to Rhea," said Sallus.

"Done! and this very night."

CHAPTER XXIII.

THE HEATHEN.

Rhea was a conundrum to herself. There had
been a love scene between her and Aleppo on the
Nile, afterward a mutual understanding, expressed
without words; but there had never been any plans
made between them, nor had the future been discussed at all. A prudent young woman, on a trip
around the world, would have renewed her journey
long since, feeling that the moonlit beauty of a
Nile love dream, was scarcely adequate to hold her
like a fixture in Cairo, when the young man, according to Mrs. Hancock, had run away of his own
accord.

The romance of idealism in a nature such as
Rhea's is beyond understanding by the conserva-
tive and worldly wise. The young lady kept herself to herself, obstinately remaining in Cairo,
without deigning to explain farther than she had
already done. The Misses Richards had departed
long since, and Mrs. Hancock, from a sense of duty,

she said, but really because it was to her pecuniary interest, had ''settled in Cairo for life.''

Rhea never for an instant harbored the idea that Aleppo had left altogether of his own accord; to be sure she knew but little about him except what he and the letters had told. Their personal acquaintance had been very short; he was three or four years younger than herself, had no prospects that she knew of, and the idea of marrying him had scarcely entered her head. This may seem improbable, yes, impossible in the light of the fact of the usual modern young lady, whose love dream is tinctured with calculation, and whose heart is balanced with jewels and gold. But Rhea, like Aleppo, was far ahead of or behind the times; they were children of romance, and suited to the days of the cavalier, or the Eden of the Golden Age.

It was love that enraptured Rhea. A man-made marriage, a humdrum existence, where crude reality should serve to check the wild beating of the heart, were scarcely dwelt upon at all. Even the presence of Aleppo was not altogether essential; she loved—she was loved; yet, though conscious of this blessedness ever with her, the green serpent of jealousy had begun to sting. Her sorrow at the disappearance of Aleppo had vanished, even her fear, but by the true instinct of woman she realized that his affection was divided, that there was something that forced him from her—his now conscience, or a divine inspiration. Whatever it

might be, it was akin to that which compelled the
Prince Siddartha to wander away from the bosom of
his wife and the shadow of the throne. She knew all
this; and the conjectures of Regan and Sallus were
as nothing to her. She felt his personal absence
to be involuntary, but there was something more
subtle which she had sensed, and which must
separate them in life—Aleppo Bracciolini was destined to scan the prospect from the Maha Meru of
being—and she? All women on earth who had
given their fathers, husbands and sons to their
country, who had sent them forth for the cause of
science and truth, who had seen them sacrificed to
religion and art, were like herself—martyrs upon
whom a Master had set the seal. Rhea was jealous
of truth, of grand ideals, of God; jealous of all
sibylline books, of mystic powers and divine possibilities; yet, though *she knew*, she waited striving
to quiet and delude herself into the belief that she
was mistaken. Then came a dark day. Sallus
requested an interview; and the mysterious letter,
delivered by Spino, was placed in her hands.

"How did you get this?" she asked in a strange
voice.

Sallus recounted all that had happened since
coming to Cairo, in regard to the search; he expressed his hopes and his doubts, his suspicions and
his expectations, telling her a great deal about
Cicily, and asking her very earnestly to judge her
for him.

"I don't know," said Rhea—still in the unnatural voice, "I should have to see her first; but about this letter I have no doubt; it is a genuine epistle to Aleppo—in this I make no mistake."

"But you haven't read it," said Sallus.

Nor do I need to, to be conscious of its intrinsic value, nor the source from which it came."

"You must be a psychic."

"Perhaps I am—will you trust me to-night with it"—still in the same strange voice.

No matter what Rhea asked, Sallus must needs grant it; he was her veritable slave.

"Certainly Miss Rhea, forever, if it gives you pleasure."

She took his hand, and gave him that peculiar look which seemed to see, yet did not. In her eyes he read misery, despair; this Sallus could not endure. That Rhea should suffer was to him incredible.

"O, Miss Nellino, please don't look that way!"

She tried to smile, but it made matters worse. Tears are pathetic enough, but there is a smile forced to the lips for friendship's sake, which is heart-breaking.

Sallus was distracted; he faced things as a rule, but this experience with Rhea completely unmanned him.

"I must do something for you—you suffer"— this in a broken way.

"Please don't bother, Sallus, I am all right"—

he knew she was lying—" the climate, Mrs. Hancock says, is not good—am a little ill to-day. Go
now, and I'll see you to-morrow and tell you what
I think of this." She smiled brightly, but the
young man was not deceived ; however he was
forced out, and went off to Regan in a state of des-
pondency quite unnatural in a person of his healthy
physique.

Rhea, frozen even to her heart, sat down to read
the letter. It was all she had expected. No matter
who had carried Aleppo off, there was a powerful
influence overshadowing him, that compelled him
to face truth; that forced him to the ultimate—the
finality of reason—the premise of philosophy, and
the foundation of religion. She heard the voice of
Jesus, as he looked upon his mother—" Woman,
what have I to do with thee?"

Love ! it was the acme, the completion, the one
thing. Away with truth, logic, attainment, power.
Love ! the soft glamour of it, the perpetual infatuation, the chaste beauty, the song sung by the
breezes, the trees, the sea—the rapture that has its
rhythm in the tide of being, rising and falling like
the waves—the passion that fired Endymion, and
spent itself in Keats—the Sapphic ecstasy that sang
its soul out to the Phaon of eternal youth. Love !
the pure flame of Vesta, burning, burning ! The
dim mist of the eye that veils earth in beauty, and
softens the blush on the rose—Love ! that wafts to
the sense the spicy breezes of a magic Ceylon, or an

enchanted garden of Araby—Love ! that brings
Adonai out of heaven to touch up the landscape of
Eden, and Aphrodite from the depths to intoxicate
the soul with the ultimate charm.

Rhea ! whose spirit was Greek, who had wandered in dream over the grassy mounds of the Helicon
who had dabbled her white fingers in the waters of
the Aegean, who had leaned against the columns of
the Parthenon—Rhea ! who knew well the stray
trees and curving beach of Mitylene, whose sandaled
feet had trod the shores of Lesbos—Rhea ! who
loved all Attica, and whose beautiful face was akin
to the marble of Praxitiles—Rhea ! the poet, whose
song was an immortal appeal to Aphrodite, whose
heathen witchery compelled the gods to descend—
Rhea ! must she tear her heart from her breast and
the laurel from her brow ? Ah the wine she had
drunk in the old time !—She felt the fiery soul of
Aspasia, and the burning lips of Sappho full upon
her own—must she destroy the love immortal—*herself*—her very self ? And *she* a Greek woman of
the ancients—Ye gods ! To put out the fire of
love was to drag the Uranian Venus from the
Celestials and bury her beneath the sod. And all
this for wisdom's sake, and an Olympic view? Ah
no ! suffer she would, as did the poet of Lesbos who
stood on the Tarpeian rock—the fire of herself was
divine; she was Eve without temptation, from
whom the serpent had hid.

Rhea was a thrilling rhapsody, a tragedy, a song;

10

and yet,—the ice peak of Olympus! the wild New England shore! In her abandon, her passion, her misery, she forgot the square brow of the thinker, over which her brown hair had its way ; she forgot the icy stream of logic with which in times past she had deluged her fiery soul; she forgot her stern New England ancestry and the bleak winds of the Atlantic.

She was in Egypt, whose azure tints and daring skies revivified the woman of history, and warmed the blood of the ancient. She loved with that immortal, deadly, love which was not of the body but of the soul. Immortal, it would not die; deadly, it sought to slay itself. And *this* is tragedy. We view the victim of the knife and ball with horror; we turn our back upon the ghastly face and prate of tragedy—ha ! ha ! the spatter of blood—ha ! ha !

Suddenly, as though a vivid thunder-shower had changed into a sweep of falling snow, she felt the ice upon her brow and the freezing logic within. She was a frozen Labrador, over which the heat of the tropics had passed in another age. With the keen mind of the thinker she remembered her situation and prospects, crushing sentiment as does the Alpine climber the flower. She reasoned without mercy, and talked out loud in the stern voice of the judge.

"Who are you, Rhea Nellino, that you stand in the way of a man younger than yourself; who may, for aught you know, be a prince destined for a royal

bride, and a throne, or, if called to some sacred and
lofty vocation, what right have you to interfere, by
your passionate rhapsody and Hellenic romance.
'Tis absurd that you hold the episode of the Nile
as any but a passing fancy of one who has other
dreams, and visions which annihilate your own.
To be sure he loves you, but what of that; are there
not others besides yourself to whom he may
respond? Why demand of him a grand absorbing
passion, when heaven is full of stars, and the eyes
of a young man rove in enraptured gaze over them
all. You are selfish, Rhea Nellino; give up—abjure
—spurn!

   "But I can not!"—The lightning flashed again
amid the drifts of snow—" Can Cupid slay himself
with his own darts, even though Psyche hover
near?

   "Love is immortal! Aleppo, seek Olympus, stand
on its icy crest and freeze, yet must thou love me!
—Fly, fly to the very verge of heaven, and part us
by the abyss of space, yet wilt thou remember!—
Learn wisdom from the Master, sit at the feet of
the teacher who shall unroll the scroll of the ages
before thy astonished gaze, yet will my face appear
in every picture, though time shall never end!—
Challenge Isis, lift the sacred veil of the future
before her outraged eyes, yet me wilt thou see, as
far as thy dim vision stretches, even to the vanishing perspective of the years ahead!—Me! me!—
Rhea Nellino, coming, going, returning, vanishing!

—Though thou rise to the dignity of a priest or the
splendor of a prince; though alone on the desert
nursing the shame of illegitimacy, or lifted to a
position of power, always my face—mine !—Though
thou aimest to the breadth of vision of the Master
of Galilee, or the teacher of Benares, though thy
wisdom inundate thee with formulas and brace thee
with facts, though truth purify as with fire, still
wilt thou see me in a never ending dream !—
Though God doth wrap thee in veils till he himself
appear in the white light of his divinity, even there
will I make my way to stand before thee! I will
haunt thee in the stars ; each eye of heaven that
greets thine own shall flash my vision at thee till
all the blue above shall tell of me !—The deeps
shall reflect me, and my name shall echo in thine
ears *forever* and *forever !* "

She paused, and held her breath like an ecstatic
of Delphi; seeming to see Aleppo, with the eyes of
an entranced soul, and to him she spoke that
which was above reason, or within the range of
experience. She prophesied a transcendentalism
unknown to the mortal, and possible alone to the
god.

Out of the veering inconsistency of variety, she
sensed the changelessness of unity, which, like a
golden thread, ran through the shimmering pearls
of life. She had risen above herself, and in her
extremity of pain had seized upon the ultimate,
which is the love that never dies. Drawn by misery

to the brink of the gulf, which separates Psyche from Eros, she discovered the bridge of gossamer, finer than a spider's web, which spanned the depths of woe.

"Henceforth, Rhea," she said softly, "thy home shall be above; thou hast wings like the bird; thou shalt fly and rest on the mountain peak, like the eagle; thine eye, thou shalt train to far sight; and thine ear, to catch the echoes that come down the ages or over the waste. Hereafter, thou shalt drink from the spring of the river of life, and grow warm at the eternal flame."

CHAPTER XXIV.

THE YANKEE AND THE JEW.

"L'amour fait beaucoup, mais l'argent fait tout;" so spake Spino; but Regan failed to understand.

"Speak in English, please, he said, with a drawl.

"I mean that you can't beat the Jew. Love is mighty, but money is almighty. Your affection for Aleppo, with your Yankee wits thrown in, will be as nothing against Issachar, who works for gold."

"Has Issachar ever loved anybody?" asked Regan, with considerable curiosity.

"He!"

"Why yes, he!"

"How on earth should I know?"—she looked very sly and peculiar.

"Why on earth should you not! you're wise as a serpent."

"And harmless as a dove," she continued with a queer laugh.

"Apparently," said Regan; "anyhow, prove your good will by putting Issachar in my way, or me in his, I don't care which; you will get your reward, Madame Spino, on earth as well as in heaven."

"What do you mean by a reward?" she asked, shrewdly.

"Money, if you wish it."

"We don't want money, we desire to be captured, Cicily and I—stolen—kidnapped; we are waiting for you and Sallus to run off with us."

Regan whistled a few pensive notes, then scrutinized Spino from head to toe. "Is your husband dead, Madame?"

"Yes," showing her one tooth in a silent laugh.

"I was thinking," went on Regan, "that if Sallus takes Cicily, I shall have to run off with you."

Spino's laugh continued, even to the interior depths of her cavernous throat. "Shouldn't like that at all," she answered; "you're not after my fancy, I prefer the young man."

"That settles it," said Regan, "Sallus will have to elope with you and I'll take Cicily."

Madame Spino was no fool; she took all this as a huge joke, and treated Regan to the airs of an arrant coquette. She had evidently learned from Cicily, and appeared much as a monkey does when aping a pretty mistress.

It was impossible not to admire Spino; she realized her absurd grotesqueness so perfectly and took it so good-naturedly, transcending it in such a masterly fashion that she forced one to pay court to her subtlety and power, whether he desired to do so or not. She was, with all, so mysterious and hard to translate, that she held others by an uncanny fascination, not unlike that of a much abused witch.

"You wish me to bring about a meeting between yourself and Issachar," she said, abruptly changing her tactics.

"I do."

"When? Where?"

"Any time. Any place."

"Night or day?"

"I'm like a restaurant that's lighted up at all hours."

"Can you crawl through a two and a half foot hole, more or less?"

"Yes, any size; why?"

"Because Issachar wiggles into his den that way, and if you want an interview you'll have to stop that hole up with yourself, there's no other means.

"Suppose I get stuck there, what then?"

"You'll have to take your chances on that.

He's in Cairo again, and goes into his lair every night."

" Where is it?' '

" It opens out of the shop where he vanishes; it has a blue curtain hanging over it, with a big yellow dragon picked out in the stuff."

" Will he be on hand to-night? "

" Most likely, after ten, so I think; but I tell you its no use, you'll get nothing from him but smiles —he's the devil."

" So am I."

" Well, good-bye," with her corkscrew bow.

This all happened in Sallus' room a few minutes after the other interview in the same place, and Regan, fully determined to " beard the lion in his den," secretly informed Sallus of his daring scheme.

" Issachar has returned, and Spino has let me into the secret of the shop, which seems to swallow his body and soul every time he enters it; he must be a veritable cat, to go in and out of a hole after that fashion. The Madame says he is guarded by a yellow dragon, picked out in blue silk."

" How do you know," said Sallus, to whom Regan had given an accurate account of his interview with Spino, "but this is another trap set by the old woman herself? "

" Can't tell ; I comprehend one thing, though, loafing round and doing nothing is too much for me; we haven't got ahead an inch. Catus played me a pretty trick too; from what Spino says, I imagine he's in with the Jew. He acted to me as though ignorant as to the whereabouts of Aleppo, while he knew well enough that the boy had been at Issachar's very house. Cæsar didn't get out of Cairo any too soon. If you want anything done, do it yourself; that's my maxim from now on."

" How are you going to manage ? "

I'll slip into the shop about ten o'clock to-night; duck my head under the dragon, and squeeze through the aperture, if I have to stretch out a yard longer. It takes a Yankee to narrow himself and elongate. If Issachar can make it, I guess I can."

" When you get into whatever is behind that cat hole, what then ? "

"I'll leave the rest to luck and chance." said Regan. "I would take you along, but 'twouldn't do, you'd be one too many."

"Sure," said Sallus, " I'll be on hand, though, within call. I know your signal—understand."

The two men parted, and promptly at ten o'clock Regan walked into the little shop; he made a few purchases of the ever present dealer and politely requested him to step to the entrance, where a gentleman desired him to make some inquiries. The merchant, apparently with great innocence, turned his back on Regan, and began a confab with Sallus, who stood outside. It was the Yankee's chance; more quickly than it takes to tell it, he ducked under the dragon and confronted a little

door about four feet square and two from the floor; it
was a thin, paralleled arrangement, swung on light
hinges, and unfastened. Opening it without hesitation, and making a hump of his back, he got
through somehow, to find himself in utter darkness.
Extending his hands, he felt a wall on either side
of him, and presumed, from this, that he was in a
narrow passage leading to Issachar's room. He
stepped cautiously, and kept going farther and
farther away from the entrance.

"Wonder if this blamed rat hole will ever end,"
he muttered, between his teeth; he had no more
than said it, when he came against a second swinging door, which flew back, and sent him sprawling
into the den of the Jew.

The lion had evidently departed, for the room,
though lighted, was vacant. It was a low apartment, about ten feet square, and so stuffed with
odds and ends of great beauty that there was
scarcely space in it to turn around.

He scrambled to his feet, and found a pile of
cushions, upon which he sank like a wily Turk. A
dim candle, scarcely sufficient to see by, was but a
poor aid to his eyes, but he succeeded in making
the place out, after a fashion, and found it typical
of the Master, who came and went in such a mysterious way. The stuffs about him were of the
richest; while gold and silver bronzes and Damascan blades, to say nothing of manuscripts and
ancient books, gave the spot an ultra appearance,

even in Cairo. The diabolism of most of the
bronze specimens constituted their art. There
were grinning and frowning faces—monstrosities
more enigmatical than the Libyan sphinx, half
animal, half man; serpents and dragons, crouched
hyenas, and a startling array of cats, in every shape
and posture; all in a small room, whose ceiling was
scarcely seven feet high. Much of the brass was
green, having a slimy and slippery look, which,
as it threw off the dim light of the dripping candle,
took on the appearance of motion and life. A
scaly dragon seemed to undulate and crawl, while
a filthy frog puffed and breathed in hideous fashion.
The eyes of a coiled serpent glittered malignantly,
and a long-legged stork opened and closed its beak.
The place allowed of but little ventilation and the
air was heavy with carbon and dust.

Regan sat in the midst of this squalid wealth,
chewing his mental quid, and shivering perceptibly, although as a rule, not given to "nerves."

There was but one way to get out, and that was
by the door through which he had entered. The
creatures about him had become so animated and
repulsive, that he half made up his mind to crawl
away from the accursed spot on the instant; this
feeling was momentary, however, and summoning
his Yankee grit he dove down into his pockets, gaining courage from the cold touch of a Colt's revolver,
concealed inside. He remembered Sallus as a far-
off reality, that it would be difficult to reach in a

hurry; so slapping an intrusive cat in the face, and kicking over a brass crane, he stretched his long legs and stood up. It was none too soon; the door opened softly, and Issachar, looming nearly to the ceiling, confronted him with his eternal smile.

"Ah! How honored am I!"

"Indeed you are," said Regan, his hand on his pocket, where the cold steel nestled, "don't get a visitor like me every day, I suspect."

The composure of Issachar was beyond describing. He snuffed the candle, and arranged the pile of cushions, from which Regan had just risen, and said with great dignity, "My humble room is at your service; what will you have?"

In spite of his good cause, Regan felt somewhat ashamed; he had forced himself upon the Jew, who had received him very graciously with no show of fear or anger. Regan had desired a stormy interview, something to rouse his blood, but the Jew was as calm as a Cairo sky. The Yankee stammered a little and took his hand from his hip, for his host was unarmed, and, marshalling his thoughts, and seducing himself into the idea that he had a good quid in his mouth, he began—

"I am led to believe that you know something of the whereabouts of the young man, Aleppo Bracciolini, upon whom you called in Venice—hem!"

"And so thou camest here to inqure," said the Jew, politely. I am not accustomed to receive guests in this apartment, I beg thee to excuse its appearance and my lack of power to entertain; if thou wilt kindly walk up-stairs, I will introduce thee to my housekeeper and niece and make thee more comfortable.''

Regan forgot himself and spat at the bronze turtle on the floor near by; he was upset by the suavity of Issachar, which was something he had not bargained for.

"No, thank you, this place is good enough for me; besides I can't stay long; just answer a few questions, will you? ''

"Please put them," said Issachar.

"In the first place, do you know anything about Aleppo Bracciolini?''

"I have sought long for one Romanes, but found him not.''

"So you took Bracciolini in his place," said Regan.   I may as well speak to the point.   If it's money you're after, I'm as good a bank as any, unless it be a Rothchild or a Rockefeller; what will you take for him? ''

"Who?''   The eyes of the Jew glittered in the dim light like gold coins.

"The young man that you kidnapped at the temple of Ammon.''

"I fail to understand; I have kidnapped no young man.''

"Then appearances are deceptive; one Cæsar

Catus came to your house to inquire after him,
when you had him concealed up-stairs."

"Ah! Cæsar Catus!—how knowest thou that?"

"Watching around of course; I'm hunting
Aleppo, and I've traced him to you; there's no use
in evading any longer. I could have you arrested,
but there's too much red tape about it. I prefer to
turn criminal myself and buy you off; how much?"

The Jew looked keenly at Regan, then, with
superb dignity, brushing a speck from his immaculate robe, said, "I understand thee not at all. I own
a shop, wouldst thou buy something, go there."

"So you prefer to deal with those who are in the
web—the spider doesn't dive after worms like a
bird."

"Thou hast the Yankee metaphor," said Issachar showing all his teeth, " the American Indian
speaks the same; is there anything more?"

"Have you Aleppo Bracciolini?"

" No."

"Do you know where he is?"

" No'"

Regan refrained from referring to the women up-
stairs, but Issachar remarked in measured accent—

"Thou hast heard the gabble of my ancient
housekeeper, whose talk is well known in Cairo.
People listen for the sake of hearing, when Spino
speaks; she tells fables and fairy tales. Ah! she is
an eloquent one!"

"Well?"

"And my beautiful niece speaks as the madame dictates; they gossip both." He smiled again.

"What could Regan say; he, himself had suspected them. Was he, after all, accusing an innocent man? He had no particle of proof that could implicate Issachar, save the gossip of these two women, who might, for aught he knew, be amusing themselves. He could get no hold on the Jew; a bribe had no more effect than a threat. Was he on the wrong track, and were these foolish women up-stairs making a greater fool of himself.

Issachar had not even a vulnerable heel, he was a dignified host and slow to anger; nor could he be seduced by the jingle of coin, so thought Regan, who forgot not the experience of Sallus, when the Jew seemed to be playing the spy. Was it but seeming after all? Sallus had been unmerciful in his judgment, but did that prove anything? The Yankee was undone. In an open game he was a match for the devil, but under cover, an angel could master him at once.

"I'm sorry," said Regan, in a half-shamed voice, "that you can tell me nothing. I would give a good deal to find my young friend."

"Didst thou ever consider," said Issachar, in an impressive voice, "that probably the young man is dead?"

Regan looked with startled eyes at the Jew, but said nothing.

"He disappeared at Karnac, murdered, undoubt-

edly, for a sum of money, by an Arab, who afterwards concealed him under-ground." The Jew's
glittering eyes were on him. "Dead," said Issachar, "*dead*."

"Don't believe it," answered Regan, though he
shivered from head to foot, while the bronze Satan,
in front of him, grinned maliciously, and the
crouching dwarf rolled up his eyes. "Don't
believe it, but excuse me, Mr. Issachar, and I will
bid you good-night; you have a queer way of getting in and out of this place."

"It is my private apartment," said Issachar, in
a stately way, that abashed the intruder.

He opened the door, and held the candle at the
end of the passage, till Regan made his exit, crawl-
ing under the yellow dragon, into the shop, as
thoroughly beat a Yankee as ever misunderstood a
mysterious Jew.

Sallus was on guard outside, and looked greatly
relieved when Regan appeared.

"How did it turn out?"

"I'll be switched if I know. They're the
deucedest puzzle that ever I've struck—the whole
lot of them. Issachar played the rôle of a white
Mahatma, top notch. Compared with the dragons,
and snakes, and imps, and frogs and cats, inside, he
looked like the driven snow, more sinned against
than sinning." .

"There's no use in facing him, that's certain,"

answered Sallus; "hereafter we'll work behind his back."

"We wont gain a thing by that either, not a thing. I believe, now, that he knew I was coming; did you notice how innocent that shop-keeper appeared—too all fired innocent! Do you suppose Spino played a dirty trick on us after all?"

"I don't suppose anything any more, except that we've got into a web of mystery that's two sticky to get out of."

"It takes a Master to fight a Master. I'm no match for that Jew; good or bad. Good night, Sal; sleep if you can, I can't."

CHAPTER XXV.

QUICK ACTION.

Cæsar Catus left Henrique Romanes at Genoa and made his headquarters at Venice; here he wrote and got letters by the hundred, to say nothing of innumerable telegrams received and sent. His manner of living in the city of the Doges was entirely different from that of Cairo. His room, at one of the chief hotels, was a barren apartment, having more the appearance of a business office than anything else. He seemed to put off one nature and take on another as he did his clothes. He scarcely touched a cigar, and was painfully abstemious as to coffee and rich food; dispatching business with marvelous rapidity, and, from the amount of work accomplished, might well have been a dozen men in one.

He arose one morning, about a month after his exit from Genoa, and looked at his watch ; it was half past five. After a cold plunge and a rapid toilet he rang for his breakfast, which was served in his room. It was a simple affair—some crusts of French bread and a tiny cup of coffee, taken straight. Then going directly to his big table, which was loaded down with papers, letters and dispatches, he tore them open and read rapidly, one after another; mastering a page at a glance. After perusing, he sifted the letters, filing some, putting a peculiar mark on others, and throwing a large proportion into the waste basket. Three out of as many dozen, received his special attention; the first was from Genoa, signed "Nita." Catus read it twice.

" Dear Mr. Jackson :

"I got your letter this morning in answer to my last. If you hadn't sent it, I should have put on my paint and powder again. I hate to look in the glass; a woman who makes up appears like a scarecrow natural. It's easy living now, while your money lasts, though it's going fast. I couldn't help it, but I got another girl just like me to lay off and be good, so we go shares. I couldn't have staid here alone for anybody, not even you. Yesterday for a half-hour I was actually happy, at least I think I was, for I felt as I did once when a child. The other girl and I went out into the country; we slept well, and had a good breakfast, and promised each other not to speak of anything bad, so we went back to the time when we were good. I listened to .the birds, I don't know when I've heard them before; and I read her your first letter; she cried and I cried; we were both very happy.

" Perhaps you think reforming is easy, but it isn't.

"Please write soon.
                                            NITA."

Cæsar laid this letter aside carefully and his eye glittered; whether it were a steely glance, or a tear, it would have been hard to tell.

The next in the pile of latest arrivals was addressed in a strange hand, which he failed to recognize, and, turning the letter over, he held it to the light. The inscription was bold and strong— " Cæsar Catus, Cairo." It had been forwarded, and evidently the writer had no knowledge of his present address. He tried to get an impression from it before opening and succeeding somewhat he tore off the seal and read:

" *Dear Mr. Catus:*

" Have you forgotton Rhea Nellino? I met you once in Cairo, and have thought often of you since. It may seem absurd, my writing this letter; I act on intuition absolutely, and though I try my best to reason myself out of it, I feel certain that you know something of Aleppo Bracciolini, and perhaps out of sympathy for my sorrow, will answer frankly that which I ask. In the first place I am very unhappy and will tell you a secret which I have breathed to no other. Why I am so bold with a stranger I do not know. That I defy all conventionality I am well aware; that I act against the sound judgment of my two true friends, Mr. Patrick Regan and Mr. Sallus Smith, I am also certain, but I can bear this pain no longer, and in my extremity I appeal to you whom I know, somehow, can help me.

"I give you my sacred confidence; I love Aleppo Bracciolini even unto death, and my heart will break if I may not be permitted to speak with him once more. I ask but to see him again, once, only once, then, forever after, till life on earth is done, I will abide alone. Though I feel that I know and understand, yet would I verify and make sure. Oh, Mr. Catus, if you have ever loved, be kind to me. I realize that you are a man of great powers and a thousand resources; *help me!* I have nowhere else to turn; am shut up in myself alone.

RHEA NELLINO."

While reading this appeal, Catus turned very white; he was a fair visaged person as a rule, but he grew fairer, till the healthy glow of his face became a deathly pallor. He read it again, and again; the same ghastly expression on his face; then, rising abruptly left the room. After an absence of two hours, he returned and resumed the pile of letters so suddenly abandoned, still having the pallid look, but otherwise quite himself. The third epistle bore the peculiar stamp, which Catus instantly understood. The contents were emphatic:

"Meet Bedouin at Cairo; lose no time. New move about to be made. Act quickly; a day's delay fatal."

Catus closed his eyes and began to reckon. This letter had come from Brindisi; it would take him some time to get back to Cairo; he knew, however, that all had been considered, and that if he started forthwith there would be no mistake.

So, bringing out a strong box from the closet, he swept the table's whole burden into it, save the last three letters; then, turning the key, he restored the safe to its place and began to write. To Nita he addressed a full sheet, enclosing a draft; to Rhea the following :

"*Dear Miss Nellino :*

"Take heart; your instinct is correct; your intuition true. Rest on this for the present, and await word from me.   Yours,

CÆSAR CATUS."

To the third correspondent, after the date, was simply this :

"Will start to-day.   C. C."

As rapidly as steam could take him, Catus travelled to Cairo and proceeded immediately to the great pyramid of Khufu. It was already night, and the monster tomb shut off everything, even the sky. It seemed to encompass him, though he stood outside, and crush him with its mass of stone and weight of years. If Catus had a tendency to brood, he put a check upon it at once, and allowed no awe-inspiring pile of matter to turn him an iota from the object upon which he was bent.

This power to annihilate one environment and substitute another, is the gift of a great soul. To turn grandeur into the commonplace, or the small to the sublime, is a hard task, but Cæsar pulled on the reins with which he guided himself, and jerked the fiery steed of his imagination till he had it in hand; then scrutinizing along the shadow at the pyramid's base, he skulked, silently like a thief, till at the sharp turn of one of the angles he met a tall, draped Bedouin, who addressed him. in a whisper, speaking but *one* word, but it transfixed Catus where he stood. For a moment there was an ominous silence, broken later by Catus, who gave the man near him a sign, for their hands touched and parted; then they walked out from the shadow into the open, where the majesty and silence of the desert could be felt.

"I must go with you to-night?" said Catus.

"Immediately; the camels are ready; the Arabs waiting; thou shalt eat and sleep to-morrow."

" Are you sure you are prepared—armed, ammunition, food and water ? "

" All," said the Bedouin.

" And the *young Master ?* " said Catus, his voice trembling.

"Great," came back the solemn voice of the Bedouin, who marched straight ahead, with long strides, his figure erect, while his flowing robes gave majesty to a stature far above that of the ordinary man.

" How know you this—what sign? "

" The test, too hard for thee, was naught to him. Thou hast had the training of a few short years; the great planet Saturn has scarce past its perihelion and returned to its distant companions in space since thou began.

" And he? " said Catus anxiously.

" Ah! " said the Bedouin, "seest thou that sun ? Already he understands El Reshid, but in time, El Reshid will gaze upward at him, as thou dost at yon dog star.

" How comes it that one so young has attained so great a height; he must indeed be immature and without experience," urged Catus.

"He matured long since; he experienced much in another life."

A silence fell between the two; the Bedouin marching on guided by instinct, without compass, track or chart, while Catus walked in his wake in a dream.

"And Issachar?" said Catus after a pause of some minutes."

"Issachar is naught to me."

"It is not so easy to count him out; El Reshid himself, knows this." Catus manifested his first impatience since leaving Venice, but the Bedouin deigned no answer and strode ahead.

In less than an hour they reached an Arab camp where camels were in readiness for immediate departure. Catus was hungry and very tired, besides this there was a worm gnawing at his heart. He felt himself abused, wronged; he had worked hard and done much and that which he most desired went easily to another who seemed to do nothing at all. But below all this surface of fretfulness and fume was the fixed purpose from which he never swerved. Reward, punishment, joy, sorrow were out of consideration in the final analysis. So mounting his camel, on which he sat familiarly, he fell into file and wended his way under the stars toward the spot where Aleppo Romanes watched for his coming with longing eyes.

It was late the next day ere they halted before a group of skin tents pitched on the waste of Libya.

Catus alighted from his camel and uncovering his head approached the largest of these; looking keenly from under his brows for some sign of Aleppo whom he had known as a Bohemian youth in the art studio in Italy. He remembered well his ideal face, dark hair, and innocence of expression, the like of which is seldom beheld in a man. As he drew near the door of the tent, he felt that there would be a difference, and was conscious of Aleppo even before he appeared, as if the very sands could speak.

' The Bedouin had passed on and only Cæsar remained to greet his friend. He waited but a moment when the young man appeared, slighter and less robust than in the days of blessed memory, yet more powerful than Catus could have deemed possible. He stood before him erect and thrilling, his eyes beaming into those of Catus, brilliant with pure love, though, save the look, he made no demonstration, except to touch his head and his heart. The two went into the tent and what was said there, none but themselves will ever know. In an hour's time Catus came forth and went straight to the quarters of the Bedouin.

" At what time do we start to night ? "

" At two o'clock." .

" Give me food," said Catus.

An Arab appeared immediately with a substantial meal, which Catus devoured as though famished; then turning to the Bedouin again,—" I must rest."

A skin tent was spread on the ground upon which Catus threw himself, to fall immediately to sleep.

The Bedouin faced the Arab—" Be ready," he said; " forget nothing." Wake this man on the minute; have the camels at hand; put thy brother

on guard; walk like a cat. The servants of Issachar
suspect nothing; travel due east; halt at the tomb
of the sacred bulls, and Allah reward thee."

The Arab threw a quick glance at the Bedouin
when he uttered the last sentence, never before
having heard him refer to Allah; but he said nothing,
and silently performed the task assigned him with
the agility of a monkey and the suppleness of a cat.
At the time designated, to the minute, he touched
the sleeper softly with his velvety hand; Catus
arose, left his tent, mounted his camel without
noise, and immediately joined the rest of the party
who were waiting near by. Upon another animal
sat Aleppo Romanes, equipped for a long ride.
When everything was in readiness the ghostly
caravan wended its way into the dark of night
headed due east.

CHAPTER XXVI.

ON THE CAMEL'S BACK.

Catus and Aleppo rode side by side, or as nearly
so as the camels allowed, exchanging now and then
a word, or keeping silent as circumstances necessitated. They had before them but a twenty hour's
journey to Cairo, as the tents of Issachar had lately
been pitched nearer civilization.

As soon as the gray light of dawn stole softly
over Libya, Catus came close to Aleppo and placed

in his hands a letter. The young man's eyes were strong and he picked out the writing, Catus watching the expression on his face while he read:—

ILLUSION.

We see men hurrying to and fro like gnats in the sunshine, and pronounce judgment with cool indifference. They are six feet tall, more or less, and from two to three feet broad, going and coming as though each were dispatched by the Absolute; a walking mass of skin and bone and sinew and blood; in so-called civilized lands subject to his tyrant—the tailor; in Barbaria, to his tyrant—the sun.

And we call this six-foot medley of flesh and garment an entity; this stiff, sharp sliver from the "tree of life," a universe; this conglomerate of molecules, darting here and there in the sunshine, an immortal.

We see him falling to pieces before our eyes ; we watch the elongated hole, as the sexton plunges his spade into earth; we behold the weeds and flowers upspringing from the soil of his vitals; and in face of this, we pronounce him eternal. Whence he came, we know not; whither he goeth, we wonder.

He crushes the little beneath his feet, while the great tramples him to earth. He steals from the universe and condenses into himself, to give back with absolute exactness that which he purloined. A shifting phenomenon, he impresses us with a sense of stability, till we take him for a fact, in spite of the sexton and the spade.

We read his age on the tomb-stone, and scornfully glance at the angel above his grave, whose spread wings are of marble which the ethers repudiate. Yet while he is rotting, and the worms are feasting, we hear his voice in our ears, and feel his touch on our cheeks.

When he is turned into ashes, we gather the handful of dust, WHICH NO FIRE CAN DESTROY, and store it away. And what of this handful of dust—listen ! the six feet of flesh—an *illusion;* the handful of dust—the *eternal.*

By the Unit of Force stands its opposite—the finality of matter—the ashes that fire cannot burn, nor effort destroy.

Within this handful of dust, energy wakes like a whirlwind. A spiral, it fleeth and gathereth, till it grows from a mite to a mountain of sinew and organs and bone—six feet of illusion, packed and bedded around the immortal—the ashes—the handful of fact, that no fire can destroy.

But man, with the blear on his eyes, sees naught but the fiction; he builds it an altar, and sits at its feet, and prays at its tomb, while the real is concealed out of sight, like the scent of the flower. It evades, it is subtle, and scorneth the fire.

We worship the fiction—the flesh and the blood; we build it a temple, a mosque; we paint it with colors, and stud it with gems; we pour our wine on

the ground at its feet; with ointment and spikenard
we deluge its head. The illusion is set on a throne,
while fact—the eternal, is hid in the urn.

But listen! Even change, which shifts like the
beams of the moon on the lake, even change is
reality masked, a chimera of law, a fiction of truth,
an enigma of unity, budding to flower; the corolla
and scent of the root underground.

Even change, translated by one who is wise, is a
verity, stripped of the false, and glittering with
gems. 'Tis Isis in color—the plumes of the
peacock, the opal, the pearl, the gem of all gems,
the Sirius in heaven—the magnet of stars.

*　　　*　　　*　　　*　　　*　　　*　　　*

But man, who beholds through the lashes of his
eyes, lives and dies in a fatal dream; he sacrifices to
the down of the peach, forgetting the bitter power
of the stone; he worships the flower, unaware of
the root; he discovers but *half* of the one, and
makes of the whole a delusion.

He chisels his wings out of marble, and
hammers his plumes out of bronze; he imprisons the
ethereal in the vault of the base, and traps his
ideal in a pit.

To the wise, the illusion lies in the crescent, when
the bulk of the moon is concealed.

*　　　*　　　*　　　*　　　*　　　*　　　*

Having studied the paper carefully, Aleppo stored
it away in a secret pocket of his garment, and

giving Catus a confidential glance, faced the rising
sun which appeared suddenly and defied his steady
eyes that dared to look straight at its heart.

"And his name is El Reshid," said Aleppo.

"Yes," answered Catus, "it signifies the pasha
—the ruler—the Master; it stands for power over
self and others; the first, as you know, implies the
last; the master of one's self has to a degree the
control of others."

"If all individuals were self-mastered there
would be no controlling of anybody," said Aleppo.

"True, but the mass of people have approxi-
mately no self control, and those who have, rule
others."

"What do you mean by self-mastery?" asked
Aleppo.

"Having one's self in hand, controlling one's
self."

"Ah no," said Aleppo; "use no more the word
control, but substitute the word guide; the Master
guides himself. Is there a man on earth that can
hold a fiery steed, if the creature determines to run?
Tug at the bit, bring your whole power of muscle
and will to bear, it is nothing to the mad brute that
spurns the earth and drags you after him. So with
yourself, in reality you admit no Master; even self
revolts against self—and takes the bit in its teeth
and runs—runs; but "—tossing his hair and smiling
in boyish confidence, "guide, that is all, and let self
realize its full speed, no matter how fast it goes,

nor with how much vim and rush it tears along the avenues of life, if it keeps out of the ditches and ruts; guide—guide.

"How queerly so much learning sets on your young head; already you wear a professor's cap."

"Learning is not after my fancy," said Aleppo. "To learn is to accumulate. I would rather have a vacant room, than one too crowded. There is an art of unknowing, as well as of knowing; of getting rid of, as well as of acquiring. Learning is a rubbish unless it be a means to an end. The learned man is seldom wise; he is pedantic, narrow, bigoted. A wise man on the contrary understands people and things, more, even life itself and its meaning."

"I suppose," said Catus, "that he has the Shakespearean quality, and reads human nature like an open book."

"True; he is one with his environment and enters to the heart, the motive, the purpose of things; he lives the life of each, of all; he grasps it specially and generally; he is everything—*he is it*."

"Will you tell me" said Catus, rather reverently for him, "how you grew suddenly to understand so well; I can't remember that in Italy you were overburdened with wisdom."

"Do you not realize," answered Aleppo, "that when you are thrown back upon pure reason that you get a revelation, not from reasons nor reasoning, but *the Reason*. Sometimes one may be stripped so naked that he beholds his very vitals—his hear 𝓣 palpitates before his eyes, his skeleton, sinews, muscles, all are revealed. He has no garment to cover him, nor even a soft padding of flesh, he is thin, transparent, the interior mechanism, with the reason thereof stares him in the face.

"Catus, dear old teacher of Italy, I began without parents, country, or name, and, as though that were not poverty enough, whatever of love and friendship were mine, were taken also. At last I stood outside of the great temple of Ammon, stripped of all, and then there flashed over me a light, as dazzling as that which struck St. Paul on the way to Damascus; in the glare of it I saw the *Reason*, the meaning of myself. Since then I have thought little of learning, and sought wisdom, which is the principal thing."

"I would that I might have such an experience," said Catus, looking aggrieved and anxious.

"The causes in your case are different. To find one limit you must be driven to another; an extreme implies its opposite. You have never been cold enough to worship fire, nor hungry enough to gnaw your own flesh; you have never been so alone that you made two of yourself, nor so frightened that courage was your last resort. I went to the very verge of fancy, to rebound to the ultimate Fact. I soared so high in my dream-balloon, that when it burst, I plunged like a falling star, clear into the bed-rock of earth. I had become such a fool that wisdom had me in its very grip—the youth and the sage are one. The Master of Syria taught the self-asserting Jew that he must become as a little child. In truth, Catus, I've been stripped of my self-conceit, that is all."

" And I have not?"

" No, you have not," answered Aleppo, gazing with great love on his friend, " but you have vast powers."

" So had Romanes," said Catus.

" Who was Romanes?" asked Aleppo, with a start, looking keenly from under his broad hat at Catus.

" Your father."

Aleppo turned very white. " I am unworthy of my father and mother. I repudiated them both. Until that time comes that I deserve, I fear to know them."

" I fail to understand you," said Catus.

" I have inwardly hated and cursed them," said Aleppo; "first, for thrusting a life of isolation upon me, and second, for casting me adrift."

" Are you still in the same mood?"

" No, Catus, in my present consciousness of life, things and ideas conventional mean but little. I realize that at the very source of my stream of existence there was a pure and sparkling spring, stronger, more crystal—because it was nature's own—than the muddy fountain of most individual existences doomed to live and die on earth. I have

11

lately learned to love my mother, my beautiful, beautiful mother." Aleppo looked earnestly at Catus, with tears in his eyes. "Do you know, my friend, I believe she is dead—I feel her presence at times, as though she touched me. She used to hate me, I am sure, but she loves me now, persistently, entirely. I believe she is dead."

"She is," said Catus.

"How know you that?"—he turned quickly.

"So said Romanes."

"Ah!"

For a full half-hour they rode silently; no word was spoken.

"Cæsar," said Aleppo, at last, "my father— shall I yet see my father?"

"If we escape this accursed Jew."

"I fail to understand you," said Aleppo.

"Of course you understand that you were kidnapped at Karnak."

"No, you mistake; I went with Issachar of my own free will. I was taken ill and he brought me down the Nile to Cairo. He may have drugged me, I presume that he did, but I had agreed to go with him to my parents. Afterward, I decided to do differently, to visit Damascus, and he objected, holding me to my original proposition, and I am simply running away. I had a horror of Issachar, but it has gone; he has been kind and just with me, and though I realise that the love of power is

the prime motive [in [his case, yet will I not condemn him unfairly.''

'' May it not be money ? '' said Catus.

'' In that you mistake him again,'' said Aleppo;
'' money with him is a means to an end; nor is he
a miser.   Power over circumstances and men, is
his aim—and revenge, perhaps, his object.''

'' I take issue with you.   Issachar is a black
magician.''

'' Nevertheless,'' answered Aleppo, '' if power is
at the base of white magic, it must be at the bottom of black also.   Even the word magic is a mis-
nomer to all save the ignorant.''

They halted for breakfast.   It was quickly
over; there was no time to lose.   Once mounted
and moving again, they renewed their conversation.

'' If we succeed in getting to Damascus you will
sit at the feet of El Reshid,'' said Catus.

'' Cæsar, you have had a good teacher,''—Aleppo
beamed on him with one of his fascinating smiles
—'' but, after all, one can help another but little.
Experience is the schoolmaster and nature is the
mother Mahatma in whose lap we sit.''

'' That is all very well, Aleppo, but everybody
is experiencing—everybody, not a soul escapes ; if
not in one way, he gets his training in another :
yet, there are but few Masters.''

'' In that you are right.   The teacher gives you
the first few rules in arithmetic, and you work out
the problems for yourself.   A master knows the for-

mulas, which are the result of empiricism ; the
novice practices by them, and possibly discovers
another receipt for himself.   The teacher is necessary, but in time he goes his way; experimental
knowledge, however, is yours while life lasts.''
   " Still you will go to El Reshid.''
   '' Still will I go to El Reshid.   I am young—but
a boy; my experience has been but slight, and in
much, negative; in all save determination and a
consciousness of my true self, I am as ignorant as
a child just learning to walk.   Ah! when first I
catch sight of the domes and minarets of Damascus; when I scent the flower-breath of Syria, and
walk by the side of El Reshid, I shall feel the joy
of one who talks with a Master and holds council
with a god.''
   '' How do you know all this; no one has told
you? ''
   '' From the touch of his letters, from the impulse,
the power.   Have you ever beheld El Reshid ? ''
   '' Yes, once, but you will be disappointed ; he is
but a simple man, even smaller in stature than
yourself.   You doubtless expect to meet an aged,
long-bearded doctor of theology, or psychology,
or religion.   El Reshid is nothing of the sort; he
is a person of affairs—a man among men; he dis-
dains the robe of a priest and dons that of a civilian ; nor does he drip sanctity from his finger-tips,
nor is he unctuous, nor sophomorically religious,
nor professional.   Altogether, I presume you have

built a man of straw, that will tumble when you look at him."

At this, Aleppo laughed—they both laughed. " Hast thou known me so long, to treat me thus?" said Aleppo, with a grandiloquent air. "Surely, thou dreamest not that I seek a Parsee priest, or a Dominican monk. After that which I have said to thee to-day, thou must be mad—but look!"

Both men stared eastward, over the desert.

" Is it a caravan ?" said Catus.

" I think not," Aleppo answered; " there seem to be many horses; they travel faster than our camels."

" Halt!" shouted Catus, bringing the five Arabs of their party, with their animals, to a sudden standstill. " To arms!"

Each man of them scrutinized his revolver, and glanced along the edge of his knife.

" I would that the Bedouin were with us," said Catus.

" And I."

"I am ignorant in this business; are you sure that these Arabs are faithful?"

" Hardly," said Aleppo, "the Bedouin was an enemy in Issachar's camp, but it is hard to fix an Arab—Ah!"

"Do you not see the stately form of Issachar? With what dignity he sits astride his horse! though I fail as yet to discern his features, about that figure I have no doubt."

'' The devil's to pay ! '' said Catus between his teeth, taking a cigar from his pocket and viciously biting off its end.

'' Even if these five Arabs are loyal and true they will be as nothing against twenty mounted men,'' said Aleppo. '' Issachar will take me by force, but have no fear, Catus, for sometimes the weak get the better of the strong.''

They were coming nearer. The five Arabs grew restless and exchanged glances, showing a woeful lack of courage and determination. In a short time the mounted men with the Jew leading rode along beside the small caravan that made no resistance whatever. '' The faithful '' had given the lie to the appellation and neither used their revolvers nor knives.

'' Shall I shoot him down ? '' said Catus to Aleppo as Issachar rode toward them.

'' For the love of El Reshid, *no!* what could you gain ? Those Arabs would tear us to pieces; our camels are but slow beasts.''

Never had Issachar appeared so superb. On a magnificent Arabian horse which he completely held in check, his outer robe abandoned, and his closely fitting undergarments exposing his matchless physique, his eyes glittering with mockery, his teeth all displayed, he glanced over the pitiful array of humpy camels and shriveled Arabs, with the imperial gaze of a conquerer, who designs no explanation and offers no excuse.

" Well " said Catus sneeringly.

" Well," came the reply with that ineffable smile.

" What would you have ?"

"Aleppo Romanes."

"How did you track us," said Catus bitter with impatience, at the same time throwing away his cigar and cocking his revolver.

" Trust Issachar for that; the bird needs no chart nor compass to cross the ocean; the bee can find its hive."

" Let me deal with him, "said Aleppo dismounting; " So you would take me again."

"I would," said the Jew; "did I not bargain to deliver thee to thy father ?   Issachar never breaks his word."

"And did I not inform you," answered Aleppo looking him full in the eyes, "that I desired first to go to Damascus; am I not a man of age ?"

" Thy birthday is of little account to me— mount !"

" A revolver was fired into the air as a signal, and Catus seized from behind and disarmed; then Aleppo was lifted into the saddle of a pawing, foaming-mouthed Arabian horse and lashed to its back; his arms being taken from him and his hands tied. The five Arabs in the meantime had yielded their pistols and knives with a willingness too suggestive to be misunderstood. Then the Jew turned to Cæsar Catus, who had lost his temper and was white with rage.

"I have no need of thee; proceed to Cairo; these Arabs are safe guides. Report to the authorities, set the hounds of Egypt on my track, yet Issachar thou wilt not find.   March on ! "

But Catus shouted over his shoulder as they rode away—"A hound there is that will be one too many for you; even *Satan* fears El Reshid."

CHAPTER XXVII.

A GRIP ON SELF.

O moon ! if but my heart were cold like thine,
If all my glow were but reflected light,
If icy heights were only mine, ah mine !
How calmly would I gaze on thee to-night.

Rhea watched the full orb ascend the wondrous blue of an Egyptian sky, and longed for the cold, the death, the calm of the moon, when desire should turn to ashes and the hot passion of the soul to ice. She strove to forget Aleppo, but found it as impossible as to annihilate self; he was the *Response* of which she had always been conscious even when she knew him by no name nor person. Alas, it was still the same—she felt him, she realized, yet with a difference. He had gone away out of the path in which she traveled to another where she longed to follow, but in vain.

They had left the great hotel and taken a little house where Mrs. Hancock was more content.

Rhea had come out to the veranda on this wonderful night, and, like a rare, cold wraith with folded hands, she sat under the flood of lunar glory, all her anguish condensed and glowing in her eyes.

A young man came rapidly toward her up the path of the yard, and removed his hat. In the vague light she failed at first to recognize him, then with a quick throb of the blood, knew it to be Cæsar Catus. She gave him both hands, then offered him a chair by her side, and waited, breathless.

If Rhea had been beautiful as a "giddy girl," she was more tantalizing and distracting now.

A woman thrilled by a grand passion, touched by the finger of destiny, doomed to tragedy, is bound by the very nature of herself to intoxicate and enthral others—She is a consuming fire and the sparks fly; she is a still frenzy that sends its vibration to the depths of man's soul.

At the touch of her hand Cæsar temporarily forgot his errand, was false to Aleppo, and repudiated the Order. As their eyes met he seemed to see the river Lethe flowing, winding, coiling, in that calm shadowy elysium where death claims its phantom bride. She was consuming herself and he longed to plunge into the flame.

The dangerous charm of such women as Rhea is more often felt than acknowledged. It is subtle, beyond analysis; and has its bases in the pure passion of soul which knows no outlet through the

channel of the gross; it is the fiery heat of the
heart's center thrown off through the glance and
touch; it is the extreme of feeling that in its reaction has power to harden to ice.

Catus should never have seen nor approached
her, for to him she was dangerous. With the demi-
monde he associated freely, striving to help and
reform; and came and went among them as unsullied as a Christ. But this living poem, Rhea,
chaste as snow, yet paradox of paradox, burning
with the inextinguishable fire of Vesta, was overwhelming to the heart of Catus. When first he saw
her, he fell in love, and since, for months he dreamed
and hoped, till that bitter day in Venice, when she
told him by letter the little secret that well nigh
broke his heart. But Catus was a man of many
sides—a diamond that flashed in all tints; he lived
numerous lives, and traversed star after star where
Eve was not.

The two, Cæsar and Aleppo, had never mentioned Rhea to each other. It is the habit of men
of fine feeling to keep silence on such subjects,
deeming them sacred.

Catus had come to Rhea to tell her of her lover,
to answer her letter in person, to put himself to the
test, and here he was by her side in the glamour of
the moon, beneath the trellis of roses, gazing into
her fathomless eyes. For the time being, she was
his; Aleppo was lost, perhaps dead, why not tell
her so, and catch the bird with broken wings as it

fell; for comfort she would lean on him—his breast;
O bliss ! · To gaze and gaze into her eyes, to read
and feel her soul day after day—away philosophy;
farewell reason ! adieu sweet dream of Damascus,
and the white peak of Olympus! A frenzy of
passion, a burning look, a kiss, outweighs them all !

But above this seething volcano of his heart sat
loyalty enthroned. He had a friend, Aleppo
Romanes, a *friend;* he had stood once in the
presence of El Reshid, and more, he had sworn
fealty to truth. He turned his eyes from Rhea to
the cold moon—a man sometimes does in a moment
the work of years;—he fixed his gaze in despera-
tion on the lunar peaks, lofty, frozen, rigid, *and
became like unto them.* Rhea felt the chill and drew
herself away; half frightened she turned her glance
from Catus and fixed it on a withered rose.

"Miss Nellino, I have lately seen Aleppo
Romanes."

She trembled, but said nothing.

"He was taken by Jacob Issachar, a Jew, and
concealed on the desert; rescued, a few days ago,
by a Bedouin and myself, to be captured again
some miles out from Cairo."

He related, in a cold business voice, what
he knew of the lover of Rhea up to the day
that Issachar had retaken him. And all the
time that he talked he kept his eyes fixed on
the lunar peaks, knowing that this rebound in
himself was only temporary, and that, later, he

would have a battle to fight. To Rhea he seemed
unsympathetic, unkind; in a sense she was indig-
nant. Strange, too, the history of Aleppo in no way
surprised her; it was as she had supposed, even to
his desire to go to Damascus, and was but a con-
firmation of the profound intuition, from which her
sorrow had sprung.

Cæsar wondered if, after all, her love for Aleppo
was but shallow, she seemed so little impressed by
the tale he had told.

" Mr. Catus,"—she was rigid, like a statue—
" does Mr. Bracciolini propose to join some mystic
order and devote his life and energy to the same ? "

" He has never so stated to me. "

" Why, then, does he seek the instructions of
one whom you call El Reshid, and fly from his
friends and me ? "

" I suppose, said Catus, " he feels that the revelation made to him by Issachar, at Karnak, has cut
him off from the world of conventional love and
friendship, and forced him to philosophy. "

" Issachar did not abduct him ? "

" So Aleppo stated; but there is no doubt about
the second taking off, it was a capture. "

" When he was here, Mr. Catus, at the house of
the Jew, why did you not call the authorities and
release Aleppo ? " said Rhea, severely.

" I was uncertain whether he were here or not ;
I had a suspicion that he might be, from some facts
that I had gathered, so I called at Issachar's shop

and met Spino. The old housekeeper informed me that a young man was above stairs. From her description of him I felt quite certain that it was he; then I went off, to return later, with a detective and officers in wake, but the woman announced that Issachar and his prisoner had departed. I instituted a private search in my own way, and later, through the help of others, with whom I associated, discovered his whereabouts. The Bedouin in charge of Issachar's tents is a spy in his camp and a friend of my own; whether Issachar knows this or not no one can tell ; Issachar's innermost thoughts are a sealed book, and his character also, for that matter." There was a long pause; Rhea said nothing and Catus looked at the moon, finally Rhea broke the silence with this startling question—

"When can I see Aleppo?"

"That is hard to answer, Miss Nellino. I have no idea where the Jew has concealed him, nor whether we are more than a match for Issachar. I shall let you know everything, however."

Catus has kept a good grip on himself thus far, but the strain was telling. To stand by this beautiful sufferer and freeze her, because he dare not do otherwise for fear of himself, was a cruelty too refined, even for a man of his nerve. He could bear his own pain, but to witness hers also, conscious that she misunderstood and accused him, was a test that he felt he had better dispense with. He

knew himself well; should he condole with her.
love would speak from his eyes, his whole being
would betray it; he rose quickly—

"Miss Nellino, everything will be done to rescue
Aleppo, by those most interested. Issachar is powerful, yet I believe there are others more so. Be
assured that I shall send you whatever encouraging news we get, good-night."

He had gone. Rhea's misery lay, not so much
in the personal absence of her lover, as in her
struggle with herself; she suffered also from the
apparent indifference of Catus. The souls of most
men she read quickly, but here was a sphinx. That
he loved her, she never dreamed; that he was cold
and unkind there was no denying; the origin of
this apparent iciness puzzled her also. Was it but
seeming—did he wear a mask?

In her generally confused state she stood dazed,
before the great problem of love and life, powerless to summon her reason or subdue her passion,
yet, in all this medley and incoherence, she was conscious that she and Aleppo loved eternally, and
were parted fatally.

"If I were to die," she said to herself, "it is
possible that we might meet—but this living—
living!" The thought struck her fancy—"if I
were to die—even though I prayed to Aleppo, even
though I forced him to remain near, he would be
wretched for my sake; though I cared not a whit
for family or name, he would care. I am not good,

like Aleppo; the spritual heights are too far.   No
power can keep me from him in thought, memory,
love—but oh, to touch his hand!   For your whole
life, Rhea Nellino, you are widowed—your husband is in heaven and you wear black.   The years
are so many.   Oh, God! is it wrong to take one's
life ? "

   "Yes, said a strange voice, apparently at her
side.   She turned quickly, there was no one near ;
the veranda was empty, save the chairs.

   "Who was that?" she asked, in a whisper; but
there came no answer, and everywhere was stillness, like the grave. She was shocked to the center
of herself, and clung to the rail for support; her
face white as the dead, her tragic, frightened eyes
glowing like twin stars; then a strange thing
happened; clairvoyantly, like a memory, there
appeared on her mental horizon the form of a man;
it was an interior picture, and to get it better, she
covered her face with her hands; his intense eyes
were fixed on her, as though to hold, in their fires,
her very soul, and under their persistent gaze she
grew serene, as if she had become himself, and
viewed all things with his far-seeing glance.   A
smile stole over her lips as she thought of the
coming years—"*so few*," he seemed to say, "so
few!" What he thought, she thought; what he
felt, she felt; and then, in the depths of her consciousness she realized El Reshid, who had com-
manded the surging flow of her soul to subside;

who had transformed the muse of tragedy to a
patron saint of song; who had brought harmony
out of chaos, and life out of death.

She neither reasoned nor questioned; the heathen
had found her idol, the Pagan her sacred shrine.

How he had impressed her, how he had reached
her, she had no idea; whether by mind's subtlety,
which, being the opposite of matter, works by
reverse laws, whether by pure will, or inexplicable
sympathy she knew not.   He had come—the sun
had flashed on the night—and lo, the day!

CHAPTER XXVIII.

THE CONFUSION OF TONGUES.

"I believe in the tower of Babel," said Regan.

"Why?" asked Sallus who had settled himself
for a comfortable evening in his den.

"Because the confusion of tongues must have
started somewhere, and Babel was as good a place
as any."

They were living together in Sallus' room
opposite to the house of Issachar; had spent a
whole day in fixing it up, and it was literally loaded
with bazaar wares picked out in a hurry.   The
place was an improvisation—a sort of four-handed
duet in which Sallus and Regan took part.

The flies had been driven out, screens placed in

the windows, and the floor covered with oriental
·rugs, while a couple of divans were so arranged
that they answered both for night and day. They
had a coffee pot, an alcohol lamp, Turkish candies
and bon bons; altogether between the two they
made a cozy place of it, and chumming as they did,
were devoted to each other. Sallus· continued to
look upon Regan as the greatest of philosophers
and drew him out on all occasions.

"No matter what kind of a study you take up,"
went on Regan, "you are pestered to death with
long names; if it's botany your memory is punished
with Leontodon, Taraxacum, Sarothamnus, Scopa-
rarius, Janipha, Manihot, etc., as though corolla
and pistils and stamen were not slanderous enough
without blaspheming flowers and plants in that
way. If you tackle biology you make your evolution even uglier than it ought to be by disgracing
the process with kinetogenesis, Brachiopoda, Cin-
cinulus, and lots more. The heavens have to suffer
too; astronomy gets in its S-Z-N-3—S-3-P-N-Z.
But psychology gives us the biggest dose, especially
when it goes around in guise of mental science,
magnetic healing and oriental occidentalism ;
under that latter we have Sanskrit words that make
our jaws ache—regular mouthfuls. I tell you Sal
the tower of Babel was no joke. For my part I
can't imagine what sort of a teacher 'twould be who
would come out and talk plain English, just speak
like other people without a sprinkling of scientific

terms, or Hindu provincialism, or Arabian dialect, to
say nothing of Pali. Wisdom looks mighty absurd
spouting such ear-splitting syllables; in fact I sometimes doubt if it is wisdom at all that does it.
Besides there's the ranting, as if a man was obliged
to lengthen his face an inch or more, and assume a
punctilious drawl whenever he talks on religion, or
life after death; the air doesn't need sawing as I
know of, when salvation's talked about, or hell.
What on earth a man rises on his toes for, to sink
on his heels, when he speaks in the vernacular of
the saints, is beyond me. Sanctimoniousness goes
along with preachers as smiles do with pretty
women, they study for it I tell you my boy, both of
them; they train their voices to oiliness and unc-
tuousness just as women teach themselves to
laugh.''

'' That's the gospel truth,'' said Sallus.

'' Sure,'' went on Regan, '' once in a while there's
an exception though, and to that blessed exception
I take off my hat—always; he's as refreshing as a
thunder shower that means business. When a man
speaks plain English or French or anything, I don't
care whether he's biologist, psychologist, archaeolo-
gist, physiologist, to say nothing of religionist, I
believe in that fellow and feel pretty certain that he's
in dead earnest. Words ought to be fired at you like
bullets; 'twould be a mighty smart man though, that
could shoot one of those Sanskrit jaw breakers so
'twould hit anywhere. Science makes a fool of itself,

too; when a man gets stuck on a problem and don't
know where he's at, whether it's the germ theory
or some other, he just fills his mouth up with big
words and spews them at you; when they are so
almighty large that they can't find entrance, he just
crawls into them, and when he's hard put, they're
a regular place of refuge.   I tell you that sort of a
person thinks he's smart, and he is too, after a
fashion; he deludes nine people out of ten every-
time, impressing them so that they hold their
breath and inwardly curse themselves for ignor-
amuses.   Talk about swearing, it is nothing, my
boy, nothing to this sort of blasphemy."

" What are you going to do about it," said
Sallus.

"That's the fix I'm in, I don't know; if ever I
find a fellow though, that can cut off a word in
regular staccato, I'll build a big hall and set him
going.—Come in ! "

The door opened, and Cæsar Catus entered.
Both Sallus and Regan received him very coldly,
neither bidding him welcome nor offering him a
chair.   Cæsar paid no attention to the breach of
courtesy, but to the inward admiration of Regan,
used but few words and went straight to the point.

" I've come to rid your mind of suspicion, and to
set myself in the right light before you, for I need
your help."

" Well? " said Regan, tersely.

" You have been led to believe that I am hand

and glove with the Jew—Jacob Issachar; you are
mistaken. I discovered and rescued Bracciolini,
to lose him again near Cairo."

There !" said Regan, turning triumphantly to
Sallus, "I told you so!" Then both men rushed
at Catus, each grabbing a hand; he was not in an
effusive humor, however, nor would he sit down,
but stood near the door, as though ready to depart.

"There's no use in your staying here to watch
for Issachár; he will not return, at least, while we
three are in Cairo. He'll get to Constantinople,
if I'm not mistaken, and hide young Romanes in
the canine capital. You know Stamboul, go back
there and hound him down."   .

"Done ! " said Regan.

"Get off as soon as possible; ten to one he'll
beat us again. I confess I'm no match for him."

"Will you go with us, Mr. Catus?" asked
Sallus."

"No; I have other work, but it bears on the
same thing. Start to-morrow or next day; simply
follow your own instincts. You know as much as I
do, except that I am confident that he is on the way
to the Bosporus." He took out a cigar and
lighted it at Regan's lamp, then, refusing their
pressing invitation to stay longer, after telling them
a few of the particulars about Aleppo's life on the
desert, hurried off, saying that time was precious
and he had much to do.

"Biz—at last," said Regan.

"I should smile," answered Sallus. Both men were excited aud delighted. Suddenly, Sallus, who was pacing the floor, brought up with a round turn. "How about Spino and Cicily?"

"Great Scott! said Regan, under his breath, "have I come to that?"

"What?"

"Eloping with Spino."

"Not necessarily,"—Sallus looked uneasy and worried. "I'm not quite sure of either of them, but I'll give that girl a fair trial if I know myself."

"If we spirit them away," answered Regan, "Issachar will find it out and take his revenge on Aleppo; "'twont do; hands off those women till that boy of ours is found."

"Shake," said Sallus, loyal unto death, though it cost him a pretty hard spasm of the heart; secretly he loved Cicily, good or bad, he loved her, but friendship first and love afterwards, though it hurt.

"Tell you what we'll do," said Regan, who felt the boy's pain, "we'll keep up a secret correspondence with them, and leave somebody here on guard, and later we'll come back and capture them both, bag and baggage; that is, if they turn out all right."

At this Sallus brightened and looked at his watch. "Guess I'll run over there and explain the whole business; I suppose we'll leave this room just as it is?"

" Sure, why not; I'll rent it indefinitely, and it'll
be here when we come back, and we can turn in
just as usual. A little run over to Stamboul is
nothing." This settled, Sallus went over to Cicily.

" Now, about Rhea?" said Regan to himself,
"what am I going to do about Rhea? Why, tell
her of course; I might as well get over with it first
as last—I'll go now."

A half hour later, he was settled in Rhea's little
parlor, relating to that young lady his plans.

" You see, Miss Nellino, we'll get back to Constantinople in a jiffy, and dig up the foundations of
the whole city, if it comes to that. I'm fond of
Aleppo, and I don't take kindly to losing him, but
being 'ᵘ ... by a Jew is worse yet. I have found
my vocation—it is just this—setting Jews and
Yankees on to each other; it suits me exactly, I'm
mighty grateful to Aleppo for giving me this
chance."

" Rhea was quite herself again and beamed on
Regan as she had done in days of old.

" Can you tell me Mr. Regan anything about the
girl Cicily, whom Sallus has taken such a liking
to?"

" Not exactly, except that she's pretty and she
knows it."

" She would be a strange woman if she didn't,"
answered Rhea laughing.

" Spino's the daisy though," said Regan; " you
had better go to see them Miss Nellino; one doesn't

meet more than one such couple in a lifetime. Tell
you, if you want to find odds and ends, stay in Cairo;
Cicily and Spino make the Alpha and Omega—the
first and the last—the best and the worst as to
looks. By the way Miss Nellino, you've grown
thinner.''

'' Have I ? ''—coloring, " I expect you are mentally drawing a contrast between me and Miss
Cicily; please don't."

'' Can't help it Miss Rhea, though it's quite in
your favor. Will you leave Cairo? ''

'' Perhaps.''

'' And where next ? ''

'' I don't know,''—looking at him pathetically
with tears gathering in her eyes.

Regan was like all tender hearted men, and
woman's tears overcame him. He dared not console
her, so he rose abruptly and decided that he must
go.

'' Now look here Miss Nellino''—he had her
hand in his—''women as a rule have mighty little
effect on me, but you've broke me of the tobacco
habit, and anybody that stops another from chewing, is pretty powerful, if I do say it. I don't want
to be a fool nor seem soft, but before we part, which
may be forever, I've got to thank you for all you've
done for me. To know a woman like you Miss
Rhea, is to be converted; and the best of it is that
you never try to do anything at all; you're just you;
'that's about the size of it; and a man like me has

got to duck his head when he comes your way, he
can't help it. There's one thing more I want to
say to you before I make my run for the Bosporus"
—all the time holding her hand in a firm grip—
"that young man, Bracciolini, or Aleppo or
Romanes or whoever he may be, is all right; he's
sound as a nut and as true as gold; he rings like
the genuine coin; I've tried him. Now don't you
worry and grow thin and all that; we'll dig him up
yet, Sallus and I; so you just go in for having a
good time, and sleeping nights and eating and singing and dancing and we'll do the rest. Lots of love
to you Miss Nellino, good bye."

Rhea was dumb for a moment, but held on to
him with tight grip, so much did she hate to see
him go—a genuine comforter, every word that he
said went straight to her heart and remained there
forever.

"Mr. Regan, I love you devotedly; you're my
friend, my brother, you make one bright spot in my
life, without any shadow—good-bye."

She followed him to the door, and threw a kiss
after him, as he went down the garden path. It
was the last time that he ever saw Rhea Nellino.

CHAPTER XXIX.

THE FIGHT IS ON.

Romanes was patient, and for the first time in his existence, allowed himself to float with the tide. His one desire was to meet and talk with his son Aleppo, yet even that he curbed, trusting to the mighty hand of El Reshid to bring about the event. He lived at his hotel in Genoa, receiving frequent letters from Cæsar Catus, but otherwise quite isolate, though surrounded by a crowd. His rooms were simple hotel apartments, bare of the books and works of art to which he had been accustomed, nor did he seem to miss them, nor all the little attentions formerly paid him by his servants at his own house. He waited upon himself, and spent a great portion of his time in introspection and deep thought. If his eyes had been less restless he would have seemed to have reached a condition of serenity, but his intense, shifting glance showed his anxiety and betrayed the secret of a fiery, oriental nature held in check but not subdued.

Though he knew that El Reshid was behind Aleppo, as for himself, he felt no influence from that quarter, nor did Catus keep him informed as

to the efforts made in regard to his son. Catus'
letters were simply philosophic and friendly, advising him to cultivate patience and endurance. At
times Romanes felt bitter over this; he was by
nature a commander, and obedience, to him was a
new role, but he understood ; he had been drilled
in the formulas, and had drank at the fountain of
wisdom ; so he continued at Genoa, passive without, fiery within.   .

One evening, weeks after Catus had left him, the
servant handed him a card.   The name inscribed
caused him a flutter of the heart, but outwardly he
showed great indifference and ordered his caller to
be admitted at once.   A moment later, Jacob
Issachar entered the room and spreading both
hands, palms outward, bowed low. Romanes greeted
him with a slight inclination of the head, not even
rising as a cordial host would do.

" I suppose you have learned," said he, without
beating about the bush in the least, " that Helene
Cressey is dead and that whatever contract she may
have made with you in regard to our son, went out
with her—"

. Issachar showed all his teeth and looked Romanes
over from head to foot.

"Furthermore I repudiate you.   Madame Cressey's Vienna property belongs to Aleppo.   You
know me of old Jacob Issachar; we crossed swords
once in the Order."

Romanes was now upon his feet and stepping

close to Issachar, challenged him with a look from which another would have shrunk; not so the Jew. With equal coolness he arranged the folds of his robe and growing slightly taller, said in a melodious voice, "Very well do I remember—I forget nothing.'

" Traitor ! '' said Romanes under his breath, " false to El Reshid and the brothers, false to Helene Cressey and my son, how dare you, knowing me as you do, come here like a bargaining Jew, to barter for the freedom of Aleppo Romanes ! ''

"And thou," answed Issachar in slightly accelerated speech, " thou, I presume, hast never failed the Order, nor broken a sacred vow. Thou who knowest something of the Rosy Cross and the moon-struck lotus, thou who realizest the completed square and the symbolic cone, thou, I presume—'' drawing his thin lips taut over his glittering teeth —"thou, of all others, hast the supreme right to call me a traitor, and thyself, a god.''

For an instant Romanes bowed his head, then rose to his full height, and, as if by magic, there came to his face and figure the virile look of youth. Slowly, each syllable vibrating with the resonance of supreme contempt, he spat at the Jew, these words.

" *Canst thou face El Reshid ?* ''

Issachar's swarthy countenance, for an instant, took on the hue of death, but bracing himself with a supreme effort of will, he stooped, till his eyes were on level with those of the man by his side, and thrusting his head forward like a reptile about to sting, hissed these venomous words in the ear of Romanes—

"I have thy son, cursed traitor to the Order! do thou my bidding, or I tighten the coils."

The two men glared—glared.

"Seest thou this knife?" drawing the slim steel from his sleeve. "I swear to thee it shall pierce the heart of Aleppo Romanes, if thou darest to defy me; I am Issachar, the Jew!"

For an instant the color left Romanes' face; a startled look came into his eyes; he clutched at the chair, threw a flash at the door, then the old fire of the autocrat blazed.

"I am without arms, or I would shoot you like a dog; had I the strength, I would tear you limb from limb. You seem my master, vile cur of Stamboul, but beware how you lay hands on Aleppo Romanes.

"You, too, know something of the Rosy Cross, and the moon-struck lotus; you, too, have realized the completed square and deadly cone. Beware, dog of a Jew! Are the powers dead that send the lightning with the thunder; are the invisible wires cut; has the Damascan blade lost its edge? Beware, I tell you, or faster than the speed of thought will come the avenger, to strike you in your tracks, and toss your rotting carcass to the carrion fiends of hell!"

"Art thou done?" said Issachar.

" No! give me the dagger."

At this, the Jew bared his arm and drew the sharp. gleaming steel quickly across his naked flesh, making three long and ghastly lines in the form of a strange symbol, from which the blood fell.

"Thy son has this vile mark upon his back, Henrique Romanes;"—he held out his bleeding arm—"'tis the 'devil's own;' he is one of us; wheresoever he goeth he is cursed, living or dead he is mine; even in hell is the sign known and Issachar feared. In face of this, I offer him release; in face of this, I abjure my right and title—a Jew can keep his word. What manner of father art thou, that for the sake of ' filthy coin ' thou canst damn thy flesh and blood forever."

" And art *thou* done ? " said Romanes.

" No,"—he wiped the blood from his arm and sheathed his dagger—" fulfill the contract of the woman, Helene Cressey, and I renounce my right and title to thy son."

They had been lunging with invisible swords in deadly contest, thrusting like experts. Romanes wiped the sweat from his dripping brow, and Issachar swathed his wounded arm.

" If I refuse, you can but kill my son; and if I yield, I grow yet blacker. Honor! To get it back, I stake Aleppo."

" What! and thou take the chance? "

" Hear me!" Romanes gripped the arm of Issa-

cher where the wound bled. "The fight is on,
tooth and nail! 'Tis a battle for life. Not so easily
can you subdue me. I will summon help at once.
Genoa shall shut its gates; in the sleeve of every
brother is a knife; in the glance of the faithful
lurketh death. I refuse you, Jacob Issachar, I
defy you; even mine own son shall paint me no
blacker. Go, you, and do your worst ! "

For the first time during the interview the Jew
concealed his teeth. The smile had vanished, and
with it the look of supreme self-confidence; something of servility appeared, hid subtly beneath his
regal bearing; while a certain fawning motion of
the hand betrayed in him the velvet suavity of the
cat.

"And so thy powers are not yet blasted," he
said, casting a shifting glance upon Romanes; "I
remember well the day when thou didst summon a
legion to thy presence. Cheat not thyself, however,
into believing that thou art still the same. Even
El Reshid came at thy command, even he removed
his hat; then wert thou Master. I sank upon my
knee before thee in the dirt, I crawled upon my
belly, like a snake, and, grovelling, swore that thy
weak spot I would yet discover, and strike thee
there. Money! Ha! ha! on every coin I wrench
from thee is cut the word *revenge*.

"So thou dost bid me go and do the devil's work,
and thou will do thy worst—thou! Ha! Genoa
hath no gates, nor are there brothers at thy elbow;

even El Reshid stands aloof! Thy powers are not yet blasted! ha! ha!''

He watched his enemy as a dog who tries to sneak away watches another; he dared not remove his eyes. A change had taken place—Romanes was erect, autocratic, intense; the imperial look was on his brow, the fire within his glance; a veritable commander, he cowed Issachar, and held him by the undying thrill of memory, fast, glued, immovable thus for a full minute; then, drawing a long, barbaric sigh, that sounded like the breathing of a dextrous tiger, Issachar grew smaller, more evasive, and backed slowly, with a snake-like motion, to the door, eye-to-eye with Romanes, undulating, gliding, till, at last, reaching his hand behind him, he twisted the latch and vanished in the dark beyond.

CHAPTER XXX.

THE PRISONER.

Bunyan wrote his immortal work while in prison. If the mind of man can stand the strain, if he have power to think deeply and imagine sublimely, though you put him behind the bars and turn the key to his cell, yet in reality he escapes you, and roams not only over earth but through the spaces above. Though his floor be of stone, his bed of straw and his bread a crust, yet will he dwell in a palace and feast like a king.

Aleppo Romanes had been closely guarded from the time of his capture on the Libyan desert till he reached Stamboul.   It is not necessary to explain here the skill with which Issachar had concealed him, nor the expedients used to enable him to travel so long a distance undetected; suffice it to say that this was but child's play to the Jew, who turned the lock finally on Aleppo in a house of his own in that best of hiding places—Constantinople. The room in which young Romanes was imprisoned was a gorgeous oriental apartment, more impressive with its subtle, evasive spices and scents than would have been a common cell in an ordinary jail.   Every comfort was supplied him, and his condition was quite different from his life in the Arab tent on the desert.

In spite of his dainty dressing room and silk oriental robes, in spite of the luxurious meals served by black attendants, in spite of the books scattered here and there, the harp, the mandolin and the organ, he felt smothered and oppressed. He had no outlook, save through the half-closed shutters of a barred window, nor chance for exercise except on the thick pile of yielding rugs.   He was surfeited with luxury—it was a positive horror. The air, though pure from careful ventilation, was loaded with a spicy incense which made its way from the adjacent apartment through cracks in the

doors, and kept his mental powers in a kind of
stupor that it took a supreme effort of the will to
throw off.   The books, too, which were ever at
hand by his couch, on the window sill, under the
cushions of the divans, or concealed in the folds of
the curtains like so many evil spirits, intruded
their sensuous rottenness upon him at all times.
The worst selections of the greatest authors, while
never mediocre as to art, but devilish in intent,
were constantly appealing to his curiosity and forcing him to wander along paths where the flowers
were poison and the trees deadly.   Nor could
Aleppo raise his eyes to the ceiling without resting
them on masterpieces that, having escaped the ac-
cusation of being obscene, were yet so closely allied
to that which is vulgar, that to pronounce judgment
upon them was no easy task.   In the great room
also, for the salon was very large, were tinted
statues entirely nude, of the hue of human flesh
and magical in their power of deluding the be-
holder into the idea that they were truly alive
—works of genius, every one, and so seductive
that he who would have destroyed them might be
termed either a brute, or a benefactor.   In the immense window, where the thick iron bars were concealed with folds of exquisite lace, were potted
plants to which the black attended assiduously ;
all voluptuous, large-flowered, crossings from
hardier specimens that brazenly challenged his
eye like the wanton prostitutes of a brothel.   Here

12

Aleppo remained week after week, seeing none but
the black servants, who seemed to have lost their
tongues.

It must be remembered that Romanes was a
young man with the warm blood of the Orient in
his veins.   Had he been incarcerated here a year
sooner he would most likely have fallen a temporary
prey to the hot novels which reached to him their
invisible hands like ghostly harlots.   The busts and
statues must needs have excited unspeakable emotions, and the pictures have raised his pulse.   The
rich food also, spiced and doctored with alcoholic
stimulants would have set him reeling, drunk with
luxury, for he was pampered with a questionable
cuisine.   Even in his present condition of mind
and aspiration, hate as he might the refined lewd-
ness of the place, yet the artist in him revelled at
times in an almost insane pleasure which inevitably
transformed itself into pain.   He sat for long hours
with his eyes closed, lest he see the pictures and
ceiling frescoes that transported him to a kind of
Bacchanalian Bohemia, where art ran riot, and love
degenerated into lust.   He gleaned here and there
from the books, covering with a clean sheet of
paper those portions not fit for an aspiring soul, as
though by so concealing he had spread a swan's
white wing on a malaria-breeding pool.

Thus Aleppo kept himself unsullied though he
suffered as never before.   He strove to combat the
enclosed environment with another which he con-

jured constautly and saw, whenever he closed his
eyes. It was always the temple of Karnak, the
blue sky of Thebes, the sinuous Nile and Rhea.
This vision purified the very statues, repainted the
frescoes and extracted the poison from the books.
Test the soul with hardship, and if it be blessed
with the combativeness and resistance, it will grow
healthy and strong under the ordeal. The majority
of people improve with adversity, becoming wild,
hardy flowers with the breath of sweet violets.
But only the *great* can endure prosperity or grow
strong in the caressing arms of luxury. Imagine
this forced upon one to the extreme of cruelty and
you obtain some idea of the diabolism of Issachar
and the danger of Aleppo.

One day he was very tired, though never for a
moment had he lost the sense of the justice of all
things, and though he seemed to be a martyr, in a
certain aspect he was not, but only realizing the
effect of a far back cause for which he himself was
responsible, yet, nevertheless, he was very tired.
He had mentally petitioned El Reshid again and
again, but that great Master had apparently turned
his back. Catus, Regan and Sallus had somehow
missed him and Issachar alone was a mighty reality,
whom he had thus far failed to escape. The languor of luxury had stolen into his blood and in a
measure paralyzed his wings. In truth it was but
temporary and seeming, his mental eye looked ever
eastward toward the rising sun, his shrine was as

fixed as the Mecca of the Arab, yet on this particular occasion he was weary, sad.

It was time for the black to bring his evening
meal, he dreaded its arrival; the slimy, dumb brute,
that fawned about him, revolted his soul. The
door opened—what! a sweet smiling face looked in,
and a melodious voice said softly in Italian, "I'll
serve you to-night."

She was a seductive little Pagan, with long
narrow eyes, tinted finger nails, and naked arms,
over which draped the folds of a Greek gown to
cover them one moment and fall away the next,
displaying their ivory whiteness even to the
shoulders. She hovered about, touching him now
and then, but saying little and exciting his curiosity
by a thousand airs and graces which both charmed
and repelled; at least she was something new, a
relief from the sensuous monstrosity of the few last
weeks and a great improvement on the dumb black.

He was a little happier for the coming of the
woman for a time. The negroes had entirely
vanished, and she in their place waited upon Aleppo
as though she were the slave of a Sultan. He had
begun to like her in a grateful way, from the first
he had admired her for her grace and artistic
beauty, for she made a new picture of herself at
each turn of her head—and was a hundred women
in one, in her postures and poses, kind as a sister,
watchful as a mother; Aleppo must indeed have

been a brute had he not longed for her coming and sighed at her departure.

This went on for days. One evening she brought his supper, and as she placed the tray at his side she threw her arms about his neck and declared that she loved him. It was a critical moment in which young Romanes, with more ease than one would have supposed possible, gently put the girl away, conscious at the same time that her so-called love was not only a false passion but a part of the game of Issachar. He urged her to fly from this house of wickedness, ere she became an absolute prisoner like himself. Then the fetid nature of the vile woman displayed itself; she laughed in his face and treated him to a volley of lingual obscenity the like of which had never struck his ears before. In all his young life he had heard nothing of this kind nor had he dreamed that it could be. He ordered the young girl from the apartment, and his eyes flashing lightning, his face a thunder cloud; he rushed to the windows and tore their mockery of spider-web lace into shreds; then he tried the iron bars, hunting for a piece of steel or something that would take its place, but the room was singularly free from anything of the kind. He had never felt so strong before in his life. If physical force failed him he would forge his brain into keys and his nerves into files; if that too were in vain, he would summon the invincible, the psychic power itself, and bring from out the universal certain means of relief.

The time for action had arrived, too long already had he lain in the arms of others and sat upon their laps; too long had he negatively received inspiration—inhaled, and closed his lips. His youth had fled; he had seen the last touch of hell—a harlot out of the infernal fires; there was nothing of evil hid, he was old—old in his knowledge of sin. He jerked the lascivious pictures from the wall and hurled them to the floor; he threw down the parian statues and shattered them to bits; he tore the vile pages from the books of the great masters, and upset the barbaric plants. His whole Unit of Energy, till now but half roused, made his muscles hard like steel and his nerves tense as the strings of a bow.

"I have been learning," he said, shaking back his hair, as would a young lion. He looked strangely like his father—the one invincible lock fell on his brow, his eyes were quick, scintillating, determined, and his pose erect. The imperial stamp was on him, in spite of the devil's mark. The black veil of his past had been rent, he had faced the extreme of sorrow, and now he stood eye to eye with the limit of sin.

The arras over the door was lifted softly, and with a cat-like motion, Issachar entered the room.

" So my prisoner, to whom I showed nothing but kindness, has rebelled,"—he glanced at the chaotic pile of statues and ictpures, and smiled—" even the beautiful woman was driven out. What next may I expect from so erratic a guest?"

" That he will vanish," answered Aleppo, scornfully.

" My guest will vanish, ha! ha! my guest will vanish. I have just come from thy father, who is in Genoa, to find my house demolished and my courtesy abused. Methinks I will try new methods—a dungeon and a chain. Your ransom moneys will fail to pay me for this wholesale destruction of these precious works of art; I must raise thy price. Thine august father cares so little for his bastard son that he refuses me a modest recompense; mayhap, however, when he discovers what a wild beast he hath bred, he will change his stubborn mind. Get rid of thy conceit henceforth; in truth thou holdest thyself of far too much account. Thy faithful friends still eat, and drink, and laugh. Miss Nellino marries soon thy bosom friend of Italy, one Cæsar Catus, who stole thee from me on the Libyan sands, in lieu of thee, takes to himself a bride. Regan, the Yankee, and that pretty boy, who dangles at his heels, are off to parts unknown, and El Reshid, the invincible, who followed thee with letters, and fired thy soul to deeds of spiritual valor, forgets that thou dost live. Bastard! in all the world thou hast but me; even the love, that thou didst deem immortal, dost fail thee now, and in the breach only the devil holds his ground. I come to barter with thee, thou hast my admiration, my esteem. I would adopt thee as my very own— my mark is on thy back—on thee I would bestow both power and wealth. Spurn thy allegiance to the past, to fickle friends and shifting dreams; dis own thy spurious sire and hopeless aim toward spiritual power, forget El Reshid, who long since deserted thee, and prince that thou most surely art, *be mine!*"

Aleppo folded his arms across his breast, and said no word.

"As I am king, so shalt thou be. In Italy, Egypt, Turkey, India, on the Sahara, even in France and the islands of the sea, on the very ground where walked the Nazarene, at the Mongolian centers, aye, everywhere my subjects are— *mine.* Long have I sought for a son and heir—one strong, defiant, like myself, who dare to look me in the eye, and cross his sword with mine. Aleppo Romanes, that man thou art."

He waited, approaching nearer to the haughty figure that stood with folded arms still as a statue, in the center of a chaos which he, himself, had made.

"What sayest thou?"

But there came no answer, save the whispers in the room, which seemed to steal from every corner, as though a legion of tempters lurked in the shadow and urged Aleppo Romanes to submit. The heart of the young man had turned to stone, through all this speech of Issachar he heard naught, save the word, Rhea—Rhea—Rhea—false! Rhea!

" Speak now ! beneath this palace is a dungeon; freedom as my son, or this black hole—speak! "

" The dungeon," said Aleppo, and the Jew felt that for once he had overshot the mark.

CHAPTER XXXI.

FACE TO FACE WITH NAKED TRUTH.

Issachar had seized upon the prevalent idea that the getting of money was the prime incentive of the Jew, and under the guise of greed was striving to accomplish the revenge for which he lived ; revenge not only upon the individual, Henrique Romanes, but upon all mankind who especially aspired to divine powers. For private reasons he particularly hated Romanes and had been waiting for years for the opportunity to strike. He had insinuated himself into the good graces of Helene Cressey and, under the cloak of a powerful magician, had stimulated her curiosity and in a certain way gained her admiration. She knew nothing of his former association with Romanes, nor aught of his history save from some few hints which her lover had thrown out not altogether favorable to the Jew. When her child was about to be sent adrift she conceived the idea of so marking him with the symbol of the Order, that wherever he

went he might find friends among the members
and, possibly, if the time arrived that she wished
to trace him, that by this means she might accomplish her desire.   So she summoned Issachar
and explained the matter clearly, giving him the
stamp upon which was the sacred seal, requesting
him to duplicate the same indelibly upon the body
of her child.   On the contrary, as is well known,
Issachar substituted a symbol of his own and
marked him with a sign of diabolism which is too
vulgar to here describe.

From his birth, Issachar had never lost sight of
Aleppo, having some one in the boy's wake wherever he went.   Knowing well enough when he introduced himself at Venice that the young
Bracciolini was the son of Henrique Romanes, he
had waited his time, feeling sure that the parental
anxiety would awaken sooner or later, when he
could strike an unerring blow.

In his stormy interview with his old commander
he had drawn the dagger and threatened to kill
Aleppo, but deep in his mind he had conceived a
subtler and far more cruel revenge which was none
other than to debauch the boy and win him to
himself; counting on the aroused paternal affection
in Romanes, he had drawn the steel and, upon discovering that the fire still burned in the oriental
nature of his former master, he felt that his
supreme opportunity had arrived.   For once he
might inflict torture, the refined cruelty of which

was sufficient to satisfy a nature like his own.   So
he ordered Aleppo to the dungeon, as he called it,
though in reality it was an immense wine cellar,
kept under lock and bolt and lighted by barred
windows which threw a dim glow through
the place. There was the conventional bed of
straw and the usual paraphernalia, of a prison, but
otherwise it might have been far worse. It was the
policy of Issachar to keep a mental crack continually open for Aleppo's escape into his arms, for he
had no desire to completely antagonize the young
man.   Should Aleppo despair and commit suicide,
the aim of the Jew would be defeated, so this tantalizing cellar, while really an exceedingly hard
place to get away from, at the same time seemed to
offer a thousand ways of escape.   Issachar's main
hope of winning him, however, lay in the stress
which young Romanes must necessarily lay on the
desertion of his friends.   If he could but once con-
vince him that they were more or less false or indifferent, a hatred would be aroused and a desire
for revenge with it, which would change his nature
from one of a god to that of a fiend.   He had fabri-
cated the lie of Rhea and Cæsar out of a spy's story,
who had seen Catus departing from the young
lady's house ; nor did he understand the nature of
Aleppo sufficiently to realize what a terrible blow
he had struck.

When the young man was left in the dungeon
the reaction was upon him ; he had rebounded from

a state of intense indignation to one of stupor
and lay upon his pallet of straw indifferent to life
itself. After a time he opened his eyes and watched
a spider as it patiently worked its web in the window, and was conscious of no other interest on
earth than that the ingenious trap should be completed, for he felt himself to be the harmless fly for
whose capture the web was spun. As he gazed, the
spider enlarged and changed till it grew to the
enormous size of Issachar and then for a long time
Aleppo knew no more. When he awoke from his
sleep of exhaustion it was nearly dawn ; a faint
gray light was visible at the windows but most of ·
the objects about him were shrouded in darkness ;
his mind was clear and refreshed, however, his
mind, I say, for his heart was apparently dead—
emotion, passion, charm, imagination had all vanished and reason sat on the throne. For the first
time in his life he determined to look cold facts in
the face. He had brought up against a skeleton
bereft of bounding blood and luxurious flesh ; he
felt its bones rattle and saw its eyeless sockets and
terrible teeth. Arising quickly, he found a broken
pitcher partly filled with water and with this
and a rough towel he managed to refresh himself.
Later, he discovered on the stone table as the light
grew clearer, a crust of bread and a glass of milk.
Having finished this simple breakfast, which must ·
have been placed at his side the night before, he
sat down upon the straw and buried his face in his

hands ; not to weep, oh no ! nor was he the victim
of despair, on the contrary, he was striving to
bring his whole mental force to bear on
the situation, in other words he strove to
concentrate. He had no desire to investigate the
premises nor to effect an escape ; preferring
the dungeon as he then felt, to any place on earth.
What had he outside ? A father who abhorred him,
friends who had forgotten, and Love who had
proved herself unfaithful. All that Aleppo asked
was that he might be left alone to think—think.
El Reshid ! even he had failed to cast his spell ove r
him ; the name brought no thrill to his heart, nor
cared he for Damascus or Paradise. The problem
had attacked his brain ; he was bound to solve it
once and for all. He would wrestle with this
giant enigma of circumstances, this combination of
strange events, and know the truth; staking his
love, his pretty dream of immortality, his Utopian
hope of eternal felicity, his trust in human nature,
his confidence in a friend's loyalty, on logic, law
and fact. He would attack the puzzle inductively
and deductively, from effects to causes, from
causes to effects ; he would weigh, measure, compare, reason. In this investigation, intuition, imagination, guess work, desire, prejudice, hope and
fear should cut no figure, he was after facts—facts.
Through his whole life thus far he had been im-
pressionable, superstitious, credulous, imaginative ;
he had lived in a land of dreams, where phantom

trees sang with zephyr voices, and visionary
streams went laughing by; he had built in this
fair country an ideal castle and put therein a bride
who knew no shadow of turning, but was loyalty
incarnate; more, he had conjured from the plains
of Syria a subtle Master, basing his existence upon
the statements of others and a few scraps of paper
written over with the well known conclusions of
the great.   What of it?   Wise sayings are not so
difficult to gather, if one but set about it.   Why
believe that El Reshid was far different from other
mortals who have their little day of effort and goodness as they also have their time of evil.   Aleppo
was far from scanning this phantasmal bank,
stocked with illusions, with the eyes of a cynic;
on the contrary, he was overlooking it with the
glance of pure reason; sorting the possibilities
from the probabilities, the fancies from the facts,
the theories and hypotheses from well known laws,
in order to get the whole bearing of the situation,
which means nothing other than the Reason of the
reasons.   He began with the Jew.   Issachar was a
mighty reality, six feet and a half in height, with
superb muscles, subtle brain and powerful will.   He
had been at the heels of Aleppo from the time of
his birth—wherefore? Plainly for a reward.   What
this reward was to be cut no figure, whether
money, love or revenge. there was no denying that
the young Romanes was as redeemable as a bank
note, or, if not that, at least he figured as a tool in

the Jew's calculations, an almost helpless means to an end.   Thus far the problem was clear enough. "Put two and two together, it makes four," said Aleppo.

The next to be weighed by the scales of justice and fact was his father.   As to Henrique Romanes being his father, he had nothing to say; whether it were he or some other man, made no difference in this question.   The author of his bodily existence according to Issachar, had refused, from pecuniary motives to ransom his son.   The Jew might have lied, yet Issachar being a prominent figure, went openly about the streets, his house in Stamboul must necessarily be known; why in the name of parental love, if such love there really were, had not his father brought the law to bear and rescued his imprisoned son?   But setting this aside, admitting that the elder Romanes had been in some way deceived, misled, there was Regan, his voluntary sire (at the thought he smiled slightly), who had vowed to guard him from the wiles of the Jew.   A Yankee, shrewd, rich, how was it possible that he and his boy friend Sallus who had in former times expressed for him such entire devotion, how was it possible that they had not succeeded in some measure in tracing him, if any effort on their part had been made?   Then Catus, who had so valiantly rescued him from the Arab tent—the mysterious Catus, in touch with the powers, what save an infatuation for Rhea could have turned him against the friend

of his aspiration and youth—Rhea—his heart
neither trembled nor fluttered; the woman who had
sung his song and made claim to an eternal affection, who had enamored him on the Nile as
Cleopatra had bewitched Antony; Rhea—if the
tale of the Jew were false, why had she not
followed him, even to the dungeon, guided by the
unerring instinct of love itself. And El Reshid, if
the wonderful powers that his admirers ascribed to
him had not in some way failed, why had he not
mastered a wily Jew who appeared boldly on the
streets of Constantinople like an honest man.
And his mother—*dead*.

Whatever of feeling was left to Aleppo manifested
itself in admiration for Issachar; evil or good he
was sublime, whether a fiery volcano spitting the
lava of death, or an icy peak of the north—grand
—or, to look upon him as a thing of motion, a royal
tiger in the jungle of life, he had struck right and
left with his velvet paws and silenced the friends of
Aleppo—his parents, his sweetheart, the man, El
Reshid, and the order of the Olympians. As he
dwelt upon Issachar his admiration grew, but resolutely putting his rising emotion aside, he began
his mental tussle again.

Here on the chess-board were arranged the men,
now for the game: First, he must remember that
the great master seldom shows his hand in the
beginning; it were possible, yes probable, that El
Reshid was waiting his time; that such a man

existed he was certain, others had seen him, then
again, if Issachar could be as great, as he had
proved himself to be, it were not unreasonable to
presume that there might be another neck and neck
with him.   In the calculation of chances the world
must hold more than *one* great man at a given time.
Conceding therefore the possibility of a being
called El Reshid, and that he were biding his time
to act, how about the executor—Cæsar Catus ?
One thing was sure, it was a fact that he had risked
his life on the desert to rescue Aleppo; it was also
true that Cæsar was a man with all the passions of
one whose temperament is intense and artistic. He·
had returned to Cairo, and—how could he help it—
fallen in love; Rhea, piqued and hopeless of regaining Aleppo, for consolation had responded. The
tale of the Jew corresponded exactly with the fickle
nature of man where Cupid flutters and hovers.
Yet on the other hand if there be such a trait as
that of loyalty, why need Catus and Rhea necessarily have been devoid of it, especially as he had
sworn fealty to a sacred order, and she to an eternal
love. About Regan and Sallus he debated less, as
he well understood that they were no match for the
Jew, and might have been making great efforts
without avail.   ·

He balanced his pros and cons, and diving
deeper into the subtleties attacked the very laws
themselves. First he asked himself, "Is there such
a thing as parental love ? Admitting that there is,

does it extend beyond the mother and its manifestation in the brute? '' He went after data, recalling
all the incidents that he could glean from memory.
Of course the animal protects its young, the mother
suckles it, but this over, the time for nursing past,
does the parental instinct disappear and another
take its place, this much boasted affection resolving
itself either into friendship or indifference? From
the data at hand he could hardly make up his mind
and became agnostic upon the question at once.

Second, ''Is there such a thing as loyalty unto
death, or can it be resolved into a temporary condi-
.tion of mind which new faces and environment are
most likely to dissipate?'' He sought for one
datum and found it in himself. About parental
love he knew nothing; personally, about loyalty he
understood a great deal. If *he* could be true, was
it not the height of egotism to presume himself to
be the only reliable person on earth? The fact that
loyalty was possible to him made it possible to
others also. He had no hesitation in deciding this
question, the trait of loyalty was a fact.

Third, ''Is love eternal?'' That love *is*, he had
proven in himself, but in face of his apparently dead
heart, could it be eternal. He recalled that his condition was now purely mental; that all his energy
was firing the furnace of his brain; that his will
was bent upon deciphering a problem and trans-
lating the cold gaze in the eyes of the sphinx. That
his heart, should grow sluggish in its beating was

nothing strange—the reaction to emotion was bound
to come, when the fever heat would be upon him.
"Is love immortal?" In the sense that it is
always somewhere, he said to himself, "yes; but to
specialize the question—is love between two beings
immortal, do they not shift their affections as they do
their clothes, can one man and one woman look into
each other's eyes forever through æons of time,
must they not, by the very nature of life itself,
which is variety, look elsewhere?" Then he
sought for data; it crowded upon and buried him.
He recalled case after case, even in his own short
existence, where man, honest in intent, had sworn
eternal fealty and been false to the vow. He had
seen a husband raining tears on the grave of the
beloved, and twining bridal wreaths in the young
hair of another, later on. An eternal love is love
forever, to which the love for a few years seems but
a dot in the circle, and yet the large proportion of
these immortal lovers were seeking divorces and
remarriage, as if a day were eternity and an hour
everlasting. Alas! the data were overwhelmingly
in favor of license and against the flimsy hypothesis of unsullied constancy. Yet he plunged
deeper into subtleties. "Did an eternal love deny
to him who experienced it a realization of another?" Because one is always the same to him,
an environment, a response that never changes in
its effect, does that imply that another may not
have its individual effect also and call forth its re-

spouse? Does a mother love but one of her children? Are they not all dear according as they appeal to and draw out the mother nature that intoxicates her heart? That no one ever takes another's place he was well aware, but the soul of man is a harp of many strings, and the musician! a Liszt plays his own melody, which is not that of a Mozart. By logic he grasped it. "Love is immortal." The individual Rhea, not the shifting phantasmal, but the true, the eternal, meant a something to him, that realized once, was his forever; though she marry Cæsar Catus, the vision of the Nile was his through the æons of time; though she doubt and apparently forget, in the still depths of memory the song of "the forever" must echo and echo as long as she were Rhea.

In this mental debate he disdained the question of a bodily marriage or a physical contact; he was delving into the logic of love, the subtlety, the principle; he was dealing with environment, which meant places and beings other than Aleppo —everlasting mirrors that threw himself back to himself eternally. He might in time meet women who would thrill his heart and reveal to him his soul, but, strange! an innumerable number must necessarily emphasize Rhea, who would throw him farewell kisses while memory lasted.

One more question — the final problem—the Propylon? "Was the flood of light a delusion—a St. Paul dream? No," he said emphatically, "no." The fact that I sit here and weigh these questions, the fact that I have my grip upon the sphinx, the fact that logic plays me true and reason holds the reins, the vanquished desert, the broken statues, the rejected harlot all verify the lightning which struck me there. Yet, he remembered the teachers of opposing cults, the leaders of contending religions, the priests of different doctrines, the worshipers of idols, the Moslem, the Buddhist, the Brahmin, the Parsee, the Christian, all claiming the same enlightment and swearing to the same experience. If light flashes in green tints on one, in yellow on another, and blue on a third, though the fire which caused the same be undeniable, the effect and condition produced is far different. One beholds naught but the yawning abyss of a sulphurous hell, while another gazes on a heavenly star; one sees but palpitating ethers, and another the sun-kissed moon. So there with his experience, he took no issue, but what the light of himself would reveal later must necessarily depend upon the strength and power of his eyes. Light implies a revelation of truth of some sort, either good or bad, while darkness necessitates ignorance and doubt.

All this time Aleppo sat with his head buried in his hands, but now, his mind strengthened by the icy tonic of thought, with an air of mastership he arose to his feet. He had been face to face with naked truth ; for the time abjuring sentiment, and

looked into the eyes of bitter fact, and he, too, had
stripped himself; tossing off one after another, his
garments of imagination, fancy, theory, hypothesis,
illusion. As nude as despoiled nature, as bare as
an athlete, he had entered the arena with his an-
tagonists and fought the battle out ; passing from
person to principle, he had wrestled at last with the
Almighty itself, which was the Reason of reasons,
and never varying law.

CHAPTER XXXII.

THE HOUNDS.

" Here's a private note from Catus," said Regan,
and finding a chair near Sallus, he read the letter
out loud.

DEAR REGAN:

I must be more explicit ; I hurried you off to
Stamboul without giving you sufficient instructions
as to the course you had better pursue. In the
first place let me say that Aleppo is in Constantinople ; it is a presumption founded on the nature of
Issachar, and what has been known of him in the
past. The Jew owns houses, stores, and bazaars
in all the great centers and has a thousand good
places in which to conceal our friend. I have said
that we believed Aleppo to be in Constantinople,
because of the nature of Issachar ; I must also add
for the sake of honesty, that through a certain let-

ter lately arrived, I have received hints that this is a fact. How many residences Issachar has in Stamboul, I do not know ; to look for the young man there, is like "searching for a needle in a hay-mow."

The properties of Issachar may be booked under another name, and should you see the Jew himself, it would be absurd to lay hands on him, as by so doing, we would put Aleppo forever out of our reach. Issachar has agents on every street in Constantinople, and has but to wink, cough, or make some diabolical signal, for swift emissaries to understand and do his bidding. So then, if you see him, and you are likely to do so, for he goes everywhere boldly, track him from haunt to haunt, and trust to instinct to do the rest, as I advised in Cairo. Shall be on the ground later.

Yours,

CÆSAR CATUS.

"I don't see as there's much of an element here, except luck and chance; it sifts itself down to this, if you see the Jew, or I see the Jew, get on his scent and hound him. We might be here till doomsday, though, and never catch sight of him ; he's a striking figure everywhere, but in Stamboul they're all striking, if I know myself. I suppose I could track him by his footprints if I were hound enough; why, of course, I have it, I'll hire an oriental detective—there're lots of them, must be—

I'll pay him a fortune, it's easy enough; get a Jew
after a Jew, of course, money'll fetch them, besides,
if I can rope one of them in, he'll locate Issachar's house, stores and so forth; a man can't own
property like that and keep in the dark.''

They had just arrived in Constantinople and
taken a room together, intending to live in
Bohemian fashion, as they had done in Cairo,
and hardly had had time to wash their faces
when Cæsar Catus' letter was handed to them.
An hour or two later they were haunting
Jew shops and certain other suggestive quarters
in search of the right man for the right
place; at last they found him, and though he spoke
in a jargon of tongues we will strive to clear the
mixture into Anglo-Saxon, and though not pidgeon
English, it is perhaps a combination of words that
can be made out.

"Have you ever done detective work?" said
Regan, after he had shown the Jew the color of his
palm, and explained the object of his call.

" Me shinning after my blasted brother on my
four legs, like a rodent."

" That's just it."

" Nay, but once I wriggled across a room on
the place where I digest."

" Ah, a worm, hey ? "

" I steal an epistle from the pocket of a dissenter
when he had not yet closed his eyes, and he was
not comprehending."

" So, so, you'll do; you must be extra."

" Extra pay, most certainly I'll do, for extra moneys—extra moneys."

He had an enormous nose, retreating chin and forehead, rat-like eyes, slim hands, and, strange to say, his name was Isaac."

" Issachar and Isaac are somewhat alike," said Sallus.

" I have the name of the patriarch; Abraham was my father and Jacob my brother."

" Do you know the Jew, Jacob Issachar?" asked Regan, getting down to business.

" Yes, I know him much; if I make no mistake he is Jehovah."

" Great Scott ! that's blasphemy," said Regan.

" He have moneys, houses and lands, he is almighty."

" Well now's your chance Isaac, I want to make the tour of premises; if you'll but show me the way, to-night we'll saunter down in this direction; be on hand; just one house after another to say nothing of the shops; understand—you shall be well paid."

" But the great man, I will not meet; I put up the fence there, nobody shall force me to see the great man."

" How much will you take to interview him?"

" Nay, nay "—Isaac shrugged his shoulders and spread his palms.

" Well so be it; remember, to-night, sharp !"

" Isaac led them a pretty life; he ferreted out

place after place which he ascribed to Issachar; spending weeks at it, and they had a taste of a side of Stamboul that they would never have taken from choice; yet the experience was wonderful, interesting. Partially disguised, assuming the greasy unwashed look of the mongrel, they haunted alley ways, stole into back yards, made friends with innumerable combines of dogs, escaped officers, were sworn at and swore, tortured their stomachs with dyspeptic viands, peeped into windows, crawled on their hands and knees, looked under the cracks of doors, tried duplicate keys, practised with burglars tools, slept in the daytime and prowled at night, learned half a dozen vernaculars, flirted with buxom Jewesses, and were as utterly Bohemian as the very dogs of the street who took great interest in their proceedings, and aided them to the extent of their powers. By this means they discovered that Isaachar had vast posessions. One house to which Isaac took them made a great impression; although hard to distinguish from the adjoining residences, it being so blent in and united to them that "which was which" was the question, this however, Isaac answered directly and to the point.

"You behold the structure," he said.

"I'll be switched if I do," answered Regan.

"It is belligerent somewhat and loaded with age; it stoops with the little window aperture, and commences with the gargoyle; it is the house of

Issachar, whose mother you have certified was Leah.''

''The blamed thing is not clear yet,'' replied Regan.

It was already twilight and the men had to strain their eyes to discover the fine distinctions which Isaac was so patiently trying to show them.

'' Come with me from behind, the alley is the near vicinity to the cellar window. I would show you that one window.''

The three men skulked around in the shadow in the rear alley, and Isaac triumphantly designated the barred glass of the wine cellar which dis: tinguished the house of Issachar from its two neighbors.

'' That one window show you the variety; that one window go to the dungeon.''

'' What! ''

''Yes, Issachar keeps the grape juice and the prisoner together ; the prisoner gets into the brandies and the brandies get into the prisoner.''

'' That is they get even,'' said Regan.

'' Yes, they even upward ; first, the prisoner crack the bottle, and then the bottle crack him ; they discover satisfaction, both.''

'' I wonder if we couldn't get into that cellar and rescue whatever prisoner might be pining,'' said Regan.

'' Wait you till the moon subside, I would recommend one barrel in which to crawl—all.''

"Not much!" said Regan, "I prefer going away and coming back later." So they strolled over the adjoining streets till the moon "subsided" and then returned to the barred window, which exerted great fascination upon them. It was on the line of the alley which, at that hour, was shrouded in darkness.

"Now you keep hushed," said Isaac in a tragic whisper. "If there be one prisoner I will exhort him."

Regan and Sallus crowded close together and put their ears to the pane, while Isaac tapped softly on the glass; silence—no answer.

"If there be one prisoner here I will inform him; you hush up your tongues."

He tapped again; they listened.

"I comprehend that I hear one sound," said Isaac; "hark, and breathe you no air—what?" he rapped faintly a third time.

"Ah! I apprehend I feel a prisoner."

"You feel him?" whispered Regan.

"Swallow your breath up," said Isaac indignantly, "I'll not get him alive this way." He tapped again.

They all heard it now—a faint answer, as though some one had thrown a bit of dirt from the inside of the cellar at the glass.

"The window must be high up from the ground," said Sallus.

"That is one dungeon; the foundation of the house of Issachar is a hole."

A half dozen dogs, more or less, started a fight in the alley contiguous to the three men, and made so much havoc and dust that it was impossible for a long time to get a fair chance at the window; when stillness was restored they renewed their efforts, but, receiving no response, postponed their investigation till the next night. On this occasion they left the Jew behind. Regan tried the tapping, but with no avail, when Sallus, crouching close to the pane, whistled an old air that he and Aleppo had often sung together; then, pressing his ear against the glass, caught what seemed like the echo of a far-off trill.

"That's Lep!" said Sallus, so excited that he could hardly speak; "nobody on earth can whistle like him—nobody."

Regan, with trembling fingers, tapped again, and a pebble from the inside answered the salute.

"There's no mistake, he remembers the song and recognizes us. I expect that before he imagined some street boy was playing him a trick."

Sallus whistled again and again, and called out responses from the depths below; to be sure they might be mistaken, possibly the prisoner was not Aleppo, "yet why on earth does he recognize and answer my signal whistle?" he said.

One thing they soon discovered, that where the window was set in the stone a small aperture, large enough to allow the passage of the body of a rat, had been left, making an opening through which the whistling was heard.

"This foolishness might go on forever," said Sallus, "let's write a note and stick it in that hole. We can push it through and come to-morrow; if the prisoner is Lep he'll manage to climb up there and put in an answer."

"Right you are, we never can see him night nor day through that ground glass window; the postoffice is the business—got a pencil, Sal?"

The two men went into an eating house, some distance away, and ordering coffee as a blind, wrote the following note:

"*Aleppo Bracciolini :*

"If you are in that cellar, for the love of God answer this note ; manage somehow to get your paper into the aperture by the window and we'll fish it out.

Loyal to the death,

REGAN AND SALLUS."

They went again to the charmed spot and crowded the little message into the opening, making sure that it had got somewhere into the depths below.

"I expect he'll not discover it till morning," said Regan, as they entered their room, "then he'll answer and manage to reach us if I know him."

"Suppose, after all, it's somebody else ? "

"If it is, we'll rescue that somebody, but it isn't; it stands to reason it is Aleppo; in the first place Issachar has got him in Stamboul; in the second, that cellar's the best hiding place we've found yet; in the third, he whistled your tune back to you; what more do you want?"

"I suppose I ought to be satisfied, but we've been disappointed so many times that I'm growing pessimistic."

"Time will tell, now you contain yourself till to-morrow night, and we'll know."

"Perhaps he's chained."

"I never thought of that, but I don't believe it. How on earth if he were, did he manage to hit the glass so true with his pebble stones? Don't you worry, it'll turn out all right, sure."

Aleppo had adapted himself to the wine cellar without difficulity; he had been deprived of his freedom for so long a time that to an extent he wrought out of his environment, wherever it might be, a new world. He investigated and explored every part of the spacious excavation, and had found innumerable things to engage and interest him. He cultivated rats and mice by feeding and other allurements, watched the artistic and wonderful spiders that seemed to be spinning things of beauty for himself alone, explored the old rubbish piles and studied out a half dozen plans for escaping, which, somehow, he had no desire to carry forward. His food, of the plainest, was served three

times a day, by a hump-backed old man, who
looked as though his mission had been that of a
rag-picker since he first began to walk. He was
slovenly, filthy and taciturn, never deigning to
answer the young man's questions except with a
grunt or a snarl. Though Aleppo fully intended to
get away from the rat-hole later, if it lay within
his power, thus far he had only made plans, because
of the work he was striving to do upon himself,
toward which he found this sombre isolation especially conducive.

The time had now arrived, however, when he
was ready for freedom and he determined to have
it. He had discovered in the cellar, barrels and
boxes sufficient to make it possible to reach the
window through which he felt sure he could make
his exit, sooner or later, and never being interrupted
except by the humpback, there were hours in which
he could work at the bars with an improvised file
that he had already secreted.

One night as he was falling asleep he dreamed
in his half doze that Sallus and Regan, beaming
with the old love and friendship, had entered the
cellar and taken him bodily, through the aperture
in the wall, out into the street. He seemed in his
vision, to have dwindled to the size of a rat, which
they found no difficulty in* dragging through the
hole ; suddenly, as though touched by some one,
he sat up in bed as wide awake as he had ever been
in his life ; the cellar was dark and he had no

means by which to strike a light ; he listened intently, for such a waking as that implied something extraordinary. In a moment he heard a faint tap, tap, tap ; it came from the direction of the casement, which was a long distance from the bed. This rapping continued, intermittently, till Aleppo arose, and finding at his feet a bit of hard earth, made his way, by instinct, in the direction of the window, and strove to hit the faint blur of glass with this lump of dirt. Once or twice he thought he had succeeded, for the tapping seemed to come in answer, but later it ceased altogether, and silence reigned as before.

There was no more sleep for young Romanes that night. At first he felt sure that some friend had discovered his prison and come to his rescue, but later, in cold thought, he concluded that he might have been too hasty ; a child, or a mischievous person, from pure wantonness, was just as likely to be at the bottom of this ; however, when the raps were repeated the next night, and the next, his hopes grew apace. The effect of Sallus' whistle was like a re-birth ; when Aleppo heard the old college tune that they had sung together, he cried like a child—"Loyal to the death," he said, as the tears gushed to his eyes. " Regan —Sallus ! And there's nothing between us but this stone wall ; once I doubted even you, O God, forgive me !"

He was so happy the next day, and his heart

13

was so light that he sang and whistled as he used
to do in the old time in Stamboul.   The hump-back
looked at him suspiciously, for Aleppo's eyes were
brilliant and his look illuminated.   He had his
boxes and barrel handy and in striving to adjust
their height to the window he discovered a bit of
paper which had a fresh look about it, quite foreign
to the condition of other articles in the place.   It
was the note of Regan.   He had known happiness
many times in his life ; like all trusting natures, he
had believed in his friends and looked upon it as a
crime to doubt them, but when he opened the
twisted billet and rested his eyes again on the well
known writing of Regan he was intoxicated with
rapture ; he wondered if he would have been so
true, so faithful, himself, if he had that same capacity of devotion which these two had shown.
Months had passed since he had vanished at Karnak, and yet they were on his track ; their trip
had been abandoned, pleasure forgotten, all for
himself.

He was intoxicated with the rapture of gratitude and, bursting with a desire to express it, he
climbed to the window, but no one was there.
Dimly, through the aperture, he beheld the dull
ground of the alley—ah ! he could write ! All day
he spent at it, tearing up one note after another, as
he found old scraps of paper, feeling that each but
feebly expressed his love and longing.   At last it
resolved itself into this, and this only :

"I am dumb with gratitude.
Yours forever,
"ALEPPO ROMANES."

He deposited the message in the secret receptacle and, when morning arrived, discovered that it had vanished.

CHAPTER XXXIII.

SATAN.

From the time that the first notes were exchanged between Regan and Aleppo a constant correspondence had been kept up and all arrangements made for the young man's escape. Regan and Sallus were obliged to work secretly and mostly in the dark, for the alley was constantly traversed by individuals whose attention was more or less attracted to them.

The night for which the escape had been planned was propitious; a drizzling, disagreeable rain was falling, the clouds above causing the alley to be shrouded in darkness. Sallus allowed himself about an hour and a half for the filing of the bars; at some distance from him, on either side, Regan and Isaac acted as sentinels, and, by a pre-arranged signal, stood in readiness to warn him of the approach of danger.

The dogs of that special locality had become so accustomed to the three prowlers that they united themselves with them as friends and allies, feeling a secret kinship which they strove silently to express.

Sallus expected to work from midnight till after one in the morning, when, as had been previously arranged, Aleppo was to break the thick window pane and make good his escape from the house of Issachar.

When Romanes heard the first rasp of the file, he thrilled with the ecstasy of liberty. He had climbed upon the boxes, placed his ear to the glass, and for an hour had remained almost rigid before any sound was heard. He felt sure that he had failed in comprehending the time, as he had no means by which to do so, save that of instinct, he rightly conjectured the cause of delay. Yet his anxiety was so intense that he thought, as he stood there, of a thousand things that might have happened to prevent his escape. His friends for aught he knew were already arrested and incarcerated, and Issachar possibly had acquired a knowledge of the whole scheme. He glued his ear to the glass and every sound in the alley set his heart to beating with alternate spasms of hope and fear. At last the dull heavy rasp of the file! He remembered the powerful muscles of Sallus and felt that his friend's very sinews were on the bars. Between him and liberty, stood the Adonis of his boyish dreams. His whole life with his young friend— their days of frolic and travel passed before his mental glance; he recalled the picture of Scutari ages ago, so it seemed, when he and Sallus had fought out the question of the flask, which the half inebriated boy had bequeathed in the irony of his bitterness to a helpless corpse. Sallus! Sallus!— and here he was risking his own liberty with every grate of the steel which ripped open the bars that cut his friend off from the joys of life. When for an instant the noise subsided, Aleppo's heart stopped with it, to start again with a bound at the welcome sound. It was the longest hour that he had ever experienced, the most tantalizing, terrible. All the memories of his past thronged upon him as though to rend him asunder. A possible future was scarcely more than formed ere it would dwindle and vanish to be replaced by Issachar—Issachar, whose hyena teeth flashed in the black deeps of his mind, like the ultimate instruments of doom; and while these hellish visions came and went, interspersed by gleams of azure skies, soft vales and swaying trees, he still heard distinctly and reassuringly, the steady rasp of the file as one iron after another yielded to the muscle and brawn of Sallus, who neither wavered nor paused for rest.

There were six bars; the last act was to be performed quickly; at a signal tap from the outside, the pane was to be broken and Aleppo drawn forth. It came—three sharp quick raps which Aleppo followed immediately by a blow that shattered the glass, when from the deeps of the dungeon, from the abyss of darkness—"ha! ha! ha! ha! ha! ha!"

Before Aleppo could realize how it was done, the structure of boxes was knocked from under him, and pinioned by two powerful men he was hurried from the place into a dimly lighted apartment where stood Issachar, immaculate, sardonic, superb.

We seek in vain for martyrs among the free. At last Romanes, who had conquered isolation and vanquished the demon of luxury, was honored with martyrdom, which is the acme test of character and the finality of pain.

He raised his eyes to Issachar—the saddest eyes the Jew had ever seen ; even he who forgot all else that throbbed with sorrow or gasped with agony, even he in after years remembered them,

"Wouldst thou know me?" said Issachar; "completely, entirely, I am Satan!" His voice grew to a full falsetto. "Be mine, and all things shall be given unto thee ; rebel, and thou art crucified."

Extremes meet. A soft glamour of happiness stole over Aleppo like the unseen kiss of spring that warms her lover's lips ; he had realized the limit of suffering, which means bliss—bliss ; again he dreamed the Syrian dream and warmed to the heart of El Reshid, as the great warm to the great.

"Ha! ha! Thou dost imagine that the God of the Jews will come to thy deliverance, or that the fabled autocrat of a fickle Order will snatch thee from the grip of Issachar—ha, ha ! Thou knowest not Satan, whose mark is on thee, and whose child thou art, By proxy he would sin through thee ; on thy gluttony and debauchery would he regale himself ; his beak he would dip into thy rotten carcass ; a dainty bit shalt thou be for one whose robe is spotless and whose body is clean.

" Aleppo Romanes, a respite, and afterward, torture—begone ! "

He was hurried away—and the light extinguished.

Outside stood Sallus ; at the smashing of the glass he had reached through the aperture and found nothing. His disappointment was terrible ; he forced his head and arms into the cellar, and daringly struck a match ; the wreck of the boxes was beneath him, and the great vault. He lighted a bit of candle, which he had purposely brought, and examined the excavation as far as his eyes could reach. The straw pallet of Aleppo, the stone table, the broken pitcher, all thrust themselves at him to torture with their pathos, but the prisoner, gone ! Then Regan jerked him by the shoulder, and said, emphatically, in an excited whisper—

" Put that light out will you—quick !—run ! "

The unusual spectacle had attracted some curious night prowlers, from whom Sallus and his colleagues escaped as best they could, to meet later, in their room, in a disheveled and unhappy condition.

"That blasted Jew has beaten me again." Regan for the first time in the hunt, looked the picture of despair.

"Now," said Sallus, a peculiar expression in his eyes, "patience, chicanery, double-dealing, and underhand play, cease to be virtuous ; from this time on, I shall go it open." He took his revolver from his pocket and looked down into the barrel— "I'll hound that Jew to hell and shoot him like a dog."

"And then you will get punished yourself," said Isaac ; "the authorities will make you dead and buried."

"I hope they will put up a headstone—" Sallus was raging.

"They will put up no tombstone ; one good moneys is better than marble. You should have the young man yet ; you have no patience ; moneys will fetch that young man ; you bribe those authorities ; money is greater than Issachar ; you give those authorities moneys and the Jew will give them the young man."

"What authorities on earth, are you talking about ?" all out of patience.

"Those officials—all ; for moneys they attack the Almighty, that is Jehovah, that is Issachar ; for moneys they dig out the bowels of the planet, and pluck those lights out of the sky ; for moneys they steal from the Satan, and burn up the mosques of Stamboul. You have much moneys, you get that young man."

At this juncture the door opened and Cæsar Catus, in his traveling attire, and dusty from a long journey, stood on the threshold and extended his hand—

"So you have lost him again?"

The hounds were a wretched pair; in muddy bedraggled garments, a sort of mongrel disguise, with dirty hands and faces, unkempt hair and half grown beards, they presented about as disreputable an appearance as any two Bohemians that ever made a night of it.

No matter about Sallus! He was bound to be handsome, but Regan had no touch of beauty left.

"I'm afraid this time it's forever," said the Yankee.

Catus teemed with energy that spoke from his very fingers, and the fagged men took new heart. He dismissed Isaac, turned up the light, and, touching a match to the wood in the grate, put a cheerful aspect on things at once. "Go and have a good wash," he said, " get into Christian garments and come back."

Mechanically they obeyed, to return in fifteen minutes, still unshaved, but otherwise looking quite themselves.

" I have come to request you to give up this hunt."

"Never !" said Sallus, shutting his teeth in bull-dog fashion.

"I urged you to go into it," went on Catus un-moved, "and now I urge you to get out of it."

"Why do you set us on in this way only to make fools of us ?"·said Sallus, still angry.

"Cool up a little and I'll tell you. In the first place, when I started you on the scent I didn't know as much as I do now, that's one reason; in the second, you've done your work, and it's a great one."

"I don't understand," said Regan.

"Do you think it is nothing to restore Aleppo's confidence in human nature and to fill his heart with gratitude ? You have done a great work, I say, and to you I shall communicate some of the secrets and objects of the Order of the Olympians and the cult of Romanes. Great in victory, for you have won. Rest now, contented, till you hear from me again."

"And shall we do nothing ?" said Sallus, much sobered, "nothing at all ?"

"You don't mean to say you have given Aleppo up, do you ?" put in Regan, alarmed.

"Never ! *he is a Romanes.*"

"I can't understand your manner of cool cer-tainty. We used to feel that way, Regan and I, but we don't any more ; the conceit has been taken out of us, every bit, hasn't it, Dad ?"

"Sal says he'll shoot the Jew; what do you think of it?" asked Regan.

"He might try, but I expect he would fail"—the same twinkle in his eyes. "Stay here in old Stamboul, rest and wait for me."

Somehow the men felt more comfortable than they had thought possible an hour before; Catus inspired great confidence.

"There's one consolation," he said, "we're in the same boat—we both had him, when *lo, he was not.*"

"Isaac says moneys will fetch him."

"Isaac judges everybody by himself, and he's not far wrong either; it's a pretty safe way; money is just as powerful here as anywhere, but Satan's not caught on a gold hook; good night."

CHAPTER XXXIV.

THE GREAT ORDER.

The following evening Regan and Sallus established themselves before a fire in their room, having arranged the most comfortable chair in expectation of Catus, who had promised to join them.

"Guess likely these cigars will be good enough," said Regan, reluctantly placing some first-class Havanas within reach. "There he is now."

Catus was in quite a different mood from that of the night before, in fact his atmosphere was as varied as the New England climate. On this particular evening he was in a communicative frame of mind—his "tongue had been oiled," he said.

"May we ask questions?" said Sallus.

"Certainly, though I'll not promise to answer them."

Catus took the easiest chair—he always did—for, though a young man, he was treated like a patriarch, then; raising his feet on a stool to the level of his hips, he "lighted up" and smiled good-naturedly on his friends.

"Now pay close attention, for I'm going to teach you something and I'm anxious that you get it correctly.

"There are any number of orders in the world as of course you know, but this society of the Olympians, while a decided factor, is the least understood of them all. In the first place, to a great extent it is hermetic, its members being exceedingly cautious in their communications. Even to you, who deserve to be on the inside, I shall tell but little, leaving you to guess as much more as you like.

"Since history, men have found that if they would think for themselves they must seal their lips, and I have no need to explain to you the reason of this. Wherever the church and state are one, or to be more exact, the religion and state, no matter whether in heathendom or christendom,

tyranny and torture prevail. Money, the base of all
evil, is the gilded foundation on which a religious
autocracy is built, and no man, or set of men, with
their senses about them, under such conditions,
dare to openly defy an invincible power. If one be
such a sublime fool, he gets the reward of a Bruno,
as sure as the sun sets. Within the last few years
the method of torture has been altered, becoming
more subtle and refined, yet the sting is there,
nevertheless, in the fang of the snake, and the
venom as deadly to-day as in ages past. Hence,
the Olympians, who banded secretly at the dawn of
history, and undying, defy time, priestly rule and
political autocracy."

" Is it a large order? " asked Regan.

"Compared with the Masons, no, though there
are many of that organization among them."

" Is it a religious body?"

" That depends on what you understand by the
word. If religion means the finality of truth,
devotion to the changeless laws of being, and the
principle of them, yes, it is a religious organization.
If, however, you define religion, as a devotional
allegiance to an anthropomorphic God, and a sibylline book, no, it is not religious. Like St. Paul,
they preach the unknown God, whose name is
never spoken ; and, as for a bible, the book of
nature is amply sufficient, both as inspirer and revealer. They are always getting new insight as
they turn the leaves, such strange revelations that

pre-conceived conventional opinions become of but small value, and all things formerly believed are found to be flashes of a truth but half revealed. It is emphatically an experimental religion and in that, is closely allied to science which some of our members claim is but another name for the same thing."

" Has the Order a chief or head ? "

" Most assuredly; now listen closely: Years and years ago, you would doubt me if I told you how many, the order of the Olympians had one of the most brilliant masters that ever sat in the imperial chair. Though I myself was unborn at the time, I have heard the members tell of Henrique Romanes, who like Pericles of ancient Hellas was called the Olympian Zeus. He had gone so far in his study of chemistry and medicine, had penetrated so keenly into the secrets of nature, knew so much of the transmutation of energy and the conservation of force, that he maintained his prime as easily as others grow old, and earned his right to Olympus by the conquest over sleep and death. He had entered the innermost shrine of the order and knew the secret of secrets; not only practically compre-hending the nirvanic poise, which means an inten-sity of life that words fail to paint, but also grasped the paradox of opposition which made him a man of affairs, a general, a commander."

" This is all Greek to me," said Sallus.

" I presume it is, my boy, however, the light may

break on you some day.   Well, as I was saying, he
was the greatest master that Olympian tradition
boasts. and had more influence in the order than
any who had preceded him.   ·

It would seem that he deliberately went out;
whether he was tired of his supremacy, or overcome by love, was never quite determined. However
this aside; the young man Aleppo is of his own
flesh, and some day, as surely as the sun rises, will
take the old man's place.''

" Old man ! "

. "Yes, old man, Henrique Romanes is very, *very*
old.''

" How many years ? "   ·

The *age of an Olympian is never told.*

''How is it that Aleppo's father is so fast breaking up?'' said Sallus.

" That is as great a secret as is the famed elixir;
to give away one would be to explain the other."

" Are the members all celibate?"

" Oh, no ; only those of the inner shrine ; and
here let me say that these words, shrine, degree,
etc., are fictitious, simply designating lines or as-
pects of life and action. In reality, if a man wants
some particular thing or power, he gives up another to get it ; in cheap language, pays for it.
Force is constant, psychically as well as physically,
mathematics and logic are at the base of Olympus;
rather than gold; the medium of exchange is anything but jingling coin.''

"Is it not a pretty cold place?" said Regan doubtfully. "Olympus has ice on the summit."

"True, but fire at its heart; it is no extinct volcano, let me assure you; as a thinking body it is at the freezing point; as an emotional, it has the passion of a Christ."

"Do you do any practical work?"

"Without boasting, certainly, and always incognito. Among fallen women we are most energetic, and have pronounced success. Let me assure you, though, that we never appear among them as preachers or philanthropists. In our study of nature we remember the inner aspect and pull people out of the ditches, rags and all; should we stop to change their garments most likely they would drown. We make no show of working nor of goodness; an Olympian who boasts or uses platitudes is thrust from the order. We find ostentation intolerable, and a show of sympathy fails to pass in our cult for the real thing."

"Have you no hypocrites among you?"

"Not at present, that we are aware of. Many years ago we entertained a traitor, so says tradition."

"How was that?"

"And Satan came among them."

"Ah! Satan!"

"Yes, Issachar. He was then a young man and succeeded in deluding the Olympians, all save

Romanes, until he wormed from them the secrets
which he utilizes to this very day.''

'' Was that long since ? ''

'' Yes,'' laughed Catus.

'' What are you so amused about ? ''

'' Time cuts no figure with us.''

'' It's the most all-fired curious combination I
ever heard of,'' said Regan; ''you talk about
nature one minute and fly into her face the next;
how the deuce can you abide by the laws of nature
and not grow old ? ''

Catus lighted another Havana, at the same time
laughing silently, much to the annoyance of Regan.

Now, there's no use in your looking so wise ;
facts tell on me every time, or, for that matter,
reason; but smiles don't go down with this Yankee,
nor any of your confounded mysteries, that are
ashamed of the light of day.''

'' There is now and then a flower that opens in
the night, you know,'' said Catus sobering.

'' All right, I'll agree to that.''

'' What is more,'' went on Catus, '' while nature
is true to her rhythmic law she has another if I'm
not mistaken, which the Masters have not told of
and the rest of humanity have not, it refers to the
supremacy of will, nirvanic poise, or the moving
equilibrium of science, but that is all out of the way
of my narrative. Mark you one thing more, there's
nothing *supernatural* in the universe; but there are
laws and laws, and a Law of them. To discover a

principle is to enhance one's power; now let us drop this and go on.''

'' Say, Catus, what has a fellow got to do to get in with the Olympians ? '' asked Regan.

'' A few more such noble deeds as you have just done. Really, I look up to you and Sallus, already; you ought to be in my place.

'' Fiddlesticks! that was for love, and it doesn't count. Love is the most selfish thing in the universe. ''

'' True, and the sublimest; henceforth, who shall dare call selfishness an evil ! ''

' Who is the chief of the order to-day? '' said Sallus.

It was rather strange, but Catus removed his cigar and stood up, then answered in a subdued and affectionate voice, '' El Reshid.''

CHAPTER XXXV.

IN OLD CAIRO AGAIN.

Left in Cairo, Rhea sought Spino and Cicily, and with her keen womanly intuition comprehended and solved them as no man had been able to do. To ''the beautiful Yankee,'' as she called her, Cicily poured out her story, begging help to escape from Issachar, of whom she was becoming more and more afraid.

As the Jew was absent, Rhea went every day to

visit her new friends and spent long hours both listening to their story and planning for their escape.

"Has the answer to my letter arrived?" she asked of Spino one afternoon, as she entered the Jew's quarters.

"Yes! yes!" and Cicely came from behind the arras, and throwing her arms about Rhea kissed her again and again. The letter which the young girl produced was from southern France, and addressed to Rhea Nellino, being an answer to one from that young lady sent to Cicily's relatives making inquiries in regard to her family and their intentions. The reply was brief but explicit, stating that Cicily was undoubtedly a daughter of their family, and also a member of a secret order to which her father belonged; that while she was ostensibly stolen for money, in reality the act was a stab at the organization, and that, though her near relatives were dead, those living were willing to take the young girl, provided she made her escape. While the letter authenticated to a great extent Spino's story, the writer was no enthusiast, and being several degrees removed in blood from the victim of Issachar, seemed actuated more from a sense of duty than a desire to help in her rescue.

The communication, however, was sufficient for the purpose of Rhea. The characters of Spino and Cicily being cleared to her satisfaction she resolved, in spite of Mrs. Hancock or Issachar, to dis-

patch the two women to France immediately ; at
the same time writing a note to Regan and Sallus,
requesting them to see that they were properly
cared for, as soon as they could get off duty at
Stamboul.

" Do you think there is any danger of the Jew's
return just about now?" asked Rhea, folding the
letter and looking anxiously at Spino.

" Issachar ! he bobs up anywhere, at any time ;
yes, there is danger; nevertheless, we must try in
the face of it, and keep on trying, no matter if we
are captured and re-captured."

" How soon can you start ? "

" Any minute," answered Spino.

" I will pay your fares to France," said Rhea.
" Get your things together directly; the longer you
wait the less chance you have; let me help you."

The three bustled about and packed the few nec-
essaries required on the trip.   Rhea, finding
Cicily's wardrobe in a barbaric condition, supplied
her with a good many sober garments, which so
transformed the girl that, instead of a dowdy oriental princess, she appeared a natty French
woman, quite chic and delightful.   However you
might fix Cicily, she was distractingly pretty; in
splendid decay or prim prosperity, washed or unwashed, the girl was a flesh and blood beauty that
forced people to turn their heads.   Rhea had given
her a quiet, gray dress of her own and a sober
traveling hat that simply enhanced the rebellious

tangle of her lovely hair and the bright glow in her cheeks.

"Here, let me tie you up in a veil; you will be followed from the first—you are altogether too lovely," said Rhea anxiously. "If I were a man I would certainly run off with you."

But the veil only made matters worse. Cicily's soft, dangerous eyes flashed through its meshes more seducingly than ever, so Rhea found a heavy, green baize and smothered the poor child's fascinations in its cruel folds.

"There, you little Venus, don't you dare, on the penalty of getting caught, to lift that mask an inch—an inch."

"But I'm positively wretched; I cannot breathe."

"Be wretched then," said Rhea, laughing; "it isn't my fault that you're so pretty; if you will persist in throwing us all in the shade, we'll have to treat you in the same way."

"Aren't you going to put a veil on me?" said Spino in a grieved tone.

"Yes, granny, I am, of course I am."

People turn around and look after me," went on the old lady; "the men stare as long as they can see, and it isn't Cicily that does it, for it's worse when I go out alone. I don't believe that there is any woman in Cairo that attracts as much attention as I do."

"That's because you're so distinguished, granny; stand still now and I'll tie you up."

But Spino never stood still in her life, and she couldn't now, nor did the veil disguise her in any sense. Her face was but a part of her; her queer shape and awkward motions betrayed Spino wherever she went, and in spite of Rhea's precautions, she looked herself from head to toe.

Whether the old fellow who kept the shop below-stairs had an inkling of the mischief brewing above was unknown to them ; at any rate he appeared very innocent, and went his usual way without interfering in the least. Mrs. Hancock, too, let Rhea severely alone, contenting herself with the remark that, "The time would come when the account would be settled, and her niece would answer at the judgment seat for her hermetic intimacy with the Egytians, who were nothing more than heathen and devils." Mrs. Hancock folded her robes of sanctity around her and sat aloof, disdaining to soil the tips of her sacred fingers with the touch of such "vile trash."

No Hindoo of the highest caste could treat a cursed pariah with more contempt than she showed to these poor prisoners of Issachar, whom she happened to meet, with her niece, on the streets of Cairo. Rhea was ashamed of her, bitterly, and a great coldness came between them, which threatened to end in separation.

To escape from Issachar as easily as they did,

seemed absurd in the face of the difficulties that had
apparently been in their way. Either the Jew was
glad to get rid of them, or was so engaged elsewhere, that he had forgotten their existence ; however this might be, they went quietly to the
station with Rhea, and kissing their friend again
and again, took the train out of Cairo, unmolested.
Rhea went as boldly back to her aunt, who asked
in an icy tone—

"Are we to stay forever, in Cairo?"

"A few weeks longer, Aunt Carrie, then we'll
take up the thread of our tour where we left it, and
spin it out to the end."

Her aunt sniffed the air suspiciously, but made
no answer.

Though Regan and Sallus had both written
many times to Rhea, they had said nothing of the
finding of Aleppo, as they dreaded to torture her
with more intense anxiety than she had already
felt. Still she waited at Cairo, putting off her departure from week to week, for a time making
Spino and Cicily her excuse, and afterward saying
to herself, "A little while longer, and something
will be discovered, then I will go."

"Spino sent Rhea a message from every available
point on her trip, and at last, news came from
France, that they had arrived safely, and were met
by Cicily's relatives, who had found the girl charm-
ing, especially a young cousin who desired to marry
her without delay. This troubled Rhea consider-

ably, as she knew Sallus' secret, and was anxious
for the happiness of her boy friend; so she wrote
him immediately; telling him of the situation, and
urging him to communicate with Cicily at once.
Sallus answered:

Dear Miss Nellino:—

" The young lady knows very well that I love
her, and that I will keep my promise as soon as
Aleppo is found. If she is true, as I believe she is,
no temptation in the shape of a French cousin can
induce her to betray my trust. Time will prove
Cicily."

While this all sounded very well, in reality Sallus
was suffering from jealousy and love combined—a
miserable gray mixture of white and black, light
and darkness. Yet, setting aside his personal joys
and sorrows, ever nearest his loyal heart was
Aleppo, whom he had vowed to champion till
freedom came, if it took forever.

In Sallus's heart were two opposing emotions·—
hatred for Issachar and love for Romanes; they
were his hell and heaven. He cared little for
psychology, philosophy, or religion, save as they
were personified and demonstrated. Aleppo was
the soul of Sallus, and stood for the psychic, the
poet, the dreamer; through him he saw visions, and
felt the thrill of rhythm·and song; through his far-
seeing glance, he watched the stars and the clouds
that veiled them; without Allepo, Sallus felt himself
to be an animal and nothing more. Rhea, who

seemed but another aspect of his friend, was his goddess, his religion; through her he worshipped and gave sacrifice. Even loyalty in its finality is selfish. We are true to that which we need, to that which wakes us out of sleep. Issachar also stirred the depths of Sallus. To hate supremely, is to thrill with a sombre ecstasy that brings potential being into active life. Any emotion that shocks a man to his feet and stirs his sluggish blood, whether it be hate or love, any excitation that lifts him out of body into mind, and stirs his inert self into action, is a breeder of life and a revealer of being to itself. Sallus then was as loyal to his personalized religion—Rhea—and his personified soul—Aleppo—as another might be to his church and his priest. He hated Issachar as most men hate the devil and was working out his own salvation in a unique way.

Life is a problem, especially to him who attempts to solve another's existence and not his own. No two are ground on the same wheel, no two are uplifted in the same direction, or by the same means. Back of each is a different causation, a spring whose source is especially its own; in its flow through the æons, it has gathered its respective debris and on its banks are its own peculiar flowers, yet, we teachers and preachers presume to judge of the sequence as though we knew the causation; of the blood, without the pedigree. We dictate but one method of progress, point out but one way of

advancement, ordering an ameba to bring forth a
giant and a mollusk a man. Evolution is a slow
process and depends entirely upon its eternal mate
—involution, from which it can never be divorced.

The marvelous variety spread before our eyes
to day—the jungle of specialization, rich, teeming,
voluptuous, seen, unseen, within reach, beyond,
above, below, beautiful, ugly, harmless, venomous;
this fetid, perfumed, gorgeous, deadly jungle,
preaches heterogeneity with a silent daring that
holds us spell-bound; each individual facing the
combined opposition of the mass, as subtly conscious of its immortality, as though logic were
expounding in a voice of thunder, and we preachers
penetrate this jungle of spiders and lilies, and toss
the lamb to the jaws of the lion, and the bird at
the fangs of the snake, saying, in unctuous ver-
bosity, ''Live ye in harmony; be one; seek the
same gleaming heaven, and flee from the identical
sulphurous hell; as though the lotus loved the sunlight, or the sun-flower adored the moon.

Should there come a Master among you, who
could, like Shakespeare, read each man as though
on earth there were no other; who could prescribe
for the *individual* a formula that would fit his special condition; who would look over the far-off past
of a man, as well as ahead; who would judge the
changing phases of his existence, as though but the
other pole of his unit of energy; should a great
specialist appear, who at the same time could realize

unity as the changeless base from which phenomena spring, and should he present you with the paradox of an altruistic individualism, you would nail him to the cross and pierce his hands and feet and side; even more, you would place the crown of thorns upon his head, and soak a sponge in hyssop and vinegar to moisten his lips. Ah, yes, for men are sheep who run in herds, so like each other that they have no names, and the priest devours them in their ignorance, lest they be startled into life by a clarion voice and a new gospel.

CHAPTER XXXVI.

FAREWELL, MY DREAM.

It was Rhea's last night in Cairo. The next day they were to continue their journey as previously planned. Why she had remained so long in Egypt she hardly knew. Her friends in Stamboul had sent no encouraging news in regard to Aleppo and the prospect of ever seeing him again was exceedingly dim.

Though she had felt the spell of El Reshid, and for a time had been roused by hope, later she became depressed and practically a skeptic regarding the whole affair. Also, about herself, her dream, her belief in love eternal, constancy, and those ideal possibilities which she had so ardently sought, she was now doubtful. Of one thing only was she sure,

and that was the love of Aleppo; but whether it
would longer be entertained by him in face of new
and more lofty aspirations, she was also doubtful.
A smouldering fire was scarcely warm enough for
an exotic nature like hers; she was a 'Psyche, and
a Cupid who went elsewhere, even to heaven, was
a sorrow rather than a joy.

  She took herself to task coldly, severely, treat-
ing her suffering heart as though it belonged to an
enemy whom she desired to torture.   Her New
England conscience showed no pity, but in its pur-
itanic cruelty troubled her night and day.   "What,
after all," she thought, "are my silly fancies and
dreams; was there ever a romantic girl without
them?   Venus makes dupes of us all ;   she whispers 'love eternal,' and seduces our sweethearts
with her voluptuous eyes.   She breathes 'constancy,' and shuffles the queen of hearts with a
reckless hand; she preaches Uranian felicity while
intoxicating us poor mortals with the wine of hell.
" Ah, I have dreamed of friendship, of happy contact, of divine delights, in the glow of which, time
and space are a chimera, and death a lie.   I have
lived in the vestal whiteness of the soul's heat, I
have felt the glamour of Adonis and the cold power
of Diana ; I have built me a castle in the blue,
from the very fleece of the clouds, which even a
zephyr has blown over; I have revelled in a dim
past, where the soul of the ancient congealed into
marble, and told its story in the Hellenic shaft;

I have wandered backward, to the very verge of being, and onward to the gate of Paradise. Alas! farewell, my dream.

"Even the Nile, with its tawny beauty, the moon, the sky, the very stars, are transfigured by my eyes; I throw a spell upon Venus, and enchantment over Mars; I behold all things through the fine mesh of illusion, which transforms a pebble into a diamond and a weed into the tree of life. My soul is a rhapsody, without measure or tune. Henceforth, remember—the Nile is but a mud-stained stream, Egypt a corpse, Hellas a vision born of false ideas, Karnak a ruin of the past, religion a superstition, love an impulse of the blood, and Aleppo—Aleppo! my other self! Then wherefore seeks he the Olympians, and the inner shrine of the sage? The great temple of Ammon has seduced him, for amid its very ruins he donned the garb of a priest; and the stars that gleam coldly on the cursed pile of the ancients have put out my eyes—mine. To love you now is to worship the ice peaks of a mountain, or the cold splendor of the moon; you are a Christ uplifted, whose feet I may not kiss; and yet are you constant—as is the generous sun that shines over all. You love me as God loves, and I—I spurn it all; I renounce you. Instead of me, embrace the world; it fills your arms even now, your heart. I am not wise. Did the marble Phryne warm the fingers of Praxiteles? Was the chisel hot that cut

the block to semblance of sweet life?   O, to know
the subtlety, the flutter of love's heart—the thrill,
the passion that sets the universe a quivering, to
feel the rapture of the soul's abandon.   Alas!
farewell, my dream ?

    " And yet shall I love you—through the years of
my life—the eternities.   Despised and rejected
—a prince and a master —you.   Somewhere in the
depths of self may you feel me, as one discovers
the beating of his heart; somewhere in the spaces
may you hear me, as one catches the echo of a
song; somewhere in the light within may you see
me, as one beholds the heavenly face; somewhere
in the universe may you know me, as self discovers self.

    ' Far back I behold the oracle of Delphi and the
pale priestess of a frenzied prophesy; far ahead,
the seeress of a resurrected Hellas and the sibyl of
an unborn age.   Till then—farewell, my dream."

CHAPTER XXXVII.

THE UNIT OF FORCE.

    " Dos moi pou sto kai tan gan kinaso "—Give
me where I may stand and I will move the earth.

    Romanes and Issachar were face to face; the Jew
had crept upon him with the slyness of a cat and
their eyes met.

    " Think not that I came to barter again," said

Issachar, "Aleppo Romānes has had his chance, henceforth he is mine." He smiled.

"You may barter till the day of doom, but not with me," said Romanes; "my son shall not be bought; I knew this well when last I scorned you, vile snake, who crept into the order of Olympus on your belly, and behind me but a moment since, as if to stab me in the back. Money! you laugh,— money! by the powers you seek revenge. I might fling you gold till I were beggared, and you would chuckle and spit upon me using my flesh and blood as but a means to pull me down—*me*. Think you I failed to understand when last you came; think you that I remember not your threat in Syria years since?—have you forgot?"

"Nay, but thou hast had thy day; my turn has come."

"So you would dare the Olympians; quite well aware are you that should you draw the knife upon Aleppo your own life's blood yon must needs forfeit; by the powers you thought to catch me napping and prick my veins. Even yet, you have done the youth no harm, nor can you; your steel has lost its temper, your blade its edge; your cursed magic rebounds upon itself. All this I knew full well when last we met."

"Thy tongue can twist itself to boasting, but acts speak louder than cheap words"—the Jew's eyes glowed like burning coals; "thon art helpless; thy son forever is far beyond thy reach; thy power

which flashes, as does a dying fire whose fuel has
been spent, is not sufficiently sustained to force me
as thou once did do, when thou wert Master of
Olympus; ha ! and I, invincible, have thee upon
thy knees spouting thy boastful prayers into my
ears—the prince of ancient time, a cheap buffoon
among the moderns, making slim use of bluff and
and verbiage, where once he opened not his lips,
and did but glance to make me tremble; ha ! ha !
Romanes, my revenge is sweet."

"Words," sneered Romanes, haughtier, taller,
" are sometimes deadly shot, whose prick you may
feel later, but mark you this : It is strange in all your
boasted prowess that as yet you have failed to discover that El Reshid is but using the paws of the
cat to pull the jewel from the fire. It amazes me
that one, so wise as you suppose yourself to be, has
not yet ascertained that you are doing a service to
Aleppo beyond price. You—the devil—have helped
a master to evolve; you have broken the husk of
the chrysalis and let loose the butterfly; you have
ground the uncut gem upon a wheel. In truth,
El Reshid owes you thanks; unconsciously have
you done service to the order and to me."

" Ha ! ha !—ha ! ha ! If I have failed to make
thee suffer, prepare for torture now ; Know then,
that the young Master, the new star of Olympus,
flashed but a day on Hellas, and sank to rise again
over the strong-hold of Issachar on the banks of
the Golden Horn. Thy son has deserted the house

of Romanes, and swears allegiance to an outcast
and a Jew. He loves thee not, but me, reverest,
who stamped him with the devil's mark.''

" 'Tis false! *You lie!*"

" Ha! ha!—the proof, words are but dirt."

The afternoon sun had sunk, and the room of
Romanes was in shadow. He struck a light, it
threw a dim glow over the apartment and brought
out the Jew like a Rembrandt. Romanes went a
step nearer, so close that he touched the immaculate robe of Issachar, and said under his breath
with deadly emphasis, "Know thou that I come to
Stamboul to demand my son ; that when the time
was ripe, I left Genoa? I give you warning that
the Powers are at my back. Would you escape
them, bring forth Aleppo."

" Ha! ha! And what if he desires thee not ; no
power can force him against his will. Should the
order insist, he will laugh in its face. Should El
Reshid command, he will turn his back. He is
vile, debauched, lost. And thou wouldst lift him
high over Olympus? Ha! ha!—revenge is sweet."

A deadly sickness struck at the heart of Romanes.
Had Aleppo failed as he had ; had the tests been
beyond him? Was Issachar, after all the Master,
and Satan, the supreme?

For an instant the Jew tasted the sweetness of
revenge ; he saw the pallor creep to the brow of
Romanes, the trembling of his hands, the startled
expression in his eyes. He had known every

14

emotion before, save this ; he had revelled in every unlawful sensation and experienced every sin, but revenge, in its exquisite finality, its intensest possibility, he had waited long to feel. The bliss of the devil was forcing his heart to quick action, the exultation of the inferno was upon him—the insane rapture. To acquire this, was to have lived supremely. To realize the terror at the paternal heart of the enemy, and to know that he, himself, was the cause ; to humble to the very dust his former Master, to behold him trembling with fear and sorrow—ah, ecstasy!

The door opened so silently that neither of them heard, and a young man, vivid, powerful, crossed the threshold. For a long minute he stood in the shadow watching the two mortal enemies. On the face of one was the look of supreme triumph, on that of the other, despair. He stepped between them.

Imagine the sky when the sun bursts through the clouds, and you get some idea of the change in the face of Romanes when his eyes caught those of El Reshid, yet, in spite of the most powerful emotion that the human heart can feel, the habit of the order controlled him, and he bowed himself nearly to the floor.

Issachar, who grew tall or short according to the state of his sensations, shrank till he seemed to be bowing also, and his eyes, as they scanned the calm figure before him, flashed with deadly fear.

"Thy haughty demeanor became thee far better than this craven aspect," said El Reshid; "of what art thou afraid?"

Issachar tried to regain himself and backed slowly toward the door.

"Halt! on the spot where thou standest; move not an inch."

The voice of El Reshid vibrated with a musical intensity that echoed long after in the soul.

"Romanes," he said, turning his back on Issachar, "the time is at hand; can'st thou face Aleppo?"

The Jew again attempted to reach the door, but a glance from the masterful eyes of El Reshid transfixed him where he stood.

"I fear not to meet Aleppo," answered Romanes, "if he be the chosen of the Olympians; but this vile Jew has thrown it in my teeth that mine own son has disgraced me, *even me*. I betrayed the order; but if this be so, he has fallen to a depth of which I have never dreamed; nor would I behold him now, or ever."

"The devil is the father of lies. Stand thou erect, Romanes." Then, turning to the Jew he said in a strange tone, so vibrating with intensity that it seemed scarcely a voice at all—

"Go thou, and bring Aleppo."

Issachar threw at him a terrified glance.

"Go thou, and bring Aleppo."

But the Jew, while shifting his eyes from point
to point, remained as before.

" *Go thou, and bring Aleppo.*"

This time El Reshid stepped nearer and touched
his spotless robe, at the same time holding the
glance of Issachar upon his own, which blazed with
the impelling heat of will. The Jew turned, as
though walking in sleep, and glided from the place,
forced by a power beyond him; while El Reshid
stood calm, immovable, with his eyes upon the
entrance. A half hour passed, an hour, and yet
the Master, cold as marble, rigid as granite, unwav-
ering, fixed, remained upon the identical spot. As
we have said before, though apparently without
motion, one might have felt a still quiver of the
nerves, that manifested itself in the power with
which he impressed his surroundings; and during
this long, tense time Romanes stood with bowed
head, a shriveled pine that the blast had bent, but
failed to break.

Could one have studied the face of El Reshid during this pregnant hour he would have noticed deli-
cate changes of expression, as though he saw at a
far distance, and forced action upon another by the
power of an overmastering will; it was evident,
however, that his whole Unit of Force was called
into action, and that the strain was telling as the
time advanced.

At last, the cat-like step of Issachar was heard
upon the stairs, and the young, springing gait of

another who followed at his heels. Still El Reshid remained rigid, energized. The Jew glided into the room like one in sleep, and behind him came Aleppo, in the beauty and strength of unsullied youth. Upon the young man Romanes cast but a glance when his eyes were blinded with tears, and he turned his head away.

"Go, thou snake of Olympus," said the same strange voice of El Reshid, " back to the Gehenna of Phallic worship and the den of the depraved; revel for once, *thyself*, in the beastliness over which thou hast gloated, and soil thine own robes with the filth of the slums—*Go !*

Even more servile, more serpentine, Issachar, recoiling upon himself and moving with the sinuosity of the reptile, vanished into the darkness, leaving the room reeking with a polluted atmosphere that is beyond analysis.

"Open the windows," said the Master ; then, bolting the doors, he retired to Romanes' inner apartment, leaving father and son together—alone.

CHAPTER XXXVIII.

THE DAWN.

Regan and Sallus lived according to Catus' instructions, quietly at Stamboul, having firm faith that to do nothing is sometimes a part of wisdom. Catus had the comet attribute of coming from unexpected quarters and disappearing to others as mysteriously as he had arrived.

"I shall simply remain here until Cæsar appears," said Regan; there's something brewing, or I'm off my base." And Sallus was faithful, too, though his life of inaction was telling on his healthy nerves. The time of suspense was short, however. They were at home one evening, indulging in a harmless game of cards, beating each other in a half-hearted way, when Catus entered. Both men sprang to their feet, for they felt rejoiced, somehow, though seemingly at nothing. He appeared the same, his face telling no special story of either good or bad import.

"Well," said Regan anxiously.

"I am sorry that you don't smoke," said Catus, lighting up. "It does a man good to have company in his vices; it relieves his conscience, makes him feel more respectable, etc."

"I should like it mighty well," said Regan, "in fact, I never have conquered the desire; but that's not the question. I simply won't, that's all. The very fact that I want it so bad makes me all the more stubborn. Do you suppose I am going to be bound by a cursed habit; for that matter, I take special pleasure in torturing myself; to get where tobacco smoke is the thickest is the most hellish delight imaginable; it's a pitched battle between will and desire. I always did enjoy a fight—like it yet, see !"

"What's the news," said Sallus, as though half afraid to ask.

Catus puffed away in the most aggravating manner, holding his two anxious inquirers in suspense a half minute, then deliberately took his cigar from his mouth, inspected the lighted end, and said slowly, "Aleppo will be here shortly."

"What!"

"Yes, he sent me ahead."

A rap, distinct and peculiar, called up in the minds of Sallus and Regan pleasant memories of other days.

An instant more, and Aleppo Romanes stood in their midst.

As we all know, there are times when words fail us utterly. Regan and Sallus were dumb, while the young man who had paralyzed their tongues looked joyfully at them. He had the old, bright, beaming smile, his eyes flashing a wordless love, and his mouth, in full sympathy with them, parting over his beautiful teeth. He was thinner, fairer, but otherwise the same—no, he had acquired a dignity, a poise, an insight, which his friends felt instantly, but failed to analyze.

He went to Regan and embraced him in oriental fashion; then to Sallus; his touch, his aspect, telling of imperishable gratitude.

What so pregnant as a silence which no one dares to shatter?

At last Catus broke the spell. He had thrown

away his cigar on the entrance of Aleppo, but
when the stillness became unendurable he struck a
match and lighted another. This loosened their
tongues, and for a couple of hours they talked with.
the condensed energy that had gathered from long
separation.

.Aleppo related his experience and spoke reverently of his father, saying in a grave tone that he
should proceed with Catus to Damascus, and he
must tear himself from those to whom he owed so
much. This, they both expected.

"It is just what we looked for," said Regan,
"we knew you would fly if we caught you; nevertheless, we were determined to beat the Jew—where
is he?"

"He has vanished," said Catus; "he was
wounded and has crawled into the jungle to recover. He has no strength at present; he
wilted in the full glare of the sun; he's a night
blossom."

"So, then, there is no danger," said Sallus.

"None, whatever. To trip a man up on his
climax of triumph is to send him headlong; he fell
far. The art of the Master who would achieve a
great victory lies in hitting his victim in his weak-
est spot.. Issachar, gloating over Romanes, was a
cat revelling with its prey; his vanity ran riot; he
lost his grip, and El Reshid, taking advantage
of an instant's weakness, threw him down from
his pinnacle of triumph, which was a point of un-

certain foothold. The art of Mastership is as accurate as any other; to bring an extreme to bear upon an extreme is the strategy of war and the secret of conquest."

All the time that Catus was talking Regan kept his glance fastened on Aleppo, for his heart was heavy ; he had dreamed a dream in his innocence and ignorance, and had hoped that he and this apparently homeless boy might be all and all to each other; but as the greatness of the young man began to dawn upon him, while his heart swelled with honest pride, and at the same time he realized that he was once more alone. Rhea had become a sweet memory, Sallus dreamed of fair France, and now Aleppo would steal away to Damascus, while he—a tear rolled down his cheek, which he shame-facedly brushed away—

"Look here Regan," said Catus, turning suddenly toward him, " what's the matter with your joining us? "

" What do you mean by us? "

" The Order, of course."

"*Me?* "

" Yes, *you ;* I'm sure most of us would duck our heads when you came on deck, we'd have to."

" Guess you would, said Sallus, "Regan is the greatest philosopher, in my opinion, that ever walked the earth ; neither you nor El Reshid can hold a candle to him ; you'll be honored, if you let him in."

Another tear forced itself from Regan's eye, down on to his swarthy cheek ; he was never so disgusted with himself before, in his life.

" It isn't exactly what a man knows that opens the door of the order, but what he does. Now Regan, and you too, have done something, and, in my opinion, are the most modest couple that I ever met. You don't seem to realize, either of you, that you have been of any use, whatever. Approbativeness is left off your heads, I imagine. El Reshid himself, would have been helpless, without you ; there's nobody almighty, you know. Yes, gentlemen, your names are both up, and there's no danger of your being black-balled, I'll warn you of that."

To Catus' chagrin this announcement made but little impression on either Regan, or Sallus ; in fact, they manifested a decided indifference.

"You see, it's this way," said Regan, "neither Sallus nor I worked for honors. We rather like that boy over there for his own sake ; and don't care a rap whether he is destined to be a Mahatma, or an archangel. We admire him for just what he is, and though I assure you that we feel honored—we, for I think I know Sallus well enough to speak for him also—shall most gladly come among you, if you so desire, yet I must warn you that all the condensed wisdom of Hellas, and the Yogi powers of India, with the Kundalini thrown in, can never take the place with me, of a little love and a loyal friendship."

Here Aleppo turned his quick, masterful glance on Regan. " This is the finality of philosophy and the secret of the fiery Nirvana," he said.

Regan made no answer; he scarcely understood.

"There is work for you in the order," said Catus. We deal especially with fallen women, because sex depravity is the worm that burrows at the root of the tree of life. Now there is Nita"—he drew a letter from his pocket—" here is another—the second this week—and she is but an example of a hundred more. We have her in good hands; she is learning to do for herself and becoming very proud of her virtues. We have agents everywhere, who help along, and furnish employment suitable for these women; work of just the right kind seems to come to them, and they are unaware from what source. Some marry, but more go as missionaries to their unfortunate sisters, and slyly help them. They make the best workers imaginable, for, knowing the inferno and the way out of it, they have sympathy and charity for that for which an immaculate, touch-not-my-garment Pharisee would have no patience."

" Yes'" said Regan, whose mind was far away from the subject, " when do you go? "

" To Damascus? "

" Yes, to Damascus."

"In a few days," answered Catus; but Aleppo pierced to the heart of the question—

"I will write to you continually, Regan, my adopted father, you know"—and he laughed. "You will never lose me; if all the others drift away, I shall become a regular bore, and torture you with letters till I come back later to take possession of you bodily—understand?"

The honors of the Order of Olympus and the prospect of future glories were as nothing compared to this. Aleppo had restored Regan's equilibrium and made his heart beat to the old tune. Herein lay the greatness of young Romanes.

"And Sallus—what about Sallus?" said Catus.

"His heart is in France," answered Regan, and I don't wonder; that little Cicily is the rosiest magnet alive."

"Who is Cicily?" said Aleppo, casting on Sallus a puzzled, reproachful glance.

"Don't you remember the house of Issachar, Lep, where you stopped for a few hours in Cairo?"

"But slightly—ah yes, a pretty girl—of course; I couldn't forget her—no man could; and another who wasn't so pretty," laughingly.

"I was half asleep, but I saw them both."

"And the beauty is Sallus' sweetheart," said Regan, boldly.

A spasm of pain contracted the brows of Aleppo. There is a selfishness in love at its best, and a slight jealousy that the philosophy of the sage has a hard tussel with. Aleppo was oriental and intense in his personal affections. Sallus was his Apollo Belvidere, and this pretty girl—ah ! love even has its dark side. Under the trees in paradise are shadowy places. Sallus saw the pained look in Aleppo's eyes, and for the first time in his life he knew supreme happiness. It is supposed that two men are incapable of love; friendship is deemed quite possible, but a pure devotion is considered a dream; nevertheless Sallus drew close to Aleppo and said in his blunt fashion—

"Lep, Cicily means a good deal to me, but not what you do; understand, you've always been first and always will be; does that suit you?"

"I'm far from greatness," said Aleppo, blushing with shame and pleasure; "about you I'm as selfish as ever." And this selfishness made Sallus so contented and Aleppo so satisfied, and Regan and Catus so good natured, that we question the evil in it after all; and wonder if a thing great could ever be realized in its size, if it failed to contrast with the small. The weakness of a man, but emphasizes his strength; for character is far from being a chain guaged by its fickle link. The roar of the wild beast may be harmless, if his teeth are gone; but woe be to him who falls into the clutches of one that has lost nothing but his voice.

The night was far spent when Catus and Aleppo left the rooms of their friends, and dawn had spread the east with a rosy haze.

"And we go next to Damascus," said Catus.

"First to Cairo," answered Aleppo.

"To Cairo?"

Romanes glanced quickly at Catus; he seemed surprised.

"I would meet Rhea Nellino," he continued.

"Ah!" A pained look passed over the countenance of Catus, and then the sun in full majesty ascending the arc of heaven, literally dazzled them with the splendor and fire of the dawn.

CHAPTER XXXIX

FRANCE.

In the old Roman city, Vinenne, by the river Rhône, on the veranda of a rather modern French dwelling house, sat the irrepressible Spino, disguised, to be sure, but Spino for all that. Cicily's relatives had stripped every "oriental rag" from off her back, and dressed her up in modern French garments, suitable to her age and condition. She had been queer before, but was queerer in her present habilaments; in fact an absurd medley, made up of a black silk gown, a corset, a watch and chain, and a shriveled personality that still displayed its one tooth and cavernous throat in defiance of civilization and Parisian dressmakers. She was painfully conscious of all this and more awkward than ever; as whatever congruity she once had with her surroundings was lost, and now, as she expressed it, she felt like "a cat in a rat's skin." There was much left bare that had once been covered; she missed the convenient draperies and folds in which she had formerly swathed herself; the silk gown drew tightly about the hips and was low at the neck, the wrists and scrawny hands were very much exposed, while her tufts of nondescript hair were strained up to a peculiar little top-knot that nearly pulled her eyes into her head; she had been decorated with gold-bowed spectacles and a pair of French ear-rings, which dangled about the shrunken tissue of her neck in tipsy fashion; while she sported a lace handkerchief, a smelling bottle, and more absurd still, a pair of high-heeled Parisian gaiters. Altogether she was remarkable, and Sallus spied her a long way off. It was queer that an old hag like that should set his heart palpitating, but it did, she thrilled the young man from head to foot, and was surpassingly beautiful, in his ardent eyes. In the rapture of love he seized her by the hands and kissed her effusively, much to the ancient dame's delight.

"And Cicily?" he said, out of breath.

But Spino was an arrant tease.

"She's off with her young man."

To have seen the lilies chase the roses from the face of Sallus would have been to pity him, but Spino was not half bad.

"To tell the truth she has watched for you ever since she came to France, and has refused no end of offers. She's a great catch here, I can tell you; her cousin's not the only one. Why didn't you come sooner?"

"Am I too late," asked Sallus, gloomily.

"You're just in the nick of time"—she took out her watch with a great flourish, and adjusted her spectacles to ascertain the hour. "She'll be back after a while; sit down can't you. When did you get here?"

"This morning; as I wrote Cicily that I would come as soon as Aleppo was found. I've kept my promise."

"So the young man turned up, did he, and Issachar, "why on earth isn't he capturing Cicily?'

"That's what's the matter; for fear of any such catastrophe I'm here to marry her—that is, if she will. Once we are married, I'll defy Issachar, or any other Jew to lay hands on her."

"What's become of the young man?"

"Oh, I bade him good-bye temporarily; he leaves soon for Damascus but comes back after a time, or I go there. I shall see him again," said Sallus with a slight contraction of the brows.

"In the mean time, you want to marry Cicily."

"Most assuredly; that is, if she is willing."

"Willing! Now let me tell you something. I've been downright angry at the girl for waiting for you; she's refused some splendid offers since you saw her last. If I had been she, I'd have jumped at the first one. It's absurd, the fool she's made of herself, and for a fellow like you, who prefers a young man's salvation to her own; who puts him first and foremost, and her second. It wasn't you who saved her, understand, but Rhea. Rhea's her angel as that Romanes is yours. She'd take her in preference to you every time, but, little fool that she is, seeing that Rhea is not to be had, she pines for you; you are the next best, that's all, and enough according to my idea. Queer couple you are, you both take up with each other because you can't get some one else; and I suppose you'll go on consoling yourself to the end of time."

" Cicily is but another name for constancy," said Sallus, very happy.

" Constancy, and you've doubted her all along; that's why you don't deserve her. You were suspicious in Cairo and in Stamboul, and here even, just because she happens to be dangerously pretty. You imagined that Issachar made a tool of her; I saw it the first time we met, in old Khem."

She stood up on her French heels and nearly toppled over.

" There, granny, sit down or you'll lose your balance."

She laughed clear down to the epiglottis, and sank back all in a heap on the veranda bench.

" You see, if I misjudged Cicily in the old days, you certainly got a wrong idea of Issachar, so we're quits."

" Please explain yourself, my heart's desire."

"You said it was money that he was after, but it wasn't; it was simply revenge."

" He managed to rake in the coin all the same," she answered, unconvinced.

" He has bled Cicily's relatives, I am pretty confident from what they tell me; however, that is neither here nor there, he's out of the way, and I'm glad of it. There's no telling how long he'll stay though," but Sallus' mind was on another subject.

" Will Cicily's relatives object to her marrying me, do you think, granny? "

"I suppose you're able to sustain her?" The old woman's expression was very severe, as though she expected this ardent suitor to plead poverty on the spot.

"I guess I've enough," he answered indifferently. "I get the income of a pretty good pile which my father has looked out for. Cicily will have to take me on trust, though, for what I am today, not for what I was." Here he blushed.

"Cicily will take you, there's no doubt about that, but in my opinion she's a fool; I wouldn't have you if you got down on your knees."

"Granny, you're cruel." His eyes were fixed on the door. Framed by a climbing honeysuckle, rosy, tantalizing, Miss Cicily, the little eavesdropper, kissed him with her saucy eyes, which had the touch-me-not, I-love-you expression. It would be

this little maiden's fate to tantalize the man she
loved, or any other, to the end of her days, and
Sallus' prospect, while bright enough, had its little
sun-tinted tortures, which it would be his fate to
endure.

"Cicily," he said, going toward her and extending his hands, "I have come to marry you—will
you have me?"

He felt like a cruel schoolboy chasing a butterfly, but the answer of the young lady quite took
away his breath.

"Yes, if you'll be quick about it."

"Are you afraid of Issachar?"

"Somewhat, but not so much as of other men;
besides, there's Spino. I've wished a hundred
times to be back in Cairo."

"We'll go there," answered Sallus, "and to
Syria and Thibet—anywhere to get to a place of
safety."

While the prettiness of Cicily was still evident,
it was not in the least enhanced by the Parisian
touch. She looked like a French fashion plate,
and Sallus mentally vowed that he would persuade
her into half-oriental garments, as soon as he had
the right.

Venus must have taken great delight in this
young couple; not the mystic Urania, but the
Aphrodite of the sea foam; and Sappho, too, would
have written them a bridal hymn, no doubt, had
she been living, for they were beautiful in flesh and

blood and burning with youth. Spino, though she scoffed and made fun, and condemned and preached, enjoyed for the time, a little earthly bliss, by proxy or sympathy, or some other emotion rather hard to understand.

Of course, the relatives of Cicily could say nothing; she was dependant on their bounty and her knight had come armed with sovereigns, which he threw at their heads. Her numerous lovers vowed vengeance, which they never attempted to carry out, and Issachar, if aware of this French idyl, made no aggressive sign. Even the father of Sallus dispatched his unqualified approval, and Regan and Aleppo wished them joy. Everything was as it should be, and were this tale to end here it would be thoroughly conventional and true to the popular demand.

On the morning on which they were married the sun was bright, the air balmy, friends and relations cordial, and Spino had flowers in her hair. There were presents, congratulations, slippers and rice. Altogether, it was a romantic love affair, ending in the good, old-fashioned way. Ending? Does love subside with marriage, and is courtship the grave of Eros? Not always.

They left France, and Spino, who though a little sore and terribly homesick for Egypt, nevertheless, refused to countenance their honeymoon with her presence. But when they had gone the old woman went by herself to a deserted graveyard and sobbed her grief out on the tombstones, as though the cold marble had a sympathetic touch and felt her woe.

So it is; too much of happiness in one direction deprives somebody—always somebody. An excess of love poured out on a fortunate head leaves a poor heart shivering. The balance seems to be lost temporarily and Justice, with her face awry, belies her name. In truth, though, the equilibrium is preserved and the instability is but apparent, for life, in its finality, is self-settling.

"I want you to know Regan better," said Sallus as he placed his young wife in a steamer chair near the ship's rail.

They were on the Mediterranean, going anywhere or nowhere, simply absorbing the blue above and below.

"Couldn't he come with us?" said Cicily naively.

"I think not." But Sallus sighed, and she took note. "He is a queer individual and the greatest philosopher on earth, but he takes the loss of Aleppo and me very hard. I wouldn't have thought it, but he does. It seems to be the fate of some folks that just as they get attached to a body and find him conducive to happiness, he is snatched away by someone else. It's hard, I tell you," and he sighed again; she made a second note. Those two pronounced sighs of Sallus' were the black wings of the raven that persisted in hovering over

her head.   She knew, through the jealous instinct
of woman, that Sallus had other loves besides herself, and, in her pique, she remembered Rhea, whom
she determined should eclipse Sallus forever in her
eyes.   Rhea was the silver moon who was fated to
put out her sun periodically as long as she drew
breath.

But the Mediterranean was blue, and the empy-
rean another sea, and they, between sky and earth,
floated outward into life, with its lights and shadows, its night and day.

CHAPTER XL.

THE SETTING SUN.

" You will go to El Reshid," said Romanes, gazing directly at his son, who had come to his apartment to bid him farewell.   There was a certain
pride in his eyes, as they rested on the young man,
which Aleppo had failed to notice, so intent was he
in admiring his father, whose dignity and reserve
excited his profound respect.   The look on Aleppo's face, his smile, a subtle something beyond analysis, called Helene to Romanes' mind and, though
he made no sign, in fact, assumed an expression of
haughtiness, within, his heart ached with the old
pain that Helene had caused him on that wild night
in Paris, when she slipped his grasp and went out
like an extinguished taper.   So, too, was Aleppo
going.   A star, flashing in the dark over Romanes'

head, was about to be extinguished, and yet, holding his feeling in hand with supreme mastership, he
impressed his son with a sense of dignity that
amounted to awe.   Aleppo felt that in all his life
he had never seen so imposing a figure; and the
consciousness that he himself was of him, bone and
muscle, mind and heart, filled him with an ambi-
tion beyond any past conjecture, and he secretly
vowed that he would make himself worthy of the
kinship, or perish in the attempt. On the contrary, this man of bone and muscle, mind and
heart, wondered if sometime, somewhere, he
should gain his lost position and become the peer
of his son; if he would yet be able to lovingly
challenge the rising stars that he beheld already
flashing in Aleppo's eyes.

We have said that Romanes saw the uplifted
beauty in his son's face which had already
charmed him in Helene, but an unbiased judge
would have said that the two men, as they stood
face to face, were strangely alike, even to the
masterful quickness of eye, which gave them both
that electric glance that is never seen save in the
faces of the great.

Romanes, masked in the reserve of silence, as
was his custom on critical occasions, so awed
Aleppo that his desire of affectionate expression
was checked also, though otherwise he would have
embraced his father and talked freely, as in his
young impulsiveness he longed to do. Before their

meeting he had thought of a thousand things that
he desired to ask him, if that happy time ever arrived ; he would speak of his mother, his memory
of her, her beauty ; but no ˙word could he bring
himself to utter on the subject; the mystery of her
life seemed too sacred to probe.

"You will go to El Reshid, and later will succeed him as master of the Olympians," said
Romanes.

With the question the consciousness of kinship
in Aleppo's mind was replaced by independent
opinion, and he gave answer with a positiveness
that amounted to a finality.

"Of that I know nothing. El Reshid is but a
man.   The order must necessarily act as a break
on individuality.   I am not prepared to commit
myself.   The teacher ceases his vocation when the
pupil is no more.   I seek neither being nor order.
Truth is my magnet, and *it* will I have."

The apparent conceit of this remark seemed
worthy of his youth.   It startled Romanes, and a
look of admiration flashed in his eyes, which he
strove to conceal."

"To El Reshid, however," continued Aleppo,
"I owe untold gratitude, and though truth in the
abstract is undoubtedly a final aim, a teacher is a
means to the end.   His letters appeal to my reason
and my instinct.   It was not so much the man back
of them as the truth behind him, that aroused
my consciousness and impelled me to seek further."

"But the man, himself, is a magnet," answered Romanes, looking keenly at his son.

"Ah, you speak of attraction for *himself*—do I love him; that bears naught on the question of his instructions save indirectly; I might adore one who could teach me nothing."

"But his powers?" Romanes stepped closer and looked even more keenly at Aleppo.

"True, I have witnessed their manifestation, and have discovered also that by no art of his can he transfer them. In no way can he graft a limb of himself on to me, as you insert the cutting of a peach tree into the body of a plum. The law, however, through which he works is as universal as is that of gravitation, and is no more his than mine."

"But he knows its secret, and you do not."

"Yet will I," said Aleppo, straightening himself. "If El Reshid deem me worthy he will so inform me; if not, I will discover it *myself*."

A smile touched and vanished from the lips of Romanes; his son's egotistic audacity, which amounted to authority, thrilled his nerves and startled them for a moment into unwonted life.

"I have no fear of you," touching his head and his heart, and drawing away from Aleppo as a signal of parting.

The young man's pulse fairly bounded; he longed to rush to this man by his side and embrace him, for he felt that on earth they would never meet

again, but his lofty demeanor, his mask of dignity
so impressed him, that he restrained all outward
manifestation like a true son of the Orient, and
returning the salute, went slowly from the room,
his eyes fastened on those of his father as long as
he remained in view.   By a strange association of
ideas Romanes remembered a hotel in Vienna and a
similar parting with Helene.   With the closing of
the door he automatically arranged a few trifles and
locked his desk; then, going to the window, he
noticed that the sun had long since crossed the
zenith and was fast descending the western sky.
Placing some letters in his pocket, and casting a
strange glance over the room, he left it and sought
the outer world.   As he passed into the street, he
walked with an unsteady gait, and the sunlight
brought out the silver in his abundant hair.   He
glanced over the Golden Horn with the same peculiar glance; at the masts and minarets, the towers
and ships; from the heights he scanned the
Bosporus, on, on to the Mysian Olympus, covered with snow; his eyes seemingly immovable,
resting for long minutes on the range, dim, beautiful, beyond him, holding his gaze with the fascination of an unapproachable ideal.   Then, slowly
turning his back on the Occident, far away England, his beloved France, the cold peaks of Switzerland and the mysterious Byzantium, he crossed to
Asia, and became to the rising west but a legend
and a dream.

CHAPTER XLI.

VANISHED.

Cæsar Catus was at home in Cairo; and all things were as they had been in his luxurious apartments, even to the Arab, who materialized and dematerialized, as in times past. He, himself, in his oriental gown and Turkish fez, looked as young and unconcerned as he had done before undertaking the role of executor and man of affairs. He had come out of severe work to luxury, unscathed, and drew hard at his Havana, undisturbed by a spasm of conscience or a pang of regret. Since last embraced by the arms of his stuffy chair he had traveled extensively, labored along numerous lines unceasingly, lived abstemiously, and suffered severely. But tonight he is as benign as the climate of Egypt, and as natural a child of luxury as the Sultan himself.

He had been seated but a short time when Regan and Aleppo entered the room, and made themselves as much at home as was Cæsar himself. They had been in Cairo but an hour or two, and Catus and Romanes were expecting to leave on the following day. Regan, who still retained his rooms there, had captured Aleppo bodily, and vowed that he would hold him until he departed for Damascus. He had accompanied him to Cairo, declaring that he should remain in the Egyptian city indefinitely, as one part of the world was as good as another, and that, besides, it was just possible that Sallus and Cicily might wander that way.

"I am going out with Aleppo," said he to Catus, "to locate Rhea's residence; I will then return to you and leave them together."

"Are you sure," said Catus, "that she is still here?"

"Not at all, though she vowed to remain till she learned something definite of Aleppo; however, it does no harm to inquire."

While Regan was talking, young Romanes stood staring, with a fixed gaze, at the cast of Miss Nellino, which stood on a pedestal, where a soft, oriental lamp threw a rosy glow on the pure Greek profile and graceful neck.

"How came you by that?" he said, lifting his large eyes to those of Catus.

"I made it from memory."

Aleppo looked searchingly at Cæsar for a moment, then turned again to the bust, and remained silent till Regan reminded him that it was time to make search for Rhea.

"Do you feel that she is here" said Regan, as they walked toward the familiar street, where he had seen her before, under the trellis of roses.

"No," answered Romanes, but beyond this he said nothing.

The house appeared at last, faintly and half defined, for the night was dark; then Regan turned abruptly and left Aleppo near the garden gate. He looked vaguely, as if in a dream, at the dim, shadowy cottage, and the faint light that stole out through the window, then went slowly to the entrance and knocked upon the door. It was opened by a servant, who ushered him into a small apartment, where he awaited the mistress, who appeared later, and, as he expected, was an entire stranger. He bowed, however, and enquired calmly if she could tell him anything of a Miss Nellino, who had recently occupied the house.

"Ah, the beautiful young lady! I am sorry sir, but I cannot, except that she left here with her aunt, at the time I took the place."

"You have no idea in what direction she went?"

"Not the slightest; but I have found a lovely picture of her which she must have forgotten; would you like that sir?"

A slightly sarcastic smile flew off from Aleppo's lips—as if a picture could take the place of Rhea—but he replied, politely, in the negative and arose to depart.

"Wait a moment please, perhaps Sahib will know; and she called her man-servant whom she found as ignorant on the subject as herself. The door closed deprecatingly after Aleppo, as if it were sorry also; and he, in the same dream, out of which he had temporarily emerged, wandered back to the room of Catus.

"She has gone?" said Regan, when Romanes entered.

He smiled an answer, which spake more emphatically than a monosyllable, and contradicted his eyes, that his friends found hard to fathom.

The next day Aleppo and Catus bade Regan farewell, and proceeded on their way to Syria and the dwelling place of El Reshid.

CHAPTER XLII.

ON THE WAY TO DAMASCUS.

The environment of ancient Joppa is rich with citrus groves, and during the spring, carpets of gorgeous flowers are spread over the far-reaching plain in oriental tints, thick and luxurious like Persian rugs. The air is heavy with the breath of orange blossoms, while the hedges of prickly cactus stand on guard; and this most ancient city, with the Mediterranean at its feet and a tropical sky overhead, was said to be the port where, in the far-off past, the famous cedars of Lebanon were landed for the building of that half mythical temple from which came the voice of the the oracle and the wisdom of Solomon.

Here young Romanes and Catus paused on their way to Damascus, meeting parties of travelers with their horses and tents returning from the famous city, and others about to start, all focussing

at the entrance of the hotel where Aleppo and
Catus stopped. For some reason, hardly understood by themselves, they had concluded to remain
over the succeeding day at Joppa, taking their trip
to Damascus leisurely, and as impulse dictated.

On the following morning after their arrival,
Aleppo strolled out into the suburbs of the city,
and seeing in the distance a gnarled and ancient
tree, that might, for aught he knew, have sheltered
the head of the sainted Paul, he walked toward it
and discovered a horse tied loosely to its trunk,
while sitting near, her seat a stone, was a woman
slender and familiar, who caused young Romanes
to pause, as though transfixed. For an instant only,
then she raised her eyes, large, beautiful, sad, and
looked into those of Aleppo, as though she had
waited long.

"Rhea!"

She arose and went toward him, in the old way,
with both hands extended, looking thinner, fairer.

Aleppo asked no question; he could not speak;
he was becoming like his father, the oriental nature
having asserted itself, and with it that powerful
enthusiasm which finds no vent in words.

Rhea trembled a little and leaned against the
half-dead tree, whose withered and scraggy
branches formed a strange canopy for her young
and beautiful head.

"I have come from Cairo," said Aleppo. "I
sought you there,"

"And I have seen El Reshid," she answered, dropping her eyes, and breaking a little twig to pieces.

The name once so magical brought a chill to his heart and froze his blood—El Reshid !

Near by, in the flower vale of Syria, stood the one of all others that expressed to him the witchery and beauty of woman. To be near her was to be in Paradise, to thrill with the rapture of nature and the passion of the muse. To touch her was to become herself, and to forget his name and race. To hear her was to listen to the Æolian harp, whose strings were swept by the fingers of the Immortals.

And *she*, with downcast eyes, has spoken the name—El Reshid—that turned him to ice. His life had been in her hands; had she, herself, not said it, he would have fallen at her feet.

Is it left always with the great among women to decide at last what man shall be? Are they not only the mothers of men, but their fate also? Had she not spoken, Aleppo Romanes would have buried the name of El Reshid in the oblivion of memory, and fled from Syria and his high destiny. The flower in his hand he would have crushed by his very passion, and the laurel of the Immortal would have been covered by the sod. No other soul on earth, nor in the universe, could have tempted him to this, save Rhea Nellino. But somehow she had caught a glimpse, with that wonderful prophetic glance, of a series of heights—

a Pelion piled on Ossa, a heaven on Paradise, a magical Maha Meru, where love itself is immortal, and where the shadow of the tomb is not. She had come out from among the cedars of Lebanon, where the flickering light is lost in shade, to the splendor of the mountain-top where earth is beneath, and the sky, endless, starry, divine.

"There is but one thing that can make me happy," she said, gazing tenderly on his sorrowful, startled face, "but one thing—*your greatness*. The farther you climb, the more enraptured shall I become. We wed upon the heights."

With a shock, similar to that felt by him at the temple of Ammon, when he passed through the sacred gates, he suddenly realized that to lose her was to find her, that to part in flesh was to meet in spirit, where time and space and death are not, in the mystical Hesperides, the charmed Elysium within the soul itself; and to do this he must be great. Already had she forestalled him, and was returning from the teacher whom he sought. Already was she above him looking down into his eyes. To reach her he must rise; *to meet her they must part.*

Since first he sought truth, he had faced the paradox. On Libya he had battled with the sphinx, and here, beneath his own Bo tree, the master puzzle, the supreme problem slowly unravelled itself in the eyes of Rhea Nellino.

*　　*　　*　　*　　*　　*　　*　　*

It was a long sweet day, and in the balance
with the life time of the rhythmic man was as gold
is to a feather.   They talked of the future, the
eternal, the divine; and when the sun went down,
Rhea Nellino left him in an after-glow of splendor,
even more thrilling than the magic orb itself.

The hurrying years may come and go,
And groups of stars spin onward in their flight,
But time and space are naught to him,
Who greets each morn the rising sun,
Where looms Olympus white and lone,
In endless waste of heavenly blue.
And here upon the wooded hill,
Whose heart with bliss did once o'erflow,
A singer sang and singeth still.

CHAPTER XLIII.

THE MASTER.

Catus and Aleppo ascended the hill on the
north, that commands a superb view of the white
and rose city of Damascus, lying like a shaded
opal in its setting of green; the outlying stretches,
a blending of garden and forest, extending away
into the distance, where miniature lakes flash like
blue gems in the morning sun.

This marvelous view of ancient Esh Sham, from
whose red virgin soil Adam is said to have sprung;
this glimpse of the land of Eden, and haven of St.
Paul, is one of the famous sights of earth.

From the high summits of Anti Lebanon one sweeps the wonderful plain, El Cuta, extending, verging even upon Paradise which is the dream of the Arab and the ideal of the poet. And Damascus, "The White Swan," with wings spread, its feet just touching the waters of the glistening Pharpar and the winding ·Abana, rises as it would seem from the living green of earth to the ethereal blue of heaven, bearing upward the mighty thoughts of the wise and aspirations of the great Damascus ! at last. Before Aleppo was spread a realized vision, a verified panorama that his inner eye had scanned again and again in the past. The great mosques, the minarets, the domes, the golden crescents, the fragile blossoms of the peach, the leaves of the somber olive, the spire-like cypress, the glow, the flash, the splendor which distance lends, even the subtle perfume of the roses, the shifting veil of lucent mist, all about him, as seen *within* a thousand times, clear, expanded, sublime.

Then Catus, who, hushed like himself, had stood entranced, turned abruptly, and said in a resolute voice, pitched, however, in a minor, melancholy key:

"I return to Cairo; you know the way; find the garden; fare you well."

He looked away from Romanes to the summit of Anti Lebanon, and extended his hands. For an instant Aleppo felt that this could not be; it had

been a series of partings; they had all gone, one
after the other, and now, even Catus. But he
mastered himself, and answering the salute of his
friend in his usual silent way, turned from Cæsar
and slowly descended toward Damascus.

He passed through "Straight Street" and
wandered on, on, till at last, before an unobtrusive,
dingy door, he paused and knocked. It was so
low that to enter he must needs stoop; but once
beyond it he heard the rush of water, and beheld a
sparkling, narrow stream, on the banks of which
were ferns and reeds, where everywhere along the
paths were shrubs and roses.

Within this garden, which seemed so familiar to
Aleppo, was a small building of four-domed
columns, through which the soft air stole, heavy
with perfume and resonant with music. A Smyrna
rug had been thrown upon the floor, and upon this
Aleppo threw himself, with the ease and natural-
ness of an oriental, and leaning his head upon his
hand he fell again into a dream. It would have
seemed a long time to another, but to him it was
but a few minutes, when a man came rapidly down
the garden path and entered the airy structure.

Romanes rose immediately to his feet and made a
profound salute, but El Reshid waved it aside with
a smile and shake of his head, and said:

"Recline please, as I shall do, and let us talk."

El Reshid changed his manner, on occasion, as he
did his garment. In the Occident he had worn the

garb of a Parisian and spoken in a dignified foreign tongue; here upon Damascan soil he wore an oriental robe and spoke with the ease of the native.

"You have come a long way," he said to Aleppo, smiling again in a familiar manner, and reclining near him. "I am sure I needed you much."

"*You needed me?*" replied Romanes, with a slightly astonished inflection.

"Understand," answered El Reshid, "that everything is fair in philosophy, the exchange is always even. Without you, I should have suffered; we give for what we get, and get for what we give."

"Yes," said Aleppo, who grasped it instantly. There seemed no need of explanation between them.

"However, you must have had some definite object in coming; you desire to obtain, I presume, what are called transcendant powers."

"I do. I would learn the formulas, and take a short cut to whatever otherwise might require a long time. But on one condition only will I study with you"—here he smiled caressingly at El Reshid, as if begging him to excuse his apparent egotism —"and that is that my individuality remain intact. *I am I*, and what this or that man says, to me is nothing except it be based on truth, that reveals itself also. Revelation, inspiration, assertion, though vouched for by a Moses or a Newton, are nothing to me unless Truth stares at me through their eyes, and speaks from their very lips."

While Aleppo's words to the uninitiated would have sounded cold and egotistic, his manner was dignified yet humble, and somehow appealed to El Reshid in a remarkable way.

"You would be the ocean grey-hound," he answered, "that cuts across the waves, and rushes straight to port in the teeth of the wind. You scorn that rare beauty of the sea—the full-rigged ship that rises and falls to the rhythm of the tide, and singing the song of the surging deep, its sails taut or its poles bare, runs a race with the gale itself, or is buffeted about, a mere pet and a plaything of the monster that treats it according to his moods. Ah! you would transcend law and master rhythm; in other words, become a god."

"I would," said Aleppo, reverently bowing his head.

"You have come to me for the formulas?"

"I have."   .

The two men looked at each other; they seemed peers—equals. El Reshid was a pure oriental, with a clear, cream-tinted skin and brilliant, passionate eyes. Romanes with his strain of western blood was wonderfully fair, and his glance while quick was steady as is that of a young sun.

"Tell me," said he to El Reshid, "in what consists your power; by what means did you acquire this transcendentalism by which you overcome rhythm and discover counter-acting laws? How earned you the title of "The Master?"'

At this series of questions El Reshid, with a smile like that of Romanes, remained silent a few moments, and no sound was heard save the ripple of the river, which scorned silence and sang incessantly, then, in slow, decisive language, drawing a little near to Aleppo, he began:

"You speak of transcendentalism; know, then, that in the finality there is nothing transcendental save will. To be sure, we apparently overcome law with law, upset principle with principle, but he who rejects the sovereignty of will is a slave of rhythm and a puppet of fate. Listen while I talk; lose no word, for to one like you, who has already learned to concentrate, I need speak this truth but once."

He leaned back against a column of the little retreat, and plucking a bit of fleur de-lis pulled the leaves to bits as he talked.

THE WILL.

"We have defined Will as desire. Will pure and simple, being an inclination in a certain way, as opposed to all other ways. To will and to wish are practically the same thing, as you understand, the strength and weakness lie in the amount of force with which you back it. This force, in the finality, is different in different individuals, and also in a single individual may be greater or less

according as he exercises his Unit Power. So, in
ordinary terminology we speak of a strong will
and a weak will, as Will and force generally go
together. But in subtle analysis we distinguish
Will entirely from force; as man may wish for a
thing and make no effort to acquire it, in fact back
his desire by no energy, except that required to
will. You may sit all day and long for China, but
if you make no effort to get there, you use no
amount of strength to back your Will; more, you
may ardently, imploringly *desire* China, at the
same time knowing .your energy inadequate, you
use no force in that direction. You may be a cast-
away on a desert island, with no timber nor means
with which to construct a boat, yet that will not in
the least prevent you from longing for home with
a heart-breaking persistency. Indeed, it is often
the case that the utter impossibility of accomplish-
ing an object makes the object all the more desired.
A thing that a man can not have he sometimes
most ardently wants. So, then, force and Will are
not the same thing as we *define* the latter.

"Coming back to the idea that Will is desire, we
get into the subtleties. If you prefer green to
blue and desire it about you, why is this? What
leads you to prefer green to blue, when another
prefers the latter? Even your power of choice
seems to be backed by causation. If. in some time
past you became accustomed to an environment of
green, having lived in a forest, or perchance hav-

ing been confined to shaded rooms on account of weak eyes, where a green light became a necessity, you got accustomed to the color, and have grown on that account to love it, wherein, then, when you delve into causes, do you find your power of choice ? Any illustration will do; take your preference in *any* direction, your liking and choosing of certain articles of food, of certain localities, of certain people, would seem to result from evolution, or the birth of cause from cause. You will be startled if you begin to trace your preferences in this way, and will be temporarily shocked into believing that after all you are but a puppet of fate, which allows of no free and *sovereign* Will; that each temporary cause having a preceding one, you are, after all, not choosing anything, but sitting on the lap of fate, and deluding yourself with the idea that you are a free agent. Even your opinions are but the normal children of *previous* opinions, which you have forgotten; farther, any change of opinion, apparently due to choice, would seem, if you trace it, to be brought about by good and sufficient reasons, by which you are forced to your present position in all honesty.

"If you accept the creation hypothesis, and posit a beginning for yourself *anywhere*, at any time, you are forced into the renunciation of free Will, as surely as you are compelled to drown when the water persistently covers your head. Start a cause anywhere, which shall farther a cause, and you are as much the puppet of fate as is the slave a tool of his master. The ghastly joke of the whole matter lies in the fact that while you in reality choose nothing you seem to be choosing everything; and man resolves himself into a travesty and nothing more.

"The question then sifts down to this: Man is absolutely without the power of choice, and is forced to every apparent spontaneous desire by a series of causes, or his Will is absolutely free, and no cause affects it. Will either precedes cause, or is the result of cause. If the second proposition be true, all things that we do, we are *forced* to do, whether they be evil or good ; murder, theft, lust are as much a part of our existence as is beauty and altruism. The terrible blunder of the idea of creation, as propounded by a false philosophy is that it is absolutely self contradictory, giving man, along with his anthropomorphic god and " beginning in time " a *Free Will*.

"The whole strength of our position lies in this : that from the point of Unity or *Beginninglessness* there *is* no cause *except Will*. Should you start to trace by causes, you could never stop, except at the point where your existence begins. Now if it *begins*, there is a *reason* for its beginning; this would be the First Cause, from which all following causes would follow, being the impetus to every choice which you would make to the time of your death. If, on the contrary, you trace back to no

First Cause, Will being primal and sovereign—the two poles of being, though simultaneous, yet in a sense resultant—we have an absolutely free and sovereign Will, in itself a cause, influenced perhaps by other free Wills, but never forced, because of its precedence *to* environment.

"We must then, either posit, that environment controls Will, or that Will controls environment; one of these positions must absolutely be maintained. Modern science is far more consistent than the (revealed?) orthodox religion, because it (not as yet, in most cases, admitting endlessness of individual being) practically eliminates free, individual Will. The Law of Selection resolving itself into apparent freedom, resulting from past causation.

"Note, then, the philosophy of the man, who believes in *free Will*, must be diametrically opposed to that of one who believes in Kismet. Recognizing no sovereignty, he practises to that end, even to the dominating of his two poles of being. He finds, that whatever the cause that led up to a thing, that he can change that liking into a hate, by *Will*, pure and simple, or a resolving to do so, in spite of all environment which would lead to the contrary. But you say, that willing to do so must have a cause, and we answer, that if Will is the cause of itself, YES. In other words, he may will to will to do so, for Will's sake, as against all

influences of environment; in other words, he may
will to test his Will.

*   *   *   *   *   *   *

"We shall bring you now to test your Will by
formulas, and lead you into some *subtle* thought.
You must now be trained to the hardest kind of
thinking, and the most rigid exercise of Will.

*   *   *   *   *   *   *

"Nature is one pole of being, God the other ;
Variety one pole, Unity the other; the Law one
pole, the laws the other. The laws mean *tendencies*,
the Law of them Unity. Will is Ego—desiring.
Rhythm is a necessity of God and nature, or Law
and laws."

"The practice, do you understand?" said El
Reshid.

"I would ask you," answered Romanes, "how,
if all things are eternal, that the Will precedes; in
other words, how can anything *become* if all things
are?"

"A wise question," replied the Master. "Know
then, that in the bosom of the eternal all things
are potential, asleep, simultaneous. But to summon these out of Unity into variety necessitates the
precedence of Will or desire, for *it* is one attribute that never sleeps. Manifestation necessitates
sequence, and, therefore, time and space. Event follows upon desire. Remember then, all things are,
and ever shall be, though in variety through desire
or Will we marshal them one at a time. In life,

then, which means action, expression, Will is the Sovereign Supreme.''

He arose, and Aleppo, conscious that the lecture was done, saluted El Reshid and went toward the entrance. As he reached it he turned about once or twice and looked lovingly at his teacher, whose eyes were fixed upon him.

''To-morrow,'' said El Reshid.

'' Romanes smiled in his rare way, and saluting once more, vanished amid the tangled shrubs.

The Master was alone. He sat in an attitude of profound thought for a moment, then, passing quickly from the garden, sought the winding Arbana, and wandering along its verdant banks, addressed the river as though it were an ancient friend.

''We have waited long, Abana; one after another has come and gone, rejected by the Order, unequal to the test. For a century have aspirants to Olympus sought to scale the heights and achieve the apparently inaccessible. Alas! in the track they stumbled, bleeding and wounded, and were carried back. It was left for a Romanes to plant the standard of the Olympians on the ice peak of pure reason, at the crater of the volcano. Not once, through the terrible ordeal after he passed the Propylon, has he failed or stumbled. We have stood aloof in agony of suspense, and watched, believing, doubting, hoping, fearing. Our eyes were fixed upon him though he knew it not. Sick unto death on the waste of Libya, he sought Osiris, and with a glance on the blazing Sirius he captured heaven. By the side of the Golden Horn, steeped in luxury, tempted through the flesh, he shattered the idols of Issachar and struck a terrible blow at the legions of hell. In the dungeon, apparently forgotten, isolate, alone, he stormed the citadel of reason, and destroyed his illusions with the relentless weapon of logic. Beneath the gnarled and ancient tree of Joppa he solved the paradox of love and the mystery of heaven."

El Reshid plucked a wild rose, as he spoke, and cast its petals, one by one, upon the flashing stream.

"Beloved Abana, we have waited long."

www.ingramcontent.com/pod-product-compliance
Lightning Source LLC
Chambersburg PA
CBHW020900130726
47900CB00014B/1232